PENGUIN BOOKS

THE PENGUIN BOOK OF
ENGLISH SHORT STORIES

The Penguin Book
of English Short Stories

EDITED BY
CHRISTOPHER DOLLEY

PENGUIN BOOKS

Penguin Books Ltd, Harmondsworth, Middlesex, England
Viking Penguin Inc., 40 West 23rd Street, New York, New York 10010, U.S.A.
Penguin Books Australia Ltd, Ringwood, Victoria, Australia
Penguin Books Canada Ltd, 2801 John Street, Markham, Ontario, Canada L3R 1B4
Penguin Books (N.Z.) Ltd, 182–190 Wairau Road, Auckland 10, New Zealand

—

This selection first published 1967
Reprinted 1967, 1968, 1969, 1970, 1971 (twice), 1972, 1973, 1974,
1975, 1976 (twice), 1977, 1978, 1979, 1980, 1981 (twice), 1983, 1984 (twice),
1985 (twice), 1986, 1987

—

—

Printed and bound in Great Britain by
Cox & Wyman Ltd, Reading
Set in Monotype Garamond

CONTENTS

Editorial Foreword   7

Acknowledgements   9

Charles Dickens (1812–70)
THE SIGNALMAN   11

Thomas Hardy (1840–1928)
THE WITHERED ARM   25

Joseph Conrad (1857–1924)
AN OUTPOST OF PROGRESS   56

Rudyard Kipling (1865–1936)
AT THE END OF THE PASSAGE   82

H. G. Wells (1866–1946)
THE COUNTRY OF THE BLIND   103

W. Somerset Maugham (1874–1965)
THE FORCE OF CIRCUMSTANCE   129

James Joyce (1882–1941)
THE DEAD   157

Virginia Woolf (1882–1941)
KEW GARDENS   201

D. H. Lawrence (1885–1930)
FANNY AND ANNIE   208

Katherine Mansfield (1888–1923)
THE VOYAGE   224

Joyce Cary (1888–1957)
THE BREAKOUT   233

Aldous Huxley (1894–1963)
THE GIOCONDA SMILE   251

V. S. Pritchett (1900–   )
THE FLY IN THE OINTMENT   283

Evelyn Waugh (1903–66)
MR LOVEDAY'S LITTLE OUTING   293

Graham Greene (1904–   )
ACROSS THE BRIDGE   302

Angus Wilson (1913–   )
RASPBERRY JAM   313

EDITORIAL FOREWORD

THIS volume of English short stories is the first in the series to be published by Penguins. The aim of this collection is to appeal to the reader at large. No attempt has been made to conduct a historical survey of the English short story, and the collection starts in the mid nineteenth century, from which date the short story developed into a recognizable genre.

Most of the stories I have included are by outstanding novelists. However, an advantage of the short story as a literary form in its own right is that it allows an essentially minor talent to fulfil itself. Katherine Mansfield is a good example, and Somerset Maugham and H.G. Wells are as likely to be remembered for their stories as for their novels. Even Virginia Woolf, notwithstanding *To the Lighthouse*, is at her best in some of her marvellous early short stories.

The short story still flourishes, and the aim of this collection is to give some idea of the variety and individuality which the genre has developed over the last hundred years.

23.3.66   C. D.

ACKNOWLEDGEMENTS

For permission to reprint the stories specified we are indebted to:

the Trustees of the Hardy Estate and Macmillan & Co. Ltd for Thomas Hardy's 'The Withered Arm' from *Wessex Tales*;

Mrs George Bambridge and Macmillan & Co. Ltd for Rudyard Kipling's 'At the End of the Passage' from *Life's Handicap*;

the Executors of H. G. Wells for his 'The Country of the Blind' from *The Short Stories of H. G. Wells*;

the late W. Somerset Maugham Esq. and William Heinemann Ltd for W. Somerset Maugham's 'The Force of Circumstance' from *The Complete Short Stories*, Volume I;

the Executors of the James Joyce Estate and Jonathan Cape Ltd for James Joyce's 'The Dead' from *Dubliners*;

Leonard Woolf Esq. for Virginia Woolf's 'Kew Gardens';

Laurence Pollinger Ltd, the Estate of the late Mrs Frieda Lawrence, and William Heinemann Ltd for D. H. Lawrence's 'Fanny and Annie' from *The Complete Short Stories of D. H. Lawrence*;

the Society of Authors, for the Estate of the late Katherine Mansfield, for her 'The Voyage' from *The Garden Party*;

the Joyce Cary Estate for Joyce Cary's 'The Breakout' from *Spring Song and Other Stories*;

the late Aldous Huxley Esq. and Chatto & Windus Ltd for Aldous Huxley's 'The Gioconda Smile' from *Mortal Coils*;

A. D. Peters & Co. and Chatto & Windus Ltd for V. S. Pritchett's 'The Fly in the Ointment' from V. S. Pritchett's *Collected Stories*;

A. D. Peters & Co. for Evelyn Waugh's 'Mr Loveday's Little Outing';

Graham Greene Esq. and William Heinemann Ltd for Graham Greene's 'Across the Bridge' from *Twenty-One Stories*;

Martin Secker & Warburg Ltd for Angus Wilson's 'Raspberry Jam' from *The Wrong Set*.

Charles Dickens

THE SIGNALMAN

'HALLOA! Below there!'

When he heard a voice thus calling to him, he was standing at the door of his box, with a flag in his hand, furled round its short pole. One would have thought, considering the nature of the ground, that he could not have doubted from what quarter the voice came; but instead of looking up to where I stood on the top of the steep cutting nearly over his head, he turned himself about and looked down the Line. There was something remarkable in his manner of doing so, though I could not have said for my life what. But I know it was remarkable enough to attract my notice, even though his figure was foreshortened and shadowed, down in the deep trench, and mine was high above him, so steeped in the glow of an angry sunset, that I had shaded my eyes with my hand before I saw him at all.

'Halloa! Below!'

From looking down the Line, he turned himself about again, and, raising his eyes, saw my figure high above him.

'Is there any path by which I can come down and speak to you?'

He looked up at me without replying, and I looked down at him without pressing him too soon with a repetition of my idle question. Just then there came a vague vibration in the earth and air, quickly changing into a violent pulsation, and an oncoming rush that caused me to start back, as though it had force to draw me down. When such vapour as rose to my height from this rapid train had passed me, and was skimming away over the landscape, I looked down again, and saw him refurling the flag he had shown while the train went by.

I repeated my inquiry. After a pause, during which he seemed to regard me with fixed attention, he motioned with his rolled-up flag towards a point on my level, some two or three hundred yards distant. I called down to him: 'All right!' and made for that point. There, by dint of looking closely about me, I found a rough zigzag descending path notched out, which I followed.

The cutting was extremely deep, and unusually precipitous. It was made through a clammy stone, that became oozier and wetter as I went down. For these reasons, I found the way long enough to give me time to recall a singular air of reluctance or compulsion with which he had pointed out the path.

When I came down low enough upon the zigzag descent to see him again, I saw that he was standing between the rails on the way by which the train had lately passed, in an attitude as if he were waiting for me to appear. He had his left hand at his chin, and his left elbow rested on his right hand, crossed over his breast. His attitude was one of such expectation and watchfulness that I stopped a moment, wondering at it.

I resumed my downward way, and stepping out upon the level of the railroad, and drawing nearer to him, saw that he was a dark sallow man, with a dark beard and rather heavy eyebrows. His post was in as solitary and dismal a place as ever I saw. On either side, a dripping-wet wall of jagged stone, excluding all view but a strip of sky; the perspective one way only a crooked prolongation of this great dungeon; the shorter perspective in the other direction terminating in a gloomy red light, and the gloomier entrance to a black tunnel, in whose massive architecture there was a barbarous, depressing, and forbidding air. So little sunlight ever found its way to this spot, that it had an earthy, deadly smell; and so much cold wind rushed through it, that it struck chill to me, as if I had left the natural world.

Before he stirred, I was near enough to him to have touched him. Not even then removing his eyes from mine, he stepped back one step, and lifted his hand.

This was a lonesome post to occupy (I said), and it had riveted my attention when I looked down from up yonder. A visitor was a rarity, I should suppose; not an unwelcome rarity, I hoped? In me, he merely saw a man who had been shut up within narrow limits all his life, and who, being at last set free, had a newly-awakened interest in these great works. To such purpose I spoke to him; but I am far from sure of the terms I used; for, besides that I am not happy in opening any conversation, there was something in the man that daunted me.

He directed a most curious look towards the red light near the tunnel's mouth, and looked all about it, as if something were missing from it, and then looked at me.

That light was part of his charge? Was it not?

He answered in a low voice: 'Don't you know it is?'

The monstrous thought came into my mind, as I perused the fixed eyes and the saturnine face, that this was a spirit, not a man. I have speculated since, whether there may have been infection in his mind.

In my turn, I stepped back. But in making the action, I detected in his eyes some latent fear of me. This put the monstrous thought to flight.

'You look at me,' I said, forcing a smile, 'as if you had a dread of me.'

'I was doubtful,' he returned, 'whether I had seen you before.'

'Where?'

He pointed to the red light he had looked at.

'There?' I said.

Intently watchful of me, he replied (but without sound), 'Yes.'

'My good fellow, what should I do there? However, be that as it may, I never was there, you may swear.'

'I think I may,' he rejoined. 'Yes; I am sure I may.'

His manner cleared, like my own. He replied to my remarks with readiness, and in well-chosen words. Had he much to do there? Yes; that was to say, he had enough responsibility to bear; but exactness and watchfulness were what was required of him, and of actual work – manual labour – he had next to none. To change that signal, to trim those lights, and to turn this iron handle now and then, was all he had to do under that head. Regarding those many long and lonely hours of which I seemed to make so much, he could only say that the routine of his life had shaped itself into that form, and he had grown used to it. He had taught himself a language down here – if only to know it by sight, and to have formed his own crude ideas of its pronunciation, could be called learning it. He had also worked at fractions and decimals, and tried a little algebra; but he was, and had been as a boy, a poor hand at figures. Was it necessary for him when on duty always to remain in that channel of damp air, and could he never rise into the sunshine from between those high stone walls? Why, that depended upon times and circumstances. Under some conditions there would be less upon the Line than under others, and the same held good as to certain hours of the day and night. In bright weather, he did choose occasions for getting a little above these lower shadows; but, being at all times liable to be called by his electric bell, and at such times listening for it with redoubled anxiety, the relief was less than I would suppose.

He took me into his box, where there was a fire, a desk for an official book in which he had to make certain entries, a telegraphic instrument with its dial, face, and needles, and the little bell of which he had spoken. On my trusting that he would excuse the remark that he had been well educated, and (I hoped I might say without offence) perhaps educated above that station, he observed that instances of slight incongruity in such wise would rarely be found wanting among large bodies of men; that he had heard it was so in workhouses, in the police force; even in that last desperate resource, the army; and that he knew it was so, more or less, in any great railway staff. He had been, when young (if I could believe it, sitting in that hut – he scarcely could), a student of natural philosophy, and had attended lectures; but he had run wild, misused his opportunities, gone down, and never risen again. He had no complaint to offer about that. He had made his bed, and he lay upon it. It was far too late to make another.

All that I have here condensed he said in a quiet manner, with his grave dark regards divided between me and the fire. He threw in the word, 'sir', from time to time, and especially when he referred to his youth – as though to request me to understand that he claimed to be nothing but what I found him.

He was several times interrupted by the little bell, and had to read off messages, and send replies. Once he had to stand without the door, and display a flag as a train passed, and make some verbal communication to the driver. In the discharge of his duties, I observed him to be remarkably exact and vigilant, breaking off his discourse at a syllable, and remaining silent until what he had to do was done.

In a word, I should have set this man down as one of the safest of men to be employed in that capacity, but for the circumstance that while he was speaking to me he twice broke off with a fallen colour, turned his face towards the little bell when it did NOT ring, opened the door of the hut (which was kept shut to exclude the unhealthy damp), and looked out towards the red light near the mouth of the tunnel. On both of those occasions, he came back to the fire with the inexplicable air upon him which I had remarked, without being able to define, when we were so far asunder.

Said I, when I rose to leave him, 'You almost make me think that I have met with a contented man.'

(I am afraid I must acknowledge that I said it to lead him on.)

'I believe I used to be so,' he rejoined, in the low voice in which he had first spoken; 'but I am troubled, sir, I am troubled.'

He would have recalled the words if he could. He had said them, however, and I took them up quickly.

'With what? What is your trouble?'

'It is very difficult to impart, sir. It is very, very difficult to speak of. If ever you make me another visit, I will try to tell you.'

'But I expressly intend to make you another visit. Say, when shall it be?'

'I go off early in the morning, and I shall be on again at ten o'clock tomorrow night, sir.'

'I will come at eleven.'

He thanked me, and went out at the door with me. 'I'll show my white light, sir,' he said, in his peculiar low voice, 'till you have found the way up. When you have found it, don't call out! And when you are at the top, don't call out!'

His manner seemed to make the place strike colder to me, but I said no more than, 'Very well'.

'And when you come down tomorrow night, don't call out! Let me ask you a parting question. What made you cry, "Halloa! Below there!" tonight?'

'Heaven knows,' said I. 'I cried something to that effect—'

'Not to that effect, sir. Those were the very words. I know them well.'

'Admit those were the very words. I said them, no doubt, because I saw you below.'

'For no other reason?'

'What other reason could I possibly have?'

'You had no feeling that they were conveyed to you in any supernatural way?'

'No.'

He wished me good night, and held up his light. I walked by the side of the down Line of rails (with a very disagreeable sensation of a train coming behind me) until I found the path. It was easier to mount than to descend, and I got back to my inn without any adventure.

Punctual to my appointment, I placed my foot on the first notch of the zigzag next night, as the distant clocks were striking eleven. He was waiting for me at the bottom, with his white light on. 'I have not called out,' I said, when we came close together; 'may I speak now?' 'By all means, sir.' 'Good night, then, and here's my hand.' 'Good night, sir, and here's mine.' With that we walked side by side to his box, entered it, closed the door, and sat down by the fire.

'I have made up my mind, sir,' he began, bending forward as soon as we were seated, and speaking in a tone but a little above a whisper, 'that you shall not have to ask me twice what troubles me. I took you for someone else yesterday evening. That troubles me.'

'That mistake?'

'No. That someone else.'

'Who is it?'

'I don't know.'

'Like me?'

'I don't know. I never saw the face. The left arm is across the face, and the right arm is waved, – violently waved. This way.'

I followed his action with my eyes, and it was the action of an arm gesticulating, with the utmost passion and vehemence, 'For God's sake, clear the way!'

'One moonlight night,' said the man, 'I was sitting here, when I heard a voice cry, "Halloa! Below there!" I started up, looked from that door, and saw this someone else standing by the red light near the tunnel, waving as I just now showed you. The voice seemed hoarse with shouting, and it cried: "Look out! Look out!" And then again: "Halloa! Below there! Look out!" I caught up my lamp, turned it on red, and ran towards the figure, calling, "What's wrong? What has happened? Where?" It stood just outside the blackness of the tunnel. I advanced so close upon it that I wondered at its keeping the sleeve across its eyes. I ran right up at it, and had my hand stretched out to pull the sleeve away, when it was gone.'

'Into the tunnel?' said I.

'No. I ran on into the tunnel, five hundred yards. I stopped, and held my lamp above my head, and saw the figures of the measured distance, and saw the wet stains stealing down the walls and trickling through the arch. I ran out again faster than I had run in (for I had a mortal abhorrence of the place upon me), and I looked all round the red light with my own red light, and I went up the iron ladder to the gallery atop of it, and I came down again, and ran back here. I telegraphed both ways. "An alarm has been given. Is anything wrong?" The answer came back, both ways, "All well."'

Resisting the slow touch of a frozen finger tracing out my spine, I showed him how that this figure must be a deception of his sense of sight; and how that figures, originating in disease of the delicate nerves that minister to the functions of the eye, were known to have often troubled patients, some of whom had become conscious of the nature of their affliction, and had even proved it by experiments upon themselves. 'As to an imaginary cry,' said I, 'do but listen for a moment to the wind in this unnatural valley while we speak so low, and to the wild harp it makes of the telegraph wires.'

That was all very well, he returned, after we had sat listening for a while, and he ought to know something of the wind and the wires – he who so often passed long winter nights there, alone and watching. But he would beg to remark that he had not finished.

I asked his pardon, and he slowly added these words, touching my arm:

'Within six hours after the Appearance, the memorable accident on this Line happened, and within ten hours the dead and wounded were brought along through the tunnel over the spot where the figure had stood.'

A disagreeable shudder crept over me, but I did my best against it. It was not to be denied, I rejoined, that this was a remarkable coincidence, calculated deeply to impress his mind. But it was unquestionable that remarkable coincidences did continually occur, and they must be taken into account in dealing with such a subject. Though to be sure I must admit, I added (for I thought I saw that he was going to bring the objection to bear upon me), men of common sense did not allow much for coincidences in making the ordinary calculations of life.

He again begged to remark that he had not finished.

I again begged his pardon for being betrayed into interruptions.

'This,' he said, again laying his hand upon my arm, and glancing over his shoulder with hollow eyes, 'was just a year ago. Six or seven months passed, and I had recovered from the surprise and shock, when one morning, as the day was breaking, I, standing at the door, looked towards the red light, and saw the spectre again.' He stopped, with a fixed look at me.

'Did it cry out?'

'No. It was silent.'

'Did it wave its arm?'

'No. It leaned against the shaft of the light, with both hands before the face. Like this.'

Once more I followed his action with my eyes. It was an action of mourning. I have seen such an attitude in stone figures on tombs.

'Did you go up to it?'

'I came in and sat down, partly to collect my thoughts, partly because it had turned me faint. When I went to the door again, daylight was above me, and the ghost was gone.'

'But nothing followed? Nothing came of this?'

He touched me on the arm with his forefinger twice or thrice, giving a ghastly nod each time:

'That very day, as a train came out of the tunnel, I noticed, at a carriage window on my side, what looked like a confusion of hands and heads, and something waved. I saw it just in time to signal the driver, Stop! He shut off, and put his brake on, but the train drifted past here a hundred and fifty yards or more. I ran after it, and, as I went along, heard terrible screams and cries. A beautiful young lady had died instantaneously in one of the compartments, and was brought in here, and laid down on this floor between us.'

Involuntarily I pushed my chair back, as I looked from the boards at which he pointed to himself.

'True, sir. True. Precisely as it happened, so I tell it you.'

I could think of nothing to say, to any purpose, and my mouth was very dry. The wind and the wires took up the story with a long lamenting wail.

He resumed. 'Now, sir, mark this, and judge how my mind is troubled. The spectre came back a week ago. Ever since, it has been there, now and again, by fits and starts.'

'At the light?'

'At the Danger-light.'

'What does it seem to do?'

He repeated, if possible with increased passion and vehemence, that former gesticulation of 'For God's sake, clear the way!'

Then he went on. 'I have no peace or rest for it. It calls to me, for many minutes together, in an agonized manner, "Below there! Look out! Look out!" It stands waving to me. It rings my little bell –'

I caught at that. 'Did it ring your bell yesterday evening when I was here, and you went to the door?'

'Twice.'

'Why, see,' said I, 'how your imagination misleads you. My eyes were on the bell, and my ears were open to the bell, and if I am a living man, it did NOT ring at those times. No, nor at any other time, except when it was rung in the natural course of physical things by the station communicating with you.'

He shook his head. 'I have never made a mistake as to that yet, sir. I have never confused the spectre's ring with the man's. The ghost's ring is a strange vibration in the bell that it derives from nothing else, and I have not asserted that the bell stirs to the eye. I don't wonder that you failed to hear it. But *I* heard it.'

'And did the spectre seem to be there, when you looked out?'

'It WAS there.'

'Both times?'

He repeated firmly: 'Both times.'

'Will you come to the door with me, and look for it now?'

He bit his under lip as though he were somewhat unwilling, but arose. I opened the door, and stood on the step, while he stood in the doorway. There was the Danger-light. There was the dismal mouth of the tunnel. There were the high, wet stone walls of the cutting. There were the stars above them.

'Do you see it?' I asked him, taking particular note of his face. His eyes were prominent and strained, but not very much more so, perhaps, than my own had been when I had directed them earnestly towards the same spot.

'No,' he answered. 'It is not there.'

'Agreed,' said I.

We went in again, shut the door, and resumed our seats. I was thinking how best to improve this advantage, if it might be called one, when he took up the conversation in such a matter-of-course way, so assuming that there could' be no serious question of fact between us, that I felt myself placed in the weakest of positions.

'By this time you will fully understand, sir,' he said, 'that what troubles me so dreadfully is the question: What does the spectre mean?'

I was not sure, I told him, that I did fully understand.

'What is its warning against?' he said, ruminating, with his eyes on the fire, and only by times turning them on me.

'What is the danger? Where is the danger? There is danger overhanging somewhere on the Line. Some dreadful calamity will happen. It is not to be doubted this third time, after what has gone before. But surely this is a cruel haunting of *me*. What can *I* do?'

He pulled out his handkerchief, and wiped the drops from his heated forehead.

'If I telegraph Danger, on either side of me, or on both, I can give no reason for it,' he went on, wiping the palms of his hands. 'I should get into trouble, and do no good. They would think I was mad. This is the way it would work: Message: "Danger! Take care!" Answer: "What Danger? Where?" Message: "Don't know. But, for God's sake, take care!" They would displace me. What else could they do?'

His pain of mind was most pitiable to see. It was the mental torture of a conscientious man, oppressed beyond endurance by an unintelligible responsibility involving life.

'When it first stood under the Danger-light,' he went on, putting his dark hair back from his head, and drawing his hands outward across and across his temples in an extremity of feverish distress, 'why not tell me where that accident was to happen – if it must happen? Why not tell me how it could be averted – if it could have been averted? When on its second coming it hid its face, why not tell me, instead, "She is going to die. Let them keep her at home"? If it came, on those two occasions, only to show me that its warnings were true, and so to prepare me for the third, why not warn me plainly now? And I, Lord help me! A mere poor signalman on this solitary station! Why not go to somebody with credit to be believed and power to act?'

When I saw him in this state, I saw that for the poor man's sake, as well as for the public safety, what I had to do for the time was to compose his mind. Therefore, setting aside all question of reality or unreality between us, I represented to him that whoever thoroughly discharged his duty must do well, and that at least it was his comfort that he understood his duty, though he did not understand these confounding Appearances. In this effort I succeeded far better than in the attempt to reason him out of his conviction. He became calm; the occupations incidental to his post as the night advanced began to make larger demands on his attention: and I left him at two in the morning. I had offered to stay through the night, but he would not hear of it.

That I more than once looked back at the red light as I ascended the pathway, that I did not like the red light, and that I should have slept but poorly if my bed had been under it, I see no reason to conceal. Nor did I like the two sequences of the accident and the dead girl. I see no reason to conceal that either.

But what ran most in my thoughts was the consideration how ought I to act, having become the recipient of this disclosure? I had proved the man to be intelligent, vigilant, painstaking, and exact; but how long might he remain so, in his state of mind? Though in a subordinate position, still he held a most important trust, and would I (for instance) like to stake my own life on the chances of his continuing to execute it with precision?

Unable to overcome a feeling that there would be something treacherous in my communicating what he had told me to his superiors in the Company, without first being plain with himself and proposing a middle course to him, I ultimately resolved to offer to accompany him (otherwise keeping his secret for the present) to the wisest medical practitioner we could hear of in those parts, and to take his opinion. A change in his time of duty would come round next night, he had apprised me, and he would be off an hour or two after sunrise, and on again soon after sunset. I had appointed to return accordingly.

Next evening was a lovely evening, and I walked out early to enjoy it. The sun was not yet quite down when I traversed the field-path near the top of the deep cutting. I would extend my walk for an hour, I said to myself, half an hour on and half an hour back, and it would then be time to go to my signalman's box.

Before pursuing my stroll, I stepped to the brink, and mechanically looked down, from the point from which I had first seen him. I cannot describe the thrill that seized upon me, when, close at the mouth of the tunnel, I saw the appearance of a man, with his left sleeve across his eyes, passionately waving his right arm.

The nameless horror that oppressed me passed in a moment, for in a moment I saw that this appearance of a man was a man indeed, and that there was a little group of other men, standing at a short distance, to whom he seemed to be rehearsing the gesture he made. The Danger-light was not yet lighted. Against its shaft, a little low hut, entirely new to me, had been made of some wooden supports and tarpaulin. It looked no bigger than a bed.

With an irresistible sense that something was wrong – with a flashing self-reproachful fear that fatal mischief had come of my leaving the man there, and causing no one to be sent to overlook or correct what he did – I descended the notched path with all the speed I could make.

'What is the matter?' I asked the men.

'Signalman killed this morning, sir.'

'Not the man belonging to that box?'

'Yes, sir.'

'Not the man I know?'

'You will recognize him, sir, if you knew him,' said the man who spoke for the others, solemnly uncovering his own head, and raising an end of the tarpaulin, 'for his face is quite composed.'

'Oh, how did this happen, how did this happen?' I asked, turning from one to another as the hut closed in again.

'He was cut down by an engine, sir. No man in England knew his work better. But somehow he was not clear of the outer rail. It was just at broad day. He had struck the light, and had the lamp in his hand. As the engine came out of the tunnel, his back was towards her, and she cut him down. That man drove her, and was showing how it happened. Show the gentleman, Tom.'

The man, who wore a rough dark dress, stepped back to his former place at the mouth of the tunnel.

'Coming round the curve in the tunnel, sir,' he said, 'I saw him at the end, like as if I saw him down a perspective glass.

There was no time to check speed, and I knew him to be very careful. As he didn't seem to take heed of the whistle, I shut it off when we were running down upon him, and called to him as loud as I could call.'

'What did you say?'

'I said, "Below there! Look out! Look out! For God's sake, clear the way!"'

I started.

'Ah! it was a dreadful time, sir. I never left off calling to him. I put this arm before my eyes not to see, and I waved this arm to the last; but it was no use.'

Without prolonging the narrative to dwell on any one of its curious circumstances more than on any other, I may, in closing it, point out the coincidence that the warning of the engine-driver included, not only the words which the unfortunate signalman had repeated to me as haunting him, but also the words which I myself – not he – had attached, and that only in my own mind, to the gesticulation he had imitated.

Thomas Hardy

THE WITHERED ARM

1 · A Lorn Milkmaid

IT was an eighty-cow dairy, and the troop of milkers, regular
and supernumerary, were all at work; for, though the time of
year was as yet but early April, the feed lay entirely in water-
meadows, and the cows were 'in full pail'. The hour was about
six in the evening, and three-fourths of the large, red, rectangular animals having been finished off, there was opportunity
for a little conversation.

'He do bring home his bride tomorrow, I hear. They've
come as far as Anglebury today.'

The voice seemed to proceed from the belly of the cow called
Cherry, but the speaker was a milking-woman, whose face was
buried in the flank of that motionless beast.

'Hav' anybody seen her?' said another.

There was a negative response from the first. 'Though they
say she's a rosy-cheeked, tisty-tosty little body enough,' she
added; and as the milkmaid spoke she turned her face so that
she could glance past her cow's tail to the other side of the
barton, where a thin, fading woman of thirty milked somewhat
apart from the rest.

'Years younger than he, they say,' continued the second,
with also a glance of reflectiveness in the same direction.

'How old do you call him, then?'

'Thirty or so.'

'More like forty,' broke in an old milkman near, in a long
white pinafore or 'wropper', and with the brim of his hat tied
down, so that he looked like a woman. ' 'A was born before our
Great Weir was builded, and I hadn't man's wages when I laved
water there.'

25

The discussion waxed so warm that the purr of the milk-streams became jerky, till a voice from another cow's belly cried with authority, 'Now then, what the Turk do it matter to us about Farmer Lodge's age, or Farmer Lodge's new mis'ess? I shall have to pay him nine pound a year for the rent of every one of these milchers, whatever his age or hers. Get on with your work, or 'twill be dark afore we have done. The evening is pinking in a'ready.' This speaker was the dairyman himself, by whom the milkmaids and men were employed.

Nothing more was said publicly about Farmer Lodge's wedding, but the first woman murmured under her cow to her next neighbour, ' 'Tis hard for *she*,' signifying the thin worn milkmaid aforesaid.

'O no,' said the second. 'He ha'n't spoke to Rhoda Brook for years.'

When the milking was done they washed their pails and hung them on a many-forked stand made as usual of the peeled limb of an oak-tree, set upright in the earth, and resembling a colossal antlered horn. The majority then dispersed in various directions homeward. The thin woman who had not spoken was joined by a boy of twelve or thereabout, and the twain went away up the field also.

Their course lay apart from that of the others, to a lonely spot high above the water-meads, and not far from the border of Egdon Heath, whose dark countenance was visible in the distance as they drew nigh to their home.

'They've just been saying down in barton that your father brings his young wife home from Anglebury tomorrow,' the woman observed. 'I shall want to send you for a few things to market, and you'll be pretty sure to meet 'em.'

'Yes, Mother,' said the boy. 'Is Father married then?'

'Yes. . . . You can give her a look, and tell me what's she's like, if you do see her.'

'Yes, Mother.'

'If she's dark or fair, and if she's tall – as tall as I. And if she seems like a woman who has ever worked for a living, or one that has been always well off, and has never done anything, and shows marks of the lady on her, as I expect she do.'

'Yes.'

They crept up the hill in the twilight, and entered the cottage. It was built of mud-walls, the surface of which had been washed by many rains into channels and depressions that left none of the original flat face visible; while here and there in the thatch above a rafter showed like a bone protruding through the skin.

She was kneeling down in the chimney-corner, before two pieces of turf laid together with the heather inwards, blowing at the red-hot ashes with her breath till the turves flamed. The radiance lit her pale cheek, and made her dark eyes, that had once been handsome, seem handsome anew. 'Yes,' she resumed, 'see if she is dark or fair, and if you can, notice if her hands be white; if not, see if they look as though she had ever done housework, or are milker's hands like mine.'

The boy again promised, inattentively this time, his mother not observing that he was cutting a notch with his pocket-knife in the beech-backed chair.

2 · *The Young Wife*

The road from Anglebury to Holmstoke is in general level; but there is one place where a sharp ascent breaks its monotony. Farmers homeward-bound from the former market-town, who trot all the rest of the way, walk their horses up this short incline.

The next evening, while the sun was yet bright, a handsome new gig, with a lemon-coloured body and red wheels, was spinning westward along the level highway at the heels of a powerful mare. The driver was a yeoman in the prime of life, cleanly shaven like an actor, his face being toned to that bluish-vermilion hue which so often graces a thriving farmer's features when returning home after successful dealings in the town. Beside him sat a woman, many years his junior – almost, indeed, a girl. Her face too was fresh in colour, but it was of a totally different quality – soft and evanescent, like the light under a heap of rose-petals.

Few people travelled this way, for it was not a main road; and the long white riband of gravel that stretched before them was empty, save of one small scarce-moving speck, which presently resolved itself into the figure of a boy, who was creeping on at a snail's pace, and continually looking behind him – the heavy bundle he carried being some excuse for, if not the reason of, his dilatoriness. When the bouncing gig-party slowed at the bottom of the incline above mentioned, the pedestrian was only a few yards in front. Supporting the large bundle by putting one hand on his hip, he turned and looked straight at the farmer's wife as though he would read her through and through, pacing along abreast of the horse.

The low sun was full in her face, rendering every feature, shade, and contour distinct, from the curve of her little nostril to the colour of her eyes. The farmer, though he seemed annoyed at the boy's persistent presence, did not order him to get out of the way; and thus the lad preceded them, his hard gaze never leaving her, till they reached the top of the ascent, when the farmer trotted on with relief in his lineaments – having taken no outward notice of the boy whatever.

'How that poor lad stared at me!' said the young wife.

'Yes, dear; I saw that he did.'

'He is one of the village, I suppose?'

'One of the neighbourhood. I think he lives with his mother a mile or two off.'

'He knows who we are, no doubt?'

'O yes. You must expect to be stared at just at first, my pretty Gertrude.'

'I do – though I think the poor boy may have looked at us in the hope we might relieve him of his heavy load, rather than from curiosity.'

'O no,' said her husband off-handedly. 'These country lads will carry a hundredweight once they get it on their backs; besides his pack had more size than weight in it. Now, then, another mile and I shall be able to show you our house in the distance – if it is not too dark before we get there.' The wheels spun round, and particles flew from their periphery as before, till a white house of ample dimensions revealed itself, with farm-buildings and ricks at the back.

Meanwhile the boy had quickened his pace, and turning up a by-lane some mile and half short of the white farmstead, ascended towards the leaner pastures, and so on to the cottage of his mother.

She had reached home after her day's milking at the outlying dairy, and was washing cabbage at the doorway in the declining light. 'Hold up the net a moment,' she said, without preface, as the boy came up.

He flung down his bundle, held the edge of the cabbage-net, and as she filled its meshes with the dripping leaves she went on, 'Well, did you see her?'

'Yes; quite plain.'

'Is she ladylike?'

'Yes; and more. A lady complete.'

'Is she young?'

'Well, she's growed up, and her ways be quite a woman's.'

'Of course. What colour is her hair and face?'

'Her hair is lightish, and her face as comely as a live doll's.'

'Her eyes, then, are not dark like mine?'

'No—of a bluish turn, and her mouth is very nice and red; and when she smiles, her teeth show white.'

'Is she tall?' said the woman sharply.

'I couldn't see. She was sitting down.'

'Then do you go to Holmstoke church tomorrow morning: she's sure to be there. Go early and notice her walking in, and come home and tell me if she's taller than I.'

'Very well, Mother. But why don't you go and see for yourself?'

'*I* go to see her! I wouldn't look up at her if she were to pass my window this instant. She was with Mr Lodge, of course. What did he say or do?'

'Just the same as usual.'

'Took no notice of you?'

'None.'

Next day the mother put a clean shirt on the boy, and started him off for Holmstoke church. He reached the ancient little pile when the door was just being opened, and he was the first to enter. Taking his seat by the font, he watched all the parishioners file in. The well-to-do Farmer Lodge came nearly last; and his young wife, who accompanied him, walked up the aisle with the shyness natural to a modest woman who had appeared thus for the first time. As all other eyes were fixed upon her, the youth's stare was not noticed now.

When he reached home his mother said, 'Well?' before he had entered the room.

'She is not tall. She is rather short,' he replied.

'Ah!' said his mother, with satisfaction.

'But she's very pretty – very. In fact, she's lovely.' The youthful freshness of the yeoman's wife had evidently made an impression even on the somewhat hard nature of the boy.

'That's all I want to hear,' said his mother quickly. 'Now, spread the table-cloth. The hare you wired is very tender; but mind that nobody catches you. – You've never told me what sort of hands she had.'

'I have never seen 'em. She never took off her gloves.'

'What did she wear this morning?'

'A white bonnet and a silver-coloured gownd. It whewed and whistled so loud when it rubbed against the pews that the lady coloured up more than ever for very shame at the noise, and pulled it in to keep it from touching; but when she pushed into her seat, it whewed more than ever. Mr Lodge, he seemed pleased, and his waistcoat stuck out, and his great golden seals hung like a lord's; but she seemed to wish her noisy gownd anywhere but on her.'

'Not she! However, that will do now.'

These descriptions of the newly-married couple were continued from time to time by the boy at his mother's request, after any chance encounter he had had with them. But Rhoda Brook, though she might easily have seen young Mrs Lodge for herself by walking a couple of miles, would never attempt an excusion towards the quarter where the farmhouse lay.

Neither did she, at the daily milking in the dairyman's yard on Lodge's outlying second farm, ever speak on the subject of the recent marriage. The dairyman, who rented the cows of Lodge, and knew perfectly the tall milkmaid's history, with manly kindliness always kept the gossip in the cow-barton from annoying Rhoda. But the atmosphere thereabout was full of the subject during the first days of Mrs Lodge's arrival; and from her boy's description and the casual words of the other milkers, Rhoda Brook could raise a mental image of the unconscious Mrs Lodge that was realistic as a photograph.

3 · A Vision

One night, two or three weeks after the bridal return, when the boy was gone to bed, Rhoda sat a long time over the turf ashes that she had raked out in front of her to extinguish them. She contemplated so intently the new wife, as presented to her in her mind's eye over the embers, that she forgot the lapse of time. At last, wearied with her day's work, she too retired.

But the figure which had occupied her so much during this and the previous days was not to be banished at night. For the first time Gertrude Lodge visited the supplanted woman in her dreams. Rhoda Brook dreamed – since her assertion that she really saw, before falling asleep, was not to be believed – that the young wife, in the pale silk dress and white bonnet, but with features shockingly distorted, and wrinkled as by age, was sitting upon her chest as she lay. The pressure of Mrs Lodge's person grew heavier; the blue eyes peered cruelly into her face; and then the figure thrust forward its left hand mockingly, so as to make the wedding-ring it wore glitter in Rhoda's eyes. Maddened mentally, and nearly suffocated by pressure, the sleeper struggled; the incubus, still regarding her, withdrew to the foot of the bed, only, however, to come forward by degrees, resume her seat, and flash her left hand as before.

Gasping for breath, Rhoda, in a last desperate effort, swung out her right hand, seized the confronting spectre by its obtrusive left arm, and whirled it backward to the floor, starting up herself as she did so with a low cry.

'O, merciful heaven!' she cried, sitting on the edge of the bed in a cold sweat; 'that was not a dream – she was here!'

She could feel her antagonist's arm within her grasp even now – the very flesh and bone of it, as it seemed. She looked on the floor whither she had whirled the spectre, but there was nothing to be seen.

Rhoda Brook slept no more that night, and when she went milking at the next dawn they noticed how pale and haggard she looked. The milk that she drew quivered into the pail; her hand had not calmed even yet, and still retained the feel of the arm. She came home to breakfast as wearily as if it had been suppertime.

'What was that noise in your chimmer, Mother, last night?' said her son. 'You fell off the bed, surely?'

'Did you hear anything fall? At what time?'

'Just when the clock struck two.'

She could not explain, and when the meal was done went silently about her household work, the boy assisting her, for he hated going afield on the farms, and she indulged his reluctance. Between eleven and twelve the garden-gate clicked, and she lifted her eyes to the window. At the bottom of the garden, within the gate, stood the woman of her vision. Rhoda seemed transfixed.

'Ah, she said she would come!' exclaimed the boy, also observing her.

'Said so – when? How does she know us?'

'I have seen and spoken to her. I talked to her yesterday.'

'I told you,' said the mother, flushing indignantly, 'never to speak to anybody in that house, or go near the place.'

'I did not speak to her till she spoke to me. And I did not go near the place. I met her in the road.'

'What did you tell her?'

'Nothing. She said, "Are you the poor boy who had to bring the heavy load from market?" And she looked at my boots, and said they would not keep my feet dry if it came on wet, because they were so cracked. I told her I lived with my mother, and we had enough to do to keep ourselves, and that's how it was; and she said then, "I'll come and bring you some better boots, and see your mother." She gives away things to other folks in the meads besides us.'

Mrs Lodge was by this time close to the door – not in her silk, as Rhoda had dreamt of in the bed-chamber, but in a morning hat, and gown of common light material, which became her better than silk. On her arm she carried a basket.

The impression remaining from the night's experience was still strong. Brook had almost expected to see the wrinkles, the scorn, and the cruelty on her visitor's face. She would have escaped an interview, had escape been possible. There was, however, no backdoor to the cottage, and in an instant the boy had lifted the latch to Mrs Lodge's gentle knock.

'I see I have come to the right house,' said she, glancing at the lad, and smiling. 'But I was not sure till you opened the door.'

The figure and action were those of the phantom; but her voice was so indescribably sweet, her glance so winning, her smile so tender, so unlike that of Rhoda's midnight visitant, that the latter could hardly believe the evidence of her senses. She was truly glad that she had not hidden away in sheer aversion, as she had been inclined to do. In her basket Mrs Lodge brought the pair of boots that she had promised to the boy, and other useful articles.

At these proofs of a kindly feeling toward her and hers Rhoda's heart reproached her bitterly. This innocent young thing should have her blessing and not her curse. When she left them a light seemed gone from the dwelling. Two days later she came again to know if the boots fitted; and less than a fortnight after that paid Rhoda another call. On this occasion the boy was absent.

'I walk a good deal,' said Mrs Lodge, 'and your house is the nearest outside our own parish. I hope you are well. You don't look quite well.'

Rhoda said she was well enough; and, indeed, though the

paler of the two, there was more of the strength that endures in her well-defined features and large frame, than in the soft-cheeked young woman before her. The conversation became quite confidential as regarded their powers and weaknesses; and when Mrs Lodge was leaving, Rhoda said, 'I hope you will find this air agree with you, ma'am, and not suffer from the damp of the water meads.'

The younger one replied that there was not much doubt of it, her general health being usually good. 'Though, now you remind me,' she added, 'I have one little ailment which puzzles me. It is nothing serious, but I cannot make it out.'

She uncovered her left hand and arm; and their outline confronted Rhoda's gaze as the exact original of the limb she had beheld and seized in her dream. Upon the pink round surface of the arm were faint marks of an unhealthy colour, as if produced by a rough grasp. Rhoda's eyes became riveted on the discolorations; she fancied that she discerned in them the shape of her own four fingers.

'How did it happen?' she said mechanically.

'I cannot tell,' replied Mrs Lodge, shaking her head. 'One night when I was sound asleep, dreaming I was away in some strange place, a pain suddenly shot into my arm there, and was so keen as to awaken me. I must have struck it in the daytime, I suppose, though I don't remember doing so.' She added, laughing, 'I tell my dear husband that it looks just as if he had flown into a rage and struck me there. O, I daresay it will soon disappear.'

'Ha, ha! Yes. . . . On what night did it come?'

Mrs Lodge considered, and said it would be a fortnight ago on the morrow. 'When I awoke I could not remember where I was,' she added, 'till the clock striking two reminded me.'

She had named the night and the hour of Rhoda's spectral encounter, and Brook felt like a guilty thing. The artless disclosure startled her; she did not reason on the freaks of coincidence; and all the scenery of that ghastly night returned with double vividness to her mind.

'O, can it be,' she said to herself, when her visitor had departed, 'that I exercise a malignant power over people against my own will?' She knew that she had been slily called a witch since her fall; but never having understood why that particular stigma had been attached to her, it had passed disregarded. Could this be the explanation, and had such things as this ever happened before?

4 · A Suggestion

The summer drew on, and Rhoda Brook almost dreaded to meet Mrs Lodge again, notwithstanding that her feeling for the young wife amounted well-nigh to affection. Something in her own individuality seemed to convict Rhoda of crime. Yet a fatality sometimes would direct the steps of the latter to the outskirts of Holmstoke whenever she left her house for any other purpose than her daily work; and hence it happened that their next encounter was out of doors. Rhoda could not avoid the subject which had so mystified her, and after the first few words she stammered, 'I hope your – arm is well again, ma'am?' She had perceived with consternation that Gertrude Lodge carried her left arm stiffly.

'No; it is not quite well. Indeed it is no better at all; it is rather worse. It pains me dreadfully sometimes.'

'Perhaps you had better go to a doctor, ma'am.'

She replied that she had already seen a doctor. Her husband had insisted upon her going to one. But the surgeon had not seemed to understand the afflicted limb at all; he had told her to bathe it in hot water, and she had bathed it, but the treatment had done no good.

'Will you let me see it?' said the milkwoman.

Mrs Lodge pushed up her sleeve and disclosed the place, which was a few inches above the wrist. As soon as Rhoda Brook saw it, she could hardly preserve her composure. There was nothing of the nature of a wound, but the arm at that point had a shrivelled look, and the outline of the four fingers appeared more distinct than at the former time. Moreover, she fancied that they were imprinted in precisely the relative position of her clutch upon the arm in the trance; the first finger towards Gertrude's wrist, and the fourth towards her elbow.

What the impress resembled seemed to have struck Gertrude herself since their last meeting. 'It looks almost like finger-marks,' she said; adding with a faint laugh, 'my husband says it is as if some witch, or the devil himself, had taken hold of me there, and blasted the flesh.'

Rhoda shivered. 'That's fancy,' she said hurriedly. 'I wouldn't mind it, if I were you.'

'I shouldn't so much mind it,' said the younger, with hesitation, 'if – if I hadn't a notion that it makes my husband – dislike me – no, love me less. Men think so much of personal appearance.'

'Some do – he for one.'

'Yes; and he was very proud of mine, at first.'

'Keep your arm covered from his sight.'

'Ah – he knows the disfigurement is there!' She tried to hide the tears that filled her eyes.

'Well, ma'am, I earnestly hope it will go away soon.'

And so the milkwoman's mind was chained anew to the subject by a horrid sort of spell as she returned home. The sense of having been guilty of an act of malignity increased, affect as she might to ridicule her superstition. In her secret heart Rhoda did not altogether object to a slight diminution of her successor's beauty, by whatever means it had come about; but she did nòt wish to inflict upon her physical pain. For though this pretty young woman had rendered impossible any reparation which Lodge might have made Rhoda for his past conduct, everything like resentment at the unconscious usurpation had quite passed away from the elder's mind.

If the sweet and kindly Gertrude Lodge only knew of the dream-scene in the bed-chamber, what would she think? Not to inform her of it seemed treachery in the presence of her friendliness; but tell she could not of her own accord – neither could she devise a remedy.

She mused upon the matter the greater part of the night;

and the next day, after the morning milking, set out to obtain another glimpse of Gertrude Lodge if she could, being held to her by a gruesome fascination. By watching the house from a distance the milkmaid was presently able to discern the farmer's wife in a ride she was taking alone – probably to join her husband in some distant field. Mrs Lodge perceived her, and cantered in her direction.

'Good morning, Rhoda!' Gertrude said, when she had come up. 'I was going to call.'

Rhoda noticed that Mrs Lodge held the reins with some difficulty.

'I hope – the bad arm,' said Rhoda.

'They tell me there is possibly one way by which I might be able to find out the cause, and so perhaps the cure, of it,' replied the other anxiously. 'It is by going to some clever man over in Egdon Heath. They did not know if he was still alive – and I cannot remember his name at this moment; but they said that you knew more of his movements than anybody else here-about, and could tell me if he were still to be consulted. Dear me – what was his name? But you know.'

'Not Conjuror Trendle?' said her thin companion, turning pale.

'Trendle – yes. Is he alive?'

'I believe so,' said Rhoda, with reluctance.

'Why do you call him conjuror?'

'Well – they say – they used to say he was a – he had powers other folks have not.'

'O, how could my people be so superstitious as to recommend a man of that sort! I thought they meant some medical man. I shall think no more of him.'

Rhoda looked relieved, and Mrs Lodge rode on. The milk-woman had inwardly seen, from the moment she heard of her having been mentioned as a reference for this man, that there must exist a sarcastic feeling among the work-folk that a sorceress would know the whereabouts of the exorcist. They suspected her, then. A short time ago this would have given no concern to a woman of her common-sense. But she had a haunting reason to be superstitious now; and she had been seized with sudden dread that this Conjuror Trendle might name her as the malignant influence which was blasting the fair person of Gertrude, and so lead her friend to hate her for ever, and to treat her as some fiend in human shape.

But all was not over. Two days after, a shadow intruded into the window-pattern thrown on Rhoda Brook's floor by the afternoon sun. The woman opened the door at once, almost breathlessly.

'Are you alone?' said Gertrude. She seemed to be no less harassed and anxious than Brook herself.

'Yes,' said Rhoda.

'The place on my arm seems worse, and troubles me!' the young farmer's wife went on. 'It is so mysterious! I do hope it will not be an incurable wound. I have again been thinking of what they said about Conjuror Trendle. I don't really believe in such men, but I should not mind just visiting him, from curiosity – though on no account must my husband know. Is it far to where he lives?'

'Yes – five miles,' said Rhoda backwardly. 'In the heart of Egdon.'

'Well, I should have to walk. Could not you go with me to show me the way – say tomorrow afternoon?'

'O, not I – that is – ' the milkwoman murmured, with a start of dismay. Again the dread seized her that something to do with her fierce act in the dream might be revealed, and her character in the eyes of the most useful friend she had ever had be ruined irretrievably.

Mrs Lodge urged, and Rhoda finally assented, though with much misgiving. Sad as the journey would be to her, she could not conscientiously stand in the way of a possible remedy for her patron's strange affliction. It was agreed that, to escape suspicion of their mystic intent, they should meet at the edge of the heath at the corner of a plantation which was visible from the spot where they now stood.

5 · Conjuror Trendle

By the next afternoon Rhoda would have done anything to escape this inquiry. But she had promised to go. Moreover, there was a horrid fascination at times in becoming instrumental in throwing such possible light on her own character as would reveal her to be something greater in the occult world than she had ever herself suspected.

She started just before the time of day mentioned between them, and half-an-hour's brisk walking brought her to the south-eastern extension of the Egdon tract of country, where the fir plantation was. A slight figure, cloaked and veiled, was already there. Rhoda recognized, almost with a shudder, that Mrs Lodge bore her left arm in a sling.

They hardly spoke to each other, and immediately set out on their climb into the interior of this solemn country, which stood high above the rich alluvial soil they had left half-an-hour before. It was a long walk; thick clouds made the atmosphere dark, though it was as yet only early afternoon; and the wind howled dismally over the slopes of the heath – not improbably the same heath which had witnessed the agony of the Wessex King Ina, presented to after-ages as Lear. Gertrude Lodge talked most, Rhoda replying with monosyllabic preoccupation. She had a strange dislike to walking on the side of her companion where hung the afflicted arm, moving round to the other when inadvertently near it. Much heather had been brushed by their feet when they descended upon a cart-track, beside which stood the house of the man they sought.

He did not profess his remedial practices openly, or care anything about their continuance, his direct interests being those of a dealer in furze, turf, 'sharp sand', and other local products. Indeed, he affected not to believe largely in his own powers, and when warts that had been shown him for cure miraculously disappeared – which it must be owned they infallibly did – he would say lightly, 'O, I only drink a glass of grog upon 'em at your expense – perhaps it's all chance', and immediately turn the subject.

He was at home when they arrived, having in fact seen them descending into his valley. He was a grey-bearded man, with a reddish face, and he looked singularly at Rhoda the first moment he beheld her. Mrs Lodge told him her errand; and then with words of self-disparagement he examined her arm.

'Medicine can't cure it,' he said promptly. ' 'Tis the work of an enemy.'

Rhoda shrank into herself, and drew back.

'An enemy? What enemy?' asked Mrs Lodge.

He shook his head. 'That's best known to yourself,' he said. 'If you like, I can show the person to you, though I shall not myself know who it is. I can do no more; and don't wish to do that.'

She pressed him; on which he told Rhoda to wait outside where she stood, and took Mrs Lodge into the room. It opened immediately from the door; and, as the latter remained ajar, Rhoda Brook could see the proceedings without taking part in them. He brought a tumbler from the dresser, nearly filled it with water, and fetching an egg, prepared it in some private way; after which he broke it on the edge of the glass, so that the white went in and the yolk remained. As it was getting gloomy, he took the glass and its contents to the window, and told Gertrude to watch the mixture closely. They leant over the table together, and the milkwoman could see the opaline hue of the egg-fluid changing form as it sank in the water, but she was not near enough to define the shape that it assumed.

'Do you catch the likeness of any face or figure as you look?' demanded the conjuror of the young woman.

She murmured a reply, in tones so low as to be inaudible to Rhoda, and continued to gaze intently into the glass. Rhoda turned, and walked a few steps away.

When Mrs Lodge came out, and her face was met by the light, it appeared exceedingly pale – as pale as Rhoda's – against the sad dun shades of the upland's garniture. Trendle shut the door behind her, and they at once started homeward together. But Rhoda perceived that her companion had quite changed.

'Did he charge much?' she asked tentatively.

'O no – nothing. He would not take a farthing,' said Gertrude.

'And what did you see?' inquired Rhoda.

'Nothing I – care to speak of.' The constraint in her manner was remarkable; her face was so rigid as to wear an oldened aspect, faintly suggestive of the face in Rhoda's bed-chamber.

'Was it you who first proposed coming here?' Mrs Lodge suddenly inquired, after a long pause. 'How very odd, if you did!'

'No. But I am not sorry we have come, all things considered,' she replied. For the first time a sense of triumph possessed her, and she did not altogether deplore that the young thing at her side should learn that their lives had been antagonized by other influences than their own.

The subject was no more alluded to during the long and dreary walk home. But in some way or other a story was whispered about the many-dairied lowland that winter that Mrs Lodge's gradual loss of the use of her left arm was owing to her being 'overlooked' by Rhoda Brook. The latter kept her own counsel about the incubus, but her face grew sadder and thinner; and in the spring she and her boy disappeared from the neighbourhood of Holmstoke.

6 · A Second Attempt

Half-a-dozen years passed away, and Mr and Mrs Lodge's married experience sank into prosiness, and worse. The farmer was usually gloomy and silent: the woman whom he had wooed for her grace and beauty was contorted and disfigured in the left limb; moreover, she had brought him no child, which rendered it likely that he would be the last of a family who had occupied that valley for some two hundred years. He thought of Rhoda Brook and her son; and feared this might be a judgement from heaven upon him.

The once blithe-hearted and enlightened Gertrude was changing into an irritable, superstitious woman, whose whole time was given to experimenting upon her ailment with every quack remedy she came across. She was honestly attached to her husband, and was ever secretly hoping against hope to win back his heart again by regaining some at least of her personal beauty. Hence it arose that her closet was lined with bottles, packets, and ointment-pots of every description – nay, bunches of mystic herbs, charms, and books of necromancy, which in her schoolgirl time she would have ridiculed as folly.

'Damned if you won't poison yourself with these apothecary messes and witch mixtures some time or other,' said her husband, when his eye chanced to fall upon the multitudinous array.

She did not reply, but turned her sad, soft glance upon him in such heart-swollen reproach that he looked sorry for his words, and added, 'I only meant it for your good, you know, Gertrude.'

'I'll clear out the whole lot, and destroy them,' said she huskily, 'and try such remedies no more!'

'You want somebody to cheer you,' he observed. 'I once thought of adopting a boy; but he is too old now. And he is gone away I don't know where.'

She guessed to whom he alluded; for Rhoda Brook's story had in the course of years become known to her; though not a word had ever passed between her husband and herself on the subject. Neither had she ever spoken to him of her visit to Conjuror Trendle, and of what was revealed to her, or she thought was revealed to her, by that solitary heathman.

She was now five-and-twenty; but she seemed older. 'Six years of marriage, and only a few months of love,' she sometimes whispered to herself. And then she thought of the apparent cause, and said, with a tragic glance at her withering limb, 'If I could only again be as I was when he first saw me!'

She obediently destroyed her nostrums and charms; but there remained a hankering wish to try something else – some other sort of cure altogether. She had never revisited Trendle since she had been conducted to the house of the solitary by Rhoda against her will; but it now suddenly occurred to Gertrude that she would, in a last desperate effort at deliverance from this seeming curse, again seek out the man, if he yet lived. He was entitled to a certain credence, for the indistinct form he had raised in the glass had undoubtedly resembled the only woman in the world who – as she now knew, though not then – could have a reason for bearing her ill-will. The visit should be paid.

This time she went alone, though she nearly got lost on the heath, and roamed a considerable distance out of her way. Trendle's house was reached at last, however: he was not indoors, and instead of waiting at the cottage, she went to where his bent figure was pointed out to her at work a long way off. Trendle remembered her, and laying down the handful of furze-roots which he was gathering and throwing into a heap, he offered to accompany her in her homeward direction, as the distance was considerable and the days were short. So they walked together, his head bowed nearly to the earth, and his form of a colour with it.

'You can send away warts and other excrescences, I know,' she said; 'why can't you send away this?' And the arm was uncovered.

'You think too much of my powers!' said Trendle; 'and I am old and weak now, too. No, no; it is too much for me to attempt in my own person. What have ye tried?'

She named to him some of the hundred medicaments and counterspells which she had adopted from time to time. He shook his head.

'Some were good enough,' he said approvingly; 'but not many of them for such as this. This is of the nature of a blight, not of the nature of a wound; and if you ever do throw it off, it will be all at once.'

'If I only could!'

'There is only one chance of doing it known to me. It has

never failed in kindred afflictions – that I can declare. But it is hard to carry out, and especially for a woman.'

'Tell me!' said she.

'You must touch with the limb the neck of a man who's been hanged.'

She started a little at the image he had raised.

'Before he's cold – just after he's cut down,' continued the conjuror impassively.

'How can that do good?'

'It will turn the blood and change the constitution. But, as I say, to do it is hard. You must go to the jail when there's a hanging, and wait for him when he's brought off the gallows. Lots have done it, though perhaps not such pretty women as you. I used to send dozens for skin complaints. But that was in former times. The last I sent was in '13 – near twelve years ago.'

He had no more to tell her; and, when he had put her into a straight track homeward, turned and left her, refusing all money as at first.

7 · A Ride

The communication sank deep into Gertrude's mind. Her nature was rather a timid one; and probably of all remedies that the white wizard could have suggested there was not one which would have filled her with so much aversion as this, not to speak of the immense obstacles in the way of its adoption.

Casterbridge, the county town, was a dozen or fifteen miles off; and though in those days, when men were executed for horse-stealing, arson, and burglary, an assize seldom passed without a hanging, it was not likely that she could get access to the body of the criminal unaided. And the fear of her husband's anger made her reluctant to breathe a word of Trendle's suggestion to him or to anybody about him.

She did nothing for months, and patiently bore her dis-

figurement as before. But her woman's nature, craving for renewed love, through the medium of renewed beauty (she was
but twenty-five), was ever stimulating her to try what, at any
rate, could hardly do her any harm. 'What came by a spell will
go by a spell surely,' she would say. Whenever her imagination
pictured the act she shrank in terror from the possibility of it:
then the words of the conjuror, 'It will turn your blood', were
seen to be capable of a scientific no less than a ghastly inter-
pretation; the mastering desire returned, and urged her on
again.

There was at this time but one county paper, and that her
husband only occasionally borrowed. But old-fashioned days
had old-fashioned means, and news was extensively conveyed
by word of mouth from market to market, or from fair to fair,
so that, whenever such an event as an execution was about to
take place, few within a radius of twenty miles were ignorant of
the coming sight; and, so far as Holmstoke was concerned,
some enthusiasts had been known to walk all the way to Casterbridge and back in one day, solely to witness the spectacle. The
next assizes were in March; and when Gertrude Lodge heard
that they had been held, she inquired stealthily at the inn as to
the result, as soon as she could find opportunity.

She was, however, too late. The time at which the sentences
were to be carried out had arrived, and to make the journey and
obtain admission at such short notice required at least her
husband's assistance. She dared not tell him, for she had found
by delicate experiment that these smouldering village beliefs
made him furious if mentioned, partly because he half enter-
tained them himself. It was therefore necessary to wait for
another opportunity.

Her determination received a fillip from learning that two
epileptic children had attended from this very village of
Holmstoke many years before with beneficial results, though
the experiment had been strongly condemned by the neighbouring clergy. April, May, June, passed; and it is no over-
statement to say that by the end of the last-named month
Gertrude well-nigh longed for the death of a fellow-creature.
Instead of her formal prayers each night, her unconscious

prayer was, 'O Lord, hang some guilty or innocent person soon!'

This time she made earlier inquiries, and was altogether more systematic in her proceedings. Moreover, the season was summer, between the haymaking and the harvest, and in the leisure thus afforded him her husband had been holiday-taking away from home.

The assizes were in July, and she went to the inn as before. There was to be one execution – only one – for arson.

Her greatest problem was not how to get to Casterbridge, but what means she should adopt for obtaining admission to the jail. Though access for such purposes had formerly never been denied, the custom had fallen into desuetude; and in contemplating her possible difficulties, she was again almost driven to fall back upon her husband. But, on sounding him about the assizes, he was so uncommunicative, so more than usually cold, that she did not proceed, and decided that whatever she did she would do alone.

Fortune, obdurate hitherto, showed her unexpected favour. On the Thursday before the Saturday fixed for the execution, Lodge remarked to her that he was going away from home for another day or two on business at a fair, and that he was sorry he could not take her with him.

She exhibited on this occasion so much readiness to stay at home that he looked at her in surprise. Time had been when she would have shown deep disappointment at the loss of such a jaunt. However, he lapsed into his usual taciturnity, and on the day named left Holmstoke.

It was now her turn. She at first had thought of driving, but on reflection held that driving would not do, since it would necessitate her keeping to the turnpike-road, and so increase by tenfold the risk of her ghastly errand being found out. She decided to ride, and avoid the beaten track, notwithstanding that in her husband's stables there was no animal just at present which by any stretch of imagination could be considered a lady's mount, in spite of his promise before marriage to always keep a mare for her. He had, however, many cart-horses, fine ones of their kind; and among the rest was a serviceable creature, an equine Amazon, with a back as broad as a sofa, on which Gertrude had occasionally taken an airing when unwell. This horse she chose.

On Friday afternoon one of the men brought it round. She was dressed, and before going down looked at her shrivelled arm. 'Ah!' she said to it, 'if it had not been for you this terrible ordeal would have been saved me!'

When strapping up the bundle in which she carried a few articles of clothing, she took occasion to say to the servant, 'I take these in case I should not get back tonight from the person I am going to visit. Don't be alarmed if I am not in by ten, and close up the house as usual. I shall be at home tomorrow for certain.' She meant then to tell her husband privately: the deed accomplished was not like the deed projected. He would almost certainly forgive her.

And then the pretty palpitating Gertrude Lodge went from her husband's homestead; but though her goal was Casterbridge she did not take the direct route thither through Stickleford. Her cunning course at first was in precisely the opposite direction. As soon as she was out of sight, however, she turned to the left, by a road which led into Egdon, and on entering the heath wheeled round, and set out in the true course, due westerly. A more private way down the county could not be imagined; and as to direction, she had merely to keep her horse's head to a point a little to the right of the sun. She knew that she would light upon a furze-cutter or cottager of some sort from time to time, from whom she might correct her bearing.

Though the date was comparatively recent, Egdon was much less fragmentary in character than now. The attempts – successful and otherwise – at cultivation on the lower slopes, which intrude and break up the original heath into small detached heaths, had not been carried far; Enclosure Acts had not taken effect, and the banks and fences which now exclude the cattle of those villagers who formerly enjoyed rights of commonage thereon, and the carts of those who had turbary privileges which kept them in firing all the year round, were not erected. Gertrude, therefore, rode along with no other obstacles than the prickly furze-bushes, the mats of heather, the white water-courses, and the natural steeps and declivities of the ground.

Her horse was sure, if heavy-footed and slow, and though a draught animal, was easy-paced; had it been otherwise, she was not a woman who could have ventured to ride over such a bit of country with a half-dead arm. It was therefore nearly eight o'clock when she drew rein to breathe her bearer on the last outlying high point of heath-land towards Casterbridge, previous to leaving Egdon for the cultivated valleys.

She halted before a pool called Rushy-pond, flanked by the ends of two hedges; a railing ran through the centre of the pond, dividing it in half. Over the railing she saw the low green country; over the green trees the roofs of the town; over the roofs a white flat façade, denoting the entrance to the county jail. On the roof of this front specks were moving about; they seemed to be workmen erecting something. Her flesh crept. She descended slowly, and was soon amid corn-fields and pastures. In another half-hour, when it was almost dusk, Gertrude reached the White Hart, the first inn of the town on that side.

Little surprise was excited by her arrival; farmers' wives rode on horseback then more than they do now; though, for that matter, Mrs Lodge was not imagined to be a wife at all; the innkeeper supposed her some harum-skarum young woman who had come to attend 'hang-fair' next day. Neither her husband nor herself ever dealt in Casterbridge market, so that she was unknown. While dismounting she beheld a crowd of boys standing at the door of a harness-maker's shop just above the inn, looking inside it with deep interest.

'What is going on there?' she asked of the ostler.

'Making the rope for tomorrow.'

She throbbed responsively, and contracted her arm.

' 'Tis sold by the inch afterwards,' the man continued. 'I could get you a bit, miss, for nothing, if you'd like?'

She hastily repudiated any such wish, all the more from a curious creeping feeling that the condemned wretch's destiny was becoming interwoven with her own; and having engaged a room for the night, sat down to think.

Up to this time she had formed but the vaguest notions about her means of obtaining access to the prison. The words of the cunning-man returned to her mind. He had implied that she should use her beauty, impaired though it was, as a pass-key. In her inexperience she knew little about jail functionaries; she had heard of a high-sheriff and an under-sheriff, but dimly only. She knew, however, that there must be a hangman, and to the hangman she determined to apply.

8 · A Water-side Hermit

At this date, and for several years after, there was a hangman to almost every jail. Gertrude found, on inquiry, that the Casterbridge official dwelt in a lonely cottage by a deep slow river flowing under the cliff on which the prison buildings were situate – the stream being the self-same one, though she did not know it, which watered the Stickleford and Holmstoke meads lower down in its course.

Having changed her dress, and before she had eaten or drunk – for she could not take her ease till she had ascertained some particulars – Gertrude pursued her way by a path along the water-side to the cottage indicated. Passing thus the out-skirts of the jail, she discerned on the level roof over the gate-way three rectangular lines against the sky, where the specks had been moving in her distant view; she recognized what the erection was, and passed quickly on. Another hundred yards brought her to the executioner's house, which a boy pointed out. It stood close to the same stream, and was hard by a weir, the waters of which emitted a steady roar.

While she stood hesitating the door opened, and an old man came forth shading a candle with one hand. Locking the door on the outside, he turned to a flight of wooden steps fixed against the end of the cottage, and began to ascend them, this being evidently the staircase to his bedroom. Gertrude hastened forward, but by the time she reached the foot of the ladder he was at the top. She called to him loudly enough to be heard above the roar of the weir; he looked down and said, 'What d'ye want here?'

'To speak to you a minute.'

The candle-light, such as it was, fell upon her imploring, pale, upturned face, and Davies (as the hangman was called) backed down the ladder. 'I was just going to bed,' he said; ' "Early to bed and early to rise", but I don't mind stopping a minute for such a one as you. Come into house.' He reopened the door, and preceded her to the room within.

The implements of his daily work, which was that of a jobbing gardener, stood in a corner, and seeing probably that she looked rural, he said, 'If you want me to undertake country work I can't come, for I never leave Casterbridge for gentle nor simple – not I. My real calling is officer of justice,' he added formally.

'Yes, yes! That's it. Tomorrow!'

'Ah! I thought so. Well, what's the matter about that? 'Tis no use to come here about the knot – folks do come continually, but I tell 'em one knot is as merciful as another if ye keep it under the ear. Is the unfortunate man a relation; or, I should say, perhaps' (looking at her dress) 'a person who's been in your employ?'

'No. What time is the execution?'

'The same as usual – twelve o'clock, or as soon after as the London mail-coach gets in. We always wait for that, in case of a reprieve.'

'O – a reprieve – I hope not!' she said involuntarily.

'Well, – hee, hee! – as a matter of business, so do I! But still, if ever a young fellow deserved to be let off, this one does; only just turned eighteen, and only present by chance when the rick was fired. Howsomever, there's not much risk of it, as they are obliged to make an example of him, there having been so much destruction of property that way lately.'

'I mean,' she explained, 'that I want to touch him for a charm, a cure of an affliction, by the advice of a man who has proved the virtue of the remedy.'

'Oh yes, miss! Now I understand. I've had such people come in past years. But it didn't strike me that you looked of a sort to require blood-turning. What's the complaint? The wrong kind for this, I'll be bound.'

'My arm.' She reluctantly showed the withered skin.

'Ah! – 'tis all a-scram!' said the hangman, examining it.

'Yes,' said she.

'Well,' he continued, with interest, 'that *is* the class o' subject, I'm bound to admit! I like the look of the wownd; it is truly as suitable for the cure as any I ever saw. 'Twas a knowing man that sent 'ee, whoever he was.'

'You can contrive for me all that's necessary?' she said breathlessly.

'You should really have gone to the governor of the jail, and your doctor with 'ee, and given your name and address – that's how it used to be done, if I recollect. Still, perhaps, I can manage it for a trifling fee.'

'Oh, thank you! I would rather do it this way, as I should like it kept private.'

'Lover not to know, eh?'

'No – husband.'

'Aha! Very well. I'll get ee' a touch of the corpse.'

'Where is it now?' she said, shuddering.

'It? – *he*, you mean; he's living yet. Just inside that little small winder up there in the glum.' He signified the jail on the cliff above.

She thought of her husband and her friends. 'Yes, of course,' she said; 'and how am I to proceed?'

He took her to the door. 'Now, do you be waiting at the little wicket in the wall, that you'll find up there in the lane, not later than one o'clock. I will open it from the inside, as I shan't come home to dinner till he's cut down. Good night. Be punctual; and if you don't want anybody to know 'ee, wear a veil. Ah – once I had such a daughter as you!'

She went away, and climbed the path above, to assure herself that she would be able to find the wicket next day. Its outline was soon visible to her – a narrow opening in the outer wall of the prison precincts. The steep was so great that, having reached the wicket, she stopped a moment to breathe; and, looking back upon the water-side cot, saw the hangman again ascending his outdoor staircase. He entered the loft or chamber to which it led, and in a few minutes extinguished his light.

The town clock struck ten, and she returned to the White Hart as she had come.

9 · A Rencounter

It was one o'clock on Saturday. Gertrude Lodge, having been admitted to the jail as above described, was sitting in a waiting-room within the second gate, which stood under a classic archway of ashlar, then comparatively modern, and bearing the inscription, 'COVNTY JAIL: 1793.' This had been the façade she saw from the heath the day before. Near at hand was a passage to the roof on which the gallows stood.

The town was thronged, and the market suspended; but Gertrude had seen scarcely a soul. Having kept her room till the hour of the appointment, she had proceeded to the spot by a way which avoided the open space below the cliff where the spectators had gathered; but she could, even now, hear the multitudinous babble of their voices, out of which rose at intervals the hoarse croak of a single voice uttering the words, 'Last dying speech and confession!' There had been no reprieve, and the execution was over; but the crowd still waited to see the body taken down.

Soon the persistent woman heard a trampling overhead, then a hand beckoned to her, and, following directions, she went out and crossed the inner paved court beyond the gate-house, her knees trembling so that she could scarcely walk. One of her arms was out of its sleeve, and only covered by her shawl.

On the spot at which she had now arrived were two trestles, and before she could think of their purpose she heard heavy feet descending stairs somewhere at her back. Turn her head she would not, or could not, and, rigid in this position, she was conscious of a rough coffin passing her shoulder, borne by four men. It was open, and in it lay the body of a young man, wearing the smockfrock of a rustic, and fustian breeches. The corpse had been thrown into the coffin so hastily that the skirt of the smockfrock was hanging over. The burden was temporarily deposited on the trestles.

By this time the young woman's state was such that a grey mist seemed to float before her eyes, on account of which, and the veil she wore, she could scarcely discern anything: it was as though she had nearly died, but was held up by a sort of galvanism.

'Now!' said a voice close at hand, and she was just conscious that the word had been addressed to her.

By a last strenuous effort she advanced, at the same time hearing persons approaching behind her. She bared her poor curst arm; and Davies, uncovering the face of the corpse, took Gertrude's hand, and held it so that her arm lay across the dead man's neck, upon a line the colour of an unripe blackberry, which surrounded it.

Gertrude shrieked: 'the turn o' the blood', predicted by the conjuror, had taken place. But at that moment a second shriek rent the air of the enclosure: it was not Gertrude's, and its effect upon her was to make her start round.

Immediately behind her stood Rhoda Brook, her face drawn, and her eyes red with weeping. Behind Rhoda stood Gertrude's own husband; his countenance lined, his eyes dim, but without a tear.

'D— you! what are you doing here?' he said hoarsely.

'Hussy – to come between us and our child now!' cried Rhoda. 'This is the meaning of what Satan showed me in the vision! You are like her at last!' And clutching the bare arm of the younger woman, she pulled her unresistingly back against the wall. Immediately Brook had loosened her hold the fragile young Gertrude slid down against the feet of her husband. When he lifted her up she was unconscious.

The mere sight of the twain had been enough to suggest to her that the dead young man was Rhoda's son. At that time the relatives of an executed convict had the privilege of claiming the body for burial, if they chose to do so; and it was for this purpose that Lodge was awaiting the inquest with Rhoda. He had been summoned by her as soon as the young man was taken in the crime, and at different times since; and he had attended in court during the trial. This was the 'holiday' he had been indulging in of late. The two wretched parents had wished to avoid exposure; and hence had come themselves for the body, a waggon and sheet for its conveyance and covering being in waiting outside.

Gertrude's case was so serious that it was deemed advisable to call to her the surgeon who was at hand. She was taken out of the jail into the town; but she never reached home alive. Her delicate vitality, sapped perhaps by the paralysed arm, collapsed under the double shock that followed the severe strain, physical and mental, to which she had subjected herself during the previous twenty-four hours. Her blood had been 'turned' indeed – too far. Her death took place in the town three days after.

Her husband was never seen in Casterbridge again; once only in the old market-place at Anglebury, which he had so much frequented, and very seldom in public anywhere. Burdened at first with moodiness and remorse, he eventually changed for the better, and appeared as a chastened and thoughtful man. Soon after attending the funeral of his poor young wife he took steps towards giving up the farms in Holmstoke and the adjoining parish, and, having sold every head of his stock, he went away to Port-Bredy, at the other end of the county, living there in solitary lodgings till his death two years later of a painless decline. It was then found that he had bequeathed the whole of his not inconsiderable property to a reformatory for boys, subject to the payment of a small annuity to Rhoda Brook, if she could be found to claim it.

For some time she could not be found; but eventually she reappeared in her old parish – absolutely refusing, however, to have anything to do with the provision made for her. Her monotonous milking at the dairy was resumed, and followed for many long years, till her form became bent, and her once abundant dark hair white and worn away at the forehead – perhaps by long pressure against the cows. Here, sometimes, those who knew her experiences would stand and observe her, and wonder what sombre thoughts were beating inside that impassive, wrinkled brow, to the rhythm of the alternating milk-streams.

Joseph Conrad

AN OUTPOST OF PROGRESS

I

THERE were two white men in charge of the trading station. Kayerts, the chief, was short and fat; Carlier, the assistant, was tall, with a large head and a very broad trunk perched upon a long pair of thin legs. The third man on the staff was a Sierra Leone nigger, who maintained that his name was Henry Price. However, for some reason or other, the natives down the river had given him the name of Makola, and it stuck to him through all his wanderings about the country. He spoke English and French with a warbling accent, wrote a beautiful hand, understood book-keeping, and cherished in his innermost heart the worship of evil spirits. His wife was a Negress from Loanda, very large and very noisy. Three children rolled about in sunshine before the door of his low, shed-like dwelling. Makola, taciturn and impenetrable, despised the two white men. He had charge of a small clay storehouse with a dried-grass roof, and pretended to keep a correct account of beads, cotton cloth, red kerchiefs, brass wire, and other trade goods it contained. Besides the storehouse and Makola's hut, there was only one large building in the cleared ground of the station. It was built neatly of reeds, with a verandah on all the four sides. There were three rooms in it. The one in the middle was the living-room, and had two rough tables and a few stools in it. The other two were the bedrooms for the white men. Each had a bedstead and a mosquito net for all furniture. The plank floor was littered with the belongings of the white men; open half-empty boxes, town wearing apparel, old boots; all the things dirty, and all the things broken, that accumulate mysteriously round untidy men. There was also another dwelling-place some distance away from the buildings. In it, under a tall cross much out of the perpendicular, slept the man who had seen the beginning of all this; who had planned and had watched the construction of this outpost of progress. He had been, at home, an unsuccessful painter who, weary of pursuing fame on an empty stomach, had gone out there through high protections. He had been the first chief of that station. Makola had watched the energetic artist die of fever in the just finished house with his usual kind of 'I told you so' indifference. Then, for a time, he dwelt alone with his family, his account books, and the Evil Spirit that rules the lands under the equator. He got on very well with his god. Perhaps he had propitiated him by a promise of more white men to play with, by and by. At any rate the director of the Great Trading Company, coming up in a steamer that resembled an enormous sardine box with a flat-roofed shed erected on it, found the station in good order, and Makola as usual quietly diligent. The director had the cross put up over the first agent's grave, and appointed Kayerts to the post. Carlier was told off as second in charge. The director was a man ruthless and efficient, who at times, but very imperceptibly, indulged in grim humour. He made a speech to Kayerts and Carlier, pointing out to them the promising aspect of their station. The nearest trading-post was about three hundred miles away. It was an exceptional opportunity for them to distinguish themselves and to earn percentages on the trade. This appointment was a favour done to beginners. Kayerts was moved almost to tears by his director's kindness. He would, he said, by doing his best, try to justify the flattering confidence, etc., etc. Kayerts had been in the Administration of the Telegraphs, and knew how to express himself correctly. Carlier, an ex-non-commissioned officer of cavalry in an army guaranteed from harm by several European Powers, was less impressed. If there were commissions to get, so much the better; and, trailing a sulky glance over the river, the forests, the impenetrable bush that seemed to cut off the station from the rest of the world, he muttered between his teeth, 'We shall see, very soon.'

Next day, some bales of cotton goods and a few cases of provisions having been thrown on shore, the sardine-box steamer went off, not to return for another six months. On the deck the director touched his cap to the two agents, who stood on the bank waving their hats, and turning to an old servant of the Company on his passage to headquarters, said, 'Look at those two imbeciles. They must be mad at home to send me such specimens. I told those fellows to plant a vegetable garden, build new storehouses and fences, and construct a landing-stage. I bet nothing will be done! They won't know how to begin. I always thought the station on this river useless, and they just fit the station!'

'They will form themselves there,' said the old stager with a quiet smile.

'At any rate, I am rid of them for six months,' retorted the director.

The two men watched the steamer round the bend, then, ascending arm in arm the slope of the bank, returned to the station. They had been in this vast and dark country only a very short time, and as yet always in the midst of other white men, under the eye and guidance of their superiors. And now, dull as they were to the subtle influences of surroundings, they felt themselves very much alone, when suddenly left unassisted to face the wilderness; a wilderness rendered more strange, more incomprehensible by the mysterious glimpses of the vigorous life it contained. They were two perfectly insignificant and incapable individuals, whose existence is only rendered possible through the high organization of civilized crowds. Few men realize that their life, the very essence of their character, their capabilities and their audacities, are only the expression of their belief in the safety of their surroundings. The courage, the composure, the confidence; the emotions and principles; every great and every insignificant thought belongs not to the individual but to the crowd: to the crowd that believes blindly in the irresistible force of its institutions and of its morals, in the power of its police and of its opinion. But the contact with pure unmitigated savagery, with primitive nature and primitive man, brings sudden and profound trouble into the heart. To the sentiment of being alone of one's kind, to the clear perception of the loneliness of one's thoughts, of one's sensations – to the negation of the habitual, which is safe, there is added the affirmation of the unusual, which is dangerous; a suggestion of things vague, uncontrollable, and repulsive, whose discomposing intrusion excites the imagination and tries the civilized nerves of the foolish and the wise alike.

Kayerts and Carlier walked arm in arm, drawing close to one another as children do in the dark; and they had the same, not altogether unpleasant, sense of danger which one half suspects to be imaginary. They chatted persistently in familiar tones. 'Our station is prettily situated,' said one. The other assented with enthusiasm, enlarging volubly on the beauties of the situation. Then they passed near the grave. 'Poor devil!' said Kayerts. 'He died of fever, didn't he?' muttered Carlier, stopping short. 'Why,' retorted Kayerts, with indignation, 'I've been told that the fellow exposed himself recklessly to the sun. The climate here, everybody says, is not at all worse than at home, as long as you keep out of the sun. Do you hear that, Carlier? I am chief here, and my orders are that you should not expose yourself to the sun!' He assumed his superiority jocularly, but his meaning was serious. The idea that he would, perhaps, have to bury Carlier and remain alone, gave him an inward shiver. He felt suddenly that this Carlier was more precious to him here, in the centre of Africa, than a brother could be anywhere else. Carlier, entering into the spirit of the thing, made a military salute and answered in a brisk tone, 'Your orders shall be attended to, chief!' Then he burst out laughing, slapped Kayerts on the back and shouted, 'We shall let life run easily here! Just sit still and gather in the ivory those savages will bring. This country has its good points, after all!' They both laughed loudly while Carlier thought: That poor Kayerts; he is so fat and unhealthy. It would be awful if I had to bury him here. He is a man I respect. ... Before they reached the verandah of their house they called one another 'my dear fellow'.

The first day they were very active, pottering about with hammers and nails and red calico, to put up curtains, make their house habitable and pretty; resolved to settle down comfortably to their new life. For them an impossible task. To grapple effectually with even purely material problems requires more serenity of mind and more lofty courage than people generally imagine. No two beings could have been more unfitted for such a struggle. Society, not from any tenderness, but because of its strange needs, had taken care of those two men, forbidding them all independent thought, all initiative, all departure from routine; and forbidding it under pain of death. They could only live on condition of being machines. And now, released from the fostering care of men with pens behind the ears, or of men with gold lace on the sleeves, they were like those lifelong prisoners who, liberated after many years, do not know what use to make of their freedom. They did not know what use to make of their faculties, being both, through want of practice, incapable of independent thought.

At the end of two months Kayerts often would say, 'If it was not for my Melie, you wouldn't catch me here.' Melie was his daughter. He had thrown up his post in the Administration of the Telegraphs, though he had been for seventeen years perfectly happy there, to earn a dowry for his girl. His wife was dead, and the child was being brought up by his sisters. He regretted the streets, the pavements, the cafés, his friends of many years; all the things he used to see, day after day; all the thoughts suggested by familiar things – the thoughts effortless, monotonous, and soothing of a government clerk; he regretted all the gossip, the small enmities, the mild venom, and the little jokes of government offices. 'If I had had a decent brother-in-law,' Carlier would remark, 'a fellow with a heart, I would not be here.' He had left the army and had made himself so obnoxious to his family by his laziness and impudence, that an exasperated brother-in-law had made superhuman efforts to procure him an appointment in the Company as a second-class agent. Having not a penny in the world he was compelled to accept this means of livelihood as soon as it became quite clear to him that there was nothing more to squeeze out of his relations. He, like Kayerts, regretted his old life. He regretted the clink of sabre and spurs on a fine afternoon, the barrack-room witticisms, the girls of garrison towns; but, besides, he had also a sense of grievance. He was evidently a much ill-used man. This made him moody, at times. But the two men got on well together in the fellowship of their stupidity and laziness. Together they did nothing, absolutely nothing, and enjoyed the sense of idleness for which they were paid. And in time they came to feel something resembling affection for one another.

They lived like blind men in a large room, aware only of what came in contact with them (and of that only imperfectly), but unable to see the general aspect of things. The river, the forest, all the great land throbbing with life, were like a great emptiness. Even the brilliant sunshine disclosed nothing intelligible. Things appeared and disappeared before their eyes in an unconnected and aimless kind of way. The river seemed to come from nowhere and flow nowhither. It flowed through a void. Out of that void, at times, came canoes, and men with spears in their hands would suddenly crowd the yard of the station. They were naked, glossy black, ornamented with snowy shells and glistening brass wire, perfect of limb. They made an uncouth babbling noise when they spoke, moved in a stately manner, and sent quick, wild glances out of their startled, never-resting eyes. Those warriors would squat in long rows, four or more deep, before the verandah, while their chiefs bargained for hours with Makola over an elephant tusk. Kayerts sat on his chair and looked down on the proceedings, understanding nothing. He stared at them with his round blue eyes, called out to Carlier, 'Here, look! look at that fellow there – and that other one, to the left. Did you ever see such a face? Oh, the funny brute!'

Carlier, smoking native tobacco in a short wooden pipe, would swagger up twirling his moustaches, and surveying the warriors with haughty indulgence, would say –

'Fine animals. Brought any bone? Yes? It's not any too soon. Look at the muscles of that fellow – third from the end. I wouldn't care to get a punch on the nose from him. Fine arms, but legs no good below the knee. Couldn't make cavalry men of them.' And after glancing down complacently at his own shanks, he always concluded: 'Pah! Don't they stink! You, Makola! Take that herd over to the fetish' (the store-house was in every station called the fetish, perhaps because of the spirit of civilization it contained) 'and give them up some of the rubbish you keep there. I'd rather see it full of bone than full of rags.'

Kayerts approved.

'Yes, yes! Go and finish that palaver over there, Mr Makola. I will come round when you are ready, to weigh the tusk. We must be careful.' Then turning to his companion: 'This is the tribe that lives down the river; they are rather aromatic. I remember, they had been once before here. D'ye hear that row? What a fellow has got to put up with in this dog of a country! My head is split.'

Such profitable visits were rare. For days the two pioneers of trade and progress would look on their empty courtyard in the vibrating brilliance of vertical sunshine. Below the high bank, the silent river flowed on glittering and steady. On the sands in the middle of the stream, hippos and alligators sunned themselves side by side. And stretching away in all directions, surrounding the insignificant cleared spot of the trading post, immense forests, hiding fateful complications of fantastic life, lay in the eloquent silence of mute greatness. The two men understood nothing, cared for nothing but for the passage of days that separated them from the steamer's return. Their predecessor had left some torn books. They took up these wrecks of novels, and, as they had never read anything of the kind before, they were surprised and amused. Then during long days there were interminable and silly discussions about plots and personages. In the centre of Africa they made acquaintance of Richelieu and of d'Artagnan, of Hawk's Eye and of Father Goriot, and of many other people. All these imaginary personages became subjects for gossip as if they had been living friends. They discounted their virtues, suspected their motives, decried their successes; were scandalized at their duplicity or were doubtful about their courage. The accounts of crimes filled them with indignation, while tender or pathetic passages moved them deeply. Carlier cleared his throat and said in a soldierly voice, 'What nonsense!' Kayerts, his round eyes suffused with tears, his fat cheeks quivering, rubbed his bald head, and declared, 'This is a splendid book. I had no idea there were such clever fellows in the world.' They also found some old copies of a home paper. That print discussed what it was pleased to call 'Our Colonial Expansion' in high-flown language. It spoke much of the rights and duties of civilization, of the sacredness of the civilizing work, and extolled the merits of those who went about bringing light, and faith and commerce to the dark places of the earth. Carlier and Kayerts read, wondered, and began to think better of themselves. Carlier said one evening, waving his hand about, 'In a hundred years, there will be perhaps a town here. Quays, and warehouses, and barracks, and – and – billiard-rooms. Civilization, my boy, and virtue – and all. And then, chaps will read that two good fellows, Kayerts and Carlier, were the first civilized men to live in this very spot!' Kayerts nodded, 'Yes, it is a consolation to think of that.' They seemed to forget their dead predecessor; but, early one day, Carlier went out and replanted the cross firmly. 'It used to make me squint whenever I walked that way,' he explained to Kayerts over the morning coffee. 'It made me squint, leaning over so much. So I just planted it upright. And solid, I promise you! I suspended myself with both hands to the cross-piece. Not a move. Oh, I did that properly.'

At times Gobila came to see them. Gobila was the chief of the neighbouring villages. He was a gray-headed savage, thin and black, with a white cloth round his loins and a mangy panther skin hanging over his back. He came up with long strides of his skeleton legs, swinging a staff as tall as himself, and, entering the common room of the station, would squat on his heels to the left of the door. There he sat, watching Kayerts, and now and then making a speech which the other did not understand. Kayerts, without interrupting his occupation, would from time to time say in a friendly manner: 'How goes it, you old image?' and they would smile at one another. The two whites had a liking for that old and incomprehensible creature, and called him Father Gobila. Gobila's manner was paternal, and he seemed really to love all white men. They all appeared to him very young, indistinguishably alike (except for stature), and he knew that they were all brothers, and also immortal. The death of the artist, who was the first white man whom he knew intimately, did not disturb this belief, because he was firmly convinced that the white stranger had pretended to die and got himself buried for some mysterious purpose of his own, into which it was useless to inquire. Perhaps it was his way of going home to his own country? At any rate, these were his brothers, and he transferred his absurd affection to them. They returned it in a way. Carlier slapped him on the back, and recklessly struck off matches for his amusement. Kayerts was always ready to let him have a sniff at the ammonia bottle. In short, they behaved just like that other white creature that had hidden itself in a hole in the ground. Gobila considered them attentively. Perhaps they were the same being with the other – or one of them was. He couldn't decide – clear up that mystery; but he remained always very friendly. In consequence of that friendship the women of Gobila's village walked in single file through the reedy grass, bringing every morning to the station, fowls, and sweet potatoes, and palm wine, and sometimes a goat. The Company never provisions the stations fully, and the agents required those local supplies to live. They had them through the good-will of Gobila, and lived well. Now and then one of them had a bout of fever, and the other nursed him with gentle devotion. They did not think much of it. It left them weaker, and their appearance changed for the worse. Carlier was hollow-eyed and irritable. Kayerts showed a drawn, flabby face above the rotundity of his stomach, which gave him a weird aspect. But being constantly together, they did not notice the change that took place gradually in their appearance, and also in their dispositions.

Five months passed in that way.

Then, one morning, as Kayerts and Carlier, lounging in their chairs under the verandah, talked about the approaching visit of the steamer, a knot of armed men came out of the forest and advanced towards the station. They were strangers to that part of the country. They were tall, slight, draped classically from neck to heel in blue fringed cloths, and carried percussion muskets over their bare right shoulders. Makola showed signs of excitement, and ran out of the storehouse (where he spent all his days) to meet these visitors. They came into the courtyard and looked about them with steady, scornful glances. Their leader, a powerful and determined-looking Negro with blood-shot eyes, stood in front of the verandah and made a long speech. He gesticulated much, and ceased very suddenly.

There was something in his intonation, in the sounds of the long sentences he used, that startled the two whites. It was like a reminiscence of something not exactly familiar, and yet resembling the speech of civilized men. It sounded like one of those impossible languages which sometimes we hear in our dreams.

'What lingo is that?' said the amazed Carlier. 'In the first moment I fancied the fellow was going to speak French. Anyway, it is a different kind of gibberish to what we ever heard.'

'Yes,' replied Kayerts. 'Hey, Makola, what does he say? Where do they come from? Who are they?'

But Makola, who seemed to be standing on hot bricks, answered hurriedly, 'I don't know. They come from very far. Perhaps Mrs Price will understand. They are perhaps bad men.'

The leader, after waiting for a while, said something sharply to Makola, who shook his head. Then the man, after looking round, noticed Makola's hut and walked over there. The next moment Mrs Makola was heard speaking with great volubility. The other strangers – they were six in all – strolled about with an air of ease, put their heads through the door of the storeroom, congregated round the grave, pointed understandingly at the cross, and generally made themselves at home.

'I don't like those chaps – and, I say, Kayerts, they must be from the coast; they've got firearms,' observed the sagacious Carlier.

Kayerts also did not like those chaps. They both, for the first time, became aware that they lived in conditions where the unusual may be dangerous, and that there was no power on earth outside of themselves to stand between them and the unusual. They became uneasy, went in and loaded their revolvers. Kayerts said, 'We must order Makola to tell them to go away before dark.'

The strangers left in the afternoon, after eating a meal prepared for them by Mrs Makola. The immense woman was excited, and talked much with the visitors. She rattled away shrilly, pointing here and there at the forests and at the river. Makola sat apart and watched. At times he got up and whispered to his wife. He accompanied the strangers across the ravine at the back of the station-ground, and returned slowly looking very thoughtful. When questioned by the white men he was very strange, seemed not to understand, seemed to have forgotten French – seemed to have forgotten how to speak altogether. Kayerts and Carlier agreed that the nigger had had too much palm wine.

There was some talk about keeping a watch in turn, but in the evening everything seemed so quiet and peaceful that they retired as usual. All night they were disturbed by a lot of drumming in the villages. A deep, rapid roll near by would be followed by another far off – then all ceased. Soon short appeals would rattle out here and there, then all mingle together, increase, become vigorous and sustained, would spread out over the forest, roll through the night, unbroken and ceaseless, near and far, as if the whole land had been one immense drum booming out steadily an appeal to heaven. And through the deep and tremendous noise sudden yells that resembled snatches of songs from a madhouse darted shrill and high in discordant jets of sound which seemed to rush far above the earth and drive all peace from under the stars.

Carlier and Kayerts slept badly. They both thought they had heard shots fired during the night – but they could not agree as to the direction. In the morning Makola was gone somewhere. He returned about noon with one of yesterday's strangers, and eluded all Kayerts's attempts to close with him: had become deaf apparently. Kayerts wondered. Carlier, who had been fishing off the bank, came back and remarked while he showed his catch, 'The niggers seem to be in a deuce of a stir; I wonder what's up. I saw about fifteen canoes cross the river during the two hours I was there fishing.' Kayerts, worried, said, 'Isn't this Makola very queer today?' Carlier advised, 'Keep all our men together in case of some trouble.'

2

There were ten station men who had been left by the Director. Those fellows, having engaged themselves to the Company for six months (without having any idea of a month in particular and only a very faint notion of time in general), had been serving the cause of progress for upwards of two years. Belonging to a tribe from a very distant part of the land of darkness and sorrow, they did not run away, naturally supposing that as wandering strangers they would be killed by the inhabitants of the country; in which they were right. They lived in straw huts on the slope of a ravine overgrown with reedy grass, just behind the station buildings. They were not happy, regretting the festive incantations, the sorceries, the human sacrifices of their own land; where they also had parents, brothers, sisters, admired chiefs, respected magicians, loved friends, and other ties supposed generally to be human. Besides, the rice rations served out by the Company did not agree with them, being a food unknown to their land, and to which they could not get used. Consequently they were unhealthy and miserable. Had they been of any other tribe they would have made up their minds to die – for nothing is easier to certain savages than suicide – and so have escaped from the puzzling difficulties of existence. But belonging, as they did, to a warlike tribe with filed teeth, they had more grit, and went on stupidly living through disease and sorrow. They did very little work, and had lost their splendid physique. Carlier and Kayerts doctored them assiduously without being able to bring them back into condition again. They were mustered every morning and told off to different tasks – grass-cutting, fence-building, tree-felling, etc., etc., which no power on earth could induce them to execute efficiently. The two whites had practically very little control over them.

In the afternoon Makola came over to the big house and found Kayerts watching three heavy columns of smoke rising above the forests. 'What is that?' asked Kayerts. 'Some villages burn,' answered Makola, who seemed to have regained his wits. Then he said abruptly: 'We have got very little ivory; bad six months' trading. Do you like get a little more ivory?'

'Yes,' said Kayerts, eagerly. He thought of percentages which were low.

'Those men who came yesterday are traders from Loanda who have got more ivory than they can carry home. Shall I buy? I know their camp.'

'Certainly,' said Kayerts. 'What are those traders?'

'Bad fellows,' said Makola, indifferently. 'They fight with people, and catch women and children. They are bad men, and got guns. There is a great disturbance in the country. Do you want ivory?'

'Yes,' said Kayerts. Makola said nothing for a while. Then: 'Those workmen of ours are no good at all,' he muttered, looking round. 'Station in very bad order, sir. Director will growl. Better get a fine lot of ivory, then he say nothing.'

'I can't help it; the men won't work,' said Kayerts. 'When will you get that ivory?'

'Very soon,' said Makola. 'Perhaps tonight. You leave it to me, and keep indoors, sir. I think you had better give some palm wine to our men to make a dance this evening. Enjoy themselves. Work better tomorrow. There's plenty palm wine— gone a little sour.'

Kayerts said yes, and Makola, with his own hands, carried big calabashes to the door of his hut. They stood there till the evening, and Mrs Makola looked into every one. The men got them at sunset. When Kayerts and Carlier retired, a big bonfire was flaring before the men's huts. They could hear their shouts and drumming. Some men from Gobila's village had joined the station hands, and the entertainment was a great success.

In the middle of the night, Carlier waking suddenly, heard a man shout loudly; then a shot was fired. Only one. Carlier ran out and met Kayerts on the verandah. They were both startled. As they went across the yard to call Makola, they saw shadows moving in the night. One of them cried, 'Don't shoot! It's me, Price.' Then Makola appeared close to them. 'Go back, go back, please,' he urged, 'you spoil all.' 'There are strange men about,' said Carlier. 'Never mind; I know,' said Makola. Then he whispered, 'All right. Bring ivory. Say nothing! I know my business.' The two white men reluctantly went back to the house, but did not sleep. They heard footsteps, whispers, some groans. It seemed as if a lot of men came in, dumped heavy things on the ground, squabbled a long time, then went away. They lay on their hard beds and thought: 'This Makola is invaluable.' In the morning Carlier came out, very sleepy, and pulled at the cord of the big bell. The station hands mustered every morning to the sound of the bell. That morning nobody came. Kayerts turned out also, yawning. Across the yard they saw Makola come out of his hut, a tin basin of soapy water in his hand. Makola, a civilized nigger, was very neat in his person. He threw the soapsuds skilfully over a wretched little yellow cur he had, then turning his face to the agent's house, he shouted from the distance, 'All the men gone last night!'

They heard him plainly, but in their surprise they both yelled out together: 'What!' Then they stared at one another. 'We are in a proper fix now,' growled Carlier. 'It's incredible!' muttered Kayerts. 'I will go to the huts and see,' said Carlier, striding off. Makola coming up found Kayerts standing alone.

'I can hardly believe it,' said Kayerts, tearfully. 'We took care of them as if they had been our children.'

'They went with the coast people,' said Makola after a moment of hesitation.

'What do I care with whom they went – the ungrateful brutes!' exclaimed the other. Then with sudden suspicion, and looking hard at Makola, he added: 'What do you know about it?'

Makola moved his shoulders, looking down on the ground. 'What do I know? I think only. Will you come and look at the ivory I've got there? It is a fine lot. You never saw such.'

He moved towards the store. Kayerts followed him mechanically, thinking about the incredible desertion of the men. On the ground before the door of the fetish lay six splendid tusks.

'What did you give for it?' asked Kayerts, after surveying the lot with satisfaction.

'No regular trade,' said Makola. 'They brought the ivory and gave it to me. I told them to take what they most wanted in the station. It is a beautiful lot. No station can show such tusks. Those traders wanted carriers badly, and our men were no good here. No trade, no entry in books; all correct.'

Kayerts nearly burst with indignation. 'Why!' he shouted, 'I believe you have sold our men for these tusks!' Makola stood impassive and silent. 'I – I – will – I,' stuttered Kayerts. 'You fiend!' he yelled out.

'I did the best for you and the Company,' said Makola, imperturbably. 'Why you shout so much? Look at this tusk.'

'I dismiss you! I will report you – I won't look at the tusk. I forbid you to touch them. I order you to throw them into the river. You – you!'

'You very red, Mr Kayerts. If you are so irritable in the sun, you will get fever and die – like the first chief!' pronounced Makola impressively.

They stood still, contemplating one another with intense eyes, as if they had been looking with effort across immense distances. Kayerts shivered. Makola had meant no more than he said, but his words seemed to Kayerts full of ominous menace! He turned sharply and went away to the house. Makola retired into the bosom of his family; and the tusks, left lying before the store, looked very large and valuable in the sunshine.

Carlier came back on the verandah. 'They're all gone, hey?' asked Kayerts from the far end of the common room in a muffled voice. 'You did not find anybody?'

'Oh, yes,' said Carlier, 'I found one of Gobila's people lying dead before the huts – shot through the body. We heard that shot last night.'

Kayerts came out quickly. He found his companion staring grimly over the yard at the tusks, away by the store. They both sat in silence for a while. Then Kayerts related his conversation with Makola. Carlier said nothing. At the midday meal they ate very little. They hardly exchanged a word that day. A great silence seemed to lie heavily over the station and press on their lips. Makola did not open the store; he spent the day playing with his children. He lay full-length on a mat outside his door, and the youngsters sat on his chest and clambered all over him. It was a touching picture. Mrs Makola was busy cooking all day as usual. The white men made a somewhat better meal in the evening. Afterwards, Carlier smoking his pipe strolled over to the store; he stood for a long time over the tusks, touched one or two with his foot, even tried to lift the largest one by its small end. He came back to his chief, who had not stirred from the verandah, threw himself in the chair and said –

'I can see it! They were pounced upon while they slept heavily after drinking all that palm wine you've allowed Makola to give them. A put-up job! See? The worst is, some of Gobila's people were there, and got carried off too, no doubt. The least drunk woke up, and got shot for his sobriety. This is a funny country. What will you do now?'

'We can't touch it, of course,' said Kayerts.

'Of course not,' assented Carlier.

'Slavery is an awful thing,' stammered out Kayerts in an unsteady voice.

'Frightful – the sufferings,' grunted Carlier with conviction.

They believed their words. Everybody shows a respectful deference to certain sounds that he and his fellows can make. But about feelings people really know nothing. We talk with indignation or enthusiasm; we talk about oppression, cruelty, crime, devotion, self-sacrifice, virtue, and we know nothing real beyond the words. Nobody knows what suffering or sacrifice mean – except, perhaps the victims of the mysterious purpose of these illusions.

Next morning they saw Makola very busy setting up in the yard the big scales used for weighing ivory. By and by Carlier said: 'What's that filthy scoundrel up to?' and lounged out into the yard. Kayerts followed. They stood watching. Makola took no notice. When the balance was swung true, he tried to lift a tusk into the scale. It was too heavy. He looked up helplessly without a word, and for a minute they stood round that balance as mute and still as three statues. Suddenly Carlier said: 'Catch hold of the other end, Makola – you beast!' and together they swung the tusk up. Kayerts trembled in every limb. He muttered, 'I say! O! I say!' and putting his hand in his pocket found there a dirty bit of paper and the stump of a pencil. He turned his back on the others, as if about to do something tricky, and noted stealthily the weights which Carlier shouted out to him with unnecessary loudness. When all was over Makola whispered to himself: 'The sun's very strong here for the tusks.' Carlier said to Kayerts in a careless tone: 'I say, chief, I might just as well give him a lift with this lot into the store.'

As they were going back to the house Kayerts observed with a sigh: 'It had to be done.' And Carlier said: 'It's deplorable, but, the men being Company's men, the ivory is Company's ivory. We must look after it.' 'I will report to the Director, of course,' said Kayerts. 'Of course; let him decide,' approved Carlier.

At midday they made a hearty meal. Kayerts sighed from time to time. Whenever they mentioned Makola's name they always added to it an opprobrious epithet. It eased their conscience. Makola gave himself a half-holiday, and bathed his children in the river. No one from Gobila's villages came near the station that day. No one came the next day, and the next, nor for a whole week. Gobila's people might have been dead and buried for any sign of life they gave. But they were only mourning for those they had lost by the witchcraft of white men, who had brought wicked people into their country. The wicked people were gone, but fear remained. Fear always remains. A man may destroy everything within himself, love and hate and belief, and even doubt; but as long as he clings to life he cannot destroy fear; the fear, subtle, indestructible, and terrible, that pervades his being; that tinges his thoughts; that lurks in his heart; that watches on his lips the struggle of his last breath. In his fear, the mild old Gobila offered extra human sacrifices to all the Evil Spirits that had taken possession of his white friends. His heart was heavy. Some warriors spoke about burning and killing, but the cautious old savage dissuaded them. Who could foresee the woe those mysterious creatures, if irritated, might bring? They should be left alone. Perhaps in time they would disappear into the earth as the first one had disappeared. His people must keep away from them, and hope for the best.

Kayerts and Carlier did not disappear, but remained above on this earth, that, somehow, they fancied had become bigger and very empty. It was not the absolute and dumb solitude of the post that impressed them so much as an inarticulate feeling that something from within them was gone, something that worked for their safety, and had kept the wilderness from interfering with their hearts. The images of home; the memory of people like them, of men that thought and felt as they used to think and feel, receded into distances made indistinct by the glare of unclouded sunshine. And out of the great silence of the surrounding wilderness, its very hopelessness and savagery seemed to approach them nearer, to draw them gently, to look upon them, to envelop them with a solicitude irresistible, familiar, and disgusting.

Days lengthened into weeks, then into months. Gobila's people drummed and yelled to every new moon, as of yore, but kept away from the station. Makola and Carlier tried once in a canoe to open communications, but were received with a shower of arrows, and had to fly back to the station for dear life. That attempt set the country up and down the river into an uproar that could be very distinctly heard for days. The steamer was late. At first they spoke of delay jauntily, then anxiously, then gloomily. The matter was becoming serious. Stores were running short. Carlier cast his lines off the bank, but the river was low, and the fish kept out in the stream. They dared not stroll far away from the station to shoot. Moreover, there was no game in the impenetrable forest. Once Carlier shot a hippo in the river. They had no boat to secure it, and it sank. When it floated up it drifted away, and Gobila's people secured the carcase. It was the occasion for a national holiday, but Carlier had a fit of rage over it and talked about the necessity of exterminating all the niggers before the country could be made habitable. Kayerts mooned about silently; spent hours looking at the portrait of his Melie. It represented a little girl with long bleached tresses and a rather sour face. His legs were much swollen, and he could hardly walk. Carlier, undermined by fever, could not swagger any more, but kept tottering about, still with a devil-may-care air, as became a man who remembered his crack regiment. He had become hoarse, sarcastic, and inclined to say unpleasant things. He called it 'being frank with you'. They had long ago reckoned their percentages on trade, including in them that last deal of 'this infamous Makola'. They had also concluded not to say anything about it. Kayerts hesitated at first – was afraid of the Director.

'He has seen worse things done on the quiet,' maintained Carlier, with a hoarse laugh. 'Trust him! He won't thank you if you blab. He is no better than you or me. Who will talk if we hold our tongues? There is nobody here.'

That was the root of the trouble! There was nobody there; and being left there alone with their weakness, they became daily more like a pair of accomplices than like a couple of devoted friends. They had heard nothing from home for eight months. Every evening they said, 'Tomorrow we shall see the steamer.' But one of the Company's steamers had been wrecked, and the Director was busy with the other, relieving very distant and important stations on the main river. He thought that the useless station, and the useless men, could wait. Meantime Kayerts and Carlier lived on rice boiled without salt, and cursed the Company, all Africa, and the day they were born. One must have lived on such diet to discover what ghastly trouble the necessity of swallowing one's food may become. There was literally nothing else in the station but rice and coffee; they drank the coffee without sugar. The last fifteen lumps Kayerts had solemnly locked away in his box, together with a half-bottle of Cognac, 'in case of sickness,' he explained. Carlier approved. 'When one is sick,' he said, 'any little extra like that is cheering.'

They waited. Rank grass began to sprout over the courtyard. The bell never rang now. Days passed, silent, exasperating, and slow. When the two men spoke, they snarled; and their silences were bitter, as if tinged by the bitterness of their thoughts.

One day after a lunch of boiled rice, Carlier put down his cup untasted, and said: 'Hang it all! Let's have a decent cup of coffee for once. Bring out that sugar, Kayerts!'

'For the sick,' muttered Kayerts, without looking up.

'For the sick,' mocked Carlier. 'Bosh! . . . Well! I am sick.'

'You are no more sick than I am, and I go without,' said Kayerts in a peaceful tone.

'Come! out with that sugar, you stingy old slave-dealer.'

Kayerts looked up quickly. Carlier was smiling with marked insolence. And suddenly it seemed to Kayerts that he had never seen that man before. Who was he? He knew nothing about him. What was he capable of? There was a surprising flash of violent emotion within him, as if in the presence of something undreamt-of, dangerous, and final. But he managed to pronounce with composure –

'That joke is in very bad taste. Don't repeat it.'

'Joke!' said Carlier, hitching himself forward on his seat. 'I am hungry – I am sick – I don't joke! I hate hypocrites. You are a hypocrite. You are a slave-dealer. I am a slave-dealer. There's nothing but slave-dealers in this cursed country. I mean to have sugar in my coffee today, anyhow!'

'I forbid you to speak to me in that way,' said Kayerts with a fair show of resolution.

'You! – What?' shouted Carlier, jumping up.

Kayerts stood up also. 'I am your chief,' he began, trying to master the shakiness of his voice.

'What?' yelled the other. 'Who's chief? There's no chief here. There's nothing here: there's nothing but you and I. Fetch the sugar – you pot-bellied ass.'

'Hold your tongue. Go out of this room,' screamed Kayerts. 'I dismiss you – you scoundrel!'

Carlier swung a stool. All at once he looked dangerously in earnest. 'You flabby, good-for-nothing civilian – take that!' he howled.

Keyerts dropped under the table, and the stool struck the grass inner wall of the room. Then, as Carlier was trying to upset the table, Kayerts in desperation made a blind rush, head low, like a cornered pig would do, and over-turning his friend, bolted along the verandah, and into his room. He locked the door, snatched his revolver, and stood panting. In less than a minute Carlier was kicking at the door furiously, howling, 'If you don't bring out that sugar, I will shoot you at sight, like a dog. Now then – one – two – three. You won't? I will show you who's the master.'

Kayerts thought the door would fall in, and scrambled through the square hole that served for a window in his room. There was then the whole breadth of the house between them. But the other was apparently not strong enough to break in the door, and Kayerts heard him running round. Then he also began to run laboriously on his swollen legs. He ran as quickly as he could, grasping the revolver, and unable yet to understand what was happening to him. He saw in succession Makola's house, the store, the river, the ravine, and the low bushes; and he saw all those things again as he ran for the second time round the house. Then again they flashed past him. That morning he could not have walked a yard without a groan.

And now he ran. He ran fast enough to keep out of sight of the other man.

Then as, weak and desperate, he thought, 'Before I finish the next round I shall die,' he heard the other man stumble heavily, then stop. He stopped also. He had the back and Carlier the front of the house, as before. He heard him drop into a chair cursing, and suddenly his own legs gave way, and he slid down into a sitting posture with his back to the wall. His mouth was as dry as a cinder, and his face was wet with perspiration – and tears. What was it all about? He thought it must be a horrible illusion; he thought he was dreaming; he thought he was going mad! After a while he collected his senses. What did they quarrel about? That sugar! How absurd! He would give it to him – didn't want it himself. And he began scrambling to his feet with a sudden feeling of security. But before he had fairly stood upright, a commonsense reflection occurred to him and drove him back into despair. He thought: If I give way now to that brute of a soldier, he will begin this horror again tomorrow – and the day after – every day – raise other pretensions, trample on me, torture me, make me his slave – and I will be lost! Lost! The steamer may not come for days – may never come. He shook so that he had to sit down on the floor again. He shivered forlornly. He felt he could not, would not move any more. He was completely distracted by the sudden perception that the position was without issue – that death and life had in a moment become equally difficult and terrible.

All at once he heard the other push his chair back; and he leaped to his feet with extreme facility. He listened and got confused. Must run again! Right or left? He heard footsteps. He darted to the left, grasping his revolver, and at the very same instant, as it seemed to him, they came into violent collision. Both shouted with surprise. A loud explosion took place between them; a roar of red fire, thick smoke; and Kayerts, deafened and blinded, rushed back thinking: I am hit – it's all over. He expected the other to come round – to gloat over his agony. He caught hold of an upright of the roof – 'All over!' Then he heard a crashing fall on the other side of the house, as if somebody had tumbled headlong over a chair – then silence. Nothing more happened. He did not die. Only his shoulder felt as if it had been badly wrenched, and he had lost his revolver. He was disarmed and helpless! He waited for his fate. The other man made no sound. It was a stratagem. He was stalking him now! Along what side? Perhaps he was taking aim this very minute!

After a few moments of an agony frightful and absurd, he decided to go and meet his doom. He was prepared for every surrender. He turned the corner, steadying himself with one hand on the wall; made a few paces, and nearly swooned. He had seen on the floor, protruding past the other corner, a pair of turned-up feet. A pair of white naked feet in red slippers. He felt deadly sick, and stood for a time in profound darkness. Then Makola appeared before him, saying quietly: 'Come along, Mr Kayerts. He is dead.' He burst into tears of gratitude; a loud, sobbing fit of crying. After a time he found himself sitting in a chair and looking at Carlier, who lay stretched on his back. Makola was kneeling over the body.

'Is this your revolver?' asked Makola, getting up.

'Yes,' said Kayerts; then he added very quickly, 'He ran after me to shoot me – you saw!'

'Yes, I saw,' said Makola. 'There is only one revolver; where's his?'

'Don't know,' whispered Kayerts in a voice that had become suddenly very faint.

'I will go and look for it,' said the other, gently. He made the round along the verandah, while Kayerts sat still and looked at the corpse. Makola came back empty-handed, stood in deep thought, then stepped quietly into the dead man's room, and came out directly with a revolver, which he held up before Kayerts. Kayerts shut his eyes. Everything was going round. He found life more terrible and difficult than death. He had shot an unarmed man.

After meditating for a while, Makola said softly, pointing at the dead man who lay there with his right eye blown out –

'He died of fever.' Kayerts looked at him with a stony stare, 'Yes,' repeated Makola, thoughtfully, stepping over the corpse– 'I think he died of fever. Bury him tomorrow.'

And he went away slowly to his expectant wife, leaving the two white men alone on the verandah.

Night came, and Kayerts sat unmoving on his chair. He sat quiet as if he had taken a dose of opium. The violence of the emotions he had passed through produced a feeling of exhausted serenity. He had plumbed in one short afternoon the depths of horror and despair, and now found repose in the conviction that life had no more secrets for him: neither had death! He sat by the corpse thinking; thinking very actively, thinking very new thoughts. He seemed to have broken loose from himself altogether. His old thoughts, convictions, likes and dislikes, things he respected and things he abhorred, appeared in their true light at last! Appeared contemptible and childish, false and ridiculous. He revelled in his new wisdom while he sat by the man he had killed. He argued with himself about all things under heaven with that kind of wrong-headed lucidity which may be observed in some lunatics. Incidentally he reflected that the fellow dead there had been a noxious beast anyway; that men died every day in thousands; perhaps in hundreds of thousands – who could tell? – and that in the number, that one death could not possibly make any difference; couldn't have any importance, at least to a thinking creature. He, Kayerts, was a thinking creature. He had been all his life, till that moment, a believer in a lot of nonsense like the rest of mankind – who are fools; but now he thought! He knew! He was at peace; he was familiar with the highest wisdom! Then he tried to imagine himself dead, and Carlier sitting in his chair watching him; and his attempt met with such unexpected success, that in a very few moments he became not at all sure who was dead and who was alive. This extraordinary achievement of his fancy startled him, however, and by a clever and timely effort of mind he saved himself just in time from becoming Carlier. His heart thumped, and he felt hot all over at the thought of that danger. Carlier! What a beastly thing! To compose his now disturbed nerves – and no wonder! – he tried to whistle a little. Then, suddenly, he fell asleep, or thought he had slept; but at any rate there was a fog, and somebody had whistled in the fog.

He stood up. The day had come, and a heavy mist had descended upon the land: the mist penetrating, enveloping, and silent; the morning mist of tropical lands; the mist that clings and kills; the mist white and deadly, immaculate and poisonous. He stood up, saw the body, and threw his arms above his head with a cry like that of a man who, waking from a trance, finds himself immured forever in a tomb. '*Help! . . . My God!*'

A shriek inhuman, vibrating and sudden, pierced like a sharp dart the white shroud of that land of sorrow. Three short, impatient screeches followed, and then, for a time, the fog-wreaths rolled on, undisturbed, through a formidable silence. Then many more shrieks rapid and piercing, like the yells of some exasperated and ruthless creature, rent the air. Progress was calling to Kayerts from the river. Progress and civilization and all the virtues. Society was calling to its accomplished child to come, to be taken care of, to be instructed, to be judged, to be condemned; it called him to return to that rubbish heap from which he had wandered away, so that justice could be done.

Kayerts heard and understood. He stumbled out of the verandah, leaving the other man quite alone for the first time since they had been thrown there together. He groped his way through the fog, calling in his ignorance upon the invisible heaven to undo its work. Makola flitted by in the mist, shouting as he ran –

'Steamer! Steamer! They can't see. They whistle for the station. I go ring the bell. Go down to the landing, sir. I ring.'

He disappeared. Kayerts stood still. He looked upwards; the fog rolled low over his head. He looked round like a man who has lost his way; and he saw a dark smudge, a cross-shaped stain, upon the shifting purity of the mist. As he began to stumble towards it, the station bell rang in a tumultuous peal its answer to the impatient clamour of the steamer.

The Managing Director of the Great Civilizing Company (since we know that civilization follows trade) landed first, and incontinently lost sight of the steamer. The fog down by the river was exceedingly dense; above, at the station, the bell rang unceasing and brazen.

The Director shouted loudly to the steamer:

'There is nobody down to meet us; there may be something wrong, though they are ringing. You had better come, too!'

And he began to toil up the steep bank. The captain and the engine-driver of the boat followed behind. As they scrambled up the fog thinned, and they could see their Director a good way ahead. Suddenly they saw him start forward, calling to them over his shoulder: 'Run! Run to the house! I've found one of them. Run, look for the other!'

He had found one of them! And even he, the man of varied and startling experience, was somewhat discomposed by the manner of this finding. He stood and fumbled in his pockets (for a knife) while he faced Kayerts, who was hanging by a leather strap from the cross. He had evidently climbed the grave, which was high and narrow, and after tying the end of the strap to the arm, had swung himself off. His toes were only a couple of inches above the ground; his arms hung stiffly down; he seemed to be standing rigidly at attention, but with one purple cheek playfully posed on the shoulder. And, irreverently, he was putting out a swollen tongue at his Managing Director.

Rudyard Kipling

AT THE END OF THE PASSAGE

The sky is lead and our faces are red,
    And the gates of Hell are opened and riven,
    And the winds of Hell are loosened and driven,
And the dust flies up in the face of Heaven,
    And the clouds come down in a fiery sheet,
Heavy to raise and hard to be borne.
    And the soul of man is turned from his meat,
Turned from the trifles for which he has striven
    Sick in his body, and heavy-hearted,
    And his soul flies up like the dust in the street,
    Breaks from his flesh and is gone and departed,
As the blasts they blow on the cholera-horn.

Himalayan

FOUR men, each entitled to 'life, liberty, and the pursuit of happiness', sat at a table playing whist. The thermometer marked – for them – 101 degrees of heat. The room was darkened till it was only just possible to distinguish the pips of the cards and the very white faces of the players. A tattered, rotten punkah of whitewashed calico was puddling the hot air and whining dolefully at each stroke. Outside lay gloom of a November day in London. There was neither sky, sun, nor horizon – nothing but a brown purple haze of heat. It was as though the earth were dying of apoplexy.

From time to time clouds of tawny dust rose from the ground without wind or warning, flung themselves table-cloth-wise among the tops of the parched trees, and came down again. Then a whirling dust-devil would scutter across the plain for a couple of miles, break, and fall outward, though there was nothing to check its flight save a long low line of piled railway-sleepers white with the dust, a cluster of huts made of mud, condemned rails, and canvas, and the one squat

four-roomed bungalow that belonged to the assistant engineer
in charge of a section of the Gaudhari State line then under
construction.

The four, stripped to the thinnest of sleeping-suits, played
whist crossly, with wranglings as to leads and returns. It was
not the best kind of whist, but they had taken some trouble to
arrive at it. Mottram of the Indian Survey had ridden thirty
and railed one hundred miles from his lonely post in the
desert since the night before; Lowndes of the Civil Service, on
special duty in the political department, had come as far to
escape for an instant the miserable intrigues of an impoverished
native State whose king alternately fawned and blustered for
more money from the pitiful revenues contributed by hard-
wrung peasants and despairing camel-breeders; Spurstow, the
doctor of the line, had left a cholera-stricken camp of coolies to
look after itself for forty-eight hours while he associated with
white men once more. Hummil, the assistant engineer, was the
host. He stood fast and received his friends thus every Sunday
if they could come in. When one of them failed to appear, he
would send a telegram to his last address, in order that he
might know whether the defaulter were dead or alive. There
are very many places in the East where it is not good or kind
to let your acquaintances drop out of sight even for one short
week.

The players were not conscious of any special regard for
each other. They squabbled whenever they met; but they
ardently desired to meet, as men without water desire to drink.
They were lonely folk who understood the dread meaning of
loneliness. They were all under thirty years of age – which is
too soon for any man to possess that knowledge.

'Pilsener?' said Spurstow, after the second rubber, mopping
his forehead.

'Beer's out, I'm sorry to say, and there's hardly enough
soda-water for tonight,' said Hummil.

'What filthy bad management!' Spurstow snarled.

'Can't help it. I've written and wired; but the trains don't
come through regularly yet. Last week the ice ran out – as
Lowndes knows.'

'Glad I didn't come. I could ha' sent you some if I had known, though. Phew! it's too hot to go on playing bumble-puppy.' This with a savage scowl at Lowndes, who only laughed. He was a hardened offender.

Mottram rose from the table and looked out of a chink in the shutters.

'What a sweet day!' said he.

The company yawned all together and betook themselves to an aimless investigation of all Hummil's possessions – guns, tattered novels, saddlery, spurs, and the like. They had fingered them a score of times before, but there was really nothing else to do.

'Got anything fresh?' said Lowndes.

'Last week's *Gazette of India*, and a cutting from a home paper. My father sent it out. It's rather amusing.'

'One of those vestrymen that call 'emselves M.P.s again, is it?' said Spurstow, who read his newspapers when he could get them.

'Yes. Listen to this. It's to your address, Lowndes. The man was making a speech to his constituents, and he piled it on. Here's a sample, "And I assert unhesitatingly that the Civil Service in India is the preserve – the pet preserve – of the aristocracy of England. What does the democracy – what do the masses – get from that country, which we have step by step fraudulently annexed? I answer, nothing whatever. It is farmed with a single eye to their own interests by the scions of the aristocracy. They take good care to maintain their lavish scale of incomes, to avoid or stifle any inquiries into the nature and conduct of their administration, while they themselves force the unhappy peasant to pay with the sweat of his brow for all the luxuries in which they are lapped." ' Hummil waved the cutting above his head. ' 'Ear! 'ear!' said his audience.

Then Lowndes, meditatively, 'I'd give – I'd give three months' pay to have that gentleman spend one month with me and see how the free and independent native prince works things. Old Timbersides' – this was his flippant title for an honoured and decorated feudatory prince – 'has been wearing my life out this week past for money. By Jove, his latest performance was to send me one of his women as a bribe!'

'Good for you! Did you accept it?' said Mottram.

'No. I rather wish I had, now. She was a pretty little person, and she yarned away to me about the horrible destitution among the king's women-folk. The darlings haven't had any new clothes for nearly a month, and the old man wants to buy a new drag from Calcutta – solid silver railings and silver lamps, and trifles of that kind. I've tried to make him understand that he has played the deuce with the revenues for the last twenty years and must go slow. He can't see it.'

'But he has the ancestral treasure-vaults to draw on. There must be three millions at least in jewels and coin under his palace,' said Hummil.

'Catch a native king disturbing the family treasure! The priests forbid it except as the last resort. Old Timbersides has added something like a quarter of a million to the deposit in his reign.'

'Where the mischief does it all come from?' said Mottram.

'The country. The state of the people is enough to make you sick. I've known the taxmen wait by a milch-camel till the foal was born and then hurry off the mother for arrears. And what can I do? I can't get the court clerks to give me any accounts; I can't raise anything more than a fat smile from the commander-in-chief when I find out the troops are three months in arrears; and old Timbersides begins to weep when I speak to him. He has taken to the King's Peg heavily – liqueur brandy for whisky, and Heidsieck for soda-water.'

'That's what the Rao of Jubela took to. Even a native can't last long at that,' said Spurstow. 'He'll go out.'

'And a good thing, too. Then I suppose we'll have a council of regency, and a tutor for the young prince, and hand him back his kingdom with ten years' accumulations.'

'Whereupon that young prince, having been taught all the vices of the English, will play ducks and drakes with the money and undo ten years' work in eighteen months. I've seen that business before,' said Spurstow. 'I should tackle the king with a light hand if I were you, Lowndes. They'll hate you quite enough under any circumstances.'

'That's all very well. The man who looks on can talk about the light hand; but you can't clean a pigsty with a pen dipped in rose-water. I know my risks; but nothing has happened yet. My servant's an old Pathan, and he cooks for me. They are hardly likely to bribe him, and I don't accept food from my true friends, as they call themselves. Oh, but it's weary work! I'd sooner be with you, Spurstow. There's shooting near your camp.'

'Would you? I don't think it. About fifteen deaths a day don't incite a man to shoot anything but himself. And the worst of it is that the poor devils look at you as though you ought to save them. Lord knows, I've tried everything. My last attempt was empirical, but it pulled an old man through. He was brought to me apparently past hope, and I gave him gin and Worcester sauce with cayenne. It cured him; but I don't recommend it.'

'How do the cases run generally?' said Hummil.

'Very simply indeed. Chlorodyne, opium pill, chlorodyne, collapse, nitre, bricks to the feet, and then – the burning-ghaut. The last seems to be the only thing that stops the trouble. It's black cholera, you know. Poor devils! But, I will say, little Bunsee Lal, my apothecary, works like a demon. I've recommended him for promotion if he comes through it all alive.'

'And what are your chances, old man?' said Mottram.

'Don't know; don't care much; but I've sent the letter in. What are you doing with yourself generally?'

'Sitting under a table in the tent and spitting on the sextant to keep it cool,' said the man of the Survey. 'Washing my eyes to avoid ophthalmia, which I shall certainly get, and try to make a sub-surveyor understand that an error of five degrees in an angle isn't quite so small as it looks. I'm altogether alone, y' know, and shall be till the end of the hot weather.'

'Hummil's the lucky man,' said Lowndes, flinging himself into a long chair. 'He has an actual roof – torn as to the ceiling-cloth, but still a roof – over his head. He sees one train daily. He can get beer and soda-water and ice 'em when God is good.

He has books, pictures' – they were torn from the *Graphic* – 'and the society of the excellent sub-contractor Jevins, besides the pleasure of receiving us weekly.'

Hummil smiled grimly. 'Yes, I'm the lucky man, I suppose. Jevins is luckier.'

'How? Not –'

'Yes. Went out. Last Monday.'

'By his own hand?' said Spurstow quickly, hinting the suspicion that was in everybody's mind. There was no cholera near Hummil's section. Even fever gives a man at least a week's grace, and sudden death generally implied self-slaughter.

'I judge no man this weather,' said Hummil. 'He had a touch of the sun, I fancy; for last week, after you fellows had left, he came into the verandah and told me that he was going home to see his wife, in Market Street, Liverpool, that evening.

'I got the apothecary in to look at him, and we tried to make him lie down. After an hour or two he rubbed his eyes and said he believed he had had a fit – hoped he hadn't said anything rude. Jevins had a great idea of bettering himself socially. He was very like Chucks in his language.'

'Well?'

'Then he went to his own bungalow and began cleaning a rifle. He told the servant that he was going to shoot buck in the morning. Naturally he fumbled with the trigger, and shot himself through the head – accidentally. The apothecary sent in a report to my chief, and Jevins is buried somewhere out there. I'd have wired to you, Spurstow, if you could have done anything.'

'You're a queer chap,' said Mottram. 'If you'd killed the man yourself you couldn't have been more quiet about the business.'

'Good Lord! what does it matter?' said Hummil calmly. 'I've got to do a lot of his overseeing work in addition to my own. I'm the only person that suffers. Jevins is out of it – by pure accident, of course, but out of it. The apothecary was going to write a long screed on suicide. Trust a babu to drivel when he gets the chance.'

'Why didn't you let it go in as suicide?' said Lowndes.

'No direct proof. A man hasn't many privileges in this country, but he might at least be allowed to mishandle his own rifle. Besides, some day I may need a man to smother up an accident to myself. Live and let live. Die and let die.'

'You take a pill,' said Spurstow, who had been watching Hummil's white face narrowly. 'Take a pill, and don't be an ass. That sort of talk is skittles. Anyhow, suicide is shirking your work. If I were Job ten times over, I should be so interested in what was going to happen next that I'd stay on and watch.'

'Ah! I've lost that curiosity,' said Hummil.

'Liver out of order?' said Lowndes feelingly.

'No. Can't sleep. That's worse.'

'By Jove, it is!' said Mottram. 'I'm that way every now and then, and the fit has to wear itself out. What do you take for it?'

'Nothing. What's the use? I haven't had ten minutes' sleep since Friday morning.'

'Poor chap! Spurstow, you ought to attend to this,' said Mottram. 'Now you mention it, your eyes are rather gummy and swollen.'

Spurstow, still watching Hummil, laughed lightly. 'I'll patch him up, later on. Is it too hot, do you think, to go for a ride?'

'Where to?' said Lowndes wearily. 'We shall have to go away at eight, and there'll be riding enough for us then. I hate a horse when I have to use him as a necessity. Oh, heavens! what is there to do?'

'Begin whist again, at chick points ['a chick' is supposed to be eight shillings] and a gold mohur on the rub,' said Spurstow promptly.

'Poker. A month's pay all round for the pool – no limit – and fifty-rupee raises. Somebody would be broken before we got up,' said Lowndes.

'Can't say that it would give me any pleasure to break any man in this company,' said Mottram. 'There isn't enough excitement in it, and it's foolish.' He crossed over to the worn and battered little camp-piano – wreckage of a married household that had once held the bungalow – and opened the case.

'It's used up long ago,' said Hummil. 'The servants have picked it to pieces.'

The piano was indeed hopelessly out of order, but Mottram managed to bring the rebellious notes into a sort of agreement, and there rose from the ragged keyboard something that might once have been the ghost of a popular music-hall song. The men in the long chairs turned with evident interest as Mottram banged the more lustily.

'That's good!' said Lowndes. 'By Jove! The last time I heard that song was in '79, or thereabouts, just before I came out.'

'Ah!' said Spurstow with pride, 'I was home in '80.' And he mentioned a song of the streets popular at that date.

Mottram executed it roughly. Lowndes criticized and volunteered emendations. Mottram dashed into another ditty, not of the music-hall character, and made as if to rise.

'Sit down,' said Hummil. 'I didn't know that you had any music in your composition. Go on playing until you can't think of anything more. I'll have that piano tuned up before you come again. Play something festive.'

Very simple indeed were the tunes to which Mottram's art and the limitations of the piano could give effect, but the men listened with pleasure, and in the pauses talked all together of what they had seen or heard when they were last at home. A dense dust-storm sprung up outside, and swept roaring over the house, enveloping it in the choking darkness of midnight, but Mottram continued unheeding, and the crazy tinkle reached the ears of the listeners above the flapping of the tattered ceiling-cloth.

In the silence after the storm he glided from the more directly personal songs of Scotland, half humming them as he played, into the Evening Hymn.

'Sunday,' said he, nodding his head.

'Go on. Don't apologize for it,' said Spurstow.

Hummil laughed long and riotously. 'Play it, by all means. You're full of surprises today. I didn't know you had such a gift of finished sarcasm. How does that thing go?'

Mottram took up the tune.

'Too slow by half. You miss the note of gratitude,' said Hummil. 'It ought to go to the "Grasshopper's Polka" – this way.' And he chanted, *prestissimo* –

> 'Glory to thee, my God, this night,
> For all the blessings of the light.

'That shows we really feel our blessings. How does it go on? –

> 'If in the night I sleepless lie,
> My soul with sacred thoughts supply;
> May n o ill dreams disturb my rest, –

'Quicker, Mottram! –

> 'Or powers of darkness me molest!'

'Bah! what an old hypocrite you are!'

'Don't be an ass,' said Lowndes. 'You are at full liberty to make fun of anything else you like, but leave that hymn alone. It's associated in my mind with the most sacred recollections –'

'Summer evenings in the country – stained-glass window – light going out, and you and she jamming your heads together over one hymnbook,' said Mottram.

'Yes, and a fat old cockchafer hitting you in the eye when you walked home. Smell of hay, and a moon as big as a bandbox sitting on the top of a haycock; bats – roses – milk and midges,' said Lowndes.

'Also mothers. I can just recollect my mother singing me to sleep with that when I was a little chap,' said Spurstow.

The darkness had fallen on the room. They could hear Hummil squirming in his chair.

'Consequently,' said he testily, 'you sing it when you are seven fathom deep in Hell! It's an insult to the intelligence of the Deity to pretend we're anything but tortured rebels.'

'Take *two* pills,' said Spurstow; 'that's tortured liver.'

'The usually placid Hummil is in a vile bad temper. I'm sorry for his coolies tomorrow,' said Lowndes, as the servants brought in the lights and prepared the table for dinner.

As they were settling into their places about the miserable

goat-chops, and the smoked tapioca pudding, Spurstow took occasion to whisper to Mottram, 'Well done, David!'

'Look after Saul, then,' was the reply.

'What are you two whispering about?' said Hummil suspiciously.

'Only saying that you are a damned poor host. This fowl can't be cut,' returned Spurstow with a sweet smile. 'Call this a dinner?'

'I can't help it. You don't expect a banquet, do you?'

Throughout that meal Hummil contrived laboriously to insult directly and pointedly all his guests in succession, and at each insult Spurstow kicked the aggrieved persons under the table; but he dared not exchange a glance of intelligence with either of them. Hummil's face was white and pinched, while his eyes were unnaturally large. No man dreamed for a moment of resenting his savage personalities, but as soon as the meal was over they made haste to get away.

'Don't go. You're just getting amusing, you fellows. I hope I haven't said anything that annoyed you. You're such touchy devils.' Then, changing the note into one of almost abject entreaty, Hummil added, 'I say, you surely aren't going?'

'In the language of the blessed Jorrocks, where I dines I sleeps,' said Spurstow. 'I want to have a look at your coolies tomorrow, if you don't mind. You can give me a place to lie down in, I suppose?'

The others pleaded the urgency of their several duties next day, and, saddling up, departed together, Hummil begging them to come next Sunday. As they jogged off, Lowndes unbosomed himself to Mottram –

'. . . And I never felt so like kicking a man at his own table in my life. He said I cheated at whist, and reminded me I was in debt! Told you you were as good as a liar to your face! You aren't half indignant enough over it.'

'Not I,' said Mottram. 'Poor devil! Did you ever know old Hummy behave like that before or within a hundred miles of it?'

'That's no excuse. Spurstow was hacking my shin all the time, so I kept a hand on myself. Else I should have –'

'No, you wouldn't. You'd have done as Hummy did about Jevins; judge no man this weather. By Jove! the buckle of my bridle is hot in my hand! Trot out a bit, and 'ware rat-holes.'

Ten minutes' trotting jerked out of Lowndes one very sage remark when he pulled up, sweating from every pore –

'Good thing Spurstow's with him tonight.'

'Ye-es. Good man, Spurstow. Our roads turn here. See you again next Sunday, if the sun doesn't bowl me over.'

'S'pose so, unless old Timbersides' finance minister manages to dress some of my food. Good night, and – God bless you!'

'What's wrong now?'

'Oh, nothing.' Lowndes gathered up his whip, and, as he flicked Mottram's mare on the flank, added, 'You're not a bad little chap, – that's all.' And the mare bolted half a mile across the sand, on the word.

In the assistant engineer's bungalow Spurstow and Hummil smoked the pipe of silence together, each narrowly watching the other. The capacity of a bachelor's establishment is as elastic as its arrangements are simple. A servant cleared away the dining-room table, brought in a couple of rude native bedsteads made of tape strung on a light wood frame, flung a square of cool Calcutta matting over each, set them side by side, pinned two towels to the punkah so that their fringes should just sweep clear of the sleeper's nose and mouth, and announced that the couches were ready.

The men flung themselves down, ordering the punkah-coolies by all the powers of Hell to pull. Every door and window was shut, for the outside air was that of an oven. The atmosphere within was only 104 degrees, as the thermometer bore witness, and heavy with the foul smell of badly-trimmed kerosene lamps; and this stench, combined with that of native tobacco, baked brick, and dried earth, sends the heart of many a strong man down to his boots, for it is the smell of the Great Indian Empire when she turns herself for six months into a house of torment. Spurstow packed his pillows craftily so that he reclined rather than lay, his head at a safe elevation above his feet. It is not good to sleep on a low pillow in the hot weather if you happen to be of thick-necked build, for you may pass with lively snores and gugglings from natural sleep into the deep slumber of heat-apoplexy.

'Pack your pillows,' said the doctor sharply, as he saw Hummil preparing to lie down at full length.

The night-light was trimmed; the shadow of the punkah wavered across the room, and the '*flick*' of the punkah-towel and the soft whine of the rope through the wall-hole followed it. Then the punkah flagged, almost ceased. The sweat poured from Spurstow's brow. Should he go out and harangue the coolie? It started forward again with a savage jerk, and a pin came out of the towels. When this was replaced, a tomtom in the coolie-lines began to beat with the steady throb of a swollen artery inside some brain-fevered skull. Spurstow turned on his side and swore gently. There was no movement on Hummil's part. The man had composed himself as rigidly as a corpse, his hands clinched at his sides. The respiration was too hurried for any suspicion of sleep. Spurstow looked at the set face. The jaws were clinched, and there was a pucker round the quivering eyelids.

'He's holding himself as tightly as ever he can,' thought Spurstow. 'What in the world is the matter with him? – Hummil!'

'Yes,' in a thick constrained voice.

'Can't you get to sleep?'

'No.'

'Head hot? Throat feeling bulgy? Or how?'

'Neither, thanks. I don't sleep much, you know.'

'Feel pretty bad?'

'Pretty bad, thanks. There is a tomtom outside, isn't there? I thought it was my head at first. . . . Oh, Spurstow, for pity's sake give me something that will put me asleep – sound asleep – if it's only for six hours!' He sprang up, trembling from head to foot. 'I haven't been able to sleep naturally for days, and I can't stand it! – I can't stand it!'

'Poor old chap!'

'That's no use. Give me something to make me sleep. I tell you I'm nearly mad. I don't know what I say half my time. For three weeks I've had to think and spell out every word that has come through my lips before I dared say it. Isn't that enough to drive a man mad? I can't see things correctly now, and I've lost my sense of touch. My skin aches – my skin aches! Make me sleep. Oh, Spurstow, for the love of God make me sleep sound. It isn't enough merely to let me dream. Let me sleep!'

'All right, old man, all right. Go slow; you aren't half as bad as you think.'

The flood-gates of reserve once broken, Hummil was clinging to him like a frightened child. 'You're pinching my arm to pieces.'

'I'll break your neck if you don't do something for me. No, I didn't mean that. Don't be angry, old fellow.' He wiped the sweat off himself as he fought to regain composure. 'I'm a bit restless and off my oats, and perhaps you could recommend some sort of sleeping mixture – bromide of potassium.'

'Bromide of skittles! Why didn't you tell me this before? Let go of my arm, and I'll see if there's anything in my cigarette-case to suit your complaint.' Spurstow hunted among his day-clothes, turned up the lamp, opened a little silver cigarette-case, and advanced on the expectant Hummil with the daintiest of fairy squirts.

'The last appeal of civilization,' said he, 'and a thing I hate to use. Hold out your arm. Well, your sleeplessness hasn't ruined your muscle; and what a thick hide it is! Might as well inject a buffalo subcutaneously. Now in a few minutes the morphia will begin working. Lie down and wait.'

A smile of unalloyed and idiotic delight began to creep over Hummil's face. 'I think,' he whispered – 'I think I'm going off now. Gad! it's positively heavenly! Spurstow, you must give me that case to keep; you – ' The voice ceased as the head fell back.

'Not for a good deal,' said Spurstow to the unconscious form. 'And now, my friend, sleeplessness of your kind being very apt to relax the moral fibre in little matters of life and death, I'll just take the liberty of spiking your guns.'

He paddled into Hummil's saddle-room in his bare feet and uncased a twelve-bore rifle, an express, and a revolver. Of the first he unscrewed the nipples and hid them in the bottom of a saddlery-case; of the second he abstracted the lever, kicking it behind a big wardrobe. The third he merely opened, and knocked the doll-head bolt of the grip up with the heel of a riding-boot.

'That's settled,' he said, as he shook the sweat off his hands. 'These little precautions will at least give you time to turn. You have too much sympathy with gun-room accidents.'

And as he rose from his knees, the thick muffled voice of Hummil cried in the doorway, 'You fool!'

Such tones they use who speak in the lucid intervals of delirium to their friends a little before they die.

Spurstow started, dropping the pistol. Hummil stood in the doorway, rocking with helpless laughter.

'That was awf'ly good of you, I'm sure,' he said, very slowly, feeling for his words. 'I don't intend to go out by my own hand at present. I say, Spurstow, that stuff won't work. What shall I do? What shall I do?' And panic terror stood in his eyes.

'Lie down and give it a chance. Lie down at once.'

'I daren't. It will only take me half-way again, and I shan't be able to get away this time. Do you know it was all I could do to come out just now? Generally I am as quick as lightning; but you had clogged my feet. I was nearly caught.'

'Oh yes, I understand. Go and lie down.'

'No, it isn't delirium; but it was an awfully mean trick to play on me. Do you know I might have died?'

As a sponge rubs a slate clean, so some power unknown to Spurstow had wiped out of Hummil's face all that stamped it for the face of a man, and he stood at the doorway in the expression of his lost innocence. He had slept back into terrified childhood.

'Is he going to die on the spot?' thought Spurstow. Then, aloud, 'All right, my son. Come back to bed, and tell me all about it. You couldn't sleep; but what was all the rest of the nonsense?'

'A place – a place down there,' said Hummil, with simple sincerity. The drug was acting on him by waves, and he was flung from the fear of a strong man to the fright of a child as his nerves gathered sense or were dulled.

'Good God! I've been afraid of it for months past, Spurstow. It has made every night hell to me; and yet I'm not conscious of having done anything wrong.'

'Be still, and I'll give you another dose. We'll stop your nightmares, you unutterable idiot!'

'Yes, but you must give me so much that I can't get away. You must make me quite sleepy – not just a little sleepy. It's so hard to run then.'

'I know it; I know it. I've felt it myself. The symptoms are exactly as you describe.'

'Oh, don't laugh at me, confound you! Before this awful sleeplessness came to me I've tried to rest on my elbow and put a spur in the bed to sting me when I fell back. Look!'

'By Jove! the man has been rowelled like a horse! Ridden by the nightmare with a vengeance! And we all thought him sensible enough. Heaven send us understanding! You like to talk, don't you?'

'Yes, sometimes. Not when I'm frightened. *Then* I want to run. Don't you?'

'Always. Before I give you your second dose try to tell me exactly what your trouble is.'

Hummil spoke in broken whispers for nearly ten minutes, whilst Spurstow looked into the pupils of his eyes and passed his hand before them once or twice.

At the end of the narrative the silver cigarette-case was produced, and the last words that Hummil said as he fell back for the second time were, 'Put me quite to sleep; for if I'm caught I die – I die!'

'Yes, yes; we all do that sooner or later – thank Heaven who has set a term to our miseries,' said Spurstow, settling the cushions under the head. 'It occurs to me that unless I drink something I shall go out before my time. I've stopped sweating, and – I wear a seventeen-inch collar.' He brewed himself scalding hot tea, which is an excellent remedy against heat-apoplexy if you take three or four cups of it in time. Then he watched the sleeper.

'A blind face that cries and can't wipe its eyes, a blind face that chases him down corridors! H'm! Decidedly, Hummil ought to go on leave as soon as possible; and, sane or otherwise, he undoubtedly did rowel himself most cruelly. Well, Heaven send us understanding!'

At midday Hummil rose, with an evil taste in his mouth, but an unclouded eye and a joyful heart.

'I was pretty bad last night, wasn't I?' said he.

'I have seen healthier men. You must have had a touch of the sun. Look here: if I write you a swingeing medical certificate, will you apply for leave on the spot?'

'No.'

'Why not? You want it.'

'Yes, but I can hold on till the weather's a little cooler.'

'Why should you, if you can get relieved on the spot?'

'Burkett is the only man who could be sent; and he's a born fool.'

'Oh, never mind about the line. You aren't so important as all that. Wire for leave, if necessary.'

Hummil looked very uncomfortable.

'I can hold on till the Rains,' he said evasively.

'You can't. Wire to headquarters for Burkett.'

'I won't. If you want to know why, particularly, Burkett is married, and his wife's just had a kid, and she's up at Simla, in the cool, and Burkett has a very nice billet that takes him into Simla from Saturday to Monday. That little woman isn't at all well. If Burkett was transferred she'd try to follow him. If she left the baby behind she'd fret herself to death. If she came – and Burkett's one of those selfish little beasts who are always talking about a wife's place being with her husband – she'd die. It's murder to bring a woman here just now. Burkett hasn't the physique of a rat. If he came here he'd go out; and I know she hasn't any money, and I'm pretty sure she'd go out too. I'm salted in a sort of way, and I'm not married. Wait till the Rains, and then Burkett can get thin down here. It'll do him heaps of good.'

'Do you mean to say that you intend to face – what you have faced, till the Rains break?'

'Oh, it won't be so bad, now you've shown me a way out of it. I can always wire to you. Besides, now I've once got into the way of sleeping, it'll be all right. Anyhow, I shan't put in for leave. That's the long and the short of it.'

'My great Scott! I thought all that sort of thing was dead and done with.'

'Bosh! You'd do the same yourself. I feel a new man, thanks to that cigarette-case. You're going over to camp now, aren't you?'

'Yes; but I'll try to look you up every other day, if I can.'

'I'm not bad enough for that. I don't want you to bother. Give the coolies gin and ketchup.'

'Then you feel all right?'

'Fit to fight for my life, but not to stand out in the sun talking to you. Go along, old man, and bless you!'

Hummil turned on his heel to face the echoing desolation of his bungalow, and the first thing he saw standing in the verandah was the figure of himself. He had met a similar apparition once before, when he was suffering from overwork and the strain of the hot weather.

'This is bad – already,' he said, rubbing his eyes. 'If the thing slides away from me all in one piece, like a ghost, I shall know it is only my eyes and stomach that are out of order. If it walks – my head is going.'

He approached the figure, which naturally kept at an unvarying distance from him, as is the use of all spectres that are born of overwork. It slid through the house and dissolved into swimming specks within the eyeball as soon as it reached the burning light of the garden. Hummil went about his business till even. When he came in to dinner he found himself sitting at the table. The vision rose and walked out hastily. Except that it cast no shadow it was in all respects real.

No living man knows what that week held for Hummil. An increase of the epidemic kept Spurstow in camp among the coolies, and all he could do was to telegraph to Mottram, bidding him go to the bungalow and sleep there. But Mottram was forty miles away from the nearest telegraph, and knew nothing of anything save the needs of the Survey till he met, early on Sunday morning, Lowndes and Spurstow heading towards Hummil's for the weekly gathering.

'Hope the poor chap's in a better temper, said the former, swinging himself off his horse at the door. 'I suppose he isn't up yet.'

'I'll just have a look at him,' said the doctor. 'If he's asleep there's no need to wake him.'

And an instant later, by the tone of Spurstow's voice calling upon them to enter, the men knew what had happened. There was no need to wake him.

The punkah was still being pulled over the bed, but Hummil had departed this life at least three hours.

The body lay on its back, hands clinched by the side, as Spurstow had seen it lying seven nights previously. In the staring eyes was written terror beyond the expression of any pen.

Mottram, who had entered behind Lowndes, bent over the dead and touched the forehead lightly with his lips. 'Oh, you lucky, lucky devil!' he whispered.

But Lowndes had seen the eyes, and withdrew shuddering to the other side of the room.

'Poor chap! poor old chap! And the last time I met him I was angry. Spurstow, we should have watched him. Has he – ?'

Deftly Spurstow continued his investigations, ending by a search round the room.

'No, he hasn't,' he snapped. 'There's no trace of anything. Call the servants.'

They came, eight or ten of them, whispering and peering over each other's shoulders.

'When did your *sahib* go to bed?' said Spurstow.

'At eleven or ten, we think,' said Hummil's personal servant.

'He was well then? But how should you know?'

'He was not ill, as far as our comprehension extended. But he had slept very little for three nights. This I know, because I saw him walking much, and specially in the heart of the night.'

As Spurstow was arranging the sheet, a big straight-necked hunting-spur tumbled on the ground. The doctor groaned. The personal servant peeped at the body.

'What do you think, Chuma?' said Spurstow, catching the look on the dark face.

'Heaven-born, in my poor opinion, this that was my master has descended into the Dark Places, and there has been caught because he was not able to escape with sufficient speed. We have the spur for evidence that he fought with Fear. Thus have I seen men of my race do with thorns when a spell was laid upon them to overtake them in their sleeping hours and they dared not sleep.'

'Chuma, you're a mud-head. Go out and prepare seals to be set on the *sahib*'s property.'

'God has made the Heaven-born. God has made me. Who are we, to inquire into the dispensations of God? I will bid the other servants hold aloof while you are reckoning the tale of the *sahib*'s property. They are all thieves, and would steal.'

'As far as I can make out, he died from – oh, anything; stoppage of the heart's action, heat-apoplexy, or some other visitation,' said Spurstow to his companions. 'We must make an inventory of his effects, and so on.'

'He was scared to death,' insisted Lowndes. 'Look at those eyes! For pity's sake don't let him be buried with them open!'

'Whatever it was, he's clear of all the trouble now,' said Mottram softly.

Spurstow was peering into the open eyes.

'Come here,' said he. 'Can you see anything there?'

'I can't face it!' whimpered Lowndes. 'Cover up the face! Is there any fear on earth that can turn a man into that likeness? It's ghastly. Oh, Spurstow, cover it up!'

'No fear – on earth,' said Spurstow. Mottram leaned over his shoulder and looked intently.

'I see nothing except some grey blurs in the pupil. There can be nothing there, you know.'

'Even so. Well, let's think. It'll take half a day to knock up any sort of coffin; and he must have died at midnight. Lowndes, old man, go out and tell the coolies to break ground next to Jevins's grave. Mottram, go round the house with Chuma and see that the seals are put on things. Send a couple of men to me here, and I'll arrange.'

The strong-armed servants when they returned to their own

kind told a strange story of the doctor *sahib* vainly trying to call their master back to life by magic arts – to wit, the holding of a little green box that clicked to each of the dead man's eyes, and of a bewildered muttering on the part of the doctor *sahib,* who took the little green box away with him.

The resonant hammering of a coffin-lid is no pleasant thing to hear, but those who have experience maintain that much more terrible is the soft swish of the bed-linen, the reeving and unreeving of the bed-tapes, when he who has fallen by the roadside is apparelled for burial, sinking gradually as the tapes are tied over, till the swaddled shape touches the floor and there is no protest against the indignity of hasty disposal.

At the last moment Lowndes was seized with scruples of conscience. 'Ought you to read the service – from beginning to end?' said he to Spurstow.

'I intend to. You're my senior as a civilian. You can take it if you like.'

'I didn't mean that for a moment. I only thought if we could get a chaplain from somewhere – I'm willing to ride anywhere – and give poor Hummil a better chance. That's all.'

'Bosh!' said Spurstow, as he framed his lips to the tremendous words that stand at the head of the burial service.

After breakfast they smoked a pipe in silence to the memory of the dead. Then Spurstow said absently –

' 'Tisn't in medical science.'

'What?'

'Things in a dead man's eye.'

'For goodness' sake leave that horror alone!' said Lowndes. 'I've seen a native die of pure fright when a tiger chivied him. I know what killed Hummil.'

'The deuce you do! I'm going to try to see.' And the doctor retreated into the bath-room with a Kodak camera. After a few minutes there was the sound of something being hammered to pieces, and he emerged, very white indeed.

'Have you got a picture?' said Mottram. 'What does the thing look like?'

'It was impossible, of course. You needn't look, Mottram.

I've torn up the films. There was nothing there. It was impossible.'

'That,' said Lowndes, very distinctly, watching the shaking hand striving to relight the pipe, 'is a damned lie.'

Mottram laughed uneasily. 'Spurstow's right,' he said. 'We're all in such a state now that we'd believe anything. For pity's sake let's try to be rational.'

There was no further speech for a long time. The hot wind whistled without, and the dry trees sobbed. Presently the daily train, winking brass, burnished steel, and spouting steam, pulled up panting in the intense glare. 'We'd better go on on that,' said Spurstow. 'Go back to work. I've written my certificate. We can't do any more good here, and work'll keep our wits together. Come on.'

No one moved. It is not pleasant to face railway journeys at midday in June. Spurstow gathered up his hat and whip, and, turning in the doorway, said –

> 'There may be Heaven – there must be Hell.
> Meantime, there is our life here. We-ell?'

Neither Mottram nor Lowndes had any answer to the question.

H. G. Wells

THE COUNTRY OF THE BLIND

THREE hundred miles and more from Chimborazo, one hundred from the snows of Cotopaxi, in the wildest wastes of Ecuador's Andes, there lies that mysterious mountain valley, cut off from the world of men, the Country of the Blind. Long years ago that valley lay so far open to the world that men might come at last through frightful gorges and over an icy pass into its equable meadows; and thither indeed men came, a family or so of Peruvian half-breeds fleeing from the lust and tyranny of an evil Spanish ruler. Then came the stupendous outbreak of Mindobamba, when it was night in Quito for seventeen days, and the water was boiling at Yaguachi and all the fish floating dying even as far as Guayaquil; everywhere along the Pacific slopes there were landslips and swift thawings and sudden floods, and one whole side of the old Arauca crest slipped and came down in thunder, and cut off the Country of the Blind for ever from the exploring feet of men. But one of these early settlers had chanced to be on the hither side of the gorges when the world had so terribly shaken itself, and he perforce had to forget his wife and his child and all the friends and possessions he had left up there, and start life over again in the lower world. He started it again but ill; blindness overtook him, and he died of punishment in the mines; but the story he told begot a legend that lingers along the length of the Cordilleras of the Andes to this day.

He told of his reason for venturing back from that fastness, into which he had first been carried lashed to a llama, beside a vast bale of gear, when he was a child. The valley, he said, had in it all that the heart of man could desire – sweet water, pasture, and even climate, slopes of rich brown soil with tangles of a shrub that bore an excellent fruit, and on one side great hanging forests of pine that held the avalanches high. Far overhead, on three sides, vast cliffs of grey-green rock were capped by cliffs of ice; but the glacier stream came not to them but flowed away by the farther slopes, and only now and then huge ice masses fell on the valley side. In this valley it neither rained nor snowed, but the abundant springs gave a rich green pasture, that irrigation would spread over all the valley space. The settlers did well indeed there. Their beasts did well and multiplied, and but one thing marred their happiness. Yet it was enough to mar it greatly. A strange disease had come upon them, and had made all the children born to them there – and, indeed, several older children also – blind. It was to seek some charm or antidote against this plague of blindness that he had with fatigue and danger and difficulty returned down the gorge. In those days, in such cases, men did not think of germs and infections but of sins; and it seemed to him that the reason of this affliction must lie in the negligence of these priestless immigrants to set up a shrine so soon as they entered the valley. He wanted a shrine – a handsome, cheap effectual shrine – to be erected in the valley; he wanted relics and such-like potent things of faith, blessed objects and mysterious medals and prayers. In his wallet he had a bar of native silver for which he would not account; he insisted there was none in the valley with something of the insistence of an inexpert liar. They had all clubbed their money and ornaments together, having little need for such treasure up there, he said, to buy them holy help against their ill. I figure this dim-eyed young mountaineer, sunburnt, gaunt, and anxious, hat-brim clutched feverishly, a man all unused to the ways of the lower world, telling this story to some keen-eyed, attentive priest before the great convulsion; I can picture him presently seeking to return with pious and infallible remedies against that trouble, and the infinite dismay with which he must have faced the tumbled vastness where the gorge had once come out. But the rest of his story of mischances is lost to me, save that I know of his evil death after several years. Poor stray from that remoteness! The stream that had once made the gorge now burst from the mouth of a rocky cave, and the legend his poor, ill-told story set going developed into the legend of a race of blind men somewhere 'over there' one may still hear today.

And amidst the little population of that now isolated and forgotten valley the disease ran its course. The old became groping and purblind, the young saw but dimly, and the children that were born to them saw never at all. But life was very easy in that snow-rimmed basin, lost to all the world, with neither thorns nor briars, with no evil insects nor any beasts save the gentle breed of llamas they had lugged and thrust and followed up the beds of the shrunken rivers in the gorges up which they had come. The seeing had become purblind so gradually that they scarcely noted their loss. They guided the sightless youngsters hither and thither until they knew the whole valley marvellously, and when at last sight died out among them the race lived on. They had even time to adapt themselves to the blind control of fire, which they made carefully in stoves of stone. They were a simple strain of people at the first, unlettered, only slightly touched with the Spanish civilization, but with something of a tradition of the arts of old Peru and of its lost philosophy. Generation followed generation. They forgot many things; they devised many things. Their tradition of the greater world they came from became mythical in colour and uncertain. In all things save sight they were strong and able; and presently the chance of birth and heredity sent one who had an original mind and who could talk and persuade among them, and then afterwards another. These two passed, leaving their effects, and the little community grew in numbers and in understanding, and met and settled social and economic problems that arose. Generation followed generation. Generation followed generation. There came a time when a child was born who was fifteen generations from that ancestor who went out of the valley with a bar of silver to seek God's aid, and who never returned. Thereabouts it chanced that a man came into this community from the outer world. And this is the story of that man.

He was a mountaineer from the country near Quito, a man who had been down to the sea and had seen the world, a reader of books in an original way, an acute and enterprising man, and he was taken on by a party of Englishmen who had come out to Ecuador to climb mountains, to replace one of their three Swiss guides who had fallen ill. He climbed here and he climbed there, and then came the attempt on Parascotopetl, the Matterhorn of the Andes, in which he was lost to the outer world. The story of the accident has been written a dozen times. Pointer's narrative is the best. He tells how the party worked their difficult and almost vertical way up to the very foot of the last and greatest precipice, and how they built a night shelter amidst the snow upon a little shelf of rock, and, with a touch of real dramatic power, how presently they found Nunez had gone from them. They shouted, and there was no reply; shouted and whistled, and for the rest of that night they slept no more.

As the morning broke they saw the traces of his fall. It seems impossible he could have uttered a sound. He had slipped eastward towards the unknown side of the mountain; far below he had struck a steep slope of snow, and ploughed his way down it in the midst of a snow avalanche. His track went straight to the edge of a frightful precipice, and beyond that everything was hidden. Far, far below, and hazy with distance, they could see trees rising out of a narrow, shut-in valley – the lost Country of the Blind. But they did not know it was the lost Country of the Blind, nor distinguish it in any way from any other narrow streak of upland valley. Unnerved by the disaster, they abandoned their attempt in the afternoon, and Pointer was called away to the war before he could make another attack. To this day Parascotopetl lifts an unconquered crest, and Pointer's shelter crumbles unvisited amidst the snows.

And the man who fell survived.

At the end of the slope he fell a thousand feet, and came down in the midst of a cloud of snow upon a snow slope even steeper than the one above. Down this he was whirled, stunned and insensible, but without a bone broken in his body; and then at last came to gentler slopes, and at last rolled out and lay still, buried amidst a softening heap of the white masses that had accompanied and saved him. He came to himself with a dim fancy that he was ill in bed; then realized his position with a mountaineer's intelligence, and worked himself loose and, after a rest or so, out until he saw the stars. He rested flat upon his chest for a space, wondering where he was and what had happened to him. He explored his limbs, and discovered that several of his buttons were gone and his coat turned over his head. His knife had gone from his pocket, and his hat was lost, though he had tied it under his chin. He recalled that he had been looking for loose stones to raise his piece of the shelter wall. His ice-axe had disappeared.

He decided he must have fallen, and looked up to see, exaggerated by the ghastly light of the rising moon, the tremendous flight he had taken. For a while he lay, gazing blankly at that vast pale cliff towering above, rising moment by moment out of a subsiding tide of darkness. Its phantasmal, mysterious beauty held him for a space, and then he was seized with a paroxysm of sobbing laughter. . . .

After a great interval of time he became aware that he was near the lower edge of the snow. Below, down what was now a moonlit and practicable slope, he saw the dark and broken appearance of rock-strewn turf. He struggled to his feet, aching in every joint and limb, got down painfully from the heaped loose snow about him, went downward until he was on the turf, and there dropped rather than lay beside a boulder, drank deep from the flask in his inner pocket, and instantly fell asleep. . . .

He was awakened by the singing of birds in the trees far below.

He sat up and perceived he was on a little alp at the foot of a vast precipice, that was grooved by the gully down which he and his snow had come. Over against him another wall of rock reared itself against the sky. The gorge between these precipices ran east and west and was full of the morning sunlight, which lit to the westward the mass of fallen mountain that closed the descending gorge. Below him it seemed there was a precipice equally steep, but behind the snow in the gully he found a sort of chimney-cleft dripping with snow-water down which a desperate man might venture. He found it easier than it seemed, and came at last to another desolate alp, and then after a rock climb of no particular difficulty to a steep slope of trees. He took his bearings and turned his face up the gorge, for he saw it opened out above upon green meadows, among which he now glimpsed quite distinctly a cluster of stone huts of unfamiliar fashion. At times his progress was like clambering along the face of a wall, and after a time the rising sun ceased to strike along the gorge, the voices of the singing birds died away, and the air grew cold and dark about him. But the distant valley with its houses was all the brighter for that. He came presently to a talus, and among the rocks he noted – for he was an observant man – an unfamiliar fern that seemed to clutch out of the crevices with intense green hands. He picked a frond or so and gnawed its stalk and found it helpful.

About midday he came at last out of the throat of the gorge into the plain and the sunlight. He was stiff and weary; he sat down in the shadow of a rock, filled up his flask with water from a spring and drank it down, and remained for a time resting before he went on to the houses.

They were very strange to his eyes, and indeed the whole aspect of that valley became, as he regarded it, queerer and more unfamiliar. The greater part of its surface was lush green meadow, starred with many beautiful flowers, irrigated with extraordinary care, and bearing evidence of systematic cropping piece by piece. High up and ringing the valley about was a wall, and what appeared to be a circumferential water-channel, from which the little trickles of water that fed the meadow plants came, and on the higher slopes above this flocks of llamas cropped the scanty herbage. Sheds, apparently shelters or feeding-places for the llamas, stood against the boundary wall here and there. The irrigation streams ran together into a main channel down the centre of the valley, and this was enclosed on either side by a wall breast high. This gave a singularly urban quality to this secluded place, a quality that was greatly enhanced by the fact that a number of paths paved with black and white stones, and each with a curious little kerb at the side, ran hither and thither in an orderly manner. The houses of the central village were quite unlike the casual and higgledy-piggledy agglomeration of the mountain villages he knew; they stood in a continuous row on either side of a central street of astonishing cleanness; here and there their parti-coloured façade was pierced by a door, and not a solitary window broke their even frontage. They were parti-coloured with extraordinary irregularity; smeared with a sort of plaster that was sometimes grey, sometimes drab, sometimes slate-coloured or dark brown; and it was the sight of this wild plastering that first brought the word 'blind' into the thoughts of the explorer. 'The good man who did that', he thought, 'must have been as blind as a bat.'

He descended a steep place, and so came to the wall and channel that ran about the valley, near where the latter spouted out its surplus contents into the deeps of the gorge in a thin and wavering thread of cascade. He could now see a number of men and women resting on piled heaps of grass, as if taking a siesta, in the remoter part of the meadow, and nearer the village a number of recumbent children, and then nearer at hand three men carrying pails on yokes along a little path that ran from the encircling wall towards the houses. These latter were clad in garments of llama cloth and boots and belts of leather, and they wore caps of cloth with back and ear flaps. They followed one another in single file, walking slowly and yawning as they walked, like men who have been up all night. There was some-thing so reassuringly prosperous and respectable in their bear-ing that after a moment's hesitation Nunez stood forward as conspicuously as possible upon his rock, and gave vent to a mighty shout that echoed round the valley.

The three men stopped, and moved their heads as though they were looking about them. They turned their faces this way and that, and Nunez gesticulated with freedom. But they did not appear to see him for all his gestures, and after a time, directing themselves towards the mountains far away to the right, they shouted as if in answer. Nunez bawled again, and then once more, and as he gestured ineffectually the word 'blind' came up to the top of his thoughts. 'The fools must be blind,' he said.

When at last, after much shouting and wrath, Nunez crossed the stream by a little bridge, came through a gate in the wall, and approached them, he was sure that they were blind. He was sure that this was the Country of the Blind of which the legends told. Conviction had sprung upon him, and a sense of great and rather enviable adventure. The three stood side by side, not looking at him, but with their ears directed towards him, judging him by his unfamiliar steps. They stood close together like men a little afraid, and he could see their eyelids closed and sunken, as though the very balls beneath had shrunk away. There was an expression near awe on their faces.

'A man,' one said, in hardly recognizable Spanish – 'a man it is – a man or a spirit – coming down from the rocks.'

But Nunez advanced with the confident steps of a youth who enters upon life. All the old stories of the lost valley and the Country of the Blind had come back to his mind, and through his thoughts ran this old proverb, as if it were a refrain –

'In the Country of the Blind the One-eyed Man is King.'

'In the Country of the Blind the One-eyed Man is King.'

And very civilly he gave them greeting. He talked to them and used his eyes.

'Where does he come from, brother Pedro?' asked one.

'Down out of the rocks.'

'Over the mountains I come,' said Nunez, 'out of the country beyond there – where men can see. From near Bogotá, where there are a hundred thousands of people, and where the city passes out of sight.'

'Sight?' muttered Pedro. 'Sight?'

'He comes,' said the second blind man, 'out of the rocks.'

The cloth of their coats Nunez saw was curiously fashioned, each with a different sort of stitching.

They startled him by a simultaneous movement towards him, each with a hand outstretched. He stepped back from the advance of these spread fingers.

'Come hither,' said the blind man, following his motion and clutching him neatly.

And they held Nunez and felt him over, saying no word further until they had done so.

'Carefully,' he cried, with a finger in his eye, and found they thought that organ, with its fluttering lids, a queer thing in him. They went over it again.

'A strange creature, Correa,' said the one called Pedro. 'Feel the coarseness of his hair. Like a llama's hair.'

'Rough he is as the rocks that begot him,' said Correa, investigating Nunez's unshaven chin with a soft and slightly moist hand. 'Perhaps he will grow finer.' Nunez struggled a little under their examination, but they gripped him firmly.

'Carefully,' he said again.

'He speaks,' said the third man. 'Certainly he is a man.'

'Ugh!' said Pedro, at the roughness of his coat.

'And you have come into the world?' asked Pedro.

'*Out* of the world. Over mountains and glaciers; right over above there, half-way to the sun. Out of the great big world that goes down, twelve days' journey to the sea.'

They scarcely seemed to heed him. 'Our fathers have told us men may be made by the forces of Nature,' said Correa. 'It is the warmth of things and moisture, and rottenness – rottenness.'

'Let us lead him to the elders,' said Pedro.

'Shout first,' said Correa, 'lest the children be afraid. This is a marvellous occasion.'

So they shouted, and Pedro went first and took Nunez by the hand to lead him to the houses.

He drew his hand away. 'I can see,' he said.

'See?' said Correa.

'Yes, see,' said Nunez, turning towards him, and stumbling against Pedro's pail.

'His senses are still imperfect,' said the third blind man. 'He stumbles, and talks unmeaning words. Lead him by the hand.'

'As you will,' said Nunez, and was led along, laughing.

It seemed they knew nothing of sight.

Well, all in good time he would teach them.

He heard people shouting, and saw a number of figures gathering together in the middle roadway of the village.

He found it taxed his nerve and patience more than he had anticipated, that first encounter with the population of the

Country of the Blind. The place seemed larger as he drew near to it, and the smeared plasterings queerer, and a crowd of children and men and women (the women and girls, he was pleased to note, had some of them quite sweet faces, for all that their eyes were shut and sunken) came about him, holding on to him, touching him with soft sensitive hands, smelling at him, and listening at every word he spoke. Some of the maidens and children, however, kept aloof as if afraid, and indeed his voice seemed coarse and rude beside their softer notes. They mobbed him. His three guides kept close to him with an effort of proprietorship, and said again and again, 'A wild man out of the rocks.'

'Bogotá,' he said. 'Bogotá. Over the mountain crests.'

'A wild man – using wild words,' said Pedro. 'Did you hear that – *Bogotá*? His mind is hardly formed yet. He has only the beginnings of speech.'

A little boy nipped his hand. 'Bogotá!' he said mockingly.

'Ay! A city to your village. I come from the great world – where men have eyes and see.'

'His name's Bogotá,' they said.

'He stumbled,' said Correa; 'stumbled twice as we came hither.'

'Bring him to the elders.'

And they thrust him suddenly through a doorway into a room as black as pitch, save at the end there faintly glowed a fire. The crowd closed in behind him and shut out all but the faintest glimmer of day, and before he could arrest himself he had fallen headlong over the feet of a seated man. His arm, out-flung, struck the face of someone else as he went down; he felt the soft impact of features and heard a cry of anger, and for a moment he struggled against a number of hands that clutched him. It was a one-sided fight. An inkling of the situation came to him, and he lay quiet.

'I fell down,' he said; 'I couldn't see in this pitchy darkness.'

There was a pause as if the unseen persons about him tried to understand his words. Then the voice of Correa said: 'He is but newly formed. He stumbles as he walks and mingles words that mean nothing with his speech.'

Others also said things about him that he heard or understood imperfectly.

'May I sit up,' he asked, in a pause. 'I will not struggle against you again.'

They consulted, and let him rise.

The voice of an older man began to question him, and Nunez found himself trying to explain the great world out of which he had fallen, and the sky and mountains and sight and such-like marvels, to these elders who sat in darkness in the Country of the Blind. And they would believe and understand nothing whatever he told them, a thing quite outside his expectation. They would not even understand many of his words. For fourteen generations these people had been blind and cut off from all the seeing world; the names for all the things of sight had faded and changed; the story of the outer world was faded and changed to a child's story; and they had ceased to concern themselves with anything beyond the rocky slopes above their encircling wall. Blind men of genius had arisen among them and questioned the shreds of belief and tradition they had brought with them from their seeing days, and had dismissed all these things as idle fancies and replaced them with new and saner explanations. Much of their imagination had shrivelled with their eyes, and they had made for themselves new imaginations with their ever more sensitive ears and finger-tips. Slowly Nunez realized this; that his expectation of wonder and reverence at his origin and his gifts was not to be borne out; and after his poor attempt to explain sight to them had been set aside as the confused version of a new-made being describing the marvels of his incoherent sensations, he subsided, a little dashed, into listening to their instruction. And the eldest of the blind men explained to him life and philosophy and religion, how that the world (meaning their valley) had been first an empty hollow in the rocks, and then had come, first, inanimate things without the gift of touch, and llamas and a few other creatures that had little sense, and then men, and at last angels, whom one could hear singing and making fluttering sounds, but whom no one could touch at all, which puzzled Nunez greatly until he thought of the birds.

He went on to tell Nunez how this time had been divided into the warm and the cold, which are the blind equivalents of day and night, and how it was good to sleep in the warm and work during the cold, so that now, but for his advent, the whole town of the blind would have been asleep. He said Nunez must have been specially created to learn and serve the wisdom they had acquired, and that for all his mental incoherency and stumbling behaviour he must have courage, and do his best to learn, and at that all the people in the doorway murmured encouragingly. He said the night – for the blind call their day night – was now far gone, and it behoved every one to go back to sleep. He asked Nunez if he knew how to sleep, and Nunez said he did, but that before sleep he wanted food.

They brought him food – llama's milk in a bowl, and rough salted bread – and led him into a lonely place to eat out of their hearing, and afterwards to slumber until the chill of the mountain evening roused them to begin their day again. But Nunez slumbered not at all.

Instead, he sat up in the place where they had left him, resting his limbs and turning the unanticipated circumstances of his arrival over and over in his mind.

Every now and then he laughed, sometimes with amusement, and sometimes with indignation.

'Unformed mind!' he said. 'Got no senses yet! They little know they've been insulting their heaven-sent king and master. I see I must bring them to reason. Let me think – let me think.'

He was still thinking when the sun set.

Nunez had an eye for all beautiful things, and it seemed to him that the glow upon the snowfields and glaciers that rose about the valley on every side was the most beautiful thing he had ever seen. His eyes went from that inaccessible glory to the village and irrigated fields, fast sinking into the twilight, and suddenly a wave of emotion took him, and he thanked God from the bottom of his heart that the power of sight had been given him.

He heard a voice calling to him from out of the village.

'Ya ho there, Bogotá! Come hither!'

At that he stood up smiling. He would show these people once and for all what sight would do for a man. They would seek him, but not find him.

'You move not, Bogotá,' said the voice.

He laughed noiselessly, and made two stealthy steps aside from the path.

'Trample not on the grass, Bogotá; that is not allowed.'

Nunez had scarcely heard the sound he made himself. He stopped amazed.

The owner of the voice came running up the piebald path towards him.

He stepped back into the pathway. 'Here I am,' he said.

'Why did you not come when I called you?' said the blind man. 'Must you be led like a child? Cannot you hear the path, as you walk?'

Nunez laughed. 'I can see it,' he said.

'There is no such word as *see*,' said the blind man, after a pause. 'Cease this folly, and follow the sound of my feet.'

Nunez followed, a little annoyed.

'My time will come,' he said.

'You'll learn,' the blind man answered. 'There is much to learn in the world.'

'Has no one told you, "In the Country of the Blind the One-eyed Man is King"?'

'What is blind?' asked the blind man carelessly over his shoulder.

Four days passed, and the fifth found the King of the Blind still incognito, as a clumsy and useless stranger among his subjects.

It was, he found, much more difficult to proclaim himself than he had supposed, and in the meantime, while he meditated his *coup d'état*, he did what he was told and learned the manners and customs of the Country of the Blind. He found working and going about at night a particularly irksome thing, and he decided that that should be the first thing he would change.

They led a simple, laborious life, these people, with all the elements of virtue and happiness, as these things can be understood by men. They toiled, but not oppressively; they had food and clothing sufficient for their needs; they had days and seasons of rest; they made much of music and singing; and there was love among them, and little children.

It was marvellous with what confidence and precision they went about their ordered world. Everything, you see, had been made to fit their needs; each of the radiating paths of the valley area had a constant angle to the others, and was distinguished by a special notch upon its kerbing; all obstacles and irregularities of path or meadow had long since been cleared away; all their methods and procedure arose naturally from their special needs. Their senses had become marvellously acute; they could hear and judge the slightest gesture of a man a dozen paces away – could hear the very beating of his heart. Intonation had long replaced expression with them, and touches gesture, and their work with hoe and spade and fork was as free and confident as garden work can be. Their sense of smell was extraordinarily fine; they could distinguish individual differences as readily as a dog can, and they went about the tending of the llamas, who lived among the rocks above and came to the wall for food and shelter, with ease and confidence. It was only when at last Nunez sought to assert himself that he found how easy and confident their movements could be.

He rebelled only after he had tried persuasion.

He tried at first on several occasions to tell them of sight. 'Look you here, you people,' he said. 'There are things you do not understand in me.'

Once or twice one or two of them attended to him; they sat with faces downcast and ears turned intelligently towards him, and he did his best to tell them what it was to see. Among his hearers was a girl, with eyelids less red and sunken than the others, so that one could almost fancy she was hiding eyes, whom especially he hoped to persuade. He spoke of the beauties of sight, of watching the mountains, of the sky and the sunrise, and they heard him with amused incredulity that presently became condemnatory. They told him there were indeed no mountains at all, but that the end of the rocks where the llamas grazed was indeed the end of the world; thence sprang a cavernous roof of the universe, from which the dew and the avalanches fell; and when he maintained stoutly the world had neither end nor roof such as they supposed, they said his thoughts were wicked. So far as he could describe sky and clouds and stars to them it seemed to them a hideous void, a terrible blankness in the place of the smooth roof to things in which they believed – it was an article of faith with them that the cavern roof was exquisitely smooth to the touch. He saw that in some manner he shocked them, and gave up that aspect of the matter altogether, and tried to show them the practical value of sight. One morning he saw Pedro in the path called Seventeen and coming towards the central houses, but still too far off for hearing or scent, and he told them as much. 'In a little while,' he prophesied, 'Pedro will be here.' An old man remarked that Pedro had no business on path Seventeen, and then, as if in confirmation, that individual as he drew near turned and went transversely into path Ten, and so back with nimble paces towards the outer wall. They mocked Nunez when Pedro did not arrive, and afterwards, when he asked Pedro questions to clear his character, Pedro denied and out-faced him, and was afterwards hostile to him.

Then he induced them to let him go a long way up the sloping meadows towards the wall with one complacent individual, and to him he promised to describe all that happened among the houses. He noted certain goings and comings, but the things that really seemed to signify to these people happened inside of or behind the windowless houses – the only things they took note of to test him by – and of these he could see or tell nothing; and it was after the failure of this attempt, and the ridicule they could not repress, that he resorted to force. He thought of seizing a spade and suddenly smiting one or two of them to earth, and so in fair combat showing the advantage of eyes. He went so far with that resolution as to seize his spade, and then he discovered a new thing about himself, and that was that it was impossible for him to hit a blind man in cold blood.

He hesitated, and found them all aware that he had snatched up the spade. They stood alert, with their heads on one side, and bent ears towards him for what he would do next.

'Put that spade down,' said one, and he felt a sort of helpless horror. He came near obedience.

Then he thrust one backwards against a house wall, and fled past him and out of the village.

He went athwart one of their meadows, leaving a track of trampled grass behind his feet, and presently sat down by the side of one of their ways. He felt something of the buoyancy that comes to all men in the beginning of a fight, but more perplexity. He began to realize that you cannot even fight happily with creatures who stand upon a different mental basis to yourself. Far away he saw a number of men carrying spades and sticks come out of the street of houses, and advance in a spreading line along the several paths towards him. They advanced slowly, speaking frequently to one another, and ever and again the whole cordon would halt and sniff the air and listen.

The first time they did this Nunez laughed. But afterwards he did not laugh.

One struck his trail in the meadow grass, and came stooping and feeling his way along it.

For five minutes he watched the slow execution of the cordon, and then his vague disposition to do something forthwith became frantic. He stood up, went a pace or so towards the circumferential wall, turned, and went back a little way. There they all stood in a crescent, still and listening.

He also stood still, gripping his spade very tightly in both hands. Should he charge them?

The pulse in his ears ran into the rhythm of 'In the Country of the Blind the One-eyed Man is King!'

Should he charge them?

He looked back at the high and unclimbable wall behind – unclimbable because of its smooth plastering, but withal pierced with many little doors, and at the approaching line of seekers. Behind these, others were now coming out of the street of houses.

Should he charge them?

'Bogotá!' called one. 'Bogotá! Where are you?'

He gripped his spade still tighter, and advanced down the

meadows towards the place of habitations and directly he moved they converged upon him. 'I'll kill them if they touch me,' he swore, 'by Heaven, I will. I'll hit.' He called aloud, 'Look here, I'm going to do what I like in this valley. Do you hear? I'm going to do what I like and go where I like!'

They were moving in upon him quickly, groping, yet moving rapidly. It was like playing blind man's buff, with everyone blindfolded except one. 'Get hold of him!' cried one. He found himself in the arc of a loose curve of pursuers. He felt suddenly he must be active and resolute.

'You don't understand,' he cried in a voice that was meant to be great and resolute, and which broke. 'You are blind, and I can see. Leave me alone!'

'Bogotá! Put down that spade, and come off the grass!'

The last order, grotesque in its urban familiarity, produced a gust of anger.

'I'll hurt you,' he said, sobbing with emotion. 'By Heaven, I'll hurt you. Leave me alone!'

He began to run, not knowing clearly where to run. He ran from the nearest blind man, because it was a horror to hit him. He stopped, and then made a dash to escape from their closing ranks. He made for where a gap was wide, and the men on either side, with quick perception of the approach of his paces, rushed in on one another. He sprang forward, and then saw he must be caught, and *swish*! the spade had struck. He felt the soft thud of hand and arm, and the man was down with a yell of pain, and he was through.

Through! And then he was close to the street of houses again, and blind men, whirling spades and stakes, were running with a sort of reasoned swiftness hither and thither.

He heard steps behind him just in time, and found a tall man rushing forward and swiping at the sound of him. He lost his nerve, hurled his spade a yard wide at his antagonist, and whirled about and fled, fairly yelling as he dodged another.

He was panic-stricken. He ran furiously to and fro, dodging when there was no need to dodge, and in his anxiety to see on every side of him at once, stumbling. For a moment, he was down and they heard his fall. Far away in the circumferential wall a little doorway looked like heaven, and he set off in a wild rush for it. He did not even look round at his pursuers until it was gained, and he had stumbled across the bridge, clambered a little way among the rocks to the surprise and dismay of a young llama, who went leaping out of sight, and lay down sobbing for breath.

And so his *coup d'état* came to an end.

He stayed outside the wall of the Valley of the Blind for two nights and days without food or shelter, and meditated upon the unexpected. During these meditations he repeated very frequently and always with a profounder note of derision the exploded proverb: 'In the Country of the Blind the One-eyed Man is King.' He thought chiefly of ways of fighting and conquering these people, and it grew clear that for him no practicable way was possible. He had no weapon, and now it would be hard to get one.

The canker of civilization had got to him even in Bogotá, and he could not find it in himself to go down and assassinate a blind man. Of course, if he did that, he might then dictate terms on the threat of assassinating them all. But – sooner or later he must sleep! . . .

He tried also to find food among the pine trees, to be comfortable under pine boughs while the frost fell at night, and – with less confidence – to catch a llama by artifice in order to try to kill it – perhaps by hammering it with a stone – and so finally, perhaps, to eat some of it. But the llamas had a doubt of him and regarded him with distrustful brown eyes, and spat when he drew near. Fear came on him the second day and fits of shivering. Finally he crawled down to the wall of the Country of the Blind and tried to make terms. He crawled along by the stream, shouting, until two blind men came out of the gate and talked to him.

'I was mad,' he said. 'But I was only newly made.'

They said that was better.

He told them he was wiser now, and repented of all he had done.

Then he wept without intention, for he was very weak and ill now, and they took that as a favourable sign.

They asked him if he still thought he could 'see'.

'No,' he said. 'That was folly. The word means nothing – less than nothing!'

They asked him what was overhead.

'About ten times ten the height of a man there is a roof above the world – of rock – and very, very smooth. . . .' He burst again into hysterical tears. 'Before you ask me any more, give me some food or I shall die.'

He expected dire punishments, but these blind people were capable of toleration. They regarded his rebellion as but one more proof of his general idiocy and inferiority; and after they had whipped him they appointed him to do the simplest and heaviest work they had for anyone to do, and he, seeing no other way of living, did submissively what he was told.

He was ill for some days, and they nursed him kindly. That refined his submission. But they insisted on his lying in the dark, and that was a great misery. And blind philosophers came and talked to him of the wicked levity of his mind, and reproved him so impressively for his doubts about the lid of rock that covered their cosmic casserole that he almost doubted whether indeed he was not the victim of hallucination in not seeing it overhead.

So Nunez became a citizen of the Country of the Blind, and these people ceased to be a generalized people and became individuals and familiar to him, while the world beyond the mountains became more and more remote and unreal. There was Yacob, his master, a kindly man when not annoyed; there was Pedro, Yacob's nephew; and there was Medina-saroté, who was the youngest daughter of Yacob. She was little esteemed in the world of the blind, because she had a clear-cut face, and lacked that satisfying, glossy smoothness that is the blind man's ideal of feminine beauty; but Nunez thought her beautiful at first, and presently the most beautiful thing in the whole creation. Her closed eyelids were not sunken and red after the common way of the valley, but lay as though they might open again at any moment; and she had long eyelashes, which were considered a grave disfigurement. And her voice was strong, and did not satisfy the acute hearing of the valley swains. So that she had no lover.

There came a time when Nunez thought that, could he win her, he would be resigned to live in the valley for all the rest of his days.

He watched for her; he sought opportunities of doing her little services, and presently he found that she observed him. Once at a rest-day gathering they sat side by side in the dim starlight, and the music was sweet. His hand came upon hers and he dared to clasp it. Then very tenderly she returned his pressure. And one day, as they were at their meal in the darkness, he felt her hand very softly seeking him, and as it chanced the fire leaped then and he saw the tenderness of her face.

He sought to speak to her.

He went to her one day when she was sitting in the summer moonlight spinning. The light made her a thing of silver and mystery. He sat down at her feet and told her he loved her, and told her how beautiful she seemed to him. He had a lover's voice, he spoke with a tender reverence that came near to awe, and she had never before been touched by adoration. She made him no definite answer, but it was clear his words pleased her.

After that he talked to her whenever he could take an opportunity. The valley became the world for him, and the world beyond the mountains where men lived in sunlight seemed no more than a fairy tale he would some day pour into her ears. Very tentatively and timidly he spoke to her of sight.

Sight seemed to her the most poetical of fancies, and she listened to his description of the stars and the mountains and her own sweet white-lit beauty as though it was a guilty indulgence. She did not believe, she could only half understand, but she was mysteriously delighted, and it seemed to him that she completely understood.

His love lost its awe and took courage. Presently he was for demanding her of Yacob and the elders in marriage, but she became fearful and delayed. And it was one of her elder sisters who first told Yacob that Medina-saroté and Nunez were in love.

There was from the first very great opposition to the marriage of Nunez and Medina-saroté; not so much because they valued her as because they held him as a being apart, an idiot, incompetent thing below the permissible level of a man. Her sisters opposed it bitterly as bringing discredit on them all; and old Yacob, though he had formed a sort of liking for his clumsy, obedient serf, shook his head and said the thing could not be. The young men were all angry at the idea of corrupting the race, and one went so far as to revile and strike Nunez. He struck back. Then for the first time he found the advantage in seeing, even by twilight, and after that fight was over no one was disposed to raise a hand against him. But they still found his marriage impossible.

Old Yacob had a tenderness for his last little daughter, and was grieved to have her weep upon his shoulder.

'You see, my dear, he's an idiot. He has delusions; he can't do anything right.'

'I know,' wept Medina-saroté. 'But he's better than he was. He's getting better. And he's strong, dear father, and kind – stronger and kinder than any other man in the world. And he loves me – and, Father, I love him.'

Old Yacob was greatly distressed to find her inconsolable, and, besides – what made it more distressing – he liked Nunez for many things. So he went and sat in the windowless council-chamber with the other elders and watched the trend of the talk, and said, at the proper time, 'He's better than he was. Very likely, some day, we shall find him as sane as ourselves.'

Then afterwards one of the elders, who thought deeply, had an idea. He was the great doctor among these people, their medicine-man, and he had a very philosophical and inventive mind, and the idea of curing Nunez of his peculiarities appealed to him. One day when Yacob was present he returned to the topic of Nunez.

'I have examined Bogotá,' he said, 'and the case is clearer to me. I think very probably he might be cured.'

'That is what I have always hoped,' said old Yacob.

'His brain is affected,' said the blind doctor.

The elders murmured assent.

'Now, *what* affects it?'

'Ah!' said old Yacob.

'*This*,' said the doctor, answering his own question. 'Those queer things that are called the eyes, and which exist to make an agreeable soft depression in the face, are diseased, in the case of Bogotá, in such a way as to affect his brain. They are greatly distended, he has eyelashes, and his eyelids move, and consequently his brain is in a state of constant irritation and destruction.'

'Yes?' said old Yacob. 'Yes?'

'And I think I may say with reasonable certainty that, in order to cure him completely, all that we need do is a simple and easy surgical operation – namely, to remove these irritant bodies.'

'And then he will be sane?'

'Then he will be perfectly sane, and a quite admirable citizen.'

'Thank heaven for science!' said old Yacob, and went forth at once to tell Nunez of his happy hopes.

But Nunez's manner of receiving the good news struck him as being cold and disappointing.

'One might think,' he said, 'from the tone you take, that you do not care for my daughter.'

It was Medina-saroté who persuaded Nunez to face the blind surgeons.

'*You* do not want me', he said, 'to lose my gift of sight?'

She shook her head.

'My world is sight.'

Her head drooped lower.

'There are the beautiful things, the beautiful little things – the flowers, the lichens among the rocks, the lightness and softness of a piece of fur, the far sky with its drifting down of clouds, the sunsets and the stars. And there is *you*. For you alone it is good to have sight, to see your sweet, serene face, your kindly lips, your dear, beautiful hands folded together. . . . It is these eyes of mine you won, these eyes that hold me to you, that these idiots seek. Instead, I must touch you, hear you, and never see you again. I must come under that roof of rock and stone and darkness, that horrible roof under which your imagination stoops. . . . No; you would not have me do that?'

A disagreeable doubt had arisen in him. He stopped, and left the thing a question.

'I wish,' she said, 'sometimes – ' She paused.

'Yes?' said he, a little apprehensively.

'I wish sometimes – you would not talk like that.'

'Like what?'

'I know it's pretty – it's your imagination. I love it, but *now* – '

He felt cold. '*Now?*' he said faintly.

She sat quite still.

'You mean – you think – I should be better, better perhaps – '

He was realizing things very swiftly. He felt anger, indeed, anger at the dull course of fate, but also sympathy for her lack of understanding – a sympathy near akin to pity.

'*Dear*,' he said, and he could see by her whiteness how intensely her spirit pressed against the things she could not say. He put his arms about her, he kissed her ear, and they sat for a time in silence.

'If I were to consent to this?' he said at last, in a voice that was very gentle.

She flung her arms about him, weeping wildly. 'Oh, if you would,' she sobbed, 'if only you would!'

For a week before the operation that was to raise him from his servitude and inferiority to the level of a blind citizen, Nunez knew nothing of sleep, and all through the warm sunlit hours, while the others slumbered happily, he sat brooding or wandered aimlessly, trying to bring his mind to bear on his dilemma. He had given his answer, he had given his consent, and still he was not sure. And at last work-time was over, the sun rose in splendour over the golden crests, and his last day of vision began for him. He had a few minutes with Medina-saroté before she went apart to sleep.

'Tomorrow,' he said, 'I shall see no more.'

'Dear heart!' she answered, and pressed his hand with all her strength.

'They will hurt you but little,' she said; 'and you are going through this pain – you are going through it, dear lover, for *me*. . . . Dear, if a woman's heart and life can do it, I will repay you. My dearest one, my dearest with the tender voice, I will repay.'

He was drenched in pity for himself and her.

He held her in his arms, and pressed his lips to hers, and looked on her sweet face for the last time. 'Good-bye!' he whispered at that dear sight, 'good-bye!'

And then in silence he turned away from her.

She could hear his slow retreating footsteps, and something in the rhythm of them threw her into a passion of weeping.

He had fully meant to go to a lonely place where the meadows were beautiful with white narcissus, and there remain until the hour of his sacrifice should come, but as he went he lifted up his eyes and saw the morning, the morning like an angel in golden armour, marching down the steeps. . . .

It seemed to him that before this splendour he, and this blind world in the valley, and his love, after all, were no more than a pit of sin.

He did not turn aside as he had meant to do, but went on, and passed through the wall of the circumference and out upon the rocks, and his eyes were always upon the sunlit ice and snow.

He saw their infinite beauty, and his imagination soared over them to the things beyond he was now to resign for ever.

He thought of that great free world he was parted from, the world that was his own, and he had a vision of those further slopes, distance beyond distance, with Bogotá, a place of multitudinous stirring beauty, a glory by day, a luminous mystery by night, a place of palaces and fountains and statues and white houses, lying beautifully in the middle distance. He thought how for a day or so one might come down through passes, drawing ever nearer and nearer to its busy streets and ways. He thought of the river journey, day by day, from great Bogotá to the still vaster world beyond, through towns and villages, forest and desert places, the rushing river day by day, until its banks receded and the big steamers came splashing by, and one had reached the sea – the limitless sea, with its thousand islands, its thousands of islands, and its ships seen dimly far away in their incessant journeyings round and about the greater world. And there, unpent by mountains, one saw the sky – the sky, not such a disc as one saw it here; but an arch of immeasurable blue, a deep of deeps in which the circling stars were floating. . . .

His eyes scrutinized the great curtain of the mountains with a keener inquiry.

For example, if one went so, up that gully and to that chimney there, then one might come out high among those stunted pines that ran round in a sort of shelf and rose still higher and higher as it passed above the gorge. And then? That talus might be managed. Thence perhaps a climb might be found to take him up to the precipice that came below the snow; and if that chimney failed, then another farther to the east might serve his purpose better. And then? Then one would be out upon the amber-lit snow there, and half-way up to the crest of those beautiful desolations.

He glanced back at the village, then turned right round and regarded it steadfastly.

He thought of Medina-saroté, and she had become small and remote.

He turned again towards the mountain wall, down which the day had come to him.

Then very circumspectly he began to climb.

When sunset came he was no longer climbing, but he was far and high. He had been higher, but he was still very high. His clothes were torn, his limbs were blood-stained, he was bruised in many places, but he lay as if he were at his ease, and there was a smile on his face.

From where he rested the valley seemed as if it were in a pit and nearly a mile below. Already it was dim with haze and shadow, though the mountain summits around him were things of light and fire. The mountain summits around him were things of light and fire, and the little details of the rocks near at hand were drenched with subtle beauty – a vein of green mineral piercing the grey, the flash of crystal faces here and there, a minute, minutely beautiful orange lichen close beside his face. There were deep mysterious shadows in the gorge, blue deepening into purple, and purple into a luminous darkness, and overhead was the illimitable vastness of the sky. But he heeded these things no longer, but lay quite inactive there, smiling as if he were satisfied merely to have escaped from the Valley of the Blind in which he had thought to be King.

The glow of the sunset passed, and the night came, and still he lay peacefully contented under the cold stars.

W. Somerset Maugham

THE FORCE OF CIRCUMSTANCE

She was sitting on the veranda waiting for her husband to come in for luncheon. The Malay boy had drawn the blinds when the morning lost its freshness, but she had partly raised one of them so that she could look at the river. Under the breathless sun of midday it had the white pallor of death. A native was paddling along in a dug-out so small that it hardly showed above the surface of the water. The colours of the day were ashy and wan. They were but the various tones of the heat. (It was like an Eastern melody, in the minor key, which exacerbates the nerves by its ambiguous monotony; and the ear awaits impatiently a resolution, but waits in vain.) The cicadas sang their grating song with a frenzied energy; it was as continual and monotonous as the rustling of a brook over the stones; but on a sudden it was drowned by the loud singing of a bird, mellifluous and rich; and for an instant, with a catch at her heart, she thought of the English blackbird.

Then she heard her husband's step on the gravel path behind the bungalow, the path that led to the court-house in which he had been working, and she rose from her chair to greet him. He ran up the short flight of steps, for the bungalow was built on piles, and at the door the boy was waiting to take his topee. He came into the room which served them as a dining-room and parlour, and his eyes lit up with pleasure as he saw her.

'Hulloa, Doris. Hungry?'

'Ravenous.'

'It'll only take me a minute to have a bath and then I'm ready.'

'Be quick,' she smiled.

He disappeared into his dressing-room and she heard him whistling cheerily while, with the carelessness with which she was always remonstrating, he tore off his clothes and flung

129

them on the floor. He was twenty-nine, but he was still a school-boy; he would never grow up. That was why she had fallen in love with him, perhaps, for no amount of affection could persuade her that he was good-looking. He was a little round man, with a red face like the full moon, and blue eyes. He was rather pimply. She had examined him carefully and had been forced to confess to him that he had not a single feature which she could praise. She had told him often that he wasn't her type at all.

'I never said I was a beauty,' he laughed.

'I can't think what it is I see in you.'

But of course she knew perfectly well. He was a gay, jolly little man, who took nothing very solemnly, and he was constantly laughing. He made her laugh too. He found life an amusing rather than a serious business, and he had a charming smile. When she was with him she felt happy and good-tempered. And the deep affection which she saw in those merry blue eyes of his touched her. It was very satisfactory to be loved like that. Once, sitting on his knees, during their honeymoon she had taken his face in her hands and said to him:

'You're an ugly, little fat man, Guy, but you've got charm. I can't help loving you.'

A wave of emotion swept over her and her eyes filled with tears. She saw his face contorted for a moment with the extremity of his feeling and his voice was a little shaky when he answered.

'It's a terrible thing for me to have married a woman who's mentally deficient,' he said.

She chuckled. It was the characteristic answer which she would have liked him to make.

It was hard to realize that nine months ago she had never even heard of him. She had met him at a small place by the seaside where she was spending a month's holiday with her mother. Doris was a secretary to a member of parliament, Guy was home on leave. They were staying at the same hotel, and he quickly told her all about himself. He was born in Sembulu, where his father had served for thirty years under the second Sultan, and on leaving school he had entered the same service. He was devoted to the country.

'After all, England's a foreign land to me,' he told her. 'My home's Sembulu.'

And now it was her home too. He asked her to marry him at the end of the month's holiday. She had known he was going to, and had decided to refuse him. She was her widowed mother's only child and she could not go so far away from her, but when the moment came she did not quite know what happened to her, she was carried off her feet by an unexpected emotion, and she accepted him. They had been settled now for four months in the little outstation of which he was in charge. She was very happy.

She told him once that she had quite made up her mind to refuse him.

'Are you sorry you didn't?' he asked, with a merry smile in his twinkling blue eyes.

'I should have been a perfect fool if I had. What a bit of luck that fate or chance or whatever it was stepped in and took the matter entirely out of my hands!'

Now she heard Guy clatter down the steps to the bath-house. He was a noisy fellow and even with bare feet he could not be quiet. But he uttered an exclamation. He said two or three words in the local dialect and she could not understand. Then she heard someone speaking to him, not aloud, but in a sibilant whisper. Really it was too bad of people to waylay him when he was going to have his bath. He spoke again and though his voice was low she could hear that he was vexed. The other voice was raised now; it was a woman's. Doris supposed it was someone who had a complaint to make. It was like a Malay woman to come in that surreptitious way. But she was evidently getting very little from Guy, for she heard him say: Get out. That at all events she understood, and then she heard him bolt the door. There was a sound of the water he was throwing over himself (the bathing arrangements still amused her; the bath-houses were under the bedrooms, on the ground; you had a large tub of water and you sluiced yourself with a little tin pail) and in a couple of minutes he was back again in the dining-room. His hair was still wet. They sat down to luncheon.

'It's lucky I'm not a suspicious or a jealous person,' she laughed. 'I don't know that I should altogether approve of your having animated conversations with ladies while you're having your bath.'

His face, usually so cheerful, had borne a sullen look when he came in, but now it brightened.

'I wasn't exactly pleased to see her.'

'So I judged by the tone of your voice. In fact, I thought you were rather short with the young person.'

'Damned cheek, waylaying me like that!'

'What did she want?'

'Oh, I don't know. It's a woman from the kampong. She's had a row with her husband or something.'

'I wonder if it's the same one who was hanging about this morning.'

He frowned a little.

'Was there someone hanging about?'

'Yes, I went into your dressing-room to see that everything was nice and tidy, and then I went down to the bath-house. I saw someone slink out of the door as I went down the steps and when I looked out I saw a woman standing there.'

'Did you speak to her?'

'I asked her what she wanted and she said something, but I couldn't understand.'

'I'm not going to have all sorts of stray people prowling about here,' he said. 'They've got no right to come.'

He smiled, but Doris, with the quick perception of a woman in love, noticed that he smiled only with his lips, not as usual with his eyes also, and wondered what it was that troubled him.

'What have you been doing this morning?' he asked.

'Oh, nothing much. I went for a little walk.'

'Through the kampong?'

'Yes. I saw a man send a chained monkey up a tree to pick coconuts, which rather thrilled me.'

'It's rather a lark, isn't it?'

'Oh, Guy, there were two little boys watching him who were much whiter than the others. I wondered if they were half-castes. I spoke to them, but they didn't know a word of English.'

'There are two or three half-caste children in the kampong,' he answered.

'Who do they belong to?'

'Their mother is one of the village girls.'

'Who is their father?'

'Oh, my dear, that's the sort of question we think it a little dangerous to ask out here.' He paused. 'A lot of fellows have native wives, and then when they go home or marry they pension them off and send them back to their village.'

Doris was silent. The indifference with which he spoke seemed a little callous to her. There was almost a frown on her frank, open, pretty English face when she replied.

'But what about the children?'

'I have no doubt they're properly provided for. Within his means, a man generally sees that there's enough money to have them decently educated. They get jobs as clerks in a government office, you know; they're all right.'

She gave him a slightly rueful smile.

'You can't expect me to think it's a very good system.'

'You mustn't be too hard,' he smiled back.

'I'm not hard. But I'm thankful you never had a Malay wife. I should have hated it. Just think if those two little brats were yours.'

The boy changed their plates. There was never much variety in their menu. They started luncheon with river fish, dull and insipid, so that a good deal of tomato ketchup was needed to make it palatable, and then went on to some kind of stew. Guy poured Worcester Sauce over it.

'The old Sultan didn't think it was a white woman's country,' he said presently. 'He rather encouraged people to – keep house with native girls. Of course things have changed now. The country's perfectly quiet and I suppose we know better how to cope with the climate.'

'But, Guy, the eldest of those boys wasn't more than seven or eight and the other was about five.'

'It's awfully lonely on an outstation. Why, often one doesn't see another white man for six months on end. A fellow comes out here when he's only a boy.' He gave her that charming smile of his which transfigured his round, plain face. 'There are excuses, you know.'

She always found that smile irresistible. It was his best argument. Her eyes grew once more soft and tender.

'I'm sure there are.' She stretched her hand across the little table and put it on his. 'I'm very lucky to have caught you so young. Honestly, it would upset me dreadfully if I were told that you had lived like that.'

He took her hand and pressed it.

'Are you happy here, darling?'

'Desperately.'

She looked very cool and fresh in her linen frock. The heat did not distress her. She had no more than the prettiness of youth, though her brown eyes were fine; but she had a pleasing frankness of expression, and her dark, short hair was neat and glossy. She gave you the impression of a girl of spirit and you felt sure that the member of parliament for whom she worked had in her a very competent secretary.

'I loved the country at once,' she said. 'Although I'm alone so much I don't think I've ever once felt lonely.'

Of course she had read novels about the Malay Archipelago and she had formed an impression of a sombre land with great ominous rivers and a silent, impenetrable jungle. When the little coasting steamer set them down at the mouth of the river, where a large boat, manned by a dozen Dyaks, was waiting to take them to the station, her breath was taken away by the beauty, friendly rather than awe-inspiring, of the scene. It had a gaiety, like the joyful singing of birds in the trees, which she had never expected. On each bank of the river were mangroves and nipah palms, and behind them the dense green of the forest. In the distance stretched blue mountains, range upon range, as far as the eye could see. She had no sense of confinement nor of gloom, but rather of openness and wide spaces where the exultant fancy could wander with delight. The green glittered in the sunshine and the sky was blithe and cheerful. The gracious land seemed to offer her a smiling welcome.

They rowed on, hugging a bank, and high overhead flew a pair of doves. A flash of colour, like a living jewel, dashed across their path. It was a kingfisher. Two monkeys, with their dangling tails, sat side by side on a branch. On the horizon, over there on the other side of the broad and turbid river, beyond the jungle, was a row of little white clouds, the only clouds in the sky, and they looked like a row of ballet-girls, dressed in white, waiting at the back of the stage, alert and merry, for the curtain to go up. Her heart was filled with joy; and now, remembering it all, her eyes rested on her husband with a grateful, assured affection.

And what fun it had been to arrange their living-room! It was very big. On the floor, when she arrived, was torn and dirty matting; on the walls of unpainted wood hung (much too high up) photogravures of Academy pictures, Dyak shields, and parangs. The tables were covered with Dyak cloth in sombre colours, and on them stood pieces of Brunei brass-ware, much in need of cleaning, empty cigarette tins, and bits of Malay silver. There was a rough wooden shelf with cheap editions of novels and a number of old travel books in battered leather; and another shelf was crowded with empty bottles. It was a bachelor's room, untidy but stiff; and though it amused her she found it intolerably pathetic. It was a dreary, comfortless life that Guy had led there, and she threw her arms round his neck and kissed him.

'You poor darling,' she laughed.

She had deft hands and she soon made the room habitable. She arranged this and that, and what she could not do with she turned out. Her wedding-presents helped. Now the room was friendly and comfortable. In glass vases were lovely orchids and in great bowls huge masses of flowering shrubs. She felt an inordinate pride because it was her house (she had never in her life lived in anything but a poky flat) and she had made it charming for him.

'Are you pleased with me?' she asked when she had finished.

'Quite,' he smiled.

The deliberate understatement was much to her mind. How jolly it was that they should understand each other so well!

They were both of them shy of displaying emotion, and it was only at rare moments that they used with one another anything but ironic banter.

They finished luncheon and he threw himself into a long chair to have a sleep. She went towards her room. She was a little surprised that he drew her to him as she passed and, making her bend down, kissed her lips. They were not in the habit of exchanging embraces at odd hours of the day.

'A full tummy is making you sentimental, my poor lamb,' she chaffed him.

'Get out and don't let me see you again for at least two hours.'

'Don't snore.'

She left him. They had risen at dawn and in five minutes were fast asleep.

Doris was awakened by the sound of her husband's splashing in the bath-house. The walls of the bungalow were like a sounding board and not a thing that one of them did escaped the other. She felt too lazy to move, but she heard the boy bring the tea things in, so she jumped up and ran down into her own bath-house. The water, not cold but cool, was deliciously refreshing. When she came into the sitting-room Guy was taking the rackets out of the press, for they played tennis in the short cool of the evening. The night fell at six.

The tennis-court was two or three hundred yards from the bungalow and after tea, anxious not to lose time, they strolled down to it.

'Oh, look,' said Doris, 'there's that girl that I saw this morning.'

Guy turned quickly. His eyes rested for a moment on a native woman, but he did not speak.

'What a pretty sarong she's got,' said Doris. 'I wonder where it comes from.'

They passed her. She was slight and small, with the large, dark, starry eyes of her race and a mass of raven hair. She did not stir as they went by, but stared at them strangely. Doris saw then that she was not quite so young as she had at first thought. Her features were a trifle heavy and her skin was dark, but she was very pretty. She held a small child in her arms. Doris smiled a little as she saw it, but no answering smile moved the woman's lips. Her face remained impassive. She did not look at Guy, she looked only at Doris, and he walked on as though he did not see her. Doris turned to him.

'Isn't that baby a duck?'

'I didn't notice.'

She was puzzled by the look of his face. It was deathly white, and the pimples which not a little distressed her were more than commonly red.

'Did you notice her hands and feet? She might be a duchess.'

'All natives have good hands and feet,' he answered, but not jovially as was his wont; it was as though he forced himself to speak.

But Doris was intrigued.

'Who is she, d'you know?'

'She's one of the girls in the kampong.'

They had reached the court now. When Guy went up to the net to see that it was taut he looked back. The girl was still standing where they had passed her. Their eyes met.

'Shall I serve?' said Doris.

'Yes, you've got the balls on your side.'

He played very badly. Generally he gave her fifteen and beat her, but today she won easily. And he played silently. Generally he was a noisy player, shouting all the time, cursing his foolishness when he missed a ball and chaffing her when he placed one out of her reach.

'You're off your game, young man,' she cried.

'Not a bit,' he said.

He began to slam the balls, trying to beat her, and sent one after the other into the net. She had never seen him with that set face. Was it possible that he was a little out of temper because he was not playing well? The light fell, and they ceased to play. The woman whom they had passed stood in exactly the same position as when they came and once more, with expressionless face, she watched them go.

The blinds on the veranda were raised now, and on the table between their two long chairs were bottles and soda-water.

This was the hour at which they had the first drink of the day and Guy mixed a couple of gin slings. The river stretched widely before them, and on the farther bank the jungle was wrapped in the mystery of the approaching night. A native was silently rowing up-stream, standing at the bow of the boat, with two oars.

'I played like a fool,' said Guy, breaking a silence. 'I'm feeling a bit under the weather.'

'I'm sorry. You're not going to have fever, are you?'

'Oh, no. I shall be all right tomorrow.'

Darkness closed in upon them. The frogs croaked loudly and now and then they heard a few short notes from some singing bird of the night. Fireflies flitted across the veranda and they made the trees that surrounded it look like Christmas trees lit with tiny candles. They sparkled softly. Doris thought she heard a little sigh. It vaguely disturbed her. Guy was always so full of gaiety.

'What is it, old man?' she said gently. 'Tell mother.'

'Nothing. Time for another drink,' he answered breezily.

Next day he was as cheerful as ever and the mail came. The coasting steamer passed the mouth of the river twice a month, once on its way to the coalfields and once on its way back. On the outward journey it brought mail, which Guy sent a boat down to fetch. Its arrival was the excitement of their uneventful lives. For the first day or two they skimmed rapidly all that had come, letters, English papers and papers from Singapore, magazines and books, leaving for the ensuing weeks a more exact perusal. They snatched the illustrated papers from one another. If Doris had not been so absorbed she might have noticed that there was a change in Guy. She would have found it hard to describe and harder still to explain. There was in his eyes a sort of watchfulness and in his mouth a slight droop of anxiety.

Then, perhaps a week later, one morning when she was sitting in the shaded room studying a Malay grammar (for she was industriously learning the language) she heard a commotion in the compound. She heard the house boy's voice, he was speaking angrily, the voice of another man, perhaps it was

the water-carrier's, and then a woman's, shrill and vituperative.
There was a scuffle. She went to the window and opened the
shutters. The water-carrier had hold of a woman's arm and
was dragging her along, while the house boy was pushing her
from behind with both hands. Doris recognized her at once as
the woman she had seen one morning loitering in the compound and later in the day outside the tennis-court. She was
holding a baby against her breast. All three were shouting
angrily.

'Stop,' cried Doris. 'What are you doing?'

At the sound of her voice the water-carrier let go suddenly
and the woman, still pushed from behind, fell to the ground.
There was a sudden silence and the house boy looked sullenly
into space. The water-carrier hesitated a moment and than
slunk away. The woman raised herself slowly to her feet, arranged the baby on her arm, and stood impassive, staring at
Doris. The boy said something to her which Doris could not
have heard even if she had understood; the woman by no
change of face showed that his words meant anything to her;
but she slowly strolled away. The boy followed her to the gate
of the compound. Doris called to him as he walked back, but
he pretended not to hear. She was growing angry now and she
called more sharply.

'Come here at once,' she cried.

Suddenly, avoiding her wrathful glance, he came towards
the bungalow. He came in and stood at the door. He looked at
her sulkily.

'What were you doing with that woman?' she asked abruptly.

'*Tuan* say she no come here.'

'You mustn't treat a woman like that. I won't have it. I shall
tell the *tuan* exactly what I saw.'

The boy did not answer. He looked away, but she felt that
he was watching her through his long eyelashes. She dismissed
him.

'That'll do.'

Without a word he turned and went back to the servants'
quarters. She was exasperated and she found it impossible to
give her attention once more to the Malay exercises. In a little

while the boy came in to lay the cloth for luncheon. On a sudden he went to the door.

'What is it?' she asked.

'*Tuan* just coming.'

He went out to take Guy's hat from him. His quick ears had caught the footsteps before they were audible to her. Guy did not as usual come up the steps immediately; he paused, and Doris at once surmised that the boy had gone down to meet him in order to tell him of the morning's incident. She shrugged her shoulders. The boy evidently wanted to get his story in first. But she was astonished when Guy came in. His face was ashy.

'Guy, what on earth's the matter?'

He flushed a sudden hot red.

'Nothing. Why?'

She was so taken aback that she let him pass into his room without a word of what she had meant to speak of at once. It took him longer than usual to have his bath and change his clothes and luncheon was served when he came in.

'Guy,' she said, as they sat down, 'that woman we saw the other day was here again this morning.'

'So I've heard,' he answered.

'The boys were treating her brutally. I had to stop them. You must really speak to them about it.'

Though the Malay understood every word she said, he made no sign that he heard. He handed her the toast.

'She's been told not to come here. I gave instructions that if she showed herself again she was to be turned out.'

'Were they obliged to be so rough?'

'She refused to go. I don't think they were any rougher than they could help.'

'It was horrible to see a woman treated like that. She had a baby in her arms.'

'Hardly a baby. It's three years old.'

'How d'you know?'

'I know all about her. She hasn't the least right to come here pestering everybody.'

'What does she want?'

'She wants to do exactly what she did. She wants to make a disturbance.'

For a little while Doris did not speak. She was surprised at her husband's tone. He spoke tersely. He spoke as though all this were no concern of hers. She thought him a little unkind. He was nervous and irritable.

'I doubt if we shall be able to play tennis this afternoon,' he said. 'It looks to me as though we were going to have a storm.'

The rain was falling when she awoke and it was impossible to go out. During tea Guy was silent and abstracted. She got her sewing and began to work. Guy sat down to read such of the English papers as he had not yet gone through from cover to cover; but he was restless; he walked up and down the large room and then went out on the veranda. He looked at the steady rain. What was he thinking of? Doris was vaguely uneasy.

It was not till after dinner that he spoke. During the simple meal he had exerted himself to be his usual gay self, but the exertion was apparent. The rain had ceased and the night was starry. They sat on the veranda. In order not to attract insects they had put out the lamp in the sitting-room. At their feet, with a mighty, formidable sluggishness, silent, mysterious, and fatal, flowed the river. It had the terrible deliberation and the relentlessness of destiny.

'Doris, I've got something to say to you,' he said suddenly.

His voice was very strange. Was it her fancy that he had difficulty in keeping it quite steady? She felt a little pang in her heart because he was in distress, and she put her hand gently into his. He drew it away.

'It's rather a long story. I'm afraid it's not a very nice one and I find it rather difficult to tell. I'm going to ask you not to interrupt me, or to say anything, till I've finished.'

In the darkness she could not see his face, but she felt that it was haggard. She did not answer. He spoke in a voice so low that it hardly broke the silence of the night.

'I was only eighteen when I came out here. I came straight from school. I spent three months in Kuala Solor, and then I was sent to a station up the Sembulu river. Of course there was a Resident there and his wife. I lived in the court-house, but I used to have my meals with them and spend the evening with them. I had an awfully good time. Then the fellow who was here fell ill and had to go home. We were short of men on account of the war and I was put in charge of this place. Of course I was very young, but I spoke the language like a native, and they remembered my father. I was as pleased as punch to be on my own.'

He was silent while he knocked the ashes out of his pipe and refilled it. When he lit a match Doris, without looking at him, noticed that his hand was unsteady.

'I'd never been alone before. Of course at home there'd been father and mother and generally an assistant. And then at school naturally there were always fellows about. On the way out, on the boat, there were people all the time, and at K.S., and the same at my first post. The people there were almost like my own people. I seemed always to live in a crowd. I like people. I'm a noisy blighter. I like to have a good time. All sorts of things make me laugh and you must have somebody to laugh with. But it was different here. Of course it was all right in the day time; I had my work and I could talk to the Dyaks. Although they were head-hunters in those days and now and then I had a bit of trouble with them, they were an awfully decent lot of fellows. I got on very well with them. Of course I should have liked a white man to gas to, but they were better than nothing, and it was easier for me because they didn't look upon me quite as a stranger. I liked the work too. It was rather lonely in the evening to sit on the veranda and drink a gin and bitters by myself, but I could read. And the boys were about. My own boy was called Abdul. He'd known my father. When I got tired of reading I could give him a shout and have a bit of a jaw with him.

'It was the nights that did for me. After dinner the boys shut up and went away to sleep in the kampong. I was all alone. There wasn't a sound in the bungalow except now and then the croak of the chik-chak. It used to come out of the silence, suddenly, so that it made me jump. Over in the kampong I heard the sound of a gong or fire-crackers. They were having a good time, they weren't so far away, but I had to stay where I was. I was tired of reading. I couldn't have been more of a prisoner if I'd been in jail. Night after night it was the same. I tried drinking three or four whiskies, but it's poor fun drinking alone, and it didn't cheer me up; it only made me feel rather rotten next day. I tried going to bed immediately after dinner, but I couldn't sleep. I used to lie in bed, getting hotter and hotter, and more wide awake, till I didn't know what to do with myself. By George, those nights were long. D'you know, I got so low, I was so sorry for myself that sometimes – it makes me laugh now when I think of it, but I was only nineteen and a half – sometimes I used to cry.

'Then, one evening, after dinner, Abdul had cleared away and was just going off, when he gave a little cough. He said, wasn't I lonely in the house all night by myself? "Oh, no, that's all right," I said. I didn't want him to know what a damned fool I was, but I expect he knew all right. He stood there without speaking, and I knew he wanted to say something to me. "What is it?" I said. "Spit it out." Then he said that if I'd like to have a girl to come and live with me he knew one who was willing. She was a very good girl and he could recommend her. She'd be no trouble and it would be someone to have about the bungalow. She'd mend my things for me. . . . I felt awfully low. It had been raining all day and I hadn't been able to get any exercise. I knew I shouldn't sleep for hours. It wouldn't cost me very much money, he said, her people were poor and they'd be quite satisfied with a small present. Two hundred Straits dollars. "You look," he said. "If you don't like her you send her away." I asked him where she was. "She's here," he said. "I call her." He went to the door. She'd been waiting on the steps with her mother. They came in and sat down on the floor. I gave them some sweets. She was shy, of course, but cool enough, and when I said something to her she gave me a smile. She was very young, hardly more than a child, they said she was fifteen. She was awfully pretty, and she had her best clothes on. We began to talk. She didn't say much, but she laughed a lot when I chaffed her. Abdul said I'd find she had plenty to say for herself when she got to know me. He told her to come and sit by me. She giggled and refused, but her mother told her to come, and I made room for her on the chair. She blushed and laughed, but she came, and then she snuggled up to me. The boy laughed too. "You see, she's taken to you already," he said. "Do you want her to stay?" he asked. "Do you want to?" I said to her. She hid her face, laughing, on my shoulder. She was very soft and small. "Very well," I said, "let her stay." '

Guy leaned forward and helped himself to a whisky and soda.

'May I speak now?' asked Doris.

'Wait a minute, I haven't finished yet. I wasn't in love with her, not even at the beginning. I only took her so as to have somebody about the bungalow. I think I should have gone mad if I hadn't, or else taken to drink. I was at the end of my tether. I was too young to be quite alone. I was never in love with anyone but you.' He hesitated a moment. 'She lived here till I went home last year on leave. It's the woman you've seen hanging about.'

'Yes, I guessed that. She had a baby in her arms. Is that your child?'

'Yes. It's a little girl.'

'Is it the only one?'

'You saw the two small boys the other day in the kampong. You mentioned them.'

'She has three children then?'

'Yes.'

'It's quite a family you've got.'

She felt the sudden gesture which her remark forced from him, but he did not speak.

'Didn't she know that you were married till you suddenly turned up here with a wife?' asked Doris.

'She knew I was going to be married.'

'When?'

'I sent her back to the village before I left here. I told her it was all over. I gave her what I'd promised. She always knew it was only a temporary arrangement. I was fed up with it. I told her I was going to marry a white woman.'

'But you hadn't even seen me then.'

'No, I know. But I'd made up my mind to marry when I was home.' He chuckled in his old manner. 'I don't mind telling you that I was getting rather despondent about it when I met you. I fell in love with you at first sight and then I knew it was either you or nobody.'

'Why didn't you tell me? Don't you think it would have been only fair to give me a chance of judging for myself? It might have occurred to you that it would be rather a shock to a girl to find out that her husband had lived for ten years with another girl and had three children.'

'I couldn't expect you to understand. The circumstances out here are peculiar. It's the regular thing. Five men out of six do it. I thought perhaps it would shock you and I didn't want to lose you. You see, I was most awfully in love with you. I am now, darling. There was no reason that you should ever know. I didn't expect to come back here. One seldom goes back to the same station after home leave. When we came here I offered her money if she'd go to some other village. First she said she would and then she changed her mind.'

'Why have you told me now?'

'She's been making the most awful scenes. I don't know how she found out that you knew nothing about it. As soon as she did she began to blackmail me. I've had to give her an awful lot of money. I gave orders that she wasn't to be allowed in the compound. This morning she made that scene just to attract your attention. She wanted to frighten me. It couldn't go on like that. I thought the only thing was to make a clean breast of it.'

There was a long silence as he finished. At last he put his hand on hers.

'You do understand, Doris, don't you? I know I've been to blame.'

She did not move her hand. He felt it cold beneath his.

'Is she jealous?'

'I dare say there were all sorts of perks when she was living here, and I don't suppose she much likes not getting them any longer. But she was never in love with me any more than I was in love with her. Native women never do really care for white men, you know.'

'And the children?'

'Oh, the children are all right. I've provided for them. As soon as the boys are old enough I shall send them to school at Singapore.'

'Do they mean nothing to you at all?'

He hesitated.

'I want to be quite frank with you. I should be sorry if anything happened to them. When the first one was expected I thought I'd be much fonder of it than I ever had been of its mother. I suppose I should have been if it had been white. Of course, when it was a baby it was rather funny and touching, but I had no particular feeling that it was mine. I think that's what it is; you see, I have no sense of their belonging to me. I've reproached myself sometimes, because it seemed rather unnatural, but the honest truth is that they're no more to me than if they were somebody else's children. Of course a lot of slush is talked about children by people who haven't got any.'

Now she had heard everything. He waited for her to speak, but she said nothing. She sat motionless.

'Is there anything more you want to ask me, Doris?' he said at last.

'No, I've got rather a headache. I think I shall go to bed.' Her voice was as steady as ever. 'I don't quite know what to say. Of course it's been all very unexpected. You must give me a little time to think.'

'Are you very angry with me?'

'No. Not at all. Only – only I must be left to myself for a while. Don't move. I'm going to bed.'

She rose from her long chair and put her hand on his shoulder.

'It's so very hot tonight. I wish you'd sleep in your dressing-room. Good night.'

She was gone. He heard her lock the door of her bedroom.

She was pale next day and he could see that she had not slept. There was no bitterness in her manner, she talked as usual, but without ease; she spoke of this and that as though she were making conversation with a stranger. They had never had a quarrel, but it seemed to Guy that so would she talk if they had had a disagreement and the subsequent reconciliation had left her still wounded. The look in her eyes puzzled him; he seemed to read in them a strange fear. Immediately after dinner she said:

'I'm not feeling very well tonight. I think I shall go straight to bed.'

'Oh, my poor darling, I'm so sorry,' he cried.

'It's nothing. I shall be all right in a day or two.'

'I shall come in and say good night to you later.'

'No, don't do that. I shall try and get straight off to sleep.'

'Well, then, kiss me before you go.'

He saw that she flushed. For an instant she seemed to hesitate; then, with averted eyes, she leaned towards him. He took her in his arms and sought her lips, but she turned her face away and he kissed her cheek. She left him quickly and again he heard the key turn softly in the lock of her door. He flung himself heavily on the chair. He tried to read, but his ear was attentive to the smallest sound in his wife's room. She had said she was going to bed, but he did not hear her move. The silence in there made him unaccountably nervous. Shading the lamp with his hand he saw that there was a glimmer under her door; she had not put out her light. What on earth was she doing? He put down his book. It would not have surprised him if she had been angry and had made him a scene, or if she had cried; he could have coped with that; but her calmness frightened him. And then what was that fear which he had seen so plainly in her eyes? He tohught once more over all he had said to her on the previous night. He didn't know how else he could have put it. After all, the chief point was that he'd done the same as everybody else, and it was all over long before he met her. Of course as things turned out he had been a fool, but anyone could be wise after the event. He put his hand to his heart. Funny how it hurt him there.

'I suppose that's the sort of thing people mean when they

say they're heartbroken,' he said to himself. 'I wonder how long it's going on like this?'

Should he knock at the door and tell her he must speak to her? It was better to have it out. He *must* make her understand. But the silence scared him. Not a sound! Perhaps it was better to leave her alone. Of course it had been a shock. He must give her as long as she wanted. After all, she knew how devotedly he loved her. Patience, that was the only thing; perhaps she was fighting it out with herself; he must give her time; he must have patience. Next morning he asked her if she had slept better.

'Yes, much,' she said.

'Are you very angry with me?' he asked piteously.

She looked at him with candid, open eyes.

'Not a bit.'

'Oh, my dear, I'm so glad. I've been a brute and a beast. I know it's been hateful for you. But do forgive me. I've been so miserable.'

'I do forgive you. I don't even blame you.'

He gave her a little rueful smile, and there was in his eyes the look of a whipped dog.

'I haven't much liked sleeping by myself the last two nights.'

She glanced away. Her face grew a trifle paler.

'I've had the bed in my room taken away. It took up so much space. I've had a little camp bed put there instead.'

'My dear, what are you talking about?'

Now she looked at him steadily.

'I'm not going to live with you as your wife again.'

'Never?'

She shook her head. He looked at her in a puzzled way. He could hardly believe he had heard aright and his heart began to beat painfully.

'But that's awfully unfair to me, Doris.'

'Don't you think it was a little unfair to me to bring me out here in the circumstances?'

'But you just said you didn't blame me.'

'That's quite true. But the other's different. I can't do it.'

'But how are we going to live together like that?'

She stared at the floor. She seemed to ponder deeply.

'When you wanted to kiss me on the lips last night I – it almost made me sick.'

'Doris.'

She looked at him suddenly and her eyes were cold and hostile.

'That bed I slept on, is that the bed in which she had her children?' She saw him flush deeply. 'Oh, it's horrible. How could you?' She wrung her hands, and her twisting, tortured fingers looked like little writhing snakes. But she made a great effort and controlled herself. 'My mind is quite made up. I don't want to be unkind to you, but there are some things that you can't ask me to do. I've thought it all over. I've been thinking of nothing else since you told me, night and day, till I'm exhausted. My first instinct was to get up and go. At once. The steamer will be here in two or three days.'

'Doesn't it mean anything to you that I love you?'

'Oh, I know you love me. I'm not going to do that. I want to give us both a chance. I have loved you so, Guy.' Her voice broke, but she did not cry. 'I don't want to be unreasonable. Heaven knows, I don't want to be unkind. Guy, will you give me time?'

'I don't know quite what you mean.'

'I just want you to leave me alone. I'm frightened by the feelings that I have.'

He had been right then; she was afraid.

'What feelings?'

'Please don't ask me. I don't want to say anything to wound you. Perhaps I shall get over them. Heaven knows, I want to. I'll try, I promise you. I'll try. Give me six months. I'll do everything in the world for you, but just that one thing.' She made a little gesture of appeal. 'There's no reason why we shouldn't be happy enough together. If you really love me you'll – you'll have patience.'

He sighed deeply.

'Very well,' he said. 'Naturally I don't want to force you to do anything you don't like. It shall be as you say.'

He sat heavily for a little, as though, on a sudden grown old, it was an effort to move; then he got up.

'I'll be getting along to the office.'

He took his topee and went out.

A month passed. Women conceal their feelings better than men and a stranger visiting them would never have guessed that Doris was in any way troubled. But in Guy the strain was obvious; his round, good-natured face was drawn, and in his eyes was a hungry, harassed look. He watched Doris. She was gay and she chaffed him as she had been used to do; they played tennis together; they chatted about one thing and another. But it was evident that she was merely playing a part, and at last, unable to contain himself, he tried to speak again of his connexions with the Malay woman.

'Oh, Guy, there's no object in going back on all that,' she answered breezily. 'We've said all we had to say about it and I don't blame you for anything.'

'Why do you punish me then?'

'My poor boy, I don't want to punish you. It's not my fault if . . .' she shrugged her shoulders. 'Human nature is very odd.'

'I don't understand.'

'Don't try.'

The words might have been harsh, but she softened them with a pleasant, friendly smile. Every night when she went to bed she leaned over Guy and lightly kissed his cheek. Her lips only touched it. It was as though a moth had just brushed his face in its flight.

A second month passed, then a third, and suddenly the six months which had seemed so interminable were over. Guy asked himself whether she remembered. He gave a strained attention now to everything she said, to every look on her face and to every gesture of her hands. She remained impenetrable. She had asked him to give her six months; well, he had.

The coasting steamer passed the mouth of the river, dropped their mail, and went on its way. Guy busily wrote the letters which it would pick up on the return journey. Two or three days passed by. It was a Tuesday and the *prahu* was to start at dawn on Thursday to await the steamer. Except at meal time when Doris exerted herself to make conversation they had not of late talked very much together; and after dinner as usual they took their books and began to read; but when the boy had finished clearing away and was gone for the night Doris put down hers.

'Guy, I have something I want to say to you,' she murmured.

His heart gave a sudden thud against his ribs and he felt himself change colour.

'Oh, my dear, don't look like that, it's not so very terrible,' she laughed.

But he thought her voice trembled a little.

'Well?'

'I want you to do something for me.'

'My darling, I'll do anything in the world for you.'

He put out his hand to take hers, but she drew it away.

'I want you to let me go home.'

'You?' he cried, aghast. 'When? Why?'

'I've borne it as long as I can. I'm at the end of my tether.'

'How long do you want to go for? For always?'

'I don't know. I think so.' She gathered determination. 'Yes, for always.'

'Oh, my God!'

His voice broke and she thought he was going to cry.

'Oh, Guy, don't blame me. It really is not my fault. I can't help myself.'

'You asked me for six months. I accepted your terms. You can't say I've made a nuisance of myself.'

'No, no.'

'I've tried not to let you see what a rotten time I was having.'

'I know. I'm very grateful to you. You've been awfully kind to me. Listen, Guy, I want to tell you again that I don't blame you for a single thing you did. After all, you were only a boy, and you did no more than the others; I know what the loneliness is here. Oh, my dear, I'm so dreadfully sorry for you. I knew all that from the beginning. That's why I asked you for six months. My common sense tells me that I'm making a mountain out of a molehill. I'm unreasonable; I'm being unfair to you. But, you see, common sense has nothing to do with it; my whole soul is in revolt. When I see the woman and her children in the village I just feel my legs shaking. Everything in this house; when I think of that bed I slept in it gives me goose-flesh. . . . You don't know what I've endured.'

'I think I've persuaded her to go away. And I've applied for a transfer.'

'That wouldn't help. She'll be there always. You belong to them, you don't belong to me. I think perhaps I could have stood it if there'd only been one child, but three; and the boys are quite big boys. For ten years you lived with her.' And now she came out with what she had been working up to. She was desperate. 'It's a physical thing, I can't help it, it's stronger than I am. I think of those thin black arms of hers round you and it fills me with a physical nausea. I think of you holding those little black babies in your arms. Oh, it's loathsome. The touch of you is odious to me. Each night, when I've kissed you, I've had to brace myself up to it, I've had to clench my hands and force myself to touch your cheek.' Now she was clasping and unclasping her fingers in a nervous agony, and her voice was out of control. 'I know it's I who am to blame now. I'm a silly, hysterical woman. I thought I'd get over it. I can't, and now I never shall. I've brought it all on myself; I'm willing to take the consequences; if you say I must stay here, I'll stay, but if I stay I shall die. I beseech you to let me go.'

And now the tears which she had restrained so long overflowed and she wept broken-heartedly. He had never seen her cry before.

'Of course I don't want to keep you here against your will,' he said hoarsely.

Exhausted, she leaned back in her chair. Her features were all twisted and awry. It was horribly painful to see the abandonment of grief on that face which was habitually so placid.

'I'm so sorry, Guy. I've broken your life, but I've broken mine too. And we might have been so happy.'

'When do you want to go? On Tuesday?'

'Yes.'

She looked at him piteously. He buried his face in his hands. At last he looked up.

'I'm tired out,' he muttered.

'May I go?'

'Yes.'

For two minutes perhaps they sat there without a word. She started when the chik-chak gave its piercing, hoarse, and strangely human cry. Guy rose and went out on to the veranda. He leaned against the rail and looked at the softly flowing water. He heard Doris go into her room.

Next morning, up earlier than usual, he went to her door and knocked.

'Yes?'

'I have to go up-river today. I shan't be back till late.'

'All right.'

She understood. He had arranged to be away all day in order not to be about while she was packing. It was heartbreaking work. When she had packed her clothes she looked round the sitting-room at the things that belonged to her. It seemed dreadful to take them. She left everything but the photograph of her mother. Guy did not come in till ten o'clock at night.

'I'm sorry I couldn't get back to dinner,' he said. 'The headman at the village I had to go to had a lot of things for me to attend to.'

She saw his eyes wander about the room and notice that her mother's photograph no longer stood in its place.

'Is everything quite ready?' he asked. 'I've ordered the boatman to be at the steps at dawn.'

'I told the boy to wake me at five.'

'I'd better give you some money.' He went to his desk and wrote out a cheque. He took some notes from a drawer. 'Here's some cash to take you as far as Singapore and at Singapore you'll be able to change the cheque.'

'Thank you.'

'Would you like me to come to the mouth of the river with you?'

'Oh, I think it would be better if we said good-bye here.'

'All right. I think I shall turn in. I've had a long day and I'm dead beat.'

He did not even touch her hand. He went into his room. In a few minutes she heard him throw himself on his bed. For a little while she sat looking for the last time round that room in which she had been so happy and so miserable. She sighed deeply. She got up and went into her own room. Everything was packed except the one or two things she needed for the night.

It was dark when the boy awakened them. They dressed hurriedly and when they were ready breakfast was waiting for them. Presently they heard the boat row up to the landing-stage below the bungalow, and then the servants carried down her luggage. It was a poor pretence they made of eating. The darkness thinned away and the river was ghostly. It was not yet day, but it was no longer night. In the silence the voices of the natives at the landing-stage were very clear. Guy glanced at his wife's untouched plate.

'If you've finished we might stroll down. I think you ought to be starting.'

She did not answer. She rose from the table. She went into her room to see that nothing had been forgotten and then side by side with him walked down the steps. A little winding path led them to the river. At the landing-stage the native guards in their smart uniform were lined up and they presented arms as Guy and Doris passed. The head boatman gave her his hand as she stepped into the boat. She turned and looked at Guy. She wanted desperately to say one last word of comfort, once more to ask for his forgiveness, but she seemed to be struck dumb.

He stretched out his hand.

'Well, good-bye, I hope you'll have a jolly journey.'

They shook hands.

Guy nodded to the head boatman and the boat pushed off. The dawn now was creeping along the river mistily, but the night lurked still in the dark trees of the jungle. He stood at the landing-stage till the boat was lost in the shadows of the morning. With a sigh he turned away. He nodded absent-mindedly when the guard once more presented arms. But when he reached the bungalow he called the boy. He went round the room picking out everything that had belonged to Doris.

'Pack all these things up,' he said. 'It's no good leaving them about.'

Then he sat down on the veranda and watched the day advance gradually like a bitter, an unmerited, and an overwhelming sorrow. At last he looked at his watch. It was time for him to go to the office.

In the afternoon he could not sleep, his head ached miserably, so he took his gun and went for a tramp in the jungle. He shot nothing, but he walked in order to tire himself out. Towards sunset he came back and had two or three drinks, and then it was time to dress for dinner. There wasn't much use in dressing now; he might just as well be comfortable; he put on a loose native jacket and a sarong. That was what he had been accustomed to wear before Doris came. He was barefoot. He ate his dinner listlessly and the boy cleared away and went. He sat down to read the *Tatler*. The bungalow was very silent. He could not read and let the paper fall on his knees. He was exhausted. He could not think and his mind was strangely vacant. The chik-chak was noisy that night and its hoarse and sudden cry seemed to mock him. You could hardly believe that this reverberating sound came from so small a throat. Presently he heard a discreet cough.

'Who's there?' he cried.

There was a pause. He looked at the door. The chik-chak laughed harshly. A small boy sidled in and stood on the threshold. It was a little half-caste boy in a tattered singlet and a sarong. It was the elder of his two sons.

'What do you want?' said Guy.

The boy came forward into the room and sat down, tucking his legs away under him.

'Who told you to come here?'

'My mother sent me. She says, do you want anything?'

Guy looked at the boy intently. The boy said nothing more. He sat and waited, his eyes cast down shyly. Then Guy in deep and bitter reflection buried his face in his hands. What was the use? It was finished. Finished! He surrendered. He sat back in his chair and sighed deeply.

'Tell your mother to pack up her things and yours. She can come back.'

'When?' asked the boy, impassively.

Hot tears trickled down Guy's funny, round spotty face.

'Tonight.'

James Joyce

THE DEAD

LILY, the caretaker's daughter, was literally run off her feet Hardly had she brought one gentleman into the little pantry behind the office on the ground floor and helped him off with his overcoat, than the wheezy hall-door bell clanged again and she had to scamper along the bare hallway to let in another guest. It was well for her she had not to attend to the ladies also. But Miss Kate and Miss Julia had thought of that and had converted the bathroom upstairs into a ladies' dressing-room. Miss Kate and Miss Julia were there, gossiping and laughing and fussing, walking after each other to the head of the stairs, peering down over the banisters and calling down to Lily to ask her who had come.

It was always a great affair, the Misses Morkan's annual dance. Everybody who knew them came to it, members of the family, old friends of the family, the members of Julia's choir, any of Kate's pupils that were grown up enough, and even some of Mary Jane's pupils too. Never once had it fallen flat. For years and years it had gone off in splendid style, as long as anyone could remember: ever since Kate and Julia, after the death of their brother Pat, had left the house in Stoney Batter and taken Mary Jane, their only niece, to live with them in the dark, gaunt house on Usher's Island, the upper part of which they had rented from Mr Fulham, the corn-factor on the ground floor. That was a good thirty years ago if it was a day. Mary Jane, who was then a little girl in short clothes, was now the main prop of the household, for she had the organ in Hadding-ton Road. She had been through the Academy and gave a pupils' concert every year in the upper room of the Antient Concert Rooms. Many of her pupils belonged to the better-class families on the Kingstown and Dalkey line. Old as they were, her aunts also did their share. Julia, though she was

JAMES JOYCE

quite grey, was still the leading soprano in Adam and Eve's, and
Kate, being too feeble to go about much, gave music lessons
to beginners on the old square piano in the back room. Lily,
the caretaker's daughter, did housemaid's work for them.
Though their life was modest, they believed in eating well; the
best of everything: diamond-bone sirloins, three-shilling tea
and the best bottled stout. But Lily seldom made a mistake in
the orders, so that she got on well with her three mistresses.
They were fussy, that was all. But the only thing they would
not stand was back answers.

Of course, they had good reason to be fussy on such a night.
And then it was long after ten o'clock and yet there was no
sign of Gabriel and his wife. Besides they were dreadfully afraid
that Freddy Malins might turn up screwed. They would not
wish for worlds that any of Mary Jane's pupils should see him
under the influence; and when he was like that it was sometimes
very hard to manage him. Freddy Malins always came late, but
they wondered what could be keeping Gabriel: and that was
what brought them every two minutes to the banisters to ask
Lily had Gabriel or Freddy come.

'Oh, Mr Conroy,' said Lily to Gabriel when she opened the
door for him, 'Miss Kate and Miss Julia thought you were
never coming. Good night, Mrs Conroy.'

'I'll engage they did,' said Gabriel, 'but they forget that my
wife here takes three mortal hours to dress herself.'

He stood on the mat, scraping the snow from his goloshes,
while Lily led his wife to the foot of the stairs and called out:

'Miss Kate, here's Mrs Conroy.'

Kate and Julia came toddling down the dark stairs at once.
Both of them kissed Gabriel's wife, said she must be perished
alive, and asked was Gabriel with her.

'Here I am as right as the mail, Aunt Kate! Go on up. I'll
follow,' called out Gabriel from the dark.

He continued scraping his feet vigorously while the three
women went upstairs, laughing, to the ladies' dressing-room.
A light fringe of snow lay like a cape on the shoulders of his
overcoat and like toecaps on the toes of his goloshes; and, as
the buttons of his overcoat slipped with a squeaking noise

through the snow-stiffened frieze, a cold, fragrant air from out-of-doors escaped from crevices and folds.

'Is it snowing again, Mr Conroy?' asked Lily.

She had preceded him into the pantry to help him off with his overcoat. Gabriel smiled at the three syllables she had given his surname and glanced at her. She was a slim, growing girl, pale in complexion and with hay-coloured hair. The gas in the pantry made her look still paler. Gabriel had known her when she was a child and used to sit on the lowest step nursing a rag doll.

'Yes, Lily,' he answered, 'and I think we're in for a night of it.'

He looked up at the pantry ceiling, which was shaking with the stamping and shuffling of feet on the floor above, listened for a moment to the piano and then glanced at the girl, who was folding his overcoat carefully at the end of a shelf.

'Tell me, Lily,' he said in a friendly tone, 'do you still go to school?'

'O no, sir,' she answered. 'I'm done schooling this year and more.'

'O, then,' said Gabriel gaily, 'I suppose we'll be going to your wedding one of these fine days with your young man, eh?'

The girl glanced back at him over her shoulder and said with great bitterness:

'The men that is now is only all palaver and what they can get out of you.'

Gabriel coloured, as if he felt he had made a mistake, and, without looking at her, kicked off his goloshes and flicked actively with his muffler at his patent-leather shoes.

He was a stout, tallish young man. The high colour of his cheeks pushed upwards even to his forehead, where it scattered itself in a few formless patches of pale red; and on his hairless face there scintillated restlessly the polished lenses and the bright gilt rims of the glasses which screened his delicate and restless eyes. His glossy black hair was parted in the middle and brushed in a long curve behind his ears where it curled slightly beneath the groove left by his hat.

When he had flicked lustre into his shoes he stood up and pulled his waistcoat down more tightly on his plump body. Then he took a coin rapidly from his pocket.

'O Lily,' he said, thrusting it into her hands, 'it's Christmas time, isn't it? Just ... here's a little ... '

He walked rapidly towards the door.

'O no, sir!' cried the girl, following him. 'Really, sir, I wouldn't take it.'

'Christmas time! Christmas time!' said Gabriel, almost trotting to the stairs and waving his hand to her in deprecation.

The girl, seeing that he had gained the stairs, called out after him:

'Well, thank you, sir.'

He waited outside the drawing-room door until the waltz should finish, listening to the skirts that swept against it and to the shuffling of feet. He was still discomposed by the girl's bitter and sudden retort. It had cast a gloom over him which he tried to dispel by arranging his cuffs and the bows of his tie. He then took from his waistcoat pocket a little paper and glanced at the headings he had made for his speech. He was undecided about the lines from Robert Browning, for he feared they would be above the heads of his hearers. Some quotation that they would recognize from Shakespeare or from the Melodies would be better. The indelicate clacking of the men's heels and the shuffling of their soles reminded him that their grade of culture differed from his. He would only make himself ridiculous by quoting poetry to them which they could not understand. They would think that he was airing his superior education. He would fail with them just as he had failed with the girl in the pantry. He had taken up a wrong tone. His whole speech was a mistake from first to last, an utter failure.

Just then his aunts and his wife came out of the ladies' dressing-room. His aunts were two small, plainly dressed old women. Aunt Julia was an inch or so the taller. Her hair, drawn low over the tops of her ears, was grey; and grey also, with darker shadows, was her large flaccid face. Though she was stout in build and stood erect, her slow eyes and parted lips gave her the appearance of a woman who did not know where she was or where she was going. Aunt Kate was more vivacious. Her face, healthier than her sister's, was all puckers and creases, like a shrivelled red apple, and her hair, braided in the same old-fashioned way, had not lost its ripe nut colour.

They both kissed Gabriel frankly. He was their favourite nephew, the son of their dead elder sister, Ellen, who had married T. J. Conroy of the Port and Docks.

'Gretta tells me you're not going to take a cab back to Monkstown tonight, Gabriel,' said Aunt Kate.

'No,' said Gabriel, turning to his wife, 'we had quite enough of that last year, hadn't we? Don't you remember, Aunt Kate, what a cold Gretta got out of it? Cab windows rattling all the way, and the east wind blowing in after we passed Merrion. Very jolly it was. Gretta caught a dreadful cold.'

Aunt Kate frowned severely and nodded her head at every word.

'Quite right, Gabriel, quite right,' she said. 'You can't be too careful.'

'But as for Gretta there,' said Gabriel, 'she'd walk home in the snow if she were let.'

Mrs Conroy laughed.

'Don't mind him, Aunt Kate,' she said. 'He's really an awful bother, what with green shades for Tom's eyes at night and making him do the dumb-bells, and forcing Eva to eat the stirabout. The poor child! And she simply hates the sight of it! . . . O, but you'll never guess what he makes me wear now!'

She broke out into a peal of laughter and glanced at her husband, whose admiring and happy eyes had been wandering from her dress to her face and hair. The two aunts laughed heartily, too, for Gabriel's solicitude was a standing joke with them.

'Goloshes!' said Mrs Conroy. 'That's the latest. Whenever it's wet underfoot I must put on my goloshes. Tonight, even, he wanted me to put them on, but I wouldn't. The next thing he'll buy me will be a diving suit.'

Gabriel laughed nervously and patted his tie reassuringly, while Aunt Kate nearly doubled herself, so heartily did she enjoy the joke. The smile soon faded from Aunt Julia's face and her mirthless eyes were directed towards her nephew's face. After a pause she asked:

'And what are goloshes, Gabriel?'

'Goloshes, Julia!' exclaimed her sister. 'Goodness me, don't you know what goloshes are? You wear them over your . . . over your boots, Gretta, isn't it?'

'Yes,' said Mrs Conroy. 'Gutta-percha things. We both have a pair now. Gabriel says everyone wears them on the Continent.'

'O, on the Continent,' murmured Aunt Julia, nodding her head slowly.

Gabriel knitted his brows and said, as if he were slightly angered:

'It's nothing very wonderful, but Gretta thinks it very funny, because she says the word reminds her of Christy Minstrels.'

'But tell me, Gabriel,' said Aunt Kate, with brisk tact. 'Of course, you've seen about the room. Gretta was saying . . . '

'O, the room is all right,' replied Gabriel. 'I've taken one in the Gresham.'

'To be sure,' said Aunt Kate, 'by far the best thing to do. And the children, Gretta, you're not anxious about them?'

'O, for one night,' said Mrs Conroy. 'Besides, Bessie will look after them.'

'To be sure,' said Aunt Kate again. 'What a comfort it is to have a girl like that, one you can depend on! There's that Lily, I'm sure I don't know what has come over her lately. She's not the girl she was at all.'

Gabriel was about to ask his aunt some questions on this point, but she broke off suddenly to gaze after her sister, who had wandered down the stairs and was craning her neck over the banisters.

'Now, I ask you,' she said almost testily, 'where is Julia going? Julia! Julia! Where are you going?'

Julia, who had gone half-way down one flight, came back and announced blandly:

'Here's Freddy.'

At the same moment a clapping of hands and a final flourish of the pianist told that the waltz had ended. The drawing-room door was opened from within and some couples came out. Aunt Kate drew Gabriel aside hurriedly and whispered into his ear:

'Slip down, Gabriel, like a good fellow and see if he's all right, and don't let him up if he's screwed. I'm sure he's screwed. I'm sure he is.'

Gabriel went to the stairs and listened over the banisters. He could hear two persons talking in the pantry. Then he recognized Freddy Malins's laugh. He went down the stairs noisily.

'It's such a relief,' said Aunt Kate to Mrs Conroy, 'that Gabriel is here. I always feel easier in my mind when he's here.... Julia, there's Miss Daly and Miss Power will take some refreshment. Thanks for your beautiful waltz, Miss Daly. It made lovely time.'

A tall wizen-faced man, with a stiff grizzled moustache and swarthy skin, who was passing out with his partner, said:

'And may we have some refreshment, too, Miss Morkan?'

'Julia,' said Aunt Kate summarily, 'and here's Mr Browne and Miss Furlong. Take them in, Julia, with Miss Daly and Miss Power.'

'I'm the man for the ladies,' said Mr Browne, pursing his lips until his moustache bristled, and smiling in all his wrinkles. 'You know, Miss Morkan, the reason they are so fond of me is – '

He did not finish his sentence, but, seeing that Aunt Kate was out of earshot, at once led the three young ladies into the back room. The middle of the room was occupied by two square tables placed end to end, and on these Aunt Julia and the caretaker were straightening and smoothing a large cloth. On the sideboard were arrayed dishes and plates, and glasses and bundles of knives and forks and spoons. The top of the closed square piano served also as a sideboard for viands and sweets. At a smaller sideboard in one corner two young men were standing, drinking hop-bitters.

Mr Browne led his charges thither and invited them all, in jest, to some ladies' punch, hot, strong, and sweet. As they said they never took anything strong, he opened three bottles of lemonade for them. Then he asked one of the young men to move aside, and, taking hold of the decanter, filled out for himself a goodly measure of whisky. The young men eyed him respectfully while he took a trial sip.

'God help me,' he said, smiling, 'it's the doctor's orders.'

His wizened face broke into a broader smile, and the three young ladies laughed in musical echo to his pleasantry, swaying their bodies to and fro, with nervous jerks of their shoulders. The boldest said:

'O, now, Mr Browne, I'm sure the doctor never ordered anything of the kind.'

Mr Browne took another sip of his whisky and said, with sidling mimicry:

'Well, you see, I'm the famous Mrs Cassidy, who is reported to have said: "Now, Mary Grimes, if I don't take it, make me take it, for I feel I want it." '

His hot face had leaned forward a little too confidentially and he had assumed a very low Dublin accent, so that the young ladies, with one instinct, received his speech in silence. Miss Furlong, who was one of Mary Jane's pupils, asked Miss Daly what was the name of the pretty waltz she had played; and Mr Browne, seeing that he was ignored, turned promptly to the two young men, who were more appreciative.

A red-faced young woman, dressed in pansy, came into the room, excitedly clapping her hands and crying:

'Quadrilles! Quadrilles!'

Close on her heels came Aunt Kate, crying:

'Two gentlemen and three ladies, Mary Jane!'

'O, here's Mr Bergin and Mr Kerrigan,' said Mary Jane. 'Mr Kerrigan, will you take Miss Power? Miss Furlong, may I get you a partner, Mr Bergin. O, that'll just do now.'

'Three ladies, Mary Jane,' said Aunt Kate.

The two young gentlemen asked the ladies if they might have the pleasure, and Mary Jane turned to Miss Daly.

'O, Miss Daly, you're really awfully good, after playing for the last two dances, but really we're so short of ladies tonight.'

'I don't mind in the least, Miss Morkan.'

'But I've a nice partner for you, Mr Bartell D'Arcy, the tenor. I'll get him to sing later on. All Dublin is raving about him.'

'Lovely voice, lovely voice!' said Aunt Kate.

As the piano had twice begun the prelude to the first figure Mary Jane led her recruits quickly from the room. They had hardly gone when Aunt Julia wandered slowly into the room, looking behind her at something.

'What is the matter, Julia?' asked Aunt Kate anxiously. Who is it?'

Julia, who was carrying in a column of table-napkins, turned to her sister and said, simply, as if the question had surprised her:

'It's only Freddy, Kate, and Gabriel with him.'

In fact, right behind her Gabriel could be seen piloting Freddy Malins across the landing. The latter, a young man of about forty, was of Gabriel's size and build, with very round shoulders. His face was fleshy and pallid, touched with colour only at the thick hanging lobes of his ears and at the wide wings of his nose. He had coarse features, a blunt nose, a convex and receding brow, tumid and protruded lips. His heavy-lidded eyes and the disorder of his scanty hair made him look sleepy. He was laughing heartily in a high key at a story which he had been telling Gabriel on the stairs and at the same time rubbing the knuckles of his left fist backwards and forwards into his left eye.

'Good evening, Freddy,' said Aunt Julia.

Freddy Malins bade the Misses Morkan good evening in what seemed an off-hand fashion by reason of the habitual catch in his voice and then, seeing that Mr Browne was grinning at him from the sideboard, crossed the room on rather shaky legs and began to repeat in an undertone the story he had just told to Gabriel.

'He's not so bad, is he?' said Aunt Kate to Gabriel.

Gabriel's brows were dark, but he raised them quickly and answered:

'O, no, hardly noticeable.'

'Now, isn't he a terrible fellow!' she said. 'And his poor mother made him take the pledge on New Year's Eve. But come on, Gabriel, into the drawing-room.'

Before leaving the room with Gabriel she signalled to Mr Browne by frowning and shaking her forefinger in warning to and fro. Mr Browne nodded in answer and, when she nad gone, said to Freddy Malins:

'Now, then, Teddy, I'm going to fill you out a good glass of lemonade just to buck you up.'

Freddy Malins, who was nearing the climax of his story, waved the offer aside impatiently, but Mr Browne, having first called Freddy Malins's attention to a disarray in his dress, filled out and handed him a full glass of lemonade. Freddy Malins's left hand accepted the glass mechanically, his right hand being engaged in the mechanical readjustment of his dress. Mr Browne, whose face was once more wrinkling with mirth, poured out for himself a glass of whisky while Freddy Malins exploded, before he had well reached the climax of his story, in a kink of high-pitched bronchitic laughter and, setting down his untasted and over-flowing glass, began to run the knuckles of his left fist backwards and forwards into his left eye, repeating words of his last phrase as well as his fit of laughter would allow him.

Gabriel could not listen while Mary Jane was playing her Academy piece, full of runs and difficult passages, to the hushed drawing-room. He liked music, but the piece she was playing had no melody for him and he doubted whether it had any melody for the other listeners, though they had begged Mary Jane to play something. Four young men, who had come from the refreshment-room to stand in the doorway at the sound of the piano, had gone away quietly in couples after a few minutes. The only persons who seemed to follow the music were Mary Jane herself, her hands racing along the keyboard or lifted from it at the pauses like those of a priestess in momentary imprecation, and Aunt Kate standing at her elbow to turn the page.

Gabriel's eyes, irritated by the floor, which glittered with beeswax under the heavy chandelier, wandered to the wall above the piano. A picture of the balcony scene in *Romeo and Juliet* hung there and beside it was a picture of the two murdered princes in the Tower which Aunt Julia had worked in red, blue, and brown wools when she was a girl. Probably in the school they had gone to as girls that kind of work had been taught for one year. His mother had worked for him as a birthday present a waistcoat of purple tabinet, with little foxes' heads upon it, lined with brown satin and having round mulberry buttons. It was strange that his mother had had no musical talent, though Aunt Kate used to call her the brains carrier of the Morkan family. Both she and Julia had always seemed a little proud of their serious and matronly sister. Her photograph stood before the pier-glass. She had an open book on her knees and was pointing out something in it to Constantine who, dressed in a man-o'-war suit, lay at her feet. It was she who had chosen the names of her sons, for she was very sensible of the dignity of family life. Thanks to her, Constantine was now senior curate in Balbriggan and, thanks to her, Gabriel himself had taken his degree in the Royal University. A shadow passed over his face as he remembered her sullen opposition to his marriage. Some slighting phrases she had used still rankled in his memory; once she had spoken of Gretta as being country cute and that was not true of Gretta at all. It was Gretta who had nursed her during all her last long illness in their house at Monkstown.

He knew that Mary Jane must be near the end of her piece, for she was playing again the opening melody with runs of scales after every bar, and while he waited for the end the resentment died down in his heart. The piece ended with a trill of octaves in the treble and a final deep octave in the bass. Great applause greeted Mary Jane as, blushing and rolling up her music nervously, she escaped from the room. The most vigorous clapping came from the four young men in the doorway who had gone away to the refreshment-room at the beginning of the piece but had come back when the piano had stopped.

Lancers were arranged. Gabriel found himself partnered

with Miss Ivors. She was a frank-mannered, talkative young lady, with a freckled face and prominent brown eyes. She did not wear a low-cut bodice, and the large brooch which was fixed in the front of her collar bore on it an Irish device and motto.

When they had taken their places she said abruptly

'I have a crow to pluck with you.'

'With me?' said Gabriel.

She nodded her head gravely.

'What is it?' asked Gabriel, smiling at her solemn manner.

'Who is G. C.?' answered Miss Ivor, turning her eyes upon him.

Gabriel coloured and was about to knit his brows, as if he did not understand, when she said bluntly:

'O, innocent Amy! I have found out that you write for the *Daily Express*. Now, aren't you ashamed of yourself?'

'Why should I be ashamed of myself?' asked Gabriel, blinking his eyes and trying to smile.

'Well, I'm ashamed of you,' said Miss Ivors frankly. 'To say you'd write for a paper like that. I didn't think you were a West Briton.'

A look of perplexity appeared on Gabriel's face. It was true that he wrote a literary column every Wednesday in the *Daily Express*, for which he was paid fifteen shillings. But that did not make him a West Briton surely. The books he received for review were almost more welcome than the paltry cheque. He loved to feel the covers and turn over the pages of newly printed books. Nearly every day when his teaching in the college was ended he used to wander down the quays to the second-hand booksellers, to Hickey's on Bachelor's Walk, to Webb's or Massey's on Aston's Quay, or to O'Clohissey's in the by-street. He did not know how to meet her charge. He wanted to say that literature was above politics. But they were friends of many years' standing and their careers had been parallel, first at the University and then as teachers: he could not risk a grandiose phrase with her. He continued blinking his eyes and trying to smile and murmured lamely that he saw nothing political in writing reviews of books.

When their turn to cross had come he was still perplexed and inattentive. Miss Ivors promptly took his hand in a warm grasp and said in a soft friendly tone:

'Of course, I was only joking. Come, we cross now.'

When they were together again she spoke of the University question and Gabriel felt more at ease. A friend of hers had shown her his review of Browning's poems. That was how she had found out the secret: but she liked the review immensely. Then she said suddenly:

'O, Mr Conroy, will you come for an excursion to the Aran Isles this summer? We're going to stay there a whole month. It will be splendid out in the Atlantic. You ought to come. Mr Clancy is coming, and Mr Kilkelly and Kathleen Kearney. It would be splendid for Gretta too if she'd come. She's from Connacht, isn't she?'

'Her people are,' said Gabriel shortly.

'But you will come, won't you?' said Miss Ivors, laying her warm hand eagerly on his arm.

'The fact is,' said Gabriel, 'I have just arranged to go –'

'Go where?' asked Miss Ivors.

'Well, you know, every year I go for a cycling tour with some fellows and so –'

'But where?' asked Miss Ivors.

'Well, we usually go to France or Belgium or perhaps Germany,' said Gabriel awkwardly.

'And why do you go to France and Belgium,' said Miss Ivors, 'instead of visiting your own land?'

'Well,' said Gabriel, 'it's partly to keep in touch with the languages and partly for a change.'

'And haven't you your own language to keep in touch with – Irish?' asked Miss Ivors.

'Well,' said Gabriel, 'if it comes to that, you know, Irish is not my language.'

Their neighbours had turned to listen to the cross-examination. Gabriel glanced right and left nervously and tried to keep his good humour under the ordeal, which was making a blush invade his forehead.

'And haven't you your own land to visit,' continued Miss

Ivors, 'that you know nothing of, your own people, and your own country?'

'O, to tell you the truth,' retorted Gabriel suddenly, 'I'm sick of my own country, sick of it!'

'Why?' asked Miss Ivors.

Gabriel did not answer, for his retort had heated him.

'Why?' repeated Miss Ivors.

They had to go visiting together and, as he had not answered her, Miss Ivors said warmly:

'Of course, you've no answer.'

Gabriel tried to cover his agitation by taking part in the dance with great energy. He avoided her eyes, for he had seen a sour expression on her face. But when they met in the long chain he was surprised to feel his hand firmly pressed. She looked at him from under her brows for a moment quizzically until he smiled. Then, just as the chain was about to start again, she stood on tiptoe and whispered into his ear:

'West Briton!'

When the lancers were over Gabriel went away to a remote corner of the room where Freddy Malins's mother was sitting. She was a stout, feeble old woman with white hair. Her voice had a catch in it like her son's and she stuttered slightly. She had been told that Freddy had come and that he was nearly all right. Gabriel asked her whether she had had a good crossing. She lived with her married daughter in Glasgow and came to Dublin on a visit once a year. She answered placidly that she had had a beautiful crossing and that the captain had been most attentive to her. She spoke also of the beautiful house her daughter kept in Glasgow, and of all the friends they had there. While her tongue rambled on Gabriel tried to banish from his mind all memory of the unpleasant incident with Miss Ivors. Of course the girl, or woman, or whatever she was, was an enthusiast, but there was a time for all things. Perhaps he ought not to have answered her like that. But she had no right to call him a West Briton before people, even in joke. She had tried to make him ridiculous before people, heckling him and staring at him with her rabbit's eyes.

He saw his wife making her way towards him through the

waltzing couples. When she reached him she said into his ear:

'Gabriel, Aunt Kate wants to know won't you carve the goose as usual. Miss Daly will carve the ham and I'll do the pudding.'

'All right,' said Gabriel.

'She's sending in the younger ones first as soon as this waltz is over so that we'll have the table to ourselves.'

'Were you dancing?' asked Gabriel.

'Of course I was. Didn't you see me? What row had you with Molly Ivors?'

'No row. Why? Did she say so?'

'Something like that. I'm trying to get that Mr D'Arcy to sing. He's full of conceit, I think.'

'There was no row,' said Gabriel moodily, 'only she wanted me to go for a trip to the west of Ireland and I said I wouldn't.'

His wife clasped her hands excitedly and gave a little jump.

'O, do go, Gabriel,' she cried. 'I'd love to see Galway again.'

'You can go if you like,' said Gabriel coldly.

She looked at him for a moment, then turned to Mrs Malins and said:

'There's a nice husband for you, Mrs Malins.'

While she was threading her way back across the room Mrs Malins, without adverting to the interruption, went on to tell Gabriel what beautiful places there were in Scotland and beautiful scenery. Her son-in-law brought them every year to the lakes and they used to go fishing. Her son-in-law was a splendid fisher. One day he caught a beautiful big fish and the man in the hotel cooked it for their dinner.

Gabriel hardly heard what she said. Now that supper was coming near he began to think again about his speech and about the quotation. When he saw Freddy Malins coming across the room to visit his mother Gabriel left the chair free for him and retired into the embrasure of the window. The room had already cleared and from the back room came the clatter of plates and knives. Those who still remained in the drawing-room seemed tired of dancing and were conversing quietly in little groups. Gabriel's warm, trembling fingers tapped the cold pane of the window. How cool it must be outside! How pleasant it would be to walk out alone, first along by the river and then through the park! The snow would be lying on the branches of the trees and forming a bright cap on the top of the Wellington Monument. How much more pleasant it would be there than at the supper-table!

He ran over the headings of his speech: Irish hospitality, sad memories, the Three Graces, Paris, the quotation from Browning. He repeated to himself a phrase he had written in his review: 'One feels that one is listening to a thought-tormented music.' Miss Ivors had praised the review. Was she sincere? Had she really any life of her own behind all her propagandism? There had never been any ill-feeling between them until that night. It unnerved him to think that she would be at the supper-table, looking up at him, while he spoke, with her critical quizzing eyes. Perhaps she would not be sorry to see him fail in his speech. An idea came into his mind and gave him courage. He would say, alluding to Aunt Kate and Aunt Julia: 'Ladies and Gentlemen, the generation which is now on the wane among us may have had its faults, but for my part I think it had certain qualities of hospitality, of humour, of humanity, which the new and very serious and hyper-educated generation that is growing up around us seems to me to lack.' Very good: that was one for Miss Ivors. What did he care that his aunts were only two ignorant old women?

A murmur in the room attracted his attention. Mr Browne was advancing from the door, gallantly escorting Aunt Julia, who leaned upon his arm, smiling and hanging her head. An irregular musketry of applause escorted her also as far as the piano and then, as Mary Jane seated herself on the stool, and Aunt Julia, no longer smiling, half turned so as to pitch her voice fairly into the room, gradually ceased. Gabriel recognized the prelude. It was that of an old song of Aunt Julia's – 'Arrayed for the Bridal'. Her voice, strong and clear in tone, attacked with great spirit the runs which embellish the air, and though she sang very rapidly she did not miss even the smallest of the grace notes. To follow the voice, without looking at the singer's face, was to feel and share the excitement of swift and secure flight. Gabriel applauded loudly with all the others at the close of the song, and loud applause was borne in from the invisible supper-table. It sounded so genuine that a little colour struggled into Aunt Julia's face as she bent to replace in the music-stand the old leather-bound song-book that had her initials on the cover. Freddy Malins, who had listened with his head perched sideways to hear her better, was still applauding when everyone else had ceased and talking animatedly to his mother, who nodded her head gravely and slowly in acquiescence. At last, when he could clap no more, he stood up suddenly and hurried across the room to Aunt Julia whose hand he seized and held in both his hands, shaking it when words failed him or the catch in his voice proved too much for him.

'I was just telling my mother,' he said, 'I never heard you sing so well, never. No, I never heard your voice so good as it is tonight. Now! Would you believe that now? That's the truth. Upon my word and honour that's the truth. I never heard your voice sound so fresh and so . . . so clear and fresh, never.'

Aunt Julia smiled broadly and murmured something about compliments as she released her hand from his grasp. Mr Browne extended his open hand towards her and said to those who were near him in the manner of a showman introducing a prodigy to an audience:

'Miss Julia Morkan, my latest discovery!'

He was laughing very heartily at this himself when Freddy Malins turned to him and said:

'Well, Browne, if you're serious you might make a worse discovery. All I can say is I never heard her sing half so well as long as I am coming here. And that's the honest truth.'

'Neither did I,' said Mr Browne. 'I think her voice has greatly improved.'

Aunt Julia shrugged her shoulders and said with meek pride:

'Thirty years ago I hadn't a bad voice as voices go.'

'I often told Julia,' said Aunt Kate emphatically, 'that she was simply thrown away in that choir. But she never would be said by me.'

She turned as if to appeal to the good sense of the others

against a refractory child, while Aunt Julia gazed in front of her, a vague smile of reminiscence playing on her face.

'No,' continued Aunt Kate, 'she wouldn't be said or led by anyone, slaving there in that choir night and day, night and day. Six o'clock on Christmas morning! And all for what?'

'Well, isn't it for the honour of God, Aunt Kate?' asked Mary Jane, twisting round on the piano-stool and smiling.

Aunt Kate turned fiercely on her niece and said:

'I know all about the honour of God, Mary Jane, but I think it's not at all honourable for the Pope to turn out the women out of the choirs that have slaved there all their lives and put little whipper-snappers of boys over their heads. I suppose it is for the good of the Church, if the Pope does it. But it's not just, Mary Jane, and it's not right.'

She had worked herself into a passion and would have continued in defence of her sister, for it was a sore subject with her, but Mary Jane, seeing that all the dancers had come back, intervened pacifically.

'Now, Aunt Kate, you're giving scandal to Mr Browne, who is of the other persuasion.'

Aunt Kate turned to Mr Browne, who was grinning at this allusion to his religion, and said hastily:

'O, I don't question the Pope's being right. I'm only a stupid old woman and I wouldn't presume to do such a thing. But there's such a thing as common everyday politeness and gratitude. And if I were in Julia's place I'd tell that Father Healey straight up to his face . . .'

'And besides, Aunt Kate,' said Mary Jane, 'we really are all hungry and when we are hungry we are all very quarrelsome.'

'And when we are thirsty we are also quarrelsome,' added Mr Browne.

'So that we had better go to supper,' said Mary Jane, 'and finish the discussion afterwards.'

On the landing outside the drawing-room Gabriel found his wife and Mary Jane trying to persuade Miss Ivors to stay for supper. But Miss Ivors, who had put on her hat and was buttoning her cloak, would not stay. She did not feel in the least hungry and she had already overstayed her time.

'But only for ten minutes, Molly,' said Mrs Conroy. 'That won't delay you.'

'To take a pick itself,' said Mary Jane, 'after all your dancing.'

'I really couldn't,' said Miss Ivors.

'I am afraid you didn't enjoy yourself at all,' said Mary Jane hopelessly.

'Ever so much, I assure you,' said Miss Ivors, 'but you really must let me run off now.'

'But how can you get home?' asked Mrs Conroy.

'O, it's only two steps up the quay.'

Gabriel hesitated a moment and said:

'If you will allow me, Miss Ivors, I'll see you home if you are really obliged to go.'

But Miss Ivors broke away from them.

'I won't hear of it,' she cried. 'For goodness' sake go in to your suppers and don't mind me. I'm quite well able to take care of myself.'

'Well, you're the comical girl, Molly,' said Mrs Conroy frankly.

'*Beannacht libh*,' cried Miss Ivors, with a laugh, as she ran down the staircase.

Mary Jane gazed after her, a moody puzzled expression on her face, while Mrs Conroy leaned over the banisters to listen for the hall-door. Gabriel asked himself was he the cause of her abrupt departure. But she did not seem to be in ill humour – she had gone away laughing. He stared blankly down the staircase.

At the moment Aunt Kate came toddling out of the supper-room, almost wringing her hands in despair.

'Where is Gabriel?' she cried. 'Where on earth is Gabriel? There's everyone waiting in there, stage to let, and nobody to carve the goose!'

'Here I am, Aunt Kate!' cried Gabriel, with sudden animation, 'ready to carve a flock of geese, if necessary.'

A fat brown goose lay at one end of the table, and at the other end, on a bed of creased paper strewn with sprigs of parsley, lay a great ham, stripped of its outer skin and peppered over with crust crumbs, a neat paper frill round its shin, and beside this was a round of spiced beef. Between these rival ends ran parallel lines of side-dishes: two little minsters of jelly, red and yellow; a shallow dish full of blocks of blancmange and red jam, a large green leaf-shaped dish with a stalk-shaped handle, on which lay bunches of purple raisins and peeled almonds, a companion dish on which lay a solid rectangle of Smyrna figs, a dish of custard topped with grated nutmeg, a small bowl full of chocolates and sweets wrapped in gold and silver papers and a glass vase in which stood some tall celery stalks. In the centre of the table there stood, as sentries to a fruit-stand which upheld a pyramid of oranges and American apples, two squat old-fashioned decanters of cut glass, one containing port and the other dark sherry. On the closed square piano a pudding in a huge yellow dish lay in waiting, and behind it were three squads of bottles of stout and ale and minerals drawn up according to the colours of their uniforms, the first two black, with brown and red labels, the third and smallest squad white, with transverse green sashes.

Gabriel took his seat boldly at the head of the table and, having looked to the edge of the carver, plunged his fork firmly into the goose. He felt quite at ease now, for he was an expert carver and liked nothing better than to find himself at the head of a well-laden table.

'Miss Furlong, what shall I send you?' he asked. 'A wing or a slice of the breast?'

'Just a small slice of the breast.'

'Miss Higgins, what for you?'

'O, anything at all, Mr Conroy.'

While Gabriel and Miss Daly exchanged plates of goose and plates of ham and spiced beef, Lily went from guest to guest with a dish of hot floury potatoes wrapped in a white napkin. This was Mary Jane's idea and she had also suggested apple sauce for the goose, but Aunt Kate had said that plain roast goose without any apple sauce had always been good enough for her and she hoped she might never eat worse. Mary Jane waited on her pupils and saw that they got the best slices, and Aunt Kate and Aunt Julia opened and carried across from the piano bottles of stout and ale for the gentlemen and bottles of minerals for the ladies. There was a great deal of confusion and laughter and noise, the noise of orders and counter-orders, of knives and forks, of corks and glass-stoppers. Gabriel began to carve second helpings as soon as he had finished the first round without serving himself. Everyone protested loudly, so that he compromised by taking a long draught of stout, for he had found the carving hot work. Mary Jane settled down quietly to her supper, but Aunt Kate and Aunt Julia were still toddling round the table, walking on each other's heels, getting in each other's way and giving each other unheeded orders. Mr Browne begged of them to sit down and eat their suppers and so did Gabriel, but they said there was time enough, so that, at last, Freddy Malins stood up and, capturing Aunt Kate, plumped her down on her chair amid general laughter.

When everyone had been well served Gabriel said, smiling:

'Now, if anyone wants a little more of what vulgar people call stuffing let him or her speak.'

A chorus of voices invited him to begin his own supper, and Lily came forward with three potatoes which she had reserved for him.

'Very well,' said Gabriel amiably, as he took another preparatory draught, 'kindly forget my existence, ladies and gentlemen, for a few minutes.'

He set to his supper and took no part in the conversation with which the table covered Lily's removal of the plates. The subject of talk was the opera company which was then at the Theatre Royal. Mr Bartell D'Arcy, the tenor, a dark-complexioned young man with a smart moustache, praised very highly the leading contralto of the company, but Miss Furlong thought she had a rather vulgar style of production. Freddy Malins said there was a Negro chieftain singing in the second part of the Gaiety pantomime who had one of the finest tenor voices he had ever heard.

'Have you heard him?' he asked Mr Bartell D'Arcy across the table.

'No,' answered Mr Bartell D'Arcy carelessly.

'Because,' Freddy Malins explained, 'now I'd be curious to hear your opinion of him. I think he has a grand voice.'

'It takes Teddy to find out the really good things,' said Mr Browne familiarly to the table.

'And why couldn't he have a voice too?' asked Freddy Malins sharply. 'Is it because he's only a black?'

Nobody answered this question and Mary Jane led the table back to the legitimate opera. One of her pupils had given her a pass for *Mignon*. Of course it was very fine, she said, but it made her think of poor Georgina Burns. Mr Browne could go back farther still, to the old Italian companies that used to come to Dublin – Tietjens, Ilma de Murzka, Campanini, the great Trebelli, Giuglini, Ravelli, Aramburo. Those were the days, he said, when there was something like singing to be heard in Dublin. He told too of how the top gallery of the old Royal used to be packed night after night, of how one night an Italian tenor had sung five encores to 'Let me like a Soldier fall', introducing a high C every time, and of how the gallery boys would sometimes in their enthusiasm unyoke the horses from the carriage of some great *prima donna* and pull her themselves through the streets to her hotel. Why did they never play the grand old operas now, he asked, *Dinorah, Lucrezia Borgia*? Because they could not get the voices to sing them: that was why.

'O, well,' said Mr Bartell D'Arcy, 'I presume there are as good singers today as there were then.'

'Where are they?' asked Mr Browne defiantly.

'In London, Paris, Milan,' said Mr Bartell D'Arcy warmly. 'I suppose Caruso, for example, is quite as good, if not better than any of the men you have mentioned.'

'Maybe so,' said Mr Browne. 'But I may tell you I doubt it strongly.'

'O, I'd give anything to hear Caruso sing,' said Mary Jane.

'For me,' said Aunt Kate, who had been picking a bone, 'there was only one tenor. To please me, I mean. But I suppose none of you ever heard of him.'

'Who was he, Miss Morkan?' asked Mr Bartell D'Arcy politely.

'His name,' said Aunt Kate, 'was Parkinson. I heard him

when he was in his prime and I think he had then the purest tenor voice that was ever put into a man's throat.'

'Strange,' said Mr Bartell D'Arcy. 'I never even heard of him.'

'Yes, yes, Miss Morkan is right,' said Mr Browne. 'I remember hearing old Parkinson, but he's too far back for me.'

'A beautiful, pure, sweet, mellow English tenor,' said Aunt Kate with enthusiasm.

Gabriel having finished, the huge pudding was transferred to the table. The clatter of forks and spoons began again. Gabriel's wife served out spoonfuls of the pudding and passed the plates down the table. Midway down they were held up by Mary Jane, who replenished them with raspberry or orange jelly or with blancmange and jam. The pudding was of Aunt Julia's making, and she received praises for it from all quarters. She herself said that it was not quite brown enough.

'Well, I hope, Miss Morkan,' said Mr Browne, 'that I'm brown enough for you because, you know, I'm all Brown.'

All the gentlemen, except Gabriel, ate some of the pudding out of compliment to Aunt Julia. As Gabriel never ate sweets the celery had been left for him. Freddy Malins also took a stalk of celery and ate it with his pudding. He had been told that celery was a capital thing for the blood and he was just then under doctor's care. Mrs Malins, who had been silent all through the supper, said that her son was going down to Mount Melleray in a week or so. The table then spoke of Mount Melleray, how bracing the air was down there, how hospitable the monks were and how they never asked for a penny-piece from their guests.

'And do you mean to say,' asked Mr Browne incredulously, 'that a chap can go down there and put up there as if it were a hotel and live on the fat of the land and then come away without paying anything?'

'O, most people give some donation to the monastery when they leave,' said Mary Jane.

'I wish we had an institution like that in our Church,' said Mr Browne candidly.

He was astonished to hear that the monks never spoke, got up at two in the morning and slept in their coffins. He asked what they did it for.

'That's the rule of the order,' said Aunt Kate firmly.

'Yes, but why?' asked Mr Browne.

Aunt Kate repeated that it was the rule, that was all. Mr Browne still seemed not to understand. Freddy Malins explained to him, as best he could, that the monks were trying to make up for the sins committed by all the sinners in the outside world. The explanation was not very clear, for Mr Browne grinned and said:

'I like that idea very much, but wouldn't a comfortable spring bed do them as well as a coffin?'

'The coffin,' said Mary Jane, 'is to remind them of their last end.'

As the subject had grown lugubrious it was buried in a silence of the table, during which Mrs Malins could be heard saying to her neighbour in an indistinct undertone:

'They are very good men, the monks, very pious men.'

The raisins and almonds and figs and apples and oranges and chocolates and sweets were now passed about the table, and Aunt Julia invited all the guests to have either port or sherry. At first Mr Bartell D'Arcy refused to take either, but one of his neighbours nudged him and whispered something to him, upon which he allowed his glass to be filled. Gradually as the last glasses were being filled the conversation ceased. A pause followed, broken only by the noise of the wine and by unsettling of chairs. The Misses Morkan, all three, looked down at the tablecloth. Someone coughed once or twice, and then a few gentlemen patted the table gently as a signal for silence. The silence came and Gabriel pushed back his chair and stood up.

The patting at once grew louder in encouragement and then ceased altogether. Gabriel leaned his ten trembling fingers on the tablecloth and smiled nervously at the company. Meeting a row of upturned faces he raised his eyes to the chandelier. The piano was playing a waltz tune and he could hear the skirts sweeping against the drawing-room door. People, perhaps, were standing in the snow on the quay outside, gazing up at the lighted windows and listening to the waltz music. The air was pure there. In the distance lay the park, where the trees were weighted with snow. The Wellington Monument wore a gleaming cap of snow that flashed westwards over the white field of Fifteen Acres.

He began:

'Ladies and Gentlemen,

'It has fallen to my lot this evening, as in years past, to perform a very pleasing task, but a task for which I am afraid my poor powers as a speaker are all too inadequate.'

'No, no!' said Mr Browne.

'But however that may be, I can only ask you tonight to take the will for the deed, and to lend me your attention for a few moments while I endeavour to express to you in words what my feelings are on this occasion.

'Ladies and Gentlemen, it is not the first time that we have gathered together under this hospitable roof, around this hospitable board. It is not the first time that we have been the recipients – or perhaps, I had better say, the victims – of the hospitality of certain good ladies.'

He made a circle in the air with his arm and paused. Everyone laughed or smiled at Aunt Kate and Aunt Julia and Mary Jane, who all turned crimson with pleasure. Gabriel went on more boldly:

'I feel more strongly with every recurring year that our country has no tradition which does it so much honour and which it should guard so jealously as that of its hospitality. It is a tradition that is unique as far as my experience goes (and I have visited not a few places abroad) among the modern nations. Some would say, perhaps, that with us it is rather a failing than anything to be boasted of. But granted even that, it is, to my mind, a princely failing, and one that I trust will long be cultivated among us. Of one thing, at least, I am sure. As long as this one roof shelters the good ladies aforesaid – and I wish from my heart it may do so for many and many a long year to come – the tradition of genuine warm-hearted courteous Irish hospitality, which our forefathers have handed down to us and which we must hand down to our descendants, is still alive among us.'

A hearty murmur of assent ran round the table. It shot through Gabriel's mind that Miss Ivors was not there and that she had gone away discourteously: and he said with confidence in himself:

'Ladies and Gentlemen,

'A new generation is growing up in our midst, a generation actuated by new ideas and new principles. It is serious and enthusiastic for these new ideas and its enthusiasm, even when it is misdirected, is, I believe, in the main sincere. But we are living in a sceptical and, if I may use the phrase, a thought-tormented age: and sometimes I fear that this new generation, educated or hyper-educated as it is, will lack those qualities of humanity, of hospitality, of kindly humour which belonged to an older day. Listening tonight to the names of all those great singers of the past it seemed to me, I must confess, that we were living in a less spacious age. Those days might, without exaggeration, be called spacious days: and if they are gone beyond recall, let us hope, at least, that in gatherings such as this we shall still speak of them with pride and affection, still cherish in our hearts the memory of those dead and gone great ones whose fame the world will not willingly let die.'

'Hear, hear!' said Mr Browne loudly.

'But yet,' continued Gabriel, his voice falling into a softer inflection, 'there are always in gatherings such as this sadder thoughts that will recur to our minds: thoughts of the past, of youth, of changes, of absent faces that we miss here tonight. Our path through life is strewn with many such sad memories: and were we to brood upon them always we could not find the heart to go on bravely with our work among the living. We have all of us living duties and living affections which claim, and rightly claim, our strenuous endeavours.

'Therefore, I will not linger on the past. I will not let any gloomy moralizing intrude upon us here tonight. Here we are gathered together for a brief moment from the bustle and rush of our everyday routine. We are met here as friends, in the spirit of good-fellowship, as colleagues, also, to a certain extent, in the true spirit of *camaraderie*, and as the guests of –

what shall I call them? – the Three Graces of the Dublin musical world.'

The table burst into applause and laughter at this allusion. Aunt Julia vainly asked each of her neighbours in turn to tell her what Gabriel had said.

'He says we are the Three Graces, Aunt Julia,' said Mary Jane.

Aunt Julia did not understand, but she looked up, smiling, at Gabriel, who continued in the same vein:

'Ladies and Gentlemen,

'I will not attempt to play tonight the part that Paris played on another occasion. I will not attempt to choose between them. The task would be an invidious one and one beyond my poor powers. For when I view them in turn, whether it be our chief hostess herself, whose good heart, whose too good heart, has become a byword with all who know her; or her sister, who seems to be gifted with perennial youth and whose singing must have been a surprise and a revelation to us all tonight; or, last but not least, when I consider our youngest hostess, talented, cheerful, hard-working and the best of nieces, I confess, Ladies and Gentlemen, that I do not know to which of them I should award the prize.'

Gabriel glanced down at his aunts and, seeing the large smile on Aunt Julia's face and the tears which had risen to Aunt Kate's eyes, hastened to his close. He raised his glass of port gallantly, while every member of the company fingered a glass expectantly, and said loudly:

'Let us toast them all three together. Let us drink to their health, wealth, long life, happiness, and prosperity and may they long continue to hold the proud and self-won position which they hold in their profession and the position of honour and affection which they hold in our hearts.'

All the guests stood up, glass in hand, and turning towards the three seated ladies, sang in unison, with Mr Browne as leader:

> 'For they are jolly gay fellows,
> For they are jolly gay fellows,
> For they are jolly gay fellows,
> Which nobody can deny.'

Aunt Kate was making frank use of her handkerchief and even Aunt Julia seemed moved. Freddy Malins beat time with his pudding-fork and the singers turned towards one another, as if in melodious conference, while they sang with emphasis:

> 'Unless he tells a lie,
> Unless he tells a lie.'

Then, turning once more towards their hostesses, they sang:

> 'For they are jolly gay fellows,
> For they are jolly gay fellows,
> For they are jolly gay fellows,
> Which nobody can deny.'

The acclamation which followed was taken up beyond the door of the supper room by many of the other guests and renewed time after time, Freddy Malins acting as officer with his fork on high.

The piercing morning air came into the hall where they were standing so that Aunt Kate said:

'Close the door, somebody. Mrs Malins will get her death of cold.'

'Browne is out there, Aunt Kate,' said Mary Jane.

'Browne is everywhere,' said Aunt Kate, lowering her voice. Mary Jane laughed at her tone.

'Really,' she said archly, 'he is very attentive.'

'He has been laid on here like the gas,' said Aunt Kate in the same tone, 'all during the Christmas.'

She laughed herself this time good-humouredly and then added quickly:

'But tell him to come in, Mary Jane, and close the door. I hope to goodness he didn't hear me.'

At that moment the hall-door was opened and Mr Browne came in from the doorstep, laughing as if his heart would break. He was dressed in a long green overcoat with mock astrakhan cuffs and collar and wore on his head an oval fur cap. He pointed down the snow-covered quay from where the sound of shrill prolonged whistling was borne in.

'Teddy will have all the cabs in Dublin out,' he said.

Gabriel advanced from the little pantry behind the office, struggling into his overcoat and, looking round the hall, said:

'Gretta not down yet?'

'She's getting on her things, Gabriel,' said Aunt Kate.

'Who's playing up there?' asked Gabriel.

'Nobody. They're all gone.'

'O no, Aunt Kate,' said Mary Jane. 'Bartell D'Arcy and Miss O'Callaghan aren't gone yet.'

'Someone is fooling at the piano anyhow,' said Gabriel.

Mary Jane glanced at Gabriel and Mr Browne and said with a shiver:

'It makes me feel cold to look at you two gentlemen muffled up like that. I wouldn't like to face your journey home at this hour.'

'I'd like nothing better this minute,' said Mr Browne stoutly, 'than a rattling fine walk in the country or a fast drive with a good spanking goer between the shafts.'

'We used to have a very good horse and trap at home,' said Aunt Julia, sadly.

'The never-to-be-forgotten Johnny,' said Mary Jane, laughing.

Aunt Kate and Gabriel laughed too.

'Why, what was wonderful about Johnny?' asked Mr Browne.

'The late lamented Patrick Morkan, our grandfather, that is,' explained Gabriel, 'commonly known in his later years as the old gentleman, was a glue-boiler.'

'O, now, Gabriel,' said Aunt Kate, laughing, 'he had a starch mill.'

'Well, glue or starch,' said Gabriel, 'the old gentleman had a horse by the name of Johnny. And Johnny used to work in the old gentleman's mill, walking round and round in order to drive the mill. That was all very well; but now comes the tragic part about Johnny. One fine day the old gentleman thought he'd like to drive out with the quality to a military review in the park.'

'The Lord have mercy on his soul,' said Aunt Kate, compassionately.

'Amen,' said Gabriel. 'So the old gentleman, as I said, harnessed Johnny and put on his very best tall hat and his very best stock collar and drove out in grand style from his ancestral mansion somewhere near Back Lane, I think.'

Everyone laughed, even Mrs Malins, at Gabriel's manner, and Aunt Kate said:

'O, now, Gabriel, he didn't live in Back Lane, really. Only the mill was there.'

'Out from the mansion of his forefathers,' continued Gabriel, 'he drove with Johnny. And everything went on beautifully until Johnny came in sight of King Billy's statue: and whether he fell in love with the horse King Billy sits on or whether he thought he was back again in the mill, anyway he began to walk round the statue.'

Gabriel paced in a circle round the hall in his goloshes amid the laughter of the others.

'Round and round he went,' said Gabriel, 'and the old gentleman, who was a very pompous old gentleman, was highly indignant. "Go on, sir! What do you mean, sir? Johnny! Johnny! Most extraordinary conduct! Can't understand the horse!"'

The peals of laughter which followed Gabriel's imitation of the incident were interrupted by a resounding knock at the hall door. Mary Jane ran to open it and let in Freddy Malins. Freddy Malins, with his hat well back on his head and his shoulders humped with cold, was puffing and steaming after his exertions.

'I could only get one cab,' he said.

'O, we'll find another along the quay,' said Gabriel.

'Yes,' said Aunt Kate. 'Better not keep Mrs Malins standing in the draught.'

Mrs Malins was helped down the front steps by her son and Mr Browne and, after many manoeuvres, hoisted into the cab. Freddy Malins clambered in after her and spent a long time settling her on the seat, Mr Browne helping him with advice. At last she was settled comfortably and Freddy Malins invited Mr Browne into the cab. There was a good deal of confused talk, and then Mr Browne got into the cab. The cabman settled his rug over his knees, and bent down for the address. The confusion grew greater and the cabman was directed differently by Freddy Malins and Mr Browne, each of whom had his head out through a window of the cab. The difficulty was to know where to drop Mr Browne along the route, and Aunt Kate, Aunt Julia, and Mary Jane helped the discussion from the doorstep with cross-directions and contradictions and abundance of laughter. As for Freddy Malins he was speechless with laughter. He popped his head in and out of the window every moment to the great danger of his hat, and told his mother how the discussion was progressing, till at last Mr Browne shouted to the bewildered cabman above the din of everybody's laughter:

'Do you know Trinity College?'

'Yes, sir,' said the cabman.

'Well, drive bang up against Trinity College gates,' said Mr Browne, 'and then we'll tell you where to go. You understand now?'

'Yes, sir,' said the cabman.

'Make like a bird for Trinity College.'

'Right, sir,' said the cabman.

The horse was whipped up and the cab rattled off along the quay amid a chorus of laughter and adieux.

Gabriel had not gone to the door with the others. He was in a dark part of the hall gazing up the staircase. A woman was standing near the top of the first flight, in the shadow also. He could not see her face but he could see the terra-cotta and salmon-pink panels of her skirt which the shadow made appear black and white. It was his wife. She was leaning on the banisters, listening to something. Gabriel was surprised at her stillness and strained his ear to listen also. But he could hear little save the noise of laughter and dispute on the front steps, a few chords struck on the piano and a few notes of a man's voice singing.

He stood still in the gloom of the hall, trying to catch the air that the voice was singing and gazing up at his wife. There was grace and mystery in her attitude as if she were a symbol of something. He asked himself what is a woman standing on the stairs in the shadow, listening to distant music, a symbol of. If he were a painter he would paint her in that attitude. Her blue felt hat would show off the bronze of her hair against the darkness and the dark panels of her skirt would show off the light ones. *Distant Music* he would call the picture if he were a painter.

The hall-door was closed, and Aunt Kate, Aunt Julia, and Mary Jane came down the hall, still laughing.

'Well, isn't Freddy terrible?' said Mary Jane. 'He's really terrible.'

Gabriel said nothing, but pointed up the stairs towards where his wife was standing. Now that the hall-door was closed the voice and the piano could be heard more clearly. Gabriel held up his hand for them to be silent. The song seemed to be in the old Irish tonality and the singer seemed uncertain both of his words and of his voice. The voice, made plaintive by distance and by the singer's hoarseness, faintly illuminated the cadence of the air with words expressing grief:

> O, the rain falls on my heavy locks
> And the dew wets my skin,
> My babe lies cold . . .

'O,' exclaimed Mary Jane. 'It's Bartell D'Arcy singing, and he wouldn't sing all the night. O, I'll get him to sing a song before he goes.'

'O, do, Mary Jane,' said Aunt Kate.

Mary Jane brushed past the others and ran to the staircase, but before she reached it the singing stopped and the piano was closed abruptly.

'Oh, what a pity!' she cried. 'Is he coming down, Gretta?'

Gabriel heard his wife answer yes and saw her come down towards them. A few steps behind her were Mr Bartell D'Arcy and Miss O'Callaghan.

'O, Mr D'Arcy,' cried Mary Jane, 'it's downright mean of you to break off like that when we were all in raptures listening to you.'

'I have been at him all the evening,' said Miss O'Callaghan, 'and Mrs Conroy, too, and he told us he had a dreadful cold and couldn't sing.'

'O, Mr D'Arcy,' said Aunt Kate, 'now that was a great fib to tell.'

'Can't you see that I'm as hoarse as a crow?' said Mr D'Arcy roughly.

He went into the pantry hastily and put on his overcoat. The others, taken back by his rude speech, could find nothing to say. Aunt Kate wrinkled her brows and made signs to the others to drop the subject. Mr D'Arcy stood swathing his neck carefully and frowning.

'It's the weather,' said Aunt Julia, after a pause.

'Yes, everybody has colds,' said Aunt Kate readily, 'everybody.'

'They say,' said Mary Jane, 'we haven't had snow like it for thirty years, and I read this morning in the newspapers that the snow is general all over Ireland.'

'I love the look of snow,' said Aunt Julia sadly.

'So do I,' said Miss O'Callaghan. 'I think Christmas is never really Christmas unless we have the snow on the ground.'

'But poor Mr D'Arcy doesn't like the snow,' said Aunt Kate, smiling.

Mr D'Arcy came from the pantry, fully swathed and buttoned, and in a repentant tone told them the history of his cold. Everyone gave him advice and said it was a great pity and urged him to be very careful of his throat in the night air. Gabriel watched his wife, who did not join in the conversation. She was standing right under the dusty fanlight and the flame of the gas lit up the rich bronze of her hair, which he had seen her drying at the fire a few days before. She was in the same attitude and seemed unaware of the talk about her. At last she turned towards them and Gabriel saw that there was colour on her cheeks and that her eyes were shining. A sudden tide of joy went leaping out of his heart.

'Mr D'Arcy,' she said, 'what is the name of that song you were singing?'

'It's called "The Lass of Aughrim",' said Mr D'Arcy, 'but

I couldn't remember it properly. Why? Do you know it?'

' "The Lass of Aughrim",' she repeated. 'I couldn't think of the name.'

'It's a very nice air,' said Mary Jane. 'I'm sorry you were not in voice tonight.'

'Now, Mary Jane,' said Aunt Kate, 'don't annoy Mr D'Arcy. I won't have him annoyed.'

Seeing that all were ready to start she shepherded them to the door, where good night was said:

'Well, good night, Aunt Kate, and thanks for the pleasant evening.'

'Good night, Gabriel. Good night, Gretta!'

'Good night, Aunt Kate, and thanks ever so much. Good night, Aunt Julia.'

'O, good night, Gretta, I didn't see you.'

'Good night, Mr D'Arcy. Good night, Miss O'Callaghan.'

'Good night, Miss Morkan.'

'Good night, again.'

'Good night, all. Safe home.'

'Good night. Good night.'

The morning was still dark. A dull, yellow light brooded over the houses and the river; and the sky seemed to be descending. It was slushy underfoot, and only streaks and patches of snow lay on the roofs, on the parapets of the quay and on the area railings. The lamps were still burning redly in the murky air and, across the river, the palace of the Four Courts stood out menacingly against the heavy sky.

She was walking on before him with Mr Bartell D'Arcy, her shoes in a brown parcel tucked under one arm and her hands holding her skirt up from the slush. She had no longer any grace of attitude, but Gabriel's eyes were still bright with happiness. The blood went bounding along his veins and the thoughts went rioting through his brain, proud, joyful, tender, valorous.

She was walking on before him so lightly and so erect that he longed to run after her noiselessly, catch her by the shoulders and say something foolish and affectionate into her ear. She seemed to him so frail that he longed to defend her against something and then to be alone with her. Moments of their secret life together burst like stars upon his memory. A heliotrope envelope was lying beside his breakfast-cup and he was caressing it with his hand. Birds were twittering in the ivy and the sunny web of the curtain was shimmering along the floor: he could not eat for happiness. They were standing on the crowded platform and he was placing a ticket inside the warm palm of her glove. He was standing with her in the cold, looking in through a grated window at a man making bottles in a roaring furnace. It was very cold. Her face, fragrant in the cold air, was quite close to his, and suddenly he called out to the man at the furnace:

'Is the fire hot, sir?'

But the man could not hear with the noise of the furnace. It was just as well. He might have answered rudely.

A wave of yet more tender joy escaped from his heart and went coursing in warm flood along his arteries. Like the tender fire of stars moments of their life together, that no one knew of or would ever know of, broke upon and illumined his memory. He longed to recall to her those moments, to make her forget the years of their dull existence together and remember only their moments of ecstasy. For the years, he felt, had not quenched his soul or hers. Their children, his writing, her household cares had not quenched all their souls' tender fire. In one letter that he had written to her then he had said: 'Why is it that words like these seem to me so dull and cold? Is it because there is no word tender enough to be your name?'

Like distant music these words that he had written years before were borne towards him from the past. He longed to be alone with her. When the others had gone away, when he and she were in the room in their hotel, then they would be alone together. He would call her softly:

'Gretta!'

Perhaps she would not hear at once: she would be undressing. Then something in his voice would strike her. She would turn and look at him . . .

At the corner of Winetavern Street they met a cab. He was

glad of its rattling noise as it saved him from conversation. She was looking out of the window and seemed tired. The others spoke only a few words, pointing out some building or street. The horse galloped along wearily under the murky morning sky, dragging his old rattling box after his heels, and Gabriel was again in a cab with her, galloping to catch the boat, galloping to their honeymoon.

As the cab drove across O'Connell Bridge Miss O'Callaghan said:

'They say you never cross O'Connell Bridge without seeing a white horse.'

'I see a white man this time,' said Gabriel.

'Where?' asked Mr Bartell D'Arcy.

Gabriel pointed to the statue, on which lay patches of snow. Then he nodded familiarly to it and waved his hand.

'Good night, Dan,' he said gaily.

When the cab drew up before the hotel, Gabriel jumped out and, in spite of Mr Bartell D'Arcy's protest, paid the driver. He gave the man a shilling over his fare. The man saluted and said:

'A prosperous New Year to you, sir.'

'The same to you,' said Gabriel cordially.

She leaned for a moment on his arm in getting out of the cab and while standing at the kerb-stone, bidding the others good night. She leaned lightly on his arm, as lightly as when she had danced with him a few hours before. He had felt proud and happy then, happy that she was his, proud of her grace and wifely carriage. But now, after the kindling again of so many memories, the first touch of her body, musical and strange and perfumed, sent through him a keen pang of lust. Under cover of her silence he pressed her arm closely to his side, and, as they stood at the hotel door, he felt that they had escaped from their lives and duties, escaped from home and friends and run away together with wild and radiant hearts to a new adventure.

An old man was dozing in a great hooded chair in the hall. He lit a candle in the office and went before them to the stairs. They followed him in silence, their feet falling in soft thuds on the thickly carpeted stairs. She mounted the stairs behind the porter, her head bowed in the ascent, her frail shoulders curved as with a burden, her skirt girt tightly about her. He could have flung his arms about her hips and held her still, for his arms were trembling with desire to seize her and only the stress of his nails against the palms of his hands held the wild impulse of his body in check. The porter halted on the stairs to settle his guttering candle. They halted, too, on the steps below him. In the silence Gabriel could hear the falling of molten wax into the tray and the thumping of his own heart against his ribs.

The porter led them along a corridor and opened a door. Then he set his unstable candle down on a toilet-table and asked at what hour they were to be called in the morning.

'Eight,' said Gabriel.

The porter pointed to the tap of the electric-light and began a muttered apology, but Gabriel cut him short.

'We don't want any light. We have light enough from the street. And I say,' he added, pointing to the candle, 'you might remove that handsome article, like a good man.'

The porter took up his candle again, but slowly, for he was surprised by such a novel idea. Then he mumbled good night and went out. Gabriel shot the lock to.

A ghastly light from the street lamp lay in a long shaft from one window to the door. Gabriel threw his overcoat and hat on a couch and crossed the room towards the window. He looked down into the street in order that his emotion might calm a little. Then he turned and leaned against a chest of drawers with his back to the light. She had taken off her hat and cloak and was standing before a large swinging mirror, unhooking her waist. Gabriel paused for a few moments, watching her, and then said:

'Gretta!'

She turned away from the mirror slowly and walked along the shaft of light towards him. Her face looked so serious and weary that the words would not pass Gabriel's lips. No, it was not the moment yet.

'You looked tired,' he said.

'I am a little,' she answered.

'You don't feel ill or weak?'

'No, tired: that's all.'

She went on to the window and stood there, looking out. Gabriel waited again and then, fearing that diffidence was about to conquer him, he said abruptly:

'By the way, Gretta!'

'What is it?'

'You know that poor fellow, Malins?' he said quickly.

'Yes. What about him?'

'Well, poor fellow, he's a decent sort of chap, after all,' continued Gabriel in a false voice. 'He gave me back that sovereign I lent him, and I didn't expect it, really. It's a pity he wouldn't keep away from that Browne, because he's not a bad fellow, really.'

He was trembling now with annoyance. Why did she seem so abstracted? He did not know how he could begin. Was she annoyed, too, about something? If she would only turn to him or come to him of her own accord! To take her as she was would be brutal. No, he must see some ardour in her eyes first. He longed to be master of her strange mood.

'When did you lend him the pound?' she asked, after a pause.

Gabriel strove to restrain himself from breaking out into brutal language about the sottish Malins and his pound. He longed to cry to her from his soul, to crush her body against his, to overmaster her. But he said:

'O, at Christmas, when he opened that little Christmas card shop, in Henry Street.'

He was in such a fever of rage and desire that he did not hear her come from the window. She stood before him for an instant, looking at him strangely. Then, suddenly raising herself on tiptoe and resting her hands lightly on his shoulders, she kissed him.

'You are a very generous person, Gabriel,' she said.

Gabriel, trembling with delight at her sudden kiss and at the quaintness of her phrase, put his hands on her hair and began smoothing it back, scarcely touching it with his fingers.

The washing had made it fine and brilliant. His heart was brimming over with happiness. Just when he was wishing for it she had come to him of her own accord. Perhaps her thoughts had been running with his. Perhaps she had felt the impetuous desire that was in him, and then the yielding mood had come upon her. Now that she had fallen to him so easily, he wondered why he had been so diffident.

He stood, holding her head between his hands. Then, slipping one arm swiftly about her body and drawing her towards him, he said softly:

'Gretta, dear, what are you thinking about?'

She did not answer nor yield wholly to his arm. He said again, softly:

'Tell me what it is, Gretta. I think I know what is the matter. Do I know?'

She did not answer at once. Then she said in an outburst of tears:

'O, I am thinking about that song, "The Lass of Aughrim".'

She broke loose from him and ran to the bed and, throwing her arms across the bed-rail, hid her face. Gabriel stood stock-still for a moment in astonishment and then followed her. As he passed in the way of the cheval-glass he caught sight of himself in full length, his broad, well-filled shirt-front, the face whose expression always puzzled him when he saw it in a mirror, and his glimmering gilt-rimmed eyeglasses. He halted a few paces from her and said:

'What about the song? Why does that make you cry?'

She raised her head from her arms and dried her eyes with the back of her hand like a child. A kinder note than he had intended went into his voice.

'Why, Gretta?' he asked.

'I am thinking about a person long ago who used to sing that song.'

'And who was the person long ago?' asked Gabriel, smiling.

'It was a person I used to know in Galway when I was living with my grandmother,' she said.

The smile passed away from Gabriel's face. A dull anger

began to gather again at the back of his mind and the dull fires of his lust began to glow angrily in his veins.

'Someone you were in love with?' he asked ironically.

'It was a young boy I used to know,' she answered, 'named Michael Furey. He used to sing that song, "The Lass of Aughrim". He was very delicate.'

Gabriel was silent. He did not wish her to think that he was interested in this delicate boy.

'I can see him so plainly,' she said, after a moment. 'Such eyes as he had: big, dark eyes! And such an expression in them – an expression!'

'O, then, you were in love with him?' said Gabriel.

'I used to go out walking with him,' she said, 'when I was in Galway.'

A thought flew across Gabriel's mind.

'Perhaps that was why you wanted to go to Galway with that Ivors girl?' he said coldly.

She looked at him and asked in surprise:

'What for?'

Her eyes made Gabriel feel awkward. He shrugged his shoulders and said:

'How do I know? To see him, perhaps.'

She looked away from him along the shaft of light towards the window in silence.

'He is dead,' she said at length. 'He died when he was only seventeen. Isn't it a terrible thing to die so young as that?'

'What was he?' asked Gabriel, still ironically.

'He was in the gasworks,' she said.

Gabriel felt humiliated by the failure of his irony and by the evocation of this figure from the dead, a boy in the gas-works. While he had been full of memories of their secret life together, full of tenderness and joy and desire, she had been comparing him in her mind with another. A shameful consciousness of his own person assailed him. He saw himself as a ludicrous figure, acting as a penny-boy for his aunts, a nervous, well-meaning sentimentalist, orating to vulgarians and idealizing his own clownish lusts, the pitiable fatuous fellow he had caught a glimpse of in the mirror. Instinctively he turned his back more to the light lest she might see the shame that burned upon his forehead.

He tried to keep up his tone of cold interrogation, but his voice when he spoke was humble and indifferent.

'I suppose you were in love with this Michael Furey, Gretta,' he said.

'I was great with him at that time,' she said.

Her voice was veiled and sad. Gabriel, feeling now how vain it would be to try to lead her whither he had purposed, caressed one of her hands and said, also sadly:

'And what did he die of so young, Gretta? Consumption, was it?'

'I think he died for me,' she answered.

A vague terror seized Gabriel at this answer, as if, at that hour when he had hoped to triumph, some impalpable and vindictive being was coming against him, gathering forces against him in its vague world. But he shook himself free of it with an effort of reason and continued to caress her hand. He did not question her again, for he felt that she would tell him of herself. Her hand was warm and moist: it did not respond to his touch, but he continued to caress it just as he had caressed her first letter to him that spring morning.

'It was in the winter,' she said, 'about the beginning of the winter when I was going to leave my grandmother's and come up here to the convent. And he was ill at the time in his lodgings in Galway and wouldn't be let out, and his people in Oughterard were written to. He was in decline, they said, or something like that. I never knew rightly.'

She paused for a moment and sighed.

'Poor fellow,' she said. 'He was very fond of me and he was such a gentle boy. We used to go out together, walking, you know, Gabriel, like the way they do in the country. He was going to study singing only for his health. He had a very good voice, poor Michael Furey.'

'Well; and then?' asked Gabriel.

'And then when it came to the time for me to leave Galway and come up to the convent he was much worse and I wouldn't be let see him, so I wrote him a letter saying I was going up to

Dublin and would be back in the summer, and hoping he would be better then.'

She paused for a moment to get her voice under control, and then went on:

'Then the night before I left, I was in my grandmother's house in Nuns' Island, packing up, and I heard gravel thrown up against the window. The window was so wet I couldn't see, so I ran downstairs as I was and slipped out the back into the garden and there was the poor fellow at the end of the garden, shivering.'

'And did you not tell him to go back?' asked Gabriel.

'I implored of him to go home at once and told him he would get his death in the rain. But he said he did not want to live. I can see his eyes as well as well! He was standing at the end of the wall where there was a tree.'

'And did he go home?' asked Gabriel.

'Yes, he went home. And when I was only a week in the convent he died and he was buried in Oughterard, where his people came from. O, the day I heard that, that he was dead!'

She stopped, choking with sobs, and, overcome by emotion, flung herself face downward on the bed, sobbing in the quilt. Gabriel held her hand for a moment longer, irresolutely, and then, shy of intruding on her grief, let it fall gently and walked quietly to the window.

She was fast asleep.

Gabriel, leaning on his elbow, looked for a few moments unresentfully on her tangled hair and half-open mouth, listening to her deep-drawn breath. So she had had that romance in her life: a man had died for her sake. It hardly pained him now to think how poor a part he, her husband, had played in her life. He watched her while she slept, as though he and she had never lived together as man and wife. His curious eyes rested long upon her face and on her hair: and, as he thought of what she must have been then, in that time of her first girlish beauty, a strange, friendly pity for her entered his soul. He did not like to say even to himself that her face was no longer beautiful, but he knew that it was no longer the face for which Michael Furey had braved death.

Perhaps she had not told him all the story. His eyes moved to the chair over which she had thrown some of her clothes. A petticoat string dangled to the floor. One boot stood upright, its limp upper fallen down: the fellow of it lay upon its side. He wondered at his riot of emotions of an hour before. From what had it proceeded? From his aunt's supper, from his own foolish speech, from the wine and dancing, the merry-making when saying good night in the hall, the pleasure of the walk along the river in the snow. Poor Aunt Julia! She, too, would soon be a shade with the shade of Patrick Morkan and his horse. He had caught that haggard look upon her face for a moment when she was singing 'Arrayed for the Bridal'. Soon, perhaps, he would be sitting in that same drawing-room, dressed in black, his silk hat on his knees. The blinds would be drawn down and Aunt Kate would be sitting beside him, crying and blowing her nose and telling him how Julia had died. He would cast about in his mind for some words that might console her, and would find only lame and useless ones. Yes, yes: that would happen very soon.

The air of the room chilled his shoulders. He stretched himself cautiously along under the sheets and lay down beside his wife. One by one, they were all becoming shades. Better pass boldly into that other world, in the full glory of some passion, than fade and wither dismally with age. He thought of how she who lay beside him had locked in her heart for so many years that image of her lover's eyes when he had told her that he did not wish to live.

Generous tears filled Gabriel's eyes. He had never felt like that himself towards any woman, but he knew that such a feeling must be love. The tears gathered more thickly in his eyes and in the partial darkness he imagined he saw the form of a young man standing under a dripping tree. Other forms were near. His soul had approached that region where dwell the vast hosts of the dead. He was conscious of, but could not apprehend, their wayward and flickering existence. His own identity was fading out into a grey impalpable world: the solid world itself, which these dead had one time reared and lived in, was dissolving and dwindling.

A few light taps upo the pane made him turn to the window. It had begun to snow again. He watched sleepily the flakes, silver and dark, falling obliquely against the lamplight. The time had come for him to set out on his journey westward. Yes, the newspapers were right: snow was general all over Ireland. It was falling on every part of the dark central plain, on the treeless hills, falling softly upon the Bog of Allen and, farther westward, softly falling into the dark mutinous Shannon waves. It was falling, too, upon every part of the lonely church-yard on the hill where Michael Furey lay buried. It lay thickly drifted on the crooked crosses and headstones, on the spears of the little gate, on the barren thorns. His soul swooned slowly as he heard the snow falling faintly through the universe and faintly falling, like the descent of their last end, upon all the living and the dead.

Virginia Woolf

KEW GARDENS

FROM the oval-shaped flower-bed there rose perhaps a hundred stalks spreading into heart-shaped or tongue-shaped leaves half-way up and unfurling at the tip red or blue or yellow petals marked with spots of colour raised upon the surface; and from the red, blue or yellow gloom of the throat emerged a straight bar, rough with gold dust and slightly clubbed at the end. The petals were voluminous enough to be stirred by the summer breeze, and when they moved, the red, blue and yellow lights passed one over the other, staining an inch of the brown earth beneath with a spot of the moist intricate colour. The light fell either upon the smooth, grey back of a pebble, or the shell of a snail with its brown, circular veins, or, falling into a raindrop, it expanded with such intensity of red, blue and yellow the thin walls of water that one expected them to burst and disappear. Instead, the drop was left in a second silver grey once more, and the light now settled upon the flesh of a leaf, revealing the branching thread of fibre beneath the surface, and again it moved on and spread its illumination in the vast green spaces beneath the dome of the heart-shaped and tongue-shaped leaves. Then the breeze stirred rather more briskly overhead and the colour was flashed into the air above, into the eyes of the men and women who walk in Kew Gardens in July.

The figures of these men and women straggled past the flower-bed with a curiously irregular movement not unlike that of the white and blue butterflies who crossed the turf in zig-zag flights from bed to bed. The man was about six inches in front of the woman, strolling carelessly, while she bore on with greater purpose, only turning her head now and then to see that the children were not too far behind. The man kept this distance in front of the woman purposely, though perhaps unconsciously, for he wished to go on with his thoughts.

'Fifteen years ago I came here with Lily,' he thought. 'We sat somewhere over there by a lake and I begged her to marry me all through the hot afternoon. How the dragonfly kept circling round us: how clearly I see the dragonfly and her shoe with the square silver buckle at the toe. All the time I spoke I saw her shoe and when it moved impatiently I knew without looking up what she was going to say: the whole of her seemed to be in her shoe. And my love, my desire, were in the dragonfly; for some reason I thought that if it settled there, on that leaf, the broad one with the red flower in the middle of it, if the dragonfly settled on the leaf she would say "Yes" at once. But the dragonfly went round and round: it never settled anywhere – of course not, happily not, or I shouldn't be walking here with Eleanor and the children. Tell me, Eleanor. D'you ever think of the past?'

'Why do you ask, Simon?'

'Because I've been thinking of the past. I've been thinking of Lily, the woman I might have married. . . . Well, why are you silent? Do you mind my thinking of the past?'

'Why should I mind, Simon? Doesn't one always think of the past, in a garden with men and women lying under the trees? Aren't they one's past, all that remains of it, those men and women, those ghosts lying under the trees, . . . one's happiness, one's reality?'

'For me, a square silver shoe buckle and a dragonfly – '

'For me, a kiss. Imagine six little girls sitting before their easels twenty years ago, down by the side of a lake, painting the water-lilies, the first red water-lilies I'd ever seen. And suddenly a kiss, there on the back of my neck. And my hand shook all the afternoon so that I couldn't paint. I took out my watch and marked the hour when I would allow myself to think of the kiss for five minutes only – it was so precious – the kiss of an old grey-haired woman with a wart on her nose, the mother of all my kisses all my life. Come, Caroline, come, Hubert.'

They walked on past the flower-bed, now walking four abreast, and soon diminished in size among the trees and

looked half transparent as the sunlight and shade swam ove
their backs in large trembling irregular patches.

In the oval flower-bed the snail, whose shell had been stained
red, blue and yellow for the space of two minutes or so, now
appeared to be moving very slightly in its shell, and next began
to labour over the crumbs of loose earth which broke away
and rolled down as it passed over them. It appeared to have a
definite goal in front of it, differing in this respect from the
singular high stepping angular green insect who attempted to
cross in front of it, and waited for a second with its antennae
trembling as if in deliberation, and then stepped off as rapidly
and strangely in the opposite direction. Brown cliffs with deep
green lakes in the hollows, flat, blade-like trees that waved from
root to tip, round boulders of grey stone, vast crumpled sur-
faces of a thin crackling texture – all these objects lay across the
snail's progress between one stalk and another to his goal.
Before he had decided whether to circumvent the arched tent of
a dead leaf or to breast it there came past the bed the feet of
other human beings.

This time they were both men. The younger of the two wore
an expression of perhaps unnatural calm; he raised his eyes and
fixed them very steadily in front of him while his companion
spoke, and directly his companion had done speaking he looked
on the ground again and sometimes opened his lips only after
a long pause and sometimes did not open them at all. The elder
man had a curiously uneven and shaky method of walking,
jerking his hand forward and throwing up his head abruptly,
rather in the manner of an impatient carriage horse tired of
waiting outside a house; but in the man these gestures were
irresolute and pointless. He talked almost incessantly; he
smiled to himself and again began to talk, as if the smile had
been an answer. He was talking about spirits – the spirits of the
dead, who, according to him, were even now telling him all
sorts of odd things about their experiences in Heaven.

'Heaven was known to the ancients as Thessaly, William,
and now, with this war, the spirit matter is rolling between the
hills like thunder.' He paused, seemed to listen, smiled, jerked
his head and continued:

'You have a small electric battery and a piece of rubber to insulate the wire – isolate? – insulate? – well, we'll skip the details, no good going into details that wouldn't be understood – and in short the little machine stands in any convenient position by the head of the bed, we will say, on a neat mahogany stand. All arrangements being properly fixed by workmen under my direction, the widow applies her ear and summons the spirit by sign as agreed. Women! Widows! Women in black – '

Here he seemed to have caught sight of a woman's dress in the distance, which in the shade looked a purple black. He took off his hat, placed his hand upon his heart, and hurried towards her muttering and gesticulating feverishly. But William caught him by the sleeve and touched a flower with the tip of his walking-stick in order to divert the old man's attention. After looking at it for a moment in some confusion the old man bent his ear to it and seemed to answer a voice speaking from it, for he began talking about the forests of Uruguay which he had visited hundreds of years ago in company with the most beautiful young woman in Europe. He could be heard murmuring about forests of Uruguay blanketed with the wax petals of tropical roses, nightingales, sea beaches, mermaids, and women drowned at sea, as he suffered himself to be moved on by William, upon whose face the look of stoical patience grew slowly deeper and deeper.

Following his steps so closely as to be slightly puzzled by his gestures came two elderly women of the lower middle class, one stout and ponderous, the other rosy cheeked and nimble. Like most people of their station they were frankly fascinated by any signs of eccentricity betokening a disordered brain, especially in the well-to-do; but they were too far off to be certain whether the gestures were merely eccentric or genuinely mad. After they had scrutinized the old man's back in silence for a moment and given each other a queer, sly look, they went on energetically piecing together their very complicated dialogue:

'Nell, Bert, Lot, Cess, Phil, Pa, he says, I says, she says, I says, I says – '

'My Bert, Sis, Bill, Grandad, the old man, sugar,
Sugar, flour, kippers, greens,
Sugar, sugar, sugar.'

The ponderous woman looked through the pattern of falling words at the flowers standing cool, firm, and upright in the earth, with a curious expression. She saw them as a sleeper waking from a heavy sleep sees a brass candlestick reflecting the light in an unfamiliar way, and closes his eyes and opens them, and seeing the brass candlestick again, finally starts broad awake and stares at the candlestick with all his powers. So the heavy woman came to a standstill opposite the oval-shaped flower bed, and ceased even to pretend to listen to what the other woman was saying. She stood there letting the words fall over her, swaying the top part of her body slowly backwards and forwards, looking at the flowers. Then she suggested that they should find a seat and have their tea.

The snail had now considered every possible method of reaching his goal without going round the dead leaf or climbing over it. Let alone the effort needed for climbing a leaf, he was doubtful whether the thin texture which vibrated with such an alarming crackle when touched even by the tip of his horns would bear his weight; and this determined him finally to creep beneath it, for there was a point where the leaf curved high enough from the ground to admit him. He had just inserted his head in the opening and was taking stock of the high brown roof and was getting used to the cool brown light when two other people came past outside on the turf. This time they were both young, a young man and a young woman. They were both in the prime of youth, or even in that season which precedes the prime of youth, the season before the smooth pink folds of the flower have burst their gummy case, when the wings of the butterfly, though fully grown, are motionless in the sun.

'Lucky it isn't Friday,' he observed.

'Why? D'you believe in luck?'

'They make you pay sixpence on Friday.'

'What's sixpence anyway? Isn't it worth sixpence?'

'What's "it" – what do you mean by "it"?'

'O, anything – I mean – you know what I mean.'

Long pauses came between each of these remarks; they were uttered in toneless and monotonous voices. The couple stood still on the edge of the flower-bed, and together pressed the end of her parasol deep down into the soft earth. The action and the fact that his hand rested on the top of hers expressed their feelings in a strange way, as these short insignificant words also expressed something, words with short wings for their heavy body of meaning, inadequate to carry them far and thus alighting awkwardly upon the very common objects that surrounded them, and were to their inexperienced touch so massive; but who knows (so they thought as they pressed the parasol into the earth) what precipices aren't concealed in them, or what slopes of ice don't shine in the sun on the other side? Who knows? Who has ever seen this before? Even when she wondered what sort of tea they gave you at Kew, he felt that something loomed up behind her words, and stood vast and solid behind them; and the mist very slowly rose and uncovered – O, Heavens, what were those shapes? – little white tables, and waitresses who looked first at her and then at him; and there was a bill that he would pay with a real two shilling piece, and it was real, all real, he assured himself, fingering the coin in his pocket, real to everyone except to him and to her; even to him it began to seem real; and then – but it was too exciting to stand and think any longer, and he pulled the parasol out of the earth with a jerk and was impatient to find the place where one had tea with other people, like other people.

'Come along, Trissie; it's time we had our tea.'

'Wherever *does* one have one's tea?' she asked with the oddest thrill of excitement in her voice, looking vaguely round and letting herself be drawn on down the grass path, trailing her parasol, turning her head this way and that way forgetting her tea, wishing to go down there and then down there, remembering orchids and cranes among wild flowers, a Chinese pagoda and a crimson crested bird; but he bore her on.

Thus one couple after another with much the same irregular and aimless movement passed the flower-bed and were enveloped in layer after layer of green blue vapour, in which at first their bodies had substance and a dash of colour, but later both substance and colour dissolved in the green-blue atmosphere. How hot it was! So hot that even the thrush chose to hop, like a mechanical bird, in the shadow of the flowers, with long pauses between one movement and the next; instead of rambling vaguely the white butterflies danced one above another, making with their white shifting flakes the outline of a shattered marble column above the tallest flowers; the glass roofs of the palm house shone as if a whole market full of shiny green umbrellas had opened in the sun; and in the drone of the aeroplane the voice of the summer sky murmured its fierce soul. Yellow and black, pink and snow white, shapes of all these colours, men, women, and children were spotted for a second upon the horizon, and then, seeing the breadth of yellow that lay upon the grass, they wavered and sought shade beneath the trees, dissolving like drops of water in the yellow and green atmosphere, staining it faintly with red and blue. It seemed as if all gross and heavy bodies had sunk down in the heat motionless and lay huddled upon the ground, but their voices went wavering from them as if they were flames lolling from the thick waxen bodies of candles. Voices. Yes, voices. Wordless voices, breaking the silence suddenly with such depth of contentment, such passion of desire, or, in the voices of children, such freshness of surprise; breaking the silence? But there was no silence; all the time the motor omnibuses were turning their wheels and changing their gear; like a vast nest of Chinese boxes all of wrought steel turning ceaselessly one within another the city murmured; on the top of which the voices cried aloud and the petals of myriads of flowers flashed their colours into the air.

D. H. Lawrence

FANNY AND ANNIE

FLAME-LURID his face as he turned among the throng of flame-lit and dark faces upon the platform. In the light of the furnace she caught sight of his drifting countenance, like a piece of floating fire. And the nostalgia, the doom of home-coming went through her veins like a drug. His eternal face, flame-lit now! The pulse and darkness of red fire from the furnace towers in the sky, lighting the desultory, industrial crowd on the wayside station, lit him and went out.

Of course he did not see her. Flame-lit and unseeing! Always the same, with his meeting eyebrows, his common cap, and his red-and-black scarf knotted round his throat. Not even a collar to meet her! The flames had sunk, there was shadow.

She opened the door of her grimy, branch-line carriage, and began to get down her bags. The porter was nowhere, of course, but there was Harry, obscure, on the outer edge of the little crowd, missing her, of course.

'Here! Harry!' she called, waving her umbrella in the twilight. He hurried forward.

'Tha's come, has ter?' he said, in a sort of cheerful welcome. She got down, rather flustered, and gave him a peck of a kiss.

'Two suitcases!' she said.

Her soul groaned within her, as he clambered into the carriage after her bags. Up shot the fire in the twilight sky, from the great furnace behind the station. She felt the red flame go across her face. She had come back, she had come back for good. And her spirit groaned dismally. She doubted if she could bear it.

There, on the sordid little station under the furnaces, she stood, tall and distinguished, in her well-made coat and skirt and her broad grey velour hat. She held her umbrella, her bead chatelaine, and a little leather case in her grey-gloved hands, while Harry staggered out of the ugly little train with her bags.

'There's a trunk at the back,' she said in her bright voice. But she was not feeling bright. The twin black cones of the iron foundry blasted their sky-high fires into the night. The whole scene was lurid. The train waited cheerfully. It would wait another ten minutes. She knew it. It was all so deadly familiar.

Let us confess it at once. She was a lady's maid, thirty years old, come back to marry her first-love, a foundry worker: after having kept him dangling, off and on, for a dozen years. Why had she come back? Did she love him? No. She didn't pretend to. She had loved her brilliant and ambitious cousin, who had jilted her, and who had died. She had had other affairs which had come to nothing. So here she was, come back suddenly to marry her first-love, who had waited – or remained single – all these years.

'Won't a porter carry those?' she said, as Harry strode with his workman's stride down the platform towards the guard's van.

'I can manage,' he said.

And with her umbrella, her chatelaine, and her little leather case, she followed him.

The trunk was there.

'We'll get Heather's greengrocer's cart to fetch it up,' he said.

'Isn't there a cab?' said Fanny, knowing dismally enough that there wasn't.

'I'll just put it aside o' the penny-in-the-slot, and Heather's greengrocer's'll fetch it about half-past eight,' he said.

He seized the box by its two handles and staggered with it across the level-crossing, bumping his legs against it as he waddled. Then he dropped it by the red sweetmeats machine.

'Will it be safe there?' she said.

'Ay – safe as houses,' he answered. He returned for the two bags. Thus laden, they started to plod up the hill, under the great long black building of the foundry. She walked beside him – workman of workmen he was, trudging with that luggage. The red lights flared over the deepening darkness. From the foundry came the horrible, slow clang, clang, clang of iron, a great noise, with an interval just long enough to make it unendurable.

Compare this with the arrival at Gloucester: the carriage for her mistress, the dog-cart for herself with the luggage; the drive out past the river, the pleasant trees of the carriage-approach; and herself sitting beside Arthur, everybody so polite to her.

She had come home – for good! Her heart nearly stopped beating as she trudged up that hideous and interminable hill, beside the laden figure. What a come-down! What a come-down! She could not take it with her usual bright cheerfulness. She knew it all too well. It is easy to bear up against the unusual, but the deadly familiarity of an old stale past!

He dumped the bags down under a lamp-post, for a rest. There they stood, the two of them, in the lamplight. Passers-by stared at her, and gave good night to Harry. Her they hardly knew, she had become a stranger.

'They're too heavy for you, let me carry one,' she said.

'They begin to weigh a bit by the time you've gone a mile,' he answered.

'Let me carry the little one,' she insisted.

'Tha can ha'e it for a minute, if ter's a mind,' he said, handing over the valise.

And thus they arrived in the streets of shops of the little ugly town on top of the hill. How everybody stared at her; my word, how they stared! And the cinema was just going in, and the queues were tailing down the road to the corner. And everybody took full stock of her. 'Night, Harry!' shouted the fellows, in an interested voice.

However, they arrived at her aunt's – a little sweet-shop in a side street. They 'pinged' the door-bell, and her aunt came running forward out of the kitchen.

'There you are, child! Dying for a cup of tea, I'm sure. How are you?'

Fanny's aunt kissed her, and it was all Fanny could do to refrain from bursting into tears, she felt so low. Perhaps it was her tea she wanted.

'You've had a drag with that luggage,' said Fanny's aunt to Harry.

'Ay – I'm not sorry to put it down,' he said, looking at his hand which was crushed and cramped by the bag handle.

Then he departed to see about Heather's greengrocery cart.

When Fanny sat at tea, her aunt, a grey-haired, fair-faced little woman, looked at her with an admiring heart, feeling bitterly sore for her. For Fanny was beautiful: tall, erect, finely coloured, with her delicately arched nose, her rich brown hair, her large lustrous grey eyes. A passionate woman – a woman to be afraid of. So proud, so inwardly violent! She came of a violent race.

It needed a woman to sympathize with her. Men had not the courage. Poor Fanny! She was such a lady, and so straight and magnificent. And yet everything seemed to do her down. Every time she seemed to be doomed to humiliation and disappointment, this handsome, brilliantly sensitive woman, with her nervous, overwrought laugh.

'So you've really come back, child?' said her aunt.

'I really have, Aunt,' said Fanny.

'Poor Harry! I'm not sure, you know, Fanny, that you're not taking a bit of an advantage of him.'

'Oh, Aunt, he's waited so long, he may as well have what he's waited for.' Fanny laughed grimly.

'Yes, child, he's waited so long, that I'm not sure it isn't a bit hard on him. You know, I *like* him, Fanny – though as you know quite well, I don't think he's good enough for you. And I think he thinks so himself, poor fellow.'

'Don't you be so sure of that, Aunt. Harry is common, but he's not humble. He wouldn't think the Queen was any too good for him, if he'd a mind to her.'

'Well – It's as well if he has a proper opinion of himself.'

'It depends what you call proper,' said Fanny. 'But he's got his good points – '

'Oh, he's a nice fellow, and I like him, I do like him. Only, as I tell you, he's not good enough for you.'

'I've made up my mind, Aunt,' said Fanny, grimly.

'Yes,' mused the aunt. 'They say all things come to him who waits – '

'More than he's bargained for, eh, Aunt?' laughed Fanny rather bitterly.

The poor aunt, this bitterness grieved her for her niece.

They were interrupted by the ping of the shop-bell, and Harry's call of 'Right!' But as he did not come in at once, Fanny, feeling solicitous for him presumably at the moment, rose and went into the shop. She saw a cart outside, and went to the door.

And the moment she stood in the doorway, she heard a woman's common vituperative voice crying from the darkness of the opposite side of the road:

'Tha'rt theer, ar ter? I'll shame thee, Mester. I'll shame thee, see if I dunna.'

Startled, Fanny stared across the darkness, and saw a woman in a black bonnet go under one of the lamps up the side street.

Harry and Bill Heather had dragged the trunk off the little dray, and she retreated before them as they came up the shop step with it.

'Wheer shalt ha'e it?' asked Harry.

'Best take it upstairs,' said Fanny.

She went up first to light the gas.

When Heather had gone, and Harry was sitting down having tea and pork pie, Fanny asked:

'Who was that woman shouting?'

'Nay, I canna tell thee. To somebody, Is'd think,' replied Harry. Fanny looked at him, but asked no more.

He was a fair-haired fellow of thirty-two, with a fair moustache. He was broad in his speech, and looked like a foundry-hand, which he was. But women always liked him. There was something of a mother's lad about him – something warm and playful and really sensitive.

He had his attractions even for Fanny. What she rebelled against so bitterly was that he had no sort of ambition. He was a moulder, but of very commonplace skill. He was thirty-two years old, and hadn't saved twenty pounds. She would have to provide the money for the home. He didn't care. He just didn't care. He had no initiative at all. He had no vices – no obvious ones. But he was just indifferent, spending as he went, and not caring. Yet he did not look happy. She remembered his face in the fire-glow: something haunted, abstracted about it. As he sat there eating his pork pie, bulging his cheek out, she felt he was like a doom to her. And she raged against the doom of him. It wasn't that he was gross. His *way* was common, almost on purpose. But he himself wasn't really common. For instance, his food was not particularly important to him, he was not greedy. He had a charm, too, particularly for women, with his blondness and his sensitiveness and his way of making a woman feel that she was a higher being. But Fanny knew him, knew the peculiar obstinate limitedness of him, that would nearly send her mad.

He stayed till about half past nine. She went to the door with him.

'When are you coming up?' he said, jerking his head in the direction, presumably, of his own home.

'I'll come tomorrow afternoon,' she said brightly. Between Fanny and Mrs Goodall, his mother, there was naturally no love lost.

Again she gave him an awkward little kiss, and said good night.

'You can't wonder, you know, child, if he doesn't seem so very keen,' said her aunt. 'It's your own fault.'

'Oh, Aunt, I couldn't stand him when he was keen. I can do with him a lot better as he is.'

The two women sat and talked far into the night. They understood each other. The aunt, too, had married as Fanny was marrying: a man who was no companion to her, a violent man, brother of Fanny's father. He was dead, Fanny's father was dead.

Poor Aunt Lizzie, she cried woefully over her bright niece, when she had gone to bed.

Fanny paid the promised visit to his people the next afternoon. Mrs Goodall was a large woman with smooth-parted hair, a common, obstinate woman, who had spoiled her four lads and her one vixen of a married daughter. She was one of those old-fashioned powerful natures that couldn't do with looks or education or any form of showing off. She fairly hated the sound of correct English. She *thee'd* and *tha'd* her prospective daughter-in-law, and said:

'I'm none as ormin' as I look, seest ta.'

Fanny did not think her prospective mother-in-law looked at all orming, so the speech was unnecessary.

'I towd him mysen,' said Mrs Goodall, ' 'Er's held back all this long, let 'er stop as 'er is. 'E'd none ha' had thee for *my* tellin' – tha hears. No, 'e's a fool, an' I know it. I says to him, "Tha looks a man, doesn't ter, at thy age, goin' an' openin' to her when ter hears her scrat' at th' gate, after she's done gallivantin' round wherever she'd a mind. That looks rare an' soft." But it's no use o' any talking: he answered that letter o' thine and made his own bad bargain.'

But in spite of the old woman's anger, she was also flattered at Fanny's coming back to Harry. For Mrs Goodall was impressed by Fanny – a woman of her own match. And more than this, everybody knew that Fanny's Aunt Kate had left her two hundred pounds: this apart from the girl's savings.

So there was high tea in Princess Street when Harry came home black from work, and a rather acrid odour of cordiality, the vixen Jinny darting in to say vulgar things. Of course Jinny lived in a house whose garden end joined the paternal garden. They were a clan who stuck together, these Goodalls.

It was arranged that Fanny should come to tea again on the Sunday, and the wedding was discussed. It should take place in a fortnight's time at Morley Chapel. Morley was a hamlet on the edge of the real country, and in its little Congregational Chapel Fanny and Harry had first met.

What a creature of habit he was! He was still in the choir of Morley Chapel – not very regular. He belonged just because he had a tenor voice, and enjoyed singing. Indeed his solos were only spoilt to local fame because when he sang he handled his aitches so hopelessly.

> 'And I saw 'eaven hopened
> And be'old, a wite 'orse – '

This was one of Harry's classics, only surpassed by the fine outburst of his heaving:

    'Hangels – hever bright an' fair – '

It was a pity, but it was inalterable. He had a good voice, and he sang with a certain lacerating fire, but his pronunciation made it all funny. And *nothing* could alter him.

So he was never heard save at cheap concerts and in the little, poorer chapels. The others scoffed.

Now the month was September, and Sunday was Harvest Festival at Morley Chapel, and Harry was singing solos. So that Fanny was to go to afternoon service, and come home to a grand spread of Sunday tea with him. Poor Fanny! One of the most wonderful afternoons had been a Sunday afternoon service, with her cousin Luther at her side, Harvest Festival in Morley Chapel. Harry had sung solos then – ten years ago. She remembered his pale blue tie, and the purple asters and the great vegetable marrows in which he was framed, and her cousin Luther at her side, young, clever, come down from London, where he was getting on well, learning his Latin and his French and German so brilliantly.

However, once again it was Harvest Festival at Morley Chapel, and once again, as ten years before, a soft, exquisite September day, with the last roses pink in the cottage gardens, the last dahlias crimson, the last sunflowers yellow. And again the little old chapel was a bower, with its famous sheaves of corn and corn-plaited pillars, its great bunches of grapes, dangling like tassels from the pulpit corners, its marrows and potatoes and pears and apples and damsons, its purple asters and yellow Japanese sunflowers. Just as before, the red dahlias round the pillars were dropping, weak-headed among the oats. The place was crowded and hot, the plates of tomatoes seemed balanced perilously on the gallery front, the Rev. Enderby was weirder than ever to look at, so long and emaciated and hairless.

The Rev. Enderby, probably forewarned, came and shook hands with her and welcomed her, in his broad northern, melancholy singsong, before he mounted the pulpit. Fanny was handsome in a gauzy dress and a beautiful lace hat. Being a little late, she sat in a chair in the side-aisle wedged in, right in front of the chapel. Harry was in the gallery above, and she could only see him from the eyes upwards. She noticed again how his eyebrows met, blond and not very marked, over his nose. He was attractive too: physically lovable, very. If only – if only her *pride* had not suffered! She felt he dragged her down.

> 'Come, ye thankful people come,
> Raise the song of harvest-home.
> All is safely gathered in
> Ere the winter storms begin –'

Even the hymn was a falsehood, as the season had been wet, and half the crops were still out, and in a poor way.

Poor Fanny! She sang little, and looked beautiful through that inappropriate hymn. Above her stood Harry – mercifully in a dark suit and dark tie, looking almost handsome. And his lacerating, pure tenor sounded well, when the words were drowned in the general commotion. Brilliant she looked, and brilliant she felt, for she was hot and angrily miserable and in-flamed with a sort of fatal despair. Because there was about him a physical attraction which she really hated, but which she could not escape from. He was the first man who had ever kissed her. And his kisses, even while she rebelled from them, had lived in her blood and sent roots down into her soul. After all this time she had come back to them. And her soul groaned, for she felt dragged down, dragged down to earth, as a bird which some dog has got down in the dust. She knew her life would be unhappy. She knew that what she was doing was fatal. Yet it was her doom. She had to come back to him.

He had to sing two solos this afternoon: one before the 'address' from the pulpit and one after. Fanny looked at him, and wondered he was not too shy to stand up there in front of all the people. But no, he was not shy. He had even a kind of assurance on his face as he looked down from the choir gallery at her: the assurance of a common man deliberately entrenched in his commonness. Oh, such a rage went through her veins as she saw the air of triumph, laconic, indifferent triumph which sat so obstinately and recklessly on his eyelids as he looked down at her. Ah, she despised him! But there he stood up in that choir gallery like Balaam's ass in front of her, and she could not get beyond him. A certain winsomeness also about him. A certain physical winsomeness, and as if his flesh were new and lovely to touch. The thorn of desire rankled bitterly in her heart.

He, it goes without saying, sang like a canary this particular afternoon, with a certain defiant passion which pleasantly crisped the blood of the congregation. Fanny felt the crisp flames go through her veins as she listened. Even the curious loud-mouthed vernacular had a certain fascination. But, oh, also, it was so repugnant. He would triumph over her, obstinately he would drag her right back into the common people: a doom, a vulgar doom.

The second performance was an anthem, in which Harry sang the solo parts. It was clumsy, but beautiful, with lovely words.

> 'They that sow in tears shall reap in joy,
> He that goeth forth and weepeth, bearing precious seed
> Shall doubtless come again with rejoicing, bringing his
> sheaves with him –'

'Shall doubtless come, Shall doubtless come – ' softly intoned the altos – 'Bringing his she-e-eaves with him,' the trebles flourished brightly, and then again began the half-wistful solo:

> 'They that sow in tears shall reap in joy –'

Yes, it was effective and moving.

But at the moment when Harry's voice sank carelessly down to his close, and the choir, standing behind him, were opening their mouths for the final triumphant outburst, a shouting female voice rose up from the body of the congregation. The organ gave one startled trump, and went silent; the choir stood transfixed.

'You look well standing there, singing in God's holy house,' came the loud, angry female shout. Everybody turned electrified. A stoutish, red-faced woman in a black bonnet was standing up denouncing the soloist. Almost fainting with shock, the congregation realized it. 'You look well, don't you, standing there singing solos in God's holy house, you, Goodall. But I said I'd shame you. You look well, bringing your young woman here with you, don't you? I'll let her know who she's dealing with. A scamp as won't take the consequences of what he's done.' The hard-faced, frenzied woman turned in the direction of Fanny. '*That's* what Harry Goodall is, if you want to know.'

And she sat down again in her seat. Fanny, startled like all the rest, had turned to look. She had gone white, and then a burning red, under the attack. She knew the woman: a Mrs Nixon, a devil of a woman, who beat her pathetic, drunken, red-nosed second husband, Bob, and her two lanky daughters, grown-up as they were. A notorious character. Fanny turned round again, and sat motionless as eternity in her seat.

There was a minute of perfect silence and suspense. The audience was open-mouthed and dumb; the choir stood like Lot's wife; and Harry, with his music-sheet, stood there uplifted, looking down with a dumb sort of indifference on Mrs Nixon, his face naïve and faintly mocking. Mrs Nixon sat defiant in her seat, braving them all.

Then a rustle, like a wood when the wind suddenly catches the leaves. And then the tall, weird minister got to his feet, and in his strong, bell-like, beautiful voice – the only beautiful thing about him – he said with infinite mournful pathos:

'Let us unite in singing the last hymn on the hymn-sheet; the last hymn on the hymn-sheet, number eleven.

> 'Fair waved the golden corn,
> In Canaan's pleasant land.'

The organ tuned up promptly. During the hymn the offertory was taken. And after the hymn, the prayer.

Mr Enderby came from Northumberland. Like Harry, he had never been able to conquer his accent, which was very broad. He was a little simple, one of God's fools, perhaps, an odd bachelor soul, emotional, ugly, but very gentle.

'And if, O our dear Lord, beloved Jesus, there should fall a shadow of sin upon our harvest, we leave it to thee to judge, for thou art judge. We lift our spirits and our sorrow, Jesus, to thee, and our mouths are dumb. O, Lord, keep us from froward speech, restrain us from foolish words and thoughts, we pray thee, Lord Jesus, who knowest all and judgest all.'

Thus the minister said in his sad, resonant voice, washed his hands before the Lord. Fanny bent forward open-eyed during the prayer. She could see the roundish head of Harry, also bent forward. His face was inscrutable and expressionless. The shock left her bewildered. Anger perhaps was her dominating emotion.

The audience began to rustle to its feet, to ooze slowly and excitedly out of the chapel, looking with wildly-interested eyes at Fanny, at Mrs Nixon, and at Harry. Mrs Nixon, shortish, stood defiant in her pew, facing the aisle, as if announcing that, without rolling her sleeves up, she was ready for anybody. Fanny sat quite still. Luckily the people did not have to pass her. And Harry, with red ears, was making his way sheepishly out of the gallery. The loud noise of the organ covered all the downstairs commotion of exit.

The minister sat silent and inscrutable in his pulpit, rather like a death's-head, while the congregation filed out. When the last lingerers had unwillingly departed, craning their necks to stare at the still seated Fanny, he rose, stalked in his hooked fashion down the little country chapel and fastened the door. Then he returned and sat down by the silent young woman.

'This is most unfortunate, most unfortunate!' he moaned. 'I am so sorry, I am so sorry, indeed, indeed, ah, indeed!' he sighed himself to a close.

'It's a sudden surprise, that's one thing,' said Fanny brightly.

'Yes – yes – indeed. Yes, a surprise, yes. I don't know the woman, I don't know her.'

'I know her,' said Fanny. 'She's a bad one.'

'Well! Well!' said the minister. 'I don't know her. I don't understand. I don't understand at all. But it is to be regretted, it is very much to be regretted. I am very sorry.'

Fanny was watching the vestry door. The gallery stairs communicated with the vestry, not with the body of the chapel. She knew the choir members had been peeping for information.

At last Harry came – rather sheepishly – with his hat in his hand.

'Well!' said Fanny, rising to her feet.

'We've had a bit of an extra,' said Harry.

'I should think so,' said Fanny.

'A most unfortunate circumstance – a most *unfortunate* circumstance. Do you understand it, Harry? I don't understand it at all.'

'Ah, I understand it. The daughter's goin' to have a childt, an' 'er lays it on to me.'

'And has she no occasion to?' asked Fanny, rather censorious.

'It's no more mine than it is some other chap's,' said Harry, looking aside.

There was a moment of pause.

'Which girl is it?' asked Fanny.

'Annie – the young one – '

There followed another silence.

'I don't think I know them, do I?' asked the minister.

'I shouldn't think so. Their name's Nixon – mother married old Bob for her second husband. She's a tanger –'s driven the gel to what she is. They live in Manners Road.'

'Why, what's amiss with the girl?' asked Fanny sharply. 'She was all right when I knew her.'

'Ay – she's all right. But she's always in an' out o' th' pubs, wi' th' fellows,' said Harry.

'A nice thing!' said Fanny.

Harry glanced towards the door. He wanted to get out.

'Most distressing, indeed!' The minister slowly shook his head.

'What about tonight, Mr Enderby?' asked Harry, in rather a small voice. 'Shall you want me?'

Mr Enderby looked up painedly, and put his hand to his brow. He studied Harry for some time, vacantly. There was the faintest sort of a resemblance between the two men.

'Yes,' he said. 'Yes, I think. I think we must take no notice, and cause as little remark as possible.'

Fanny hesitated. Then she said to Harry.

'But *will* you come?'

He looked at her.

'Ay, I s'll come,' he said.

Then he turned to Mr Enderby.

'Well, good afternoon, Mr Enderby,' he said.

'Good afternoon, Harry, good afternoon,' replied the mournful minister. Fanny followed Harry to the door, and for some time they walked in silence through the late afternoon.

'And it's yours as much as anybody else's?' she said.

'Ay,' he answered shortly.

And they went without another word, for the long mile or so, till they came to the corner of the street where Harry lived. Fanny hesitated. Should she go on to her aunt's? Should she? It would mean leaving all this, for ever. Harry stood silent.

Some obstinacy made her turn with him along the road to his own home. When they entered the house-place, the whole family was there, mother and father and Jinny, with Jinny's husband and children and Harry's two brothers.

'You've been having your ears warmed, they tell me,' said Mrs Goodall grimly.

'Who told thee?' asked Harry shortly.

'Maggie and Luke's both been in.'

'You look well, don't you!' said interfering Jinny.

Harry went and hung his hat up, without replying.

'Come upstairs and take your hat off,' said Mrs Goodall to Fanny, almost kindly. It would have annoyed her very much if Fanny had dropped her son at this moment.

'What's 'er say, then?' asked the father secretly of Harry, jerking his head in the direction of the stairs whence Fanny had disappeared.

'Nowt yet,' said Harry.

'Serve you right if she chucks you now,' said Jinny. 'I'll bet it's right about Annie Nixon an' you.'

'Tha bets so much,' said Harry.

'Yi – but you can't deny it,' said Jinny.

'I can if I've a mind.'

His father looked at him inquiringly.

'It's no more mine than it is Bill Bower's, or Ted Slaney's, or six or seven on 'em,' said Harry to his father.

And the father nodded silently.

'That'll not get you out of it, in court,' said Jinny.

Upstairs Fanny evaded all the thrusts made by his mother, and did not declare her hand. She tidied her hair, washed her hands, and put the tiniest bit of powder on her face, for coolness, there in front of Mrs Goodall's indignant gaze. It was like a declaration of independence. But the old woman said nothing.

They came down to Sunday tea, with sardines and tinned salmon and tinned peaches, besides tarts and cakes. The chatter was general. It concerned the Nixon family and the scandal.

'Oh, she's a foul-mouthed woman,' said Jinny of Mrs Nixon. 'She may well talk about God's holy house, *she* had. It's first time she's set foot in it, ever since she dropped off from being converted. She's a devil and she always was one. Can't you remember how she treated Bob's children, mother, when we lived down in the Buildings? I can remember when I was a little girl she used to bathe them in the yard, in the cold, so that they shouldn't splash the house. She'd half kill them if they made a mark on the floor, and the language she'd use! And one Saturday I can remember Garry, that was Bob's own girl, she ran off when her stepmother was going to bathe her – ran off without a rag of clothes on – can you remember, mother? And she hid in Smedley's closes – it was the time of mowing-grass – and nobody could find her. She hid out there all night, didn't she, mother? Nobody could find her. My word, there was a talk. They found her on Sunday morning – '

'Fred Coutts threatened to break every bone in the woman's body, if she touched the children again,' put in the father.

'Anyhow, they frightened her,' said Jinny. 'But she was nearly as bad with her own two. And anybody can see that she's driven old Bob till he's gone soft.'

'Ah, soft as mush,' said Jack Goodall. ' 'E'd never addle a week's wage, nor yet a day's if th' chaps didn't make it up to him.'

'My word, if he didn't bring her a week's wage, she'd pull his head off,' said Jinny.

'But a clean woman, and respectable, except for her foul mouth,' said Mrs Goodall. 'Keeps to herself like a bull-dog. Never lets anybody come near the house, and neighbours with nobody.'

'Wanted it thrashed out of her,' said Mr Goodall, a silent, evasive sort of man.

'Where Bob gets the money for his drink from is a mystery,' said Jinny.

'Chaps treats him,' said Harry.

'Well, he's got the pair of frightenedest rabbit-eyes you'd wish to see,' said Jinny.

'Ay, with a drunken man's murder in them, *I* think,' said Mrs Goodall.

So the talk went on after tea, till it was practically time to start off to chapel again.

'You'll have to be getting ready, Fanny,' said Mrs Goodall.

'I'm not going tonight,' said Fanny abruptly. And there was a sudden halt in the family. 'I'll stop with *you* tonight, Mother,' she added.

'Best you had, my gel,' said Mrs Goodall, flattered and assured.

Katherine Mansfield

THE VOYAGE

THE Picton boat was due to leave at half past eleven. It was a beautiful night, mild, starry, only when they got out of the cab and started to walk down the Old Wharf that jutted out into the harbour, a faint wind blowing off the water ruffled under Fenella's hat, and she put up her hand to keep it on. It was dark on the Old Wharf, very dark; the wool sheds, the cattle trucks, the cranes standing up so high, the little squat railway engine, all seemed carved out of solid darkness. Here and there on a rounded wood-pile, that was like the stalk of a huge black mushroom, there hung a lantern, but it seemed afraid to unfurl its timid, quivering light in all that blackness; it burned softly, as if for itself.

Fenella's father pushed on with quick, nervous strides. Beside him her grandma bustled along in her crackling black ulster; they went so fast that she had now and again to give an undignified little skip to keep up with them. As well as her luggage strapped into a neat sausage, Fenella carried clasped to her her grandma's umbrella, and the handle, which was a swan's head, kept giving her shoulder a sharp little peck as if it too wanted her to hurry.... Men, their caps pulled down, their collars turned up, swung by; a few women all muffled scurried along; and one tiny boy, only his little black arms and legs showing out of a white woolly shawl, was jerked along angrily between his father and mother; he looked like a baby fly that had fallen into the cream.

Then suddenly, so suddenly that Fenella and her grandma both leapt, there sounded from behind the largest wool shed, that had a trail of smoke hanging over it, *Mia-oo-oo-O-O!*

'First whistle,' said her father briefly, and at that moment they came in sight of the Picton boat. Lying beside the dark wharf, all strung, all beaded with round golden lights, the

Picton boat looked as if she was more ready to sail among stars than out into the cold sea. People pressed along the gangway. First went her grandma, then her father, then Fenella. There was a high step down on to the deck, and an old sailor in a jersey standing by gave her his dry, hard hand. They were there; they stepped out of the way of the hurrying people, and standing under a little iron stairway that led to the upper deck they began to say good-bye.

'There, mother, there's your luggage!' said Fenella's father, giving Grandma another strapped-up sausage.

'Thank you, Frank.'

'And you've got your cabin tickets safe?'

'Yes, dear.'

'And your other tickets?'

Grandma felt for them inside her glove and showed him the tips.

'That's right.'

He sounded stern, but Fenella, eagerly watching him, saw that he looked tired and sad. *Mia-oo-oo-O-O!* The second whistle blared just above their heads, and a voice like a cry shouted, 'Any more for the gangway?'

'You'll give my love to Father,' Fenella saw her father's lips say. And her grandma, very agitated, answered, 'Of course I will, dear. Go now. You'll be left. Go now, Frank. Go now.'

'It's all right, Mother. I've got another three minutes.' To her surprise Fenella saw her father take off his hat. He clasped Grandma in his arms and pressed her to him. 'God bless you, Mother!' she heard him say.

And Grandma put her hand, with the black thread glove that was worn through on her ring finger, against his cheek, and she sobbed, 'God bless you, my own brave son!'

This was so awful that Fenella quickly turned her back on them, swallowed once, twice, and frowned terribly at a little green star on a mast head. But she had to turn round again; her father was going.

'Good-bye, Fenella. Be a good girl.' His cold wet moustache brushed her cheek. But Fenella caught hold of the lapels of his coat.

'How long am I going to stay?' she whispered anxiously. He wouldn't look at her. He shook her off gently, and gently said, 'We'll see about that. Here! Where's your hand?' He pressed something into her palm. 'Here's a shilling in case you should need it.'

A shilling! She must be going away for ever! 'Father!' cried Fenella. But he was gone. He was the last off the ship. The sailors put their shoulders to the gangway. A huge coil of dark rope went flying through the air and fell 'thump' on the wharf. A bell rang; a whistle shrilled. Silently the dark wharf began to slip, to slide, to edge away from them. Now there was a rush of water between. Fenella strained to see with all her might. 'Was that Father turning round?' – or waving? – or standing alone? – or walking off by himself? The strip of water grew broader, darker. Now the Picton boat began to swing round steady, pointing out to sea. It was no good looking any longer. There was nothing to be seen but a few lights, the face of the town clock hanging in the air, and more lights, little patches of them, on the dark hills.

The freshening wind tugged at Fenella's skirts; she went back to her grandma. To her relief Grandma seemed no longer sad. She had put the two sausages of luggage one on top of the other, and she was sitting on them, her hands folded, her head a little on one side. There was an intent, bright look on her face. Then Fenella saw that her lips were moving and guessed that she was praying. But the old woman gave her a bright nod as if to say the prayer was nearly over. She unclasped her hands, sighed, clasped them again, bent forward, and at last gave herself a soft shake.

'And now, child,' she said, fingering the bow of her bonnet-strings, 'I think we ought to see about our cabins. Keep close to me, and mind you don't slip.'

'Yes, Grandma!'

'And be careful the umbrellas aren't caught in the stair rail. I saw a beautiful umbrella broken in half like that on my way over.'

'Yes, Grandma.'

Dark figures of men lounged against the rails. In the glow

of their pipes a nose shone out, or the peak of a cap, or a pair of surprised-looking eyebrows. Fenella glanced up. High in the air, a little figure, his hand thrust in his short jacket pockets, stood staring out to sea. The ship rocked ever so little, and she thought the stars rocked too. And now a pale steward in a linen coat, holding a tray high in the palm of his hand, stepped out of a lighted doorway and skimmed past them. They went through that doorway. Carefully over the high brass-bound step on to the rubber mat and then down such a terribly steep flight of stairs that Grandma had to put both feet on each step, and Fenella clutched the clammy brass rail and forgot all about the swan-necked umbrella.

At the bottom Grandma stopped; Fenella was rather afraid she was going to pray again. But no, it was only to get out the cabin tickets. They were in the saloon. It was glaring bright and stifling; the air smelled of paint and burnt chop-bones and india-rubber. Fenella wished her grandma would go on, but the old woman was not to be hurried. An immense basket of ham sandwiches caught her eye. She went up to them and touched the top one delicately with her finger.

'How much are the sandwiches?' she asked.

'Tuppence!' bawled a rude steward, slamming down a knife and fork.

Grandma could hardly believe it.

'Twopence *each*?' she asked.

'That's right,' said the steward, and he winked at his companion.

Grandma made a small, astonished face. Then she whispered primly to Fenella. 'What wickedness!' And they sailed out at the further door and along a passage that had cabins on either side. Such a very nice stewardess came to meet them. She was dressed all in blue, and her collar and cuffs were fastened with large brass buttons. She seemed to know Grandma well.

'Well, Mrs Crane,' said she, unlocking their washstand. 'We've got you back again. It's not often you give yourself a cabin.'

'No,' said Grandma. 'But this time my dear son's thoughtfulness – '

'I hope – ' began the stewardess. Then she turned round and took a long mournful look at Grandma's blackness and at Fenella's black coat and skirt, black blouse, and hat with a crape rose.

Grandma nodded. 'It was God's will,' said she.

The stewardess shut her lips and, taking a deep breath, she seemed to expand.

'What I always say is,' she said, as though it was her own discovery, 'sooner or later each of us has to go, and that's a certingty.' She paused. 'Now, can I bring you anything, Mrs Crane? A cup of tea? I know it's no good offering you a little something to keep the cold out.'

Grandma shook her head. 'Nothing, thank you. We've got a few wine biscuits, and Fenella has a very nice banana.'

'Then I'll give you a look later on,' said the stewardess, and she went out, shutting the door.

What a very small cabin it was! It was like being shut up in a box with Grandma. The dark round eye above the washstand gleamed at them dully. Fenella felt shy. She stood against the door, still clasping her luggage and the umbrella. Were they going to get undressed in here? Already her grandma had taken off her bonnet, and, rolling up the strings, she fixed each with a pin to the lining before she hung the bonnet up. Her white hair shone like silk; the little bun at the back was covered with a black net. Fenella hardly ever saw her grandma with her head uncovered; she looked strange.

'I shall put on the woollen fascinator your dear mother crocheted for me,' said Grandma, and, unstrapping the sausage, she took it out and wound it round her head; the fringe of grey bobbles danced at her eyebrows as she smiled tenderly and mournfully at Fenella. Then she undid her bodice, and something under that, and something else underneath that. Then there seemed a short, sharp tussle, and Grandma flushed faintly. Snip! Snap! She had undone her stays. She breathed a sigh of relief, and sitting on the plush couch, she slowly and carefully pulled off her elastic-sided boots and stood them side by side.

By the time Fenella had taken off her coat and skirt and put on her flannel dressing-gown Grandma was quite ready.

'Must I take off my boots, Grandma? They're lace.'

Grandma gave them a moment's deep consideration. 'You'd feel a great deal more comfortable if you did, child,' said she. She kissed Fenella. 'Don't forget to say your prayers. Our dear Lord is with us when we are at sea even more than when we are on dry land. And because I am an experienced traveller,' said Grandma briskly, 'I shall take the upper berth.'

'But, Grandma, however will you get up there?'

Three little spider-like steps were all Fenella saw. The old woman gave a small silent laugh before she mounted them nimbly, and she peered over the high bunk at the astonished Fenella.

'You didn't think your grandma could do that, did you?' said she. And as she sank back Fenella heard her light laugh again.

The hard square of brown soap would not lather, and the water in the bottle was like a kind of blue jelly. How hard it was, too, to turn down those stiff sheets; you simply had to tear your way in. If everything had been different, Fenella might have got the giggles. . . . At last she was inside, and while she lay there panting, there sounded from above a long, soft whispering, as though someone was gently, gently rustling among tissue paper to find something. It was Grandma saying her prayers. . . .

A long time passed. Then the stewardess came in; she trod softly and leaned her hand on Grandma's bunk.

'We're just entering the Straits,' she said.

'Oh!'

'It's a fine night, but we're rather empty. We may pitch a little.'

And indeed at that moment the Picton boat rose and rose and hung in the air just long enough to give a shiver before she swung down again, and there was the sound of heavy water slapping against her sides. Fenella remembered she had left that swan-necked umbrella standing up on the little couch. If it fell over, would it break? But Grandma remembered too, at the same time.

'I wonder if you'd mind, stewardess, laying down my umbrella,' she whispered.

'Not at all, Mrs Crane.' And the stewardess, coming back to Grandma, breathed, 'Your little granddaughter's in such a beautiful sleep.'

'God be praised for that!' said Grandma.

'Poor little motherless mite!' said the stewardess. And Grandma was still telling the stewardess all about what happened when Fenella fell asleep.

But she hadn't been asleep long enough to dream before she woke up again to see something waving in the air above her head. What was it? What could it be? It was a small grey foot. Now another joined it. They seemed to be feeling about for something; there came a sigh.

'I'm awake, Grandma,' said Fenella.

'Oh, dear, am I near the ladder?' asked Grandma. 'I thought it was this end.'

'No, Grandma, it's the other. I'll put your foot on it. Are we there?' asked Fenella.

'In the harbour,' said Grandma. 'We must get up, child. You'd better have a biscuit to steady yourself before you move.'

But Fenella had hopped out of her bunk. The lamp was still burning, but night was over, and it was cold. Peering through that round eye, she could see far off some rocks. Now they were scattered over with foam; now a gull flipped by; and now there came a long piece of real land.

'It's land, Grandma,' said Fenella, wonderingly, as though they had been at sea for weeks together. She hugged herself; she stood on one leg and rubbed it with the toes of the other foot; she was trembling. Oh, it had all been so sad lately. Was it going to change? But all her Grandma said was, 'Make haste, child. I should leave your nice banana for the stewardess as you haven't eaten it.' And Fenella put on her black clothes again, and a button sprang off one of her gloves and rolled to where she couldn't reach it. They went up on deck.

But if it had been cold in the cabin, on deck it was like ice. The sun was not up yet, but the stars were dim, and the cold

pale sky was the same colour as the cold pale sea. On the land
a white mist rose and fell. Now they could see quite plainly
dark bush. Even the shapes of the umbrella ferns showed, and
those strange silvery withered trees that are like skeletons. . . .
Now they could see the landing-stage and some little houses,
pale too, clustered together, like shells on the lid of a box. The
other passengers tramped up and down, but more slowly than
they had the night before, and they looked gloomy.

And now the landing-stage came out to meet them. Slowly
it swam towards the Picton boat, and a man holding a coil of
rope, and a cart with a small drooping horse and another man
sitting on the step, came too.

'It's Mr Penreddy, Fenella, come for us,' said Grandma. She
sounded pleased. Her white waxen cheeks were blue with cold,
her chin trembled, and she had to keep wiping her eyes and her
little pink nose.

'You've got my –'

'Yes, Grandma.' Fenella showed it to her.

The rope came flying through the air, and 'smack' it fell
on to the deck. The gangway was lowered. Again Fenella
followed her grandma on to the wharf over to the little cart,
and a moment later they were bowling away. The hooves of
the little horse drummed over the wooden piles, then sank
softly into the sandy road. Not a soul was to be seen; there was
not even a feather of smoke. The mist rose and fell, and the sea
still sounded asleep as slowly it turned on the beach.

'I seen Mr Crane yestiddy,' said Mr Penreddy. 'He looked himself then. Missus knocked him up a batch of scones last week.'

And now the little horse pulled up before one of the shell-
like houses. They got down. Fenella put her hand on the gate,
and the big, trembling dewdrops soaked through her glove-
tips. Up a little path of round white pebbles they went, with
drenched sleeping flowers on either side. Grandma's delicate
white picotees were so heavy with dew that they were fallen,
but their sweet smell was part of the cold morning. The blinds
were down in the little house; they mounted the steps on to the
veranda. A pair of old bluchers was on one side of the door, and
a large red water-can on the other.

'Tut! tut! Your grandpa,' said Grandma. She turned the handle. Not a sound. She called, 'Walter!' And immediately a deep voice that sounded half stifled called back, 'Is that you, Mary?'

'Wait, dear,' said Grandma. 'Go in there.' She pushed Fenella gently into a small dusky sitting-room.

On the table a white cat, that had been folded up like a camel, rose, stretched itself, yawned, and then sprang on to the tips of its toes. Fenella buried one cold little hand in the white, warm fur, and smiled timidly while she stroked and listened to Grandma's gentle voice and the rolling tones of Grandpa.

A door creaked. 'Come in, dear.' The old woman beckoned, Fenella followed. There, lying to one side of an immense bed, lay Grandpa. Just his head with a white tuft, and his rosy face and long silver beard showed over the quilt. He was like a very old wide-awake bird.

'Well, my girl!' said Grandpa. 'Give us a kiss!' Fenella kissed him. 'Ugh!' said Grandpa. 'Her little nose is as cold as a button. What's that she's holding? Her grandma's umbrella?'

Fenella smiled again, and crooked the swan neck over the bed-rail. Above the bed there was a big text in a deep-black frame:

> Lost! One Golden Hour
> Set with Sixty Diamond Minutes.
> No Reward Is Offered
> For It Is GONE FOR EVER!

'Yer grandma painted that,' said Grandpa. And he ruffled his white tuft and looked at Fenella so merrily she almost thought he winked at her.

Joyce Cary

THE BREAKOUT

TOM SPONSON, at fifty-three, was a thoroughly successful man. He had worked up a first-class business, married a charming wife, and built himself a good house in the London suburbs that was neither so modern as to be pretentious nor so conventional as to be dull. He had good taste. His son, Bob, nineteen, was doing well at Oxford; his daughter, April, aged sixteen, who was at a good school, had no wish to use make-up, to wear low frocks, or to flirt. She still regarded herself as too young for these trifling amusements. Yet she was gay, affectionate, and thoroughly enjoyed life. All the same, for some time Tom had been aware that he was working very hard for very little. His wife, Louie, gave him a peck in the morning when he left for the office and, if she were not at a party, a peck in the evening when he came home. And it was obvious that her life was completely filled with the children, with her clothes, with keeping her figure slim, with keeping the house clean and smart, with her charities, her bridge, her tennis, her friends, and her parties.

The children were even more preoccupied – the boy with his own work and his own friends, the girl with hers. They were polite to Tom, but if he came into the room when they were entertaining a friend, there was at once a feeling of constraint. Even if they were alone together, he perceived that when he came upon them they were slightly embarrassed, and changed the subject of their conversation, whatever it was. Yet they did not seem to do this when they were with their mother. He would find them all three, for instance, laughing at something, and when he came in they would stop laughing and gaze at him as if he had shot up through the floor. In fact, if he asked what the joke was his wife would say, 'You wouldn't understand' or 'Nothing' or 'I'll tell you afterwards', but she never did tell him afterwards; she would put him off with some remark like, 'Oh, it's perfectly silly, about something April said'.

He said to himself, 'It isn't only that they don't need me, but I'm a nuisance to them. I'm in the way. I'm superfluous.' One morning when he was just going to get into his car and his wife had come out to say good-bye, he suddenly made an excuse, saying, 'Just a moment, I've left a letter', and went back to his desk, and then dashed out to the car and drove off, pretending to forget that good-bye had not been said.

Immediately he felt that he could not stand any more of this existence; it was nonsense. It was not as though his wife and children were depending any more on the business; he could sell it to a combine tomorrow, and it would support all of them in comfort. Actually he would miss the business; it was his chief interest. But if he had to give it up for the sake of freedom, of a break in this senseless life, he could do even that. Yes, joyfully.

As he circled Trafalgar Square, that is to say, as he came within the last few hundred yards from his office, he told himself that he could not go on. It was as though that moment when he dodged the customary good-bye had broken a contact. The conveyor belt on which his life had been caught up had stopped as if at a short circuit, a break in a switch. No, he could not go on. So, instead of turning down the Strand out of the Square, he drove straight on to a West End garage.

An hour later, he was in the train for Westford, a seaside place where he had once spent a summer holiday before his marriage, with three friends from college. On the luggage rack was a new suitcase containing new pyjamas, shoes, a new kit, as for a holiday by the sea – even new paperbacks for a wet day.

It was February, but when he reached Westford he was surprised, for a moment, to find that both its hotels were closed. Only the village pub, The Case Is Altered, was still open for visitors, and as he sat in the coffee-room, he appeared to be the only visitor, except for a commercial traveller, one Sims, a dignified young man who addressed him with the most formal politeness and showed a strong tendency to talk politics – politics on what he called the 'highest level'.

In his view, he said, what parliaments did and what dictators talked about did not really matter; what mattered was population statistics and economics. 'You can put over anything with the wireless and the telly – that's the way these dictators do it – but you can't feed people on words. They'll swallow all the lies you like, but they can't live on hot air. Sooner or later most of these chaps have to face facts.'

'Yes,' said Tom. 'A lot later – generally too late. Look at what Hitler did with his little yarn – and called it the Big Lie all the time. Look at all the people eating lies now and getting poison all the time. What can they do, poor devils? So long as the big noise has a really tough police.'

Tom was a Liberal, a strong supporter of the United Nations. A week before, he had been saying just the same things as Mr Sims; probably they had come out of the same papers. But now all at once he was revolted, quite furious with Mr Sims, with all those nice chaps at the club and the golf course, who had been so ready to talk this nonsense with him, who simply refused to face facts, especially the enormous, obvious fact that civilization was going to smash just because of all this cant, this wangling, this political gabble, this nonsense.

Mr Sims shook his head and remarked that the police hadn't saved the Tsar.

'No,' Tom said. 'What knocked him out was a superior brand of cant. He thought the people loved him, and sent his Guards to the front. But the Bolshies told the people they'd bring in the golden age right off. And they won. They had a bigger lie and they were smarter swindlers. The poor old Tsar only cheated himself; they cheated everybody.'

Suddenly Tom caught Mr Sims's eye fixed upon him with a speculative alarm. The man was shocked. He was so used to the regular nonsense, to the old, worn records grinding out the same old popular tune, that he was bewildered by this contradiction.

'Quite a new idea,' Mr Sims murmured. 'Very interesting.'
He was growing more and more alarmed.

'Excuse me,' Tom muttered, and hurried out into the front
hall. It was almost a run. He was afraid of losing his temper
with Mr Sims, who was obviously a nice chap, a very nice chap,
who read all the best papers, the best nonsense.

What especially angered him in Mr Sims was that Mr Sims's
nonsense was his own nonsense of a week before. Sims was a
looking-glass in which he saw his own silly face. And it made
it no better that, as he now perceived, he had always known his
nonsense to be nonsense. All that time when he had been talking it at business luncheons, at the club, in the train, at breakfast to his own family, he had had the same deep feeling: My
God, what nonsense!

For years he had been hiding this knowledge, just as he
had always pretended that he enjoyed nothing so much as his
family life. How often had he boasted of the sympathetic
devotion of his wife and children, saying how lucky he was
compared with so many others, who found themselves ciphers
in their own homes. Why, why had he gone on telling himself
these lies, living a life of hypocrisy? It was as if he had been
drugged – or was it simply that the air was so thick with nonsense, with cant, that it was almost impossible for any man to
see the truth, even the biggest, the most obvious truth?
Wasn't it simply by a stroke of luck that he had broken out
into clear air? And as if the words themselves demanded the
action, he put on his mackintosh and went out.

It was raining still, but the opposite side of the bay was
sharp and clear, as though seen through a lens. The grey sky
was brilliant with diffused light, and the breeze had a taste of
sea salt. The whole world seemed washed as clean as the
pebbles on the beach.

He walked along the front. Westford's great charm in the
old days had been its smallness, its lack of enterprise. Apart
from the two hotels, both old-fashioned, and even forbidding
to strangers, there were only a dozen or so boarding-houses
along the front, and almost the entire town was in the twenty
or so buildings facing the sea, and in the main street of the old

village branching off at right angles. There was what was called a Marine Parade, but it was simply a paved path along the front road with, on the seaward side, a strip of rough grass where half a dozen seats had been provided. Below, the magnificent beach had neither pier nor bathing huts. The great landlord who owned Westford was against huts, and summer visitors were expected to use tents that they could hire from the town council. There were no municipal gardens, bandstands, putting courses, or sideshows to vulgarize the place, which, apart from the absence of bathing machines, might have been existing still in the eighteen-sixties.

The wind was rising and big waves were thumping on the beach. The sea turned almost black, and the wet fronts of the houses, in spite of their gay colours, began to have a dreary look. The town seemed absolutely empty; not a human being was in sight. The only living creature to be seen was a dog with its nose in the gutter – as Tom appeared from around a corner, it jumped and looked at him, uttered one sharp bark, and cantered away, completely shocked by the intrusion. But the very dreariness of the scene, the monotonous pounding of the waves, the hiss of the rain in the pools, gave Tom the kind of pleasure that one gets from the defiance of an enemy. He was stimulated, excited. He felt his strength; he felt that he had done well. He had made a big decision and saved his life, and he went down to the beach and walked up and down close to the waves until the rain grew heavy. His shoes filled with sand and he remembered that he had only one suit with him. He turned back to the pub, intending to read one of his new crime novels.

In the little hall of the private entrance, the clerk, who was also the barman, was waiting for him with the register, and, upon an impulse that, for the moment, he did not understand and did not examine, he hesitated and then wrote down the name Charles Stone and gave a false address. He was surprised at himself – he detested such trickery – but it was only twenty minutes later that, lying upstairs on his bed with his book, he realized how necessary it had been, how wisely he had followed his impulse. 'In the first excitement,' he said to himself, 'they might well ask the B.B.C. or the newspapers to start a hunt; the last thing I want is any publicity. I'll write to Louie at once and get things settled in a sensible manner.'

That evening – in fact, as soon as he could, with decent politeness, separate himself from Mr Sims, who was anxious to make him realize that if you can fool the people, you can't fool population statistics, so long, of course, as they are reliable – he slipped off to his room to write to Louie. There was no writing-table in the room, or any provision for writing, so he set his new suitcase on his knee and proceeded to draft a letter on the flyleaf of his paper-back.

'Darling Louie', he began, but stopped immediately. He had always written 'Darling Louie', but how could he begin a letter of farewell, an ultimatum proposing an end to their marriage, with 'Darling Louie'? He crossed it out and wrote 'My dear Louie'. This also struck him as false. She was not his dear Louie. And was he going to start a new life of truth, of sincerity, by writing this criminal lie? 'Dear So-and-so.' What hundreds of letters to total strangers, to touts, to frauds and crooks, to people who were, in fact, absolutely detestable to him, he had started with this lying formula, this stereotyped nonsense. Louie was simply the woman who lived in his house, like a creature dropped from Mars, more strange to him than any stranger. A woman whom he supported and who had no real contact with him at all, who did not even speak the same language. He began again, without preamble: 'I dare say you wonder where I am, but it does not really matter. As far as you and the children are concerned, I have not existed anywhere for a long time. I'm not blaming anyone for this state of affairs. I imagine it's a very common one for married couples in our situation. The children are practically grown up and don't need us any more; they certainly have not needed me for years past, and your life is entirely full of your own private interests. For a long time, I have been aware that I was only in the way. You would be much happier, much freer, as a widow. You could make one of those marriages that women in their forties do make after their children cease to need them, a marriage with a man suited to the new woman you have become. There is something to be said for a change of partners at our age. After all, people don't stop growing and changing simply because they are married. I agree that they have a duty to their children, but when that duty has been discharged it is absurd to make them waste the rest of their lives in pretending to a community of interests which they no longer possess. It's even bad for the children, now they are old enough to think for themselves, to live in this atmosphere of fake and hypocrisy. They get infected, too, and so the nonsense goes on to another generation.' It was a good letter; he was surprised how good it was. He realized that it expressed for him feelings that had been present for years, and that he had been, unnoticed by himself, collecting all kinds of information bearing on his argument. It was a good letter, but he did not send it that evening. He had no notepaper or envelopes with him. He could not make a fair copy and he was not sure that he had not said too much. The whole thing, as read through, had a somewhat professorial air. It lacked the conviction that moved him so strongly. It gave no hint of the bitterness that he felt to be justifiable. He had been a good husband, a good father, and he could not help feeling that he had been treated with ingratitude. He lay awake half the night thinking of new things that he could put in this letter. Once he even turned on the light to write a phrase in another of his crime novels.

Next day he rewrote the letter. It was not till Thursday, three days after his flight, that he went out in the town to seek notepaper and envelopes. Then he found that the one stationer's had nothing to his taste – only stationery sets done up in ribbon and containing deckle-edged paper of the most vulgar type, or the cheapest blocks. Both, he felt, were quite impossible for his letter. He had always been particular about notepaper. However, Westford was only ten miles from the large seaside town of Lilmouth, and he would enjoy a visit there, too. He and his college friends had spent a very happy afternoon and evening at Lilmouth at the annual fair. He called, therefore, at the garage, to hire a car, and found that there was one that would be available the next day. He gave the order and returned to the pub. He was in no hurry to write his letter.

Why, Louie knew that he was all right. He had phoned the office to tell them that he had to go away for a while, that he would send his address in due course, and he had asked them to inform his wife.

A letter from or to Louie would start all sorts of trouble, and meanwhile he was only just beginning to enjoy his new life. He had found out how to dodge Mr Sims – simply by having his meals earlier. And time was passing far more quickly than he had expected. It was astonishing how this lounging, thoughtful, careless existence had already fallen into a routine. A late breakfast, a stroll along the front, coffee at eleven in a little café that remained open apparently for the use of unemployed landladies, who came there to discuss their bookings for the next season. Then to the stationer's for the London papers, then early luncheon with the papers to read. After luncheon, a doze in his room. Then another stroll along the front, or, if it were fine, over the headland and along the coast for a mile or two. The sea breeze was unequalled for giving one an appetite. He had not for years so much enjoyed either the prospect of dinner or dinner itself. The Case Is Altered did not attempt French cooking. All the better. It provided excellent meat, beer, and cheese, and plenty of them. After dinner he was ready for a pipe and another look at the papers, and then to bed, where he read himself to sleep in a few minutes. Even for luncheon he found that he had an appetite, and he was sniffing the smell of chops in the hall, the smell that not many months before would have turned him away from such a place in the first moment, when a large, dark figure, which seemed to have been waiting in the coffee-room doorway, stepped out and said, 'Mr Sponson?'

Tom, without thought, answered, 'My name is Stone,' and then, indignant to see himself confronted by a policeman, went on, 'What do you want here? Why should I answer your questions?'

The policeman, a large West Country man with a red face, answered, in a deprecating manner, as if to say 'Excuse me', that he had not asked any questions. He was holding his helmet in front of his stomach in the manner of a shy man who wants to occupy his hands. Tom saw at once that this polite, apologetic manner was merely assumed. It was hypocritical nonsense.

He said shortly, 'Well, don't, because I don't intend to answer any.'

'That's all right, sir,' said the policeman. 'No offence, I hope.' And he went out. Even his gesture, as, turning the corner, he threw up his chin and replaced his helmet on his head, annoyed Tom. It seemed to carry all that confidence of authority, that calm superiority of power, that is so offensive to the private citizen.

He went upstairs to his room in a rage and began to pack. He must get away at once. What enraged him was the thought that he had been followed, spied upon. Louie must have gone to the police. What right had they to pursue him like this? He had done no wrong; in fact, he was trying to do the right thing, the sensible thing. No doubt, Louie felt offended; perhaps she was hurt in her pride. She didn't want her friends to know that her marriage had failed. But if there were any publicity now it would be entirely her own fault. He had done everything to avoid publicity. He rang the bell for his bill before he remembered that it did not ring; none of the bells rang. But almost at once a maid, as if summoned by telepathy, appeared. She looked with surprise at his suitcase, half packed, and said that luncheon was ready and that someone was waiting for him.

'Someone waiting?' he demanded. 'Who's waiting?'

'In the coffee-room, sir – a gentleman.'

'What gentleman?'

The maid did not know, and seemed startled by the question. She hurried away almost at a run, and he realized that he had been shouting at her.

Tom banged his suitcase shut. The maid was obviously a spy, just as Mr Sims had certainly been a spy, and all barmen like to keep in with the police. That policeman had certainly talked to the barman, and how had the police got to know about him except from spies in the place? All at once Westford seemed to him almost as loathsome as his own suburb at home, full of people making demands upon him, thinking about him, discussing him. Certainly everyone in the pub would be discussing him – this mysterious affair, Mr Sponson's disappearance.

And who was this gentleman? Probably a detective. It must be a detective. He took his suitcase with him down the back stairs. He would escape by the yard. But the barman was at the bottom of the stairs, looking up at him with a thoughtful air, and when he turned towards the front hall, there was his brother, Fred. Fred was shaking hands with him before he realized who he was.

'Hullo, old chap, how are you? This is a bit of luck, to find you here,' Fred said.

'What do you mean, find me here? What do you take me for? You've come after me – I suppose Louie sent you?'

'My dear old chap, that's none of my business. It's only that – there's one or two small points about our own family affairs – about some of our father's things.'

Fred was in the Army, a major. Tom and he had always been good friends, but they had no family interests in common except their memories. Fred was married, with three children, the paternal estate had been divided long ago, and Tom suddenly lost his temper. 'Look, Fred,' he said. 'I don't know how you got on my tracks – I suppose I'm being spied on all the time – but it's no good coming after me like this. You won't get me to go back.'

'My dear chap, I wouldn't dream of it. In fact, I'm all for this idea of taking a holiday, a real holiday. You've not had a real holiday for years. Why not come ski-ing with me in Norway?' He slapped Tom on the shoulder with a smile that was just a little too hearty, too brotherly.

Tom pushed the hand from his shoulder. 'Don't talk nonsense,' he said. 'The thing is to humour the lunatic, isn't it? Go along with the poor chap in his wildest fantods.'

'Good heavens, no, old boy. I never saw you looking better.'

'Because the fact is that I've just got sane – for the first time in years. I've just waked up to the kind of imbecile nonsense that my life had become.'

'Exactly. I couldn't agree more. All work and no play – a real holiday –'

'Of course I want a holiday – for the rest of my life. You think this is a breakdown. It isn't. It's a breakout. What do you suppose my life is like at home – as they call it? Bob and April stopped being my children years ago when they went away to school, and as for Louie, I often wonder whether she ever has been my real wife. Certainly I've never known just what she was after or what she thought of me. And these last two years I've simply been a nuisance to her. This is a break, in fact, for her as well as for me. It isn't so much a new life we need as a real life. As it is, we just carry on this marriage by habit. It's just an imitation marriage, a robot marriage. We go through the gestures because we've been wound up and can't stop the machinery. Well, now I *have* stopped the machinery and I'm going to have some life on my own and give Louie some life, too. She needn't be afraid she will be left flat. There's plenty of money for both of us.'

Fred made a face as if to say, 'Really, I don't want all this talk,' and said, 'Quite. I quite see your point, old chap, though, in fact, I gather she's upset, quite ill, they say – But what about some lunch? I'm hungry.' He sat down at a table in the coffee-room and called the waiter.

But Tom was not going to be wangled in this manner. He wasn't going to have Fred go on pretending that this act of justice and sincerity was a trifle. He would not even sit down at the table. He bent over it towards Fred and said, 'So she's made herself ill. She would, but why? Because she's upset at what people will say. Because she may have to give up a few parties. Because her routine is changed – like someone who's knocked off cigarettes and doesn't know how to pass the time.'

The waiter had arrived with Fred's chop, mashed potato, and brussels sprouts, the standard lunch at the pub. Fred took a mouthful and then shouted, 'Waiter, half a can of old and mild!'

This affectation of ease still more irritated Tom. 'You don't believe me,' he said. 'But what do you know about it? I tell you I'm nothing to Louie but a provider and I'm going on providing. That's to say, she'll get exactly the same income as before.'

The waiter came with the beer. Fred took a sip and said, 'Might be worse', and then, sticking his fork in the chop, remarked, 'The children.'

'Yes, the children. And if I'm nothing much to Louie, I'm still less to the children. They have their own lives, they've had 'em for years.' And when Fred went on eating his chop, Tom, now very exasperated, began a long speech about the children. He wasn't blaming them, he said. They were nice children. It was, in fact, quite right that they should be having their own lives. What was wrong and perfectly stupid was this pretence that he was needed any more – this hypocrisy, which was just as bad for them as for him, and all for nothing. His own life was simply being wasted for nothing.

Fred still went on eating, and Tom, leaning across the table on his knuckles, felt like some village orator addressing a meeting so bored that it cannot even listen. Abruptly he stopped. He was so angry that for a moment he had an impulse to take up Fred's beer and throw it in his face. The impulse was so strong that he hastily turned away and went out of the room, and, catching up his suitcase, hat and coat, made for the door. But before he could escape, the barman popped out from the saloon bar. 'Your bill, sir.' When he had paid the bill, Fred had picked up the suitcase and was saying, 'Let me give you a hand, old chap. What about the old heart?' Fred carried the suitcase all the way to the bus. He talked of their childhood. Some old album of photographs had turned up in his attic. Would Tom like to see them? There ought to be a share-out.

Tom said nothing; he could not speak for fear of screaming his rage at Fred. He knew that if he began to speak, if he said a word to him, it would be a shriek, and he dared not shriek.

The bus was standing in front of The Lobster Pot, the village beerhouse, but it was not to leave for half an hour yet. Fred proposed that they should go in for a parting glass, but Tom hastily climbed into the empty bus and took his seat. For a moment he was afraid, he was terrified, that Fred would sit down beside him and go on talking, go on trying to smooth him down, to make him feel that nothing was really wrong, that all this that had happened was quite an ordinary event.

But Fred apparently had more sense, or possibly better instructions. He put down the suitcase beside Tom and held out his hand. 'Well, old chap, I suppose you don't want me here, but if there's anything I can do, I hope you'll send along and let me know.' Tom did not take the hand. He wanted to do so, he was fond of Fred, but it seemed to him now that if he touched his hand he would be acknowledging that Fred's mission was not completely nonsense, that after all there was something in the conventional shibboleth of family unity that had sent him to Westford. He could not touch his hand, and after a moment Fred said good-bye again and went off. What a relief. Tom felt such a sense of release that he was full of gratitude to his brother. He thought, I must write to him, I must tell him that I didn't want to be rude. It wasn't a personal matter; it was just a question of principle.

That night he was in Liverpool, at a quiet back-street hotel, a commercial hotel. His plan was to go abroad, to Eire or Europe. He had sent to the office for a letter of credit, addressed Poste Restante. But when he called at the Central Post Office, there was only a note from his chief clerk saying the credit was on its way. When it had not arrived by next morning, he wrote again, with some indignation. And on the next day, the fourth, as he came from the hotel to go to the post office, Louie stepped out of a taxi that had been waiting at the kerb. She threw her arms round his neck and broke into tears. She said nothing – after that warm embrace she only stood gazing at him with an anxious and embarrassed smile. Louie's smile through her tears struck Tom as especially artificial and disgusting. How ridiculous to try to get round him in this manner. As if he were a child to be wangled by caresses and 'darlings'.

'What exactly do you want?' he demanded. 'Didn't you get my letter?' Just then he remembered that he'd never sent that letter. He'd never quite decided how to finish it. So he added quickly and impatiently, 'What's the point of chasing me about like this? *That* can't do any good to anybody.'

Louie only continued to gaze with the same tearful and exasperating look of grief.

Another person had now descended from the taxi – Tom's family doctor, Bewley, an earnest young man, whose long, solemn face had caused Tom to say that he was more fitted to be an undertaker. He was much valued by all those valuable private patients who like to have their kinks taken seriously. Tom did not care for him, and shouted, 'Good God, and what do *you* think you're doing here?'

Bewley did not seem to hear. He did not even look at Tom but addressed himself to a stranger standing a couple of paces behind Louie – a man with very large and very black horn-rims, and very high, square shoulders. His face was square, too, with a pug nose and a large mouth, which was fixed in that habitual, professional smile that marks a floor manager in a store or the master of ceremonies at a *palais de danse*.

Tom had hardly wondered who the fellow was and where he had come from before he noticed, just behind, as if to take cover from his broad back, both the children. And a little to their right, he suddenly recognized, in a mysterious skulker with an immense coat collar turned up almost to the brim of a bowler hat, the long white nose and little steel goggles of his chief clerk. His whole life seemed to have gathered about him again in this back street – all those ties that had gradually bound him and wrapped him round in that cocoon of dead matter, that dusty nonsense, which, if he could not break through it now, once for all, would smother him.

'What on earth is all this about?' he asked Louie.

She opened her mouth to speak, and then lost courage and looked round at the stranger. It was he, with a slight extension of that professional smile, who answered, 'It's all right, Mr Sponson. We don't want to bother you in any way. We're just going.'

'The sooner the better,' Tom said, and, with a sudden conviction, added, 'So you're the private eye that's been spying on me.'

'Not at all, Mr Sponson.' The man stepped forward with outstretched hand. 'I don't suppose you remember me.'

'No, I'm damned if I do. Who the devil are you?'

The stranger did not answer, and for some reason Tom did not press him for an answer. He was too angry, too infuriated by that professional, confident grin. What had the brute got to be pleased about? He wanted to hit him, to knock that grin off his pug face. But he saw that this would be a giveaway; it would be just what the brute wanted. To see him rattled. He ignored the fellow, and said to Louie, with an easy, nonchalant air, 'Now, Louie, you're a sensible woman. You know perfectly well that all this fuss is completely unnecessary. It's not helping either of us to see straight. Do realize,' he went on, in a sympathetic tone, 'that I'm not accusing you of any *conscious* hypocrisy, of putting on an act. Not at all. I realize perfectly well that you *think* you're doing the right thing. For instance, I'm prepared to bet that you *think* you need me at home. Don't you?' Louie didn't answer. She only gazed sadly, anxiously. Tom thought, 'She's not even listening,' and he became more urgent. 'But don't you *see* all this is simply because you won't stop to ask yourself what you're *really* doing – what we're all playing at?'

His voice rose, and he wanted to wave his hands. But he kept them firmly under control. He smiled in a nonchalant, lazy manner. 'My dear old girl, really, you know – '

At this moment, he noticed that the party had closed on him. As the stranger had moved in, they had followed, as if drawn by some magnetic centre of attraction. The children were within a yard; the clerk, on the other side, was at his elbow. All at once he lost the thread of his calm discussion with Louie. He started back. He had actually been on the brink of running away, declaring himself a fugitive. And what from? Nonsense? To run away from nonsense, just pretence, a made-up delusion – that would be simply madness. And what enraged him as he looked round at all these nonsense-mongers was their nonsense looks. The children seemed even more terrified than Louie – the self-confident Bob, the popular and rather too successful freshman, now wore the face of a child who has seen a spectre, and April, a plump girl, whose cheeks were normally round and rather too rosy, seemed lank and pale. The lugubrious

247

Bewley had a ferocious glare, as if affronted, and the chief clerk, a highly respectable and rather timid person whose favourite recreation was dominoes, had that desperate frown of resolution that one sees in dentists' parlours.

Tom waved one hand and muttered, 'But it's perfectly stupid', then turned on the girl. 'Why aren't you at school?'

The girl looked frightened, as if she were going to cry, and all the rest turned their faces towards her, as if imploring her to do the wise, the intelligent thing. And obviously, she felt her responsibility but hadn't an idea of what was expected of her. Then abruptly she stepped forward, gave her father a timid peck on the cheek, quite unlike her usual vigorous embrace, and said, 'I was so worried about you, Daddy.'

'But why, why, why?' He appealed to this child of whom he was so fond. 'Look at me – I'm all right.' He laughed gaily. 'It's you who are worried, darling, it's you who are running about with looks of horror simply because I've told the truth for once.' He laughed again, and now both his arms were waving, but he didn't care. Why care? Why pretend? What hypocrisy, what nonsense! 'It's so f-funny,' he said. 'Look at you. Chasing me all over England – and why? You don't want me, you know – you haven't wanted me for years.'

Suddenly he grew disgusted. What was the good of talking? They absolutely refused to understand. They had simply sold themselves to nonsense. They simply didn't want to understand truth any more. Talking to them was like talking to Chinese. They were so completely foreign that they could not interpret even his looks, his tone.

'I'm so so-sorry,' said the girl, and she gave a sob.

The sob had a kind of echo in Tom's breast, a physical echo. He took a long breath. He wanted to console the poor child, but he didn't know how. She was too strange, too cut off from him.

And then, catching the stranger's eye, noting again his smile, he saw that the fellow quite understood the situation. He was a brute but not a fool. Tom found himself smiling at him in a confidential manner.

The stranger at once stepped forward and opened the taxi

door. Tom, perceiving at once how right he had been about the fellow's intelligence, climbed in and joyfully took his seat. He was surprised for only a moment when the stranger followed him; he saw at once that this, too, was an intelligent act. He had a lot to say to him – he wanted to explain the whole ridiculous affair. As the taxi drove off, he said with a cheerful and knowing air, 'I spotted you at once – one of Louie's psychiatrists.' The stranger simply smiled, in fact, beamed at him. He now looked like a floor manager who has made a good sale. 'But all the same,' said Tom, 'I'm not having a breakdown. I'm simply fed up with nonsense.'

'I know. I know. So am I. So's everybody. You just want to get away.'

'Get away from the nonsense,' Tom said. 'But it comes after you all the time. And it won't even listen when you tell it it's nonsense. It won't even believe it's nonsense. It's so absolutely soaked in its own nonsense that it can't take in anything else. Like fish.' He didn't stop to explain this point; he was quite sure that the stranger understood. He smiled hastily to show this confidence. 'Or whisky. If you cut it off, they'd get the shakes, they couldn't breathe.'

The stranger's very spectacles were full of understanding, and Tom waved his hands and leaned towards him. 'Words,' he said. 'It's all words, words, words. They live on words – they can't understand anything but words. They think words. You talk to them, but you might as well be burbling in a madhouse to a lot of tape recorders – they only get a lot of noises. You saw that poor child – all the family in tears – for nothing. For absolute nonsense. For words. It makes you laugh.' And to his horror, he began to cry.

The stranger patted his shoulder and said, 'All over now', in a professional but understanding tone.

The taxi drove up in front of a large, discreet building standing back from the road in a surburban street.

'Is this an asylum?' Tom asked.

The stranger actually laughed. 'No, no, no. What nonsense. It's just a place where you *can* get away. That's all you need – to get away.'

Twenty minutes later, Tom was in bed; the stranger was giving instructions to a nurse. Tom had had an injection and was sinking happily into a doze. What joy, what peace. At last he had got away. But just as he closed his eyes, he muttered again, in protest, 'This isn't a breakdown, you know. It's only – I got fed up with all the words, the nonsense.'

The stranger laid a large, cool hand on his head. 'I know. I know.' And he really seemed to know.

That was six weeks ago. Tom is now back at work, back with his family. He has been back a fortnight and already life is exactly the same as before. Louie no longer hovers about him with anxious affection; the children no longer come into the room on tiptoe and try to talk sympathetically about his long day at the office. He has found it especially trying to keep up this absurd kind of conversation. With the arrears at the office, he has been far too busy to want anything at home but peace. And why should Louie tell him about her day's amusements or the children pretend to take an interest in a business of which they have never comprehended a detail? What nonsense. Thank God they've got over it. That first week back at home had almost driven him *really* mad.

And suddenly, at the club, talking to an old friend, he hears himself say, 'Yes, I've been lucky, it's been a wonderful marriage. Well, you know Louie, and the children *stay* so nice, so affectionate. You couldn't find nicer, more affectionate children. After all, family life is everything, and mine has been a marvellous success.' He stops, startled by some echo from that holiday, now almost forgotten. The word 'nonsense' has jumped into his brain.

Neither Tom nor his family has ever admitted that he has had a breakdown – it is called a holiday, a rest cure. And no nonsense about it. But if that wasn't nonsense, what is this – all these words that he is uttering with such earnestness? But no, *not* nonsense – God forbid. More like a prayer.

Aldous Huxley

THE GIOCONDA SMILE

I

'MISS SPENCE will be down directly, sir.'

'Thank you,' said Mr Hutton, without turning round. Janet
Spence's parlourmaid was so ugly – ugly on purpose, it always
seemed to him, malignantly, criminally ugly – that he could not
bear to look at her more than was necessary. The door closed.
Left to himself, Mr Hutton got up and began to wander round
the room, looking with meditative eyes at the familiar objects
it contained.

Photographs of Greek statuary, photographs of the Roman
Forum, coloured prints of Italian masterpieces, all very safe and
well known. Poor, dear Janet, what a prig – what an intellectual
snob! Her real taste was illustrated in that water-colour by the
pavement artist, the one she had paid half a crown for (and
thirty-five shillings for the frame). How often he had heard her
tell the story, how often expatiate on the beauties of that skilful
imitation of an oleograph! 'A real Artist in the streets', and you
could hear the capital A in Artist as she spoke the words. She
made you feel that part of his glory had entered into Janet
Spence when she tendered him that half-crown for the copy of
the oleograph. She was implying a compliment to her own
taste and penetration. A genuine Old Master for half a crown.
Poor, dear Janet!

Mr Hutton came to a pause in front of a small oblong mirror.
Stopping a little to get a full view of his face, he passed a white,
well-manicured finger over his moustache. It was as curly, as
freshly auburn as it had been twenty years ago. His hair still
retained its colour, and there was no sign of baldness yet – only a
certain elevation of the brow. 'Shakespearean', thought Mr

Hutton, with a smile, as he surveyed the smooth and polished expanse of his forehead.

Others abide our question, thou are free. . . . Footsteps in the sea . . . Majesty. . . . Shakespeare, thou shouldst be living at this hour. No, that was Milton, wasn't it? Milton, the Lady of Christ's. There was no lady about him. He was what the women would call a manly man. That was why they liked him – for the curly auburn moustache and the discreet redolence of tobacco. Mr Hutton smiled again; he enjoyed making fun of himself. Lady of Christ's? No, no. He was the Christ of Ladies. Very pretty, very pretty. The Christ of Ladies. Mr Hutton wished there were somebody he could tell the joke to. Poor, dear Janet wouldn't appreciate it, alas!

He straightened himself up, patted his hair, and resumed his peregrination. Damn the Roman Forum; he hated those dreary photographs.

Suddenly he became aware that Janet Spence was in the room, standing near the door. Mr Hutton started, as though he had been taken in some felonious act. To make these silent and spectral appearances was one of Janet Spence's peculiar talents. Perhaps she had been there all the time, had seen him looking at himself in the mirror. Impossible! But, still, it was disquieting.

'Oh, you gave me such a surprise,' said Mr Hutton, recovering his smile and advancing with outstretched hand to meet her.

Miss Spence was smiling too: her Gioconda smile, he had once called it in a moment of half-ironical flattery. Miss Spence had taken the compliment seriously, and always tried to live up to the Leonardo standard. She smiled on in silence while Mr Hutton shook hands; that was part of the Gioconda business.

'I hope you're well,' said Mr Hutton. 'You look it.'

What a queer face she had! That small mouth pursed forward by the Gioconda expression into a little snout with a round hole in the middle as though for whistling – it was like a penholder seen from the front. Above the mouth a well-shaped nose, finely aquiline. Eyes large, lustrous, and dark, with the largeness, lustre, and darkness that seems to invite sties and an occasional bloodshot suffusion. They were fine eyes, but unchangingly grave. The penholder might do its Gioconda trick, but the eyes never altered in their earnestness. Above them, a pair of boldly arched, heavily pencilled black eyebrows lent a surprising air of power, as of a Roman matron, to the upper portion of the face. Her hair was dark and equally Roman; Agrippina from the brows upward.

'I thought I'd just look in on my way home,' Mr Hutton went on. 'Ah, it's good to be back here' – he indicated with a wave of his hand the flowers in the vases, the sunshine and greenery beyond the windows – 'it's good to be back in the country after a stuffy day of business in town.'

Miss Spence, who had sat down, pointed to a chair at her side.

'No, really, I can't sit down,' Mr Hutton protested. 'I must get back to see how poor Emily is. She was rather seedy this morning.' He sat down, nevertheless. 'It's these wretched liver chills. She's always getting them. Women – ' He broke off and coughed, so as to hide the fact that he had uttered. He was about to say that women with weak digestions ought not to marry; but the remark was too cruel, and he didn't really believe it. Janet Spence, moreover, was a believer in eternal flames and spiritual attachments. 'She hopes to be well enough,' he added, 'to see you at luncheon tomorrow. Can you come? Do I' He smiled persuasively. 'It's my invitation too, you know.'

She dropped her eyes, and Mr Hutton almost thought that he detected a certain reddening of the cheek. It was a tribute; he stroked his moustache.

'I should like to come if you think Emily's really well enough to have a visitor.'

'Of course. You'll do her good. You'll do us both good. In married life three is often better company than two.'

'Oh, you're cynical.'

Mr Hutton always had a desire to say 'Bow-wow-wow' whenever that last word was spoken. It irritated him more than any other word in the language. But instead of barking he made haste to protest.

'No, no. I'm only speaking a melancholy truth. Reality doesn't always come up to the ideal, you know. But that doesn't make me believe any the less in the ideal. Indeed, I believe in it passionately – the ideal of a matrimony between two people in perfect accord. I think it's realizable. I'm sure it is.'

He paused significantly and looked at her with an arch expression. A virgin of thirty-six, but still unwithered; she had her charms. And there was something really rather enigmatic about her. Miss Spence made no reply, but continued to smile. There were times when Mr Hutton got rather bored with the Gioconda. He stood up.

'I must really be going now. Farewell, mysterious Gioconda.' The smile grew intenser, focused itself, as it were, in a narrower snout. Mr Hutton made a Cinquecento gesture, and kissed her extended hand. It was the first time he had done such a thing; the action seemed not to be resented. 'I look forward to tomorrow.'

'Do you?'

For answer Mr Hutton once more kissed her hand, then turned to go. Miss Spence accompanied him to the porch.

'Where's your car?' she asked.

'I left it at the gate of the drive.'

'I'll come and see you off.'

'No, no.' Mr Hutton was playful, but determined. 'You must do no such thing. I simply forbid you.'

'But I should like to come,' Miss Spence protested, throwing a rapid Gioconda at him.

Mr Hutton held up his hand. 'No,' he repeated, and then, with a gesture that was almost the blowing of a kiss, he started to run down the drive, lightly, on his toes, with long, bounding strides like a boy's. He was proud of that run; it was quite marvellously youthful. Still, he was glad the drive was no longer. At the last bend, before passing out of sight of the house, he halted and turned round. Miss Spence was still standing on the steps, smiling her smile. He waved his hand, and this time quite definitely and overtly wafted a kiss in her direction. Then, breaking once more into his magnificent canter, he rounded the last dark promontory of trees. Once out of sight of the house he let his high paces decline to a trot, and finally to a walk. He took out his handkerchief and began wiping his neck inside his collar. What fools, what fools! Had there ever been such an ass as poor, dear Janet Spence? Never, unless it was himself. Decidedly he was the more malignant fool, since he, at least, was aware of his folly and still persisted in it. Why did he persist? Ah, the problem that was himself, the problem that was other people . . .

He had reached the gate. A large prosperous-looking motor was standing at the side of the road.

'Home, M'Nab.' The chauffeur touched his cap. 'And stop at the cross-roads on the way, as usual,' Mr Hutton added, as he opened the door of the car. 'Well?' he said, speaking into the obscurity that lurked within.

'Oh, Teddy Bear, what an age you've been!' It was a fresh and childish voice that spoke the words. There was the faintest hint of Cockney impurity about the vowel sounds.

Mr Hutton bent his large form and darted into the car with the agility of an animal regaining its burrow.

'Have I?' he said, as he shut the door. The machine began to move. 'You must have missed me a lot if you found the time so long.' He sat back in the low seat; a cherishing warmth enveloped him.

'Teddy Bear . . . ' and with a sigh of contentment a charming little head declined on to Mr Hutton's shoulder. Ravished, he looked down sideways at the round, babyish face.

'Do you know, Doris, you look like the pictures of Louise de Kéroual.' He passed his fingers through a mass of curly hair.

'Who's Louise de Kera-whatever-it-is?' Doris spoke from remote distances.

'She was, alas! *Fuit*. We shall all be "was" one of these days. Meanwhile . . . '

Mr Hutton covered the babyish face with kisses. The car rushed smoothly along. M'Nab's back, through the front window, was stonily impressive, the back of a statue.

'Your hands,' Doris whispered. 'Oh, you mustn't touch me. They give me electric shocks.'

Mr Hutton adored her for the virgin imbecility of the words. How late in one's existence one makes the discovery of one's body!

'The electricity isn't in me, it's in you.' He kissed her again, whispering her name several times: Doris, Doris, Doris. The scientific appellation of the sea-mouse, he was thinking as he kissed the throat she offered him, white and extended like the throat of a victim awaiting the sacrificial knife. The sea-mouse was a sausage with iridescent fur: very peculiar. Or was Doris the sea-cucumber, which turns itself inside out in moments of alarm? He would really have to go to Naples again, just to see the aquarium. These sea creatures were fabulous, unbelievably fantastic.

'Oh, Teddy Bear!' (More zoology; but he was only a land animal. His poor little jokes!) 'Teddy Bear, I'm so happy.'

'So am I,' said Mr Hutton. Was it true?

'But I wish I knew if it were right. Tell me, Teddy Bear, is it right or wrong?'

'Ah, my dear, that's just what I've been wondering for the last thirty years.'

'Be serious, Teddy Bear. I want to know if this is right; if it's right that I should be here with you and that we should love one another, and that it should give me electric shocks when you touch me.'

'Right? Well, it's certainly good that you should have electric shocks rather than sexual repressions. Read Freud; repressions are the devil.'

'Oh, you don't help me. Why aren't you ever serious? If only you knew how miserable I am sometimes, thinking it's not right. Perhaps, you know, there is a hell, and all that. I don't know what to do. Sometimes I think I ought to stop loving you.'

'But could you?' asked Mr Hutton, confident in the powers of his seduction and his moustache.

'No, Teddy Bear, you know I couldn't. But I could run away, I could hide from you, I could lock myself up and force myself not to come to you.'

'Silly little thing!' He tightened his embrace.

'Oh, dear, I hope it isn't wrong. And there are times when I don't care if it is.'

Mr Hutton was touched. He had a certain protective affection for this little creature. He laid his cheek against her hair and so, interlaced, they sat in silence, while the car, swaying and pitching a little as it hastened along, seemed to draw in the white road and the dusty hedges towards it devouringly.

'Good-bye, good-bye.'

The car moved on, gathered speed, vanished round a curve, and Doris was left standing by the sign-post at the cross-roads, still dizzy and weak with the languor born of those kisses and the electrical touch of those gentle hands. She had to take a deep breath, to draw herself up deliberately, before she was strong enough to start her homeward walk. She had half a mile in which to invent the necessary lies.

Alone, Mr Hutton suddenly found himself the prey of an appalling boredom.

2

Mrs Hutton was lying on the sofa in her boudoir, playing patience. In spite of the warmth of the July evening a wood fire was burning on the hearth. A black Pomeranian, extenuated by the heat and the fatigues of digestion, slept before the blaze.

'Phew! Isn't it rather hot in here?' Mr Hutton asked as he entered the room.

'You know I have to keep warm, dear.' The voice seemed breaking on the verge of tears. 'I get so shivery.'

'I hope you're better this evening.'

'Not much, I'm afraid.'

The conversation stagnated. Mr Hutton stood leaning his back against the mantelpiece. He looked down at the Pomeranian lying at his feet, and with the toe of his right boot he rolled the little dog over and rubbed its white-flecked chest and belly. The creature lay in an inert ecstasy. Mrs Hutton continued to play patience. Arrived at an *impasse*, she altered the position of one card, took back another, and went on playing. Her patiences always came out.

'Dr Libbard thinks I ought to go to Llandrindod Wells this summer.'

'Well, go, my dear – go, most certainly.'

Mr Hutton was thinking of the events of the afternoon: how they had driven, Doris and he, up to the hanging wood, had left the car to wait for them under the shade of the trees, and walked together out into the windless sunshine of the chalk down.

'I'm to drink the waters for my liver, and he thinks I ought to have massage and electric treatment, too.'

Hat in hand, Doris had stalked four blue butterflies that were dancing together round a scabious flower with a motion that was like the flickering of blue fire. The blue fire burst and scattered into whirling sparks; she had given chase, laughing and shouting like a child.

'I'm sure it will do you good, my dear.'

'I was wondering if you'd come with me, dear.'

'But you know I'm going to Scotland at the end of the month.'

Mrs Hutton looked up at him entreatingly. 'It's the journey,' she said. 'The thought of it is such a nightmare. I don't know if I can manage it. And you know I can't sleep in hotels. And then there's the luggage and all the worries. I can't go alone.'

'But you won't be alone. You'll have your maid with you.' He spoke impatiently. The sick woman was usurping the place of the healthy one. He was being dragged back from the memory of the sunlit down and the quick, laughing girl, back to this unhealthy, overheated room and its complaining occupant.

'I don't think I shall be able to go.'

'But you must, my dear, if the doctor tells you to. And, besides, a change will do you good.'

'I don't think so.'

'But Libbard thinks so, and he knows what he's talking about.'

'No, I can't face it. I'm too weak. I can't go alone.' Mrs Hutton pulled a handkerchief out of her black silk bag, and put it to her eyes.

'Nonsense, my dear, you must make the effort.'

'I had rather be left in peace to die here.' She was crying in earnest now.

'O Lord! Now do be reasonable. Listen now, please.' Mrs

Hutton only sobbed more violently. 'Oh, what is one to do?'
He shrugged his shoulders and walked out of the room.

Mr Hutton was aware that he had not behaved with proper
patience; but he could not help it. Very early in his manhood he
had discovered that not only did he not feel sympathy for the
poor, the weak, the diseased, and deformed; he actually hated
them. Once, as an undergraduate, he spent three days at a
mission in the East End. He had returned, filled with a profound and ineradicable disgust. Instead of pitying, he loathed
the unfortunate. It was not, he knew, a very comely emotion,
and he had been ashamed of it at first. In the end he had decided
that it was temperamental, inevitable, and had felt no further
qualms. Emily had been healthy and beautiful when he married
her. He had loved her then. But now – was it his fault that she
was like this?

Mr Hutton dined alone. Food and drink left him more bene-
volent than he had been before dinner. To make amends for his
show of exasperation he went up to his wife's room and offered
to read to her. She was touched, gratefully accepted the offer,
and Mr Hutton, who was particularly proud of his accent,
suggested a little light reading in French.

'French? I am so fond of French.' Mrs Hutton spoke of the
language of Racine as though it were a dish of green peas.

Mr Hutton ran down to the library and returned with a yellow
volume. He began reading. The effort of pronouncing perfectly
absorbed his whole attention. But how good his accent was!
The fact of its goodness seemed to improve the quality of the
novel he was reading.

At the end of fifteen pages an unmistakable sound aroused
him. He looked up; Mrs Hutton had gone to sleep. He sat still
for a little while, looking with a dispassionate curiosity at the
sleeping face. Once it had been beautiful; once, long ago, the
sight of it, the recollection of it, had moved him with an
emotion profounder, perhaps, than any he had felt before or
since. Now it was lined and cadaverous. The skin was stretched
tightly over the cheekbones, across the bridge of the sharp,
bird-like nose. The closed eyes were set in profound bone-
rimmed sockets. The lamplight striking on the face from the

side emphasized with light and shade its cavities and projections. It was the face of a dead Christ by Morales.

> *Le squelette était invisible*
> *Au temps heureux de l'art païen.*

He shivered a little, and tiptoed out of the room.

On the following day Mrs Hutton came down to luncheon. She had had some unpleasant palpitations during the night, but she was feeling better now. Besides, she wanted to do honour to her guest. Miss Spence listened to her complaints about Llandrindod Wells, and was loud in sympathy, lavish with advice. Whatever she said was always said with intensity. She leaned forward, aimed, so to speak, like a gun, and fired her words. Bang! the charge in her soul was ignited, the words whizzed forth at the narrow barrel of her mouth. She was a machine-gun riddling her hostess with sympathy. Mr Hutton had undergone similar bombardments, mostly of a literary or philosophic character – bombardments of Maeterlinck, of Mrs Besant, of Bergson, of William James. Today the missiles were medical. She talked about insomnia, she expatiated on the virtues of harmless drugs and beneficent specialists. Under the bombardment Mrs Hutton opened out, like a flower in the sun.

Mr Hutton looked on in silence. The spectacle of Janet Spence evoked in him an unfailing curiosity. He was not romantic enough to imagine that every face masked an interior physiognomy of beauty or strangeness, that every woman's small talk was like a vapour hanging over mysterious gulfs. His wife, for example, and Doris; they were nothing more than what they seemed to be. But with Janet Spence it was somehow different. Here one could be sure that there was some kind of a queer face behind the Gioconda smile and the Roman eyebrows. The only question was: What exactly was there? Mr Hutton could never quite make out.

'But perhaps you won't have to go to Llandrindod after all,' Miss Spence was saying. 'If you get well quickly Dr Libbard will let you off.'

'I only hope so. Indeed, I do really feel rather better today.'

Mr Hutton felt ashamed. How much was it his own lack of sympathy that prevented her from feeling well every day? But he comforted himself by reflecting that it was only a case of feeling, not of being better. Sympathy does not mend a diseased liver or a weak heart.

'My dear, I wouldn't eat those red currants if I were you,' he said, suddenly solicitous. 'You know that Libbard has banned everything with skins and pips.'

'But I am so fond of them,' Mrs Hutton protested, 'and I feel so well today.'

'Don't be a tyrant,' said Miss Spence, looking first at him and then at his wife. 'Let the poor invalid have what she fancies; it will do her good.' She laid her hand on Mrs Hutton's arm and patted it affectionately two or three times.

'Thank you, my dear.' Mrs Hutton helped herself to the stewed currants.

'Well, don't blame me if they make you ill again.'

'Do I ever blame you, dear?'

'You have nothing to blame me for,' Mr Hutton answered playfully. 'I am the perfect husband.'

They sat in the garden after luncheon. From the island of shade under the old cypress tree they looked out across a flat expanse of lawn, in which the parterres of flowers shone with a metallic brilliance.

Mr Hutton took a deep breath of the warm and fragrant air. 'It's good to be alive,' he said.

'Just to be alive,' his wife echoed, stretching one pale, knot-jointed hand into the sunlight.

A maid brought the coffee; the silver pots and the little blue cups were set on a folding table near the group of chairs.

'Oh, my medicine!' exclaimed Mrs Hutton. 'Run in and fetch it, Clara, will you? The white bottle on the sideboard.'

'I'll go,' said Mr Hutton. 'I've got to go and fetch a cigar in any case.'

He ran in towards the house. On the threshold he turned round for an instant. The maid was walking back across the lawn. His wife was sitting up in her deck-chair, engaged in opening her white parasol. Miss Spence was bending over the table, pouring out the coffee. He passed into the cool obscurity of the house.

'Do you like sugar in your coffee?' Miss Spence inquired.

'Yes, please. Give me rather a lot. I'll drink it after my medicine to take the taste away.'

Mrs Hutton leaned back in her chair, lowering the sunshade over her eyes, so as to shut out from her vision the burning sky.

Behind her, Miss Spence was making a delicate clinking among the coffee-cups.

'I've given you three large spoonfuls. That ought to take the taste away. And here comes the medicine.'

Mr Hutton had reappeared, carrying a wine-glass, half full of a pale liquid.

'It smells delicious,' he said, as he handed it to his wife.

'That's only the flavouring.' She drank it off at a gulp, shuddered, and made a grimace. 'Ugh, it's so nasty. Give me my coffee.'

Miss Spence gave her the cup; she sipped at it. 'You've made it like syrup. But it's very nice, after that atrocious medicine.'

At half past three Mrs Hutton complained that she did not feel as well as she had done, and went indoors to lie down. Her husband would have said something about the red currants, but checked himself; the triumph of an 'I told you so' was too cheaply won. Instead, he was sympathetic, and gave her his arm to the house.

'A rest will do you good,' he said. 'By the way, I shan't be back till after dinner.'

'But why? Where are you going?'

'I promised to go to Johnson's this evening. We have to discuss the war memorial, you know.'

'Oh, I wish you weren't going.' Mrs Hutton was almost in tears. 'Can't you stay? I don't like being alone in the house.'

'But, my dear, I promised – weeks ago.' It was a bother having to lie like this. 'And now I must get back and look after Miss Spence.'

He kissed her on the forehead and went out again into the garden. Miss Spence received him aimed and intense.

'Your wife is dreadfully ill,' she fired off at him.

'I thought she cheered up so much when you came.'

'That was purely nervous, purely nervous. I was watching her closely. With a heart in that condition and her digestion wrecked – yes, wrecked – anything might happen.'

'Libbard doesn't take so gloomy a view of poor Emily's health.' Mr Hutton held open the gate that led from the garden into the drive; Miss Spence's car was standing by the front door.

'Libbard is only a country doctor. You ought to see a specialist.'

He could not refrain from laughing. 'You have a macabre passion for specialists.'

Miss Spence held up her hand in protest. 'I am serious. I think poor Emily is in a very bad state. Anything might happen – at any moment.'

He handed her into the car and shut the door. The chauffeur started the engine and climbed into his place, ready to drive off.

'Shall I tell him to start?' He had no desire to continue the conversation.

Miss Spence leaned forward and shot a Gioconda in his direction. 'Remember, I expect you to come and see me again soon.'

Mechanically he grinned, made a polite noise, and, as the car moved forward, waved his hand. He was happy to be alone.

A few minutes afterwards Mr Hutton himself drove away. Doris was waiting at the cross-roads. They dined together twenty miles from home, at a roadside hotel. It was one of those bad, expensive meals which are only cooked in country hotels frequented by motorists. It revolted Mr Hutton, but Doris enjoyed it. She always enjoyed things. Mr Hutton ordered a not very good brand of champagne. He was wishing he had spent the evening in his library.

When they started homewards Doris was a little tipsy and extremely affectionate. It was very dark inside the car, but looking forward, past the motionless form of M'Nab, they could see a bright and narrow universe of forms and colours scooped out of the night by the electric head-lamps.

It was after eleven when Mr Hutton reached home. Dr Libbard met him in the hall. He was a small man with delicate hands and well-formed features that were almost feminine. His brown eyes were large and melancholy. He used to waste a great deal of time sitting at the bedside of his patients, looking sadness through those eyes and talking in a sad, low voice about nothing in particular. His person exhaled a pleasing odour, decidedly antiseptic but at the same time suave and discreetly delicious.

'Libbard?' said Mr Hutton in surprise. 'You here? Is my wife ill?'

'We tried to fetch you earlier,' the soft, melancholy voice replied. 'It was thought you were at Mr Johnson's, but they had no news of you there.'

'No, I was detained. I had a break-down,' Mr Hutton answered irritably. It was tiresome to be caught out in a lie.

'Your wife wanted to see you urgently.'

'Well, I can go now.' Mr Hutton moved towards the stairs. Dr Libbard laid a hand on his arm. 'I am afraid it's too late.'

'Too late?' He began fumbling with his watch; it wouldn't come out of the pocket.

'Mrs Hutton passed away half an hour ago.'

The voice remained even in its softness, the melancholy of the eyes did not deepen. Dr Libbard spoke of death as he would speak of a local cricket match. All things were equally vain and equally deplorable.

Mr Hutton found himself thinking of Janet Spence's words. At any moment – at any moment. She had been extraordinarily right.

'What happened?' he asked. 'What was the cause?'

Dr Libbard explained. It was heart failure brought on by a violent attack of nausea, caused in its turn by the eating of something of an irritant nature. Red currants? Mr Hutton suggested. Very likely. It had been too much for the heart. There was chronic valvular disease: something had collapsed under the strain. It was all over; she could not have suffered much.

3

'It's a pity they should have chosen the day of the Eton and Harrow match for the funeral,' old General Grego was saying as he stood, his top hat in his hand, under the shadow of the lich-gate, wiping his face with his handkerchief.

Mr Hutton overheard the remark and with difficulty restrained a desire to inflict grievous bodily pain on the General. He would have liked to hit the old brute in the middle of his big red face. Monstrous great mulberry, spotted with meal! Was there no respect for the dead? Did nobody care? In theory he didn't much care; let the dead bury their dead. But here, at the graveside, he had found himself actually sobbing. Poor Emily, they had been pretty happy once. Now she was lying at the bottom of a seven-foot hole. And here was Grego complaining that he couldn't go to the Eton and Harrow match.

Mr Hutton looked round at the groups of black figures that were drifting slowly out of the churchyard towards the fleet of cabs and motors assembled in the road outside. Against the brilliant background of the July grass and flowers and foliage, they had a horribly alien and unnatural appearance. It pleased him to think that all these people would soon be dead too.

That evening Mr Hutton sat up late in his library reading the life of Milton. There was no particular reason why he should have chosen Milton; it was the book that first came to hand, that was all. It was after midnight when he had finished. He got up from his armchair, unbolted the French windows, and stepped out on to the little paved terrace. The night was quiet and clear. Mr Hutton looked at the stars and at the holes between them, dropped his eyes to the dim lawns and hueless flowers of the garden, and let them wander over the farther landscape, black and grey under the moon.

He began to think with a kind of confused violence. There were the stars, there was Milton. A man can be somehow the peer of stars and night. Greatness, nobility. But is there seriously a difference between the noble and the ignoble? Milton, the stars, death, and himself – himself. The soul, the body; the higher and the lower nature. Perhaps there was something in it, after all. Milton had a god on his side and righteousness. What had he? Nothing, nothing whatever. There were only Doris's little breasts. What was the point of it all? Milton, the stars, death, and Emily in her grave, Doris and himself – always himself. . . .

Oh, he was a futile and disgusting being. Everything convinced him of it. It was a solemn moment. He spoke aloud: 'I will, I will.' The sound of his own voice in the darkness was appalling; it seemed to him that he had sworn that infernal oath which binds even the gods: 'I will, I will.' There had been New Year's days and solemn anniversaries in the past, when he had felt the same contritions and recorded similar resolutions. They had all thinned away, these resolutions, like smoke, into nothingness. But this was a greater moment and he had pronounced a more fearful oath. In the future it was to be different. Yes, he would live by reason, he would be industrious, he would curb his appetites, he would devote his life to some good purpose. It was resolved and it would be so.

In practice he was himself spending his mornings in agricultural pursuits, riding round with the bailiff, seeing that his land was farmed in the best modern way – silos and artificial manures and continuous cropping, and all that. The remainder of the day should be devoted to serious study. There was that book he had been intending to write for so long–*The Effect of Diseases on Civilization.*

Mr Hutton went to bed humble and contrite, but with a sense that grace had entered into him. He slept for seven and a half hours, and woke to find the sun brilliantly shining. The emotions of the evening before had been transformed by a good night's rest into his customary cheerfulness. It was not until a good many seconds after his return to conscious life that he remembered his resolution, his Stygian oath. Milton and death seemed somehow different in the sunlight. As for the stars, they were not there. But the resolutions good; even in the daytime he could see that. He had his horse saddled after breakfast, and rode round the farm with the bailiff. After luncheon he read Thucydides on the plague at Athens. In the evening he made a few notes on malaria in Southern Italy. While he was undressing he remembered that there was a good anecdote in Skelton's jest-book about the Sweating Sickness. He would have made a note of it if only he could have found a pencil.

On the sixth morning of his new life Mr Hutton found among his correspondence an envelope addressed in that peculiarly vulgar handwriting which he knew to be Doris's. He opened it, and began to read. She didn't know what to say; words were so inadequate. His wife dying like that, and so suddenly – it was too terrible. Mr Hutton sighed, but his interest revived somewhat as he read on:

Death is so frightening, I never think of it when I can help it. But when something like this happens, or when I am feeling ill or depressed, then I can't help remembering it is there so close, and I think about all the wicked things I have done and about you and me, and I wonder what will happen, and I am so frightened. I am so lonely, Teddy Bear, and so unhappy, and I don't know what to do. I can't get rid of the idea of dying, I am so wretched and help- less without you. I didn't mean to write to you; I meant to wait till you were out of mourning and could come and see me again, but I was so lonely and miserable, Teddy Bear, I had to write. I couldn't help it. Forgive me, I want you so much; I have nobody in the world but you. You are so good and gentle and understanding; there is nobody like you. I shall never forget how good and kind you have been to me, and you are so clever and know so much, I can't under- stand how you ever came to pay any attention to me, I am so dull and stupid, much less like me and love me, because you do love me a little, don't you, Teddy Bear?

Mr Hutton was touched with shame and remorse. To be thanked like this, worshipped for having seduced the girl – it was too much. It had just been a piece of imbecile wantonness. Imbecile, idiotic: there was no other way to describe it. For, when all was said, he had derived very little pleasure from it. Taking all things together, he had probably been more bored than amused. Once upon a time he had believed himself to be a hedonist. But to be a hedonist implies a certain process of reasoning, a deliberate choice of known pleasure, a rejection of known pains. This had been done without reason, against it. For he knew beforehand – so well, so well – that there was no interest or pleasure to be derived from these wretched affairs. And yet each time the vague itch came upon him he succumbed, involving himself once more in the old stupidity. There had been Maggie, his wife's maid, and Edith, the girl on the farm, and Mrs Pringle, and the waitress in London, and others – there seemed to be dozens of them. It had all been so stale and boring. He knew it would be; he always knew. And yet, and yet. . . . Experience doesn't teach.

Poor little Doris! He would write to her kindly, comfortingly, but he wouldn't see her again. A servant came to tell him that his horse was saddled and waiting. He mounted and rode off. That morning the old bailiff was more irritating than usual.

Five days later Doris and Mr Hutton were sitting together on the pier at Southend; Doris, in white muslin with pink garnishings, radiated happiness; Mr Hutton, legs outstretched and chair tilted, had pushed the panama back from his forehead, and was trying to feel like a tripper. That night, when Doris was asleep, breathing and warm by his side, he recaptured, in this moment of darkness and physical fatigue, the rather cosmic emotion which had possessed him that evening, not a fortnight ago, when he had made his great resolution. And so his solemn oath had already gone the way of so many other resolutions. Unreason had triumphed; at the first itch of desire he had given way. He was hopeless, hopeless.

For a long time he lay with closed eyes, ruminating his humiliation. The girl stirred in her sleep. Mr Hutton turned over and looked in her direction. Enough faint light crept in between the half-drawn curtains to show her bare arm and shoulder, her neck, and the dark tangle of hair on the pillow. She was beautiful, desirable. Why did he lie there moaning over his sins? What did it matter? If he were hopeless, then so be it; he would make the best of his hopelessness. A glorious sense of irresponsibility suddenly filled him. He was free, magnificently free. In a kind of exaltation he drew the girl towards him. She woke, bewildered, almost frightened under his rough kisses.

The storm of his desire subsided into a kind of serene merriment. The whole atmosphere seemed to be quivering with enormous silent laughter.

'Could anyone love you as much as I do, Teddy Bear?' The question came faintly from distant worlds of love.

'I think I know somebody who does,' Mr Hutton replied. The submarine laughter was swelling, rising, ready to break the surface of silence and resound.

'Who? Tell me. What do you mean?' The voice had come very close; charged with suspicion, anguish, indignation, it belonged to this immediate world.

'A - ah!'

'Who?'

'You'll never guess.' Mr Hutton kept up the joke until it began to grow tedious, and then pronounced the name: 'Janet Spence.'

Doris was incredulous. 'Miss Spence of the Manor? That old woman?' It was too ridiculous. Mr Hutton laughed too.

'But it's quite true,' he said. 'She adores me.' Oh, the vast joke! He would go and see her as soon as he returned – see and conquer. 'I believe she wants to marry me,' he added.

'But you wouldn't ... you don't intend ...'

The air was fairly crepitating with humour. Mr Hutton laughed aloud. 'I intend to marry you,' he said. It seemed to him the best joke he had ever made in his life.

When Mr Hutton left Southend he was once more a married man. It was agreed that, for the time being, the fact should be kept secret. In the autumn they would go abroad together, and the world should be informed. Meanwhile he was to go back to his own house and Doris to hers.

The day after his return he walked over in the afternoon to see Miss Spence. She received him with the old Gioconda.

'I was expecting you to come.'

'I couldn't keep away,' Mr Hutton gallantly replied.

They sat in the summer-house. It was a pleasant place – a little old stucco temple bowered among dense bushes of evergreen. Miss Spence had left her mark on it by hanging up over the seat a blue-and-white Della Robbia plaque.

'I am thinking of going to Italy this autumn,' said Mr Hutton. He felt like a ginger-beer bottle, ready to pop with bubbling humorous excitement.

'Italy. . . . ' Miss Spence closed her eyes ecstatically. 'I feel drawn there too.'

'Why not let yourself be drawn?'

'I don't know. One somehow hasn't the energy and initiative to set out alone.'

'Alone. . . . ' Ah, sound of guitars and throaty singing! 'Yes, travelling alone isn't much fun.'

Miss Spence lay back in her chair without speaking. Her eyes were still closed. Mr Hutton stroked his moustache. The silence prolonged itself for what seemed a very long time.

Pressed to stay to dinner, Mr Hutton did not refuse. The fun had hardly started. The table was laid in the loggia. Through its arches they looked out on to the sloping garden, to the valley below and the farther hills. Light ebbed away; the heat and silence were oppressive. A huge cloud was mounting up the sky, and there were distant breathings of thunder. The thunder drew nearer, a wind began to blow, and the first drops of rain fell. The table was cleared. Miss Spence and Mr Hutton sat on in the growing darkness.

Miss Spence broke a long silence by saying meditatively:

'I think everyone has a right to a certain amount of happiness, don't you?'

'Most certainly.' But what was she leading up to? Nobody makes generalizations about life unless they mean to talk about themselves. Happiness: he looked back on his own life, and saw a cheerful, placid existence disturbed by no great griefs or discomforts or alarms. He had always had money and freedom; he had been able to do very much as he wanted. Yes, he supposed he had been happy – happier than most men. And now he was not merely happy; he had discovered in irresponsibility the secret of gaiety. He was about to say something about his happiness when Miss Spence went on speaking.

'People like you and me have a right to be happy some time in our lives.'

'Me?' said Mr Hutton, surprised.

'Poor Henry! Fate hasn't treated either of us very well.'

'Oh, well, it might have treated me worse.'

'You're being cheerful. That's brave of you. But don't think I can't see behind the mask.'

Miss Spence spoke louder and louder as the rain came down more and more heavily. Periodically the thunder cut across her utterances. She talked on, shouting against the noise.

'I have understood you so well and for so long.'

A flash revealed her, aimed and intent, leaning towards him. Her eyes were two profound and menacing gun-barrels. The darkness re-engulfed her.

'You were a lonely soul seeking a companion soul. I could sympathize with you in your solitude. Your marriage . . . '

The thunder cut short the sentence. Miss Spence's voice became audible once more with the words:

' . . . could offer no companionship to a man of your stamp. You needed a soul-mate.'

A soul-mate – he! a soul-mate. It was incredibly fantastic. 'Georgette Leblanc, the ex-soul-mate of Maurice Maeterlinck.' He had seen that in the paper a few days ago. So it was thus that Janet Spence had painted him in her imagination – as a soul-mater. And for Doris he was a picture of goodness and the cleverest man in the world. And actually, really, he was what? – Who knows?

'My heart went out to you. I could understand; I was lonely, too.' Miss Spence laid her hand on his knee. 'You were so patient.' Another flash. She was still aimed, dangerously. 'You never complained. But I could guess – I could guess.'

'How wonderful of you!' So he was an *âme incomprise*. 'Only a woman's intuition . . . '

The thunder crashed and rumbled, died away, and only the

sound of the rain was left. The thunder was his laughter, magnified, externalized. Flash and crash, there it was again, right on top of them.

'Don't you feel that you have within you something that is akin to this storm?' He could imagine her leaning forward as she uttered the words. 'Passion makes one the equal of the elements.'

What was his gambit now? Why, obviously, he should have said 'Yes', and ventured on some unequivocal gesture. But Mr Hutton suddenly took fright. The ginger beer in him had gone flat. The woman was serious – terribly serious. He was appalled.

Passion? 'No,' he desperately answered. 'I am without passion.'

But his remark was either unheard or unheeded, for Miss Spence went on with a growing exaltation, speaking so rapidly, however, and in such a burningly intimate whisper that Mr Hutton found it very difficult to distinguish what she was saying. She was telling him, as far as he could make out, the story of her life. The lightning was less frequent now, and there were long intervals of darkness. But at each flash he saw her still aiming towards him, still yearning forward with a terrifying intensity. Darkness, the rain, and then flash! her face was there, close at hand. A pale mask, greenish white; the large eyes, the narrow barrel of the mouth, the heavy eyebrows. Agrippina, or wasn't it rather – yes, wasn't it rather George Robey?'

He began devising absurd plans for escaping. He might suddenly jump up, pretending he had seen a burglar – Stop thief! stop thief! – and dash off into the night in pursuit. Or should he say that he felt faint, a heart attack? Or that he had seen a ghost – Emily's ghost – in the garden? Absorbed in his childish plotting, he had ceased to pay any attention to Miss Spence's words. The spasmodic clutching of her hand recalled his thoughts.

'I honoured you for that, Henry,' she was saying.

Honoured him for what?

'Marriage is a sacred tie, and your respect for it, even when the marriage was, as it was in your case, an unhappy one, made me respect you and admire you, and – shall I dare say the word? – '

Oh, the burglar, the ghost in the garden! But it was too late.

' . . . yes, love you, Henry, all the more. But we're free now, Henry.'

Free? There was a movement in the dark, and she was kneeling on the floor by his chair.

'Oh, Henry, Henry, I have been unhappy too.'

Her arms embraced him, and by the shaking of her body he could feel that she was sobbing. She might have been a suppliant crying for mercy.

'You mustn't, Janet,' he protested. Those tears were terrible, terrible. 'Not now, not now! You must be calm; you must go to bed.' He patted her shoulder, then got up, disengaging himself from her embrace. He left her still crouching on the floor beside the chair on which he had been sitting.

Groping his way into the hall, and without waiting to look for his hat, he went out of the house, taking infinite pains to close the front door noiselessly behind him. The clouds had blown over, and the moon was shining from a clear sky. There were puddles all along the road, and a noise of running water rose from the gutters and ditches. Mr Hutton splashed along, not caring if he got wet.

How heartrendingly she had sobbed! With the emotions of pity and remorse that the recollection evoked in him there was a certain resentment: why couldn't she have played the game that he was playing – the heartless, amusing game? Yes, but he had known all the time that she wouldn't, she couldn't, play that game; he had known and persisted.

What had she said about passion and the elements? Something absurdly stale, but true, true. There she was, a cloud black-bosomed and charged with thunder, and he, like some absurd little Benjamin Franklin, had sent up a kite into the heart of the menace. Now he was complaining that his toy had drawn the lightning.

She was probably still kneeling by that chair in the loggia, crying.

But why hadn't he been able to keep up the game? Why had his irresponsibility deserted him, leaving him suddenly sober in a cold world? There were no answers to any of his questions. One idea burned steady and luminous in his mind – the idea of flight. He must get away at once.

4

'What are you thinking about, Teddy Bear?'

'Nothing.'

There was a silence. Mr Hutton remained motionless, his elbows on the parapet of the terrace, his chin in his hands, looking down over Florence. He had taken a villa on one of the hilltops to the south of the city. From a little raised terrace at the end of the garden one looked down a long fertile valley on to the town and beyond it to the bleak mass of Monte Morello and, eastward of it, to the peopled hill of Fiesole, dotted with white houses. Everything was clear and luminous in the September sunshine.

'Are you worried about anything?'

'No, thank you.'

'Tell me, Teddy Bear.'

'But, my dear, there's nothing to tell.' Mr Hutton turned round, smiled, and patted the girl's hand. 'I think you'd better go in and have your siesta. It's too hot for you here.'

'Very well, Teddy Bear. Are you coming too?'

'When I've finished my cigar.'

'All right. But do hurry up and finish it, Teddy Bear.' Slowly, reluctantly, she descended the steps of the terrace and walked towards the house.

Mr Hutton continued his contemplation of Florence. He had need to be alone. It was good sometimes to escape from Doris and the restless solicitude of her passion. He had never known the pains of loving hopelessly, but he was experiencing now the pains of being loved. These last weeks had been a period of growing discomfort. Doris was always with him, like an obsession, like a guilty conscience. Yes, it was good to be alone.

He pulled an envelope out of his pocket and opened it, not without reluctance. He hated letters; they always contained something unpleasant – nowadays, since his second marriage. This was from his sister. He began skimming through the insulting home-truths of which it was composed. The words 'indecent haste', 'social suicide', 'scarcely cold in her grave', 'person of the lower classes', all occurred. They were inevitable now in any communication from a well-meaning and right-thinking relative. Impatient, he was about to tear the stupid letter to pieces when his eye fell on a sentence at the bottom of the third page. His heart beat with uncomfortable violence as he read it. It was too monstrous! Janet Spence was going about telling everyone that he had poisoned his wife in order to marry Doris. What damnable malice! Ordinarily a man of the suavest temper, Mr Hutton found himself trembling with rage. He took the childish satisfaction of calling names – he cursed the woman.

Then suddenly he saw the ridiculous side of the situation. The notion that he should have murdered anyone in order to marry Doris! If they only knew how miserably bored he was. Poor, dear Janet! She had tried to be malicious; she had only succeeded in being stupid.

A sound of footsteps aroused him; he looked round. In the garden below the little terrace the servant girl of the house was picking fruit. A Neapolitan, strayed somehow as far north as Florence, she was a specimen of the classical type – a little debased. Her profile might have been taken from a Sicilian coin of a bad period. Her features, carved floridly in the grand tradition, expressed an almost perfect stupidity. Her mouth was the most beautiful thing about her; the calligraphic hand of nature had richly curved it into an expression of mulish bad temper. . . . Under her hideous black clothes, Mr Hutton divined a powerful body, firm and massive. He had looked at her before with a vague interest and curiosity. Today the curiosity defined and focused itself into a desire. An idyll of Theocritus. Here was the woman; he, alas, was not precisely like a goatherd on the volcanic hills. He called to her.

'Armida!'

The smile with which she answered him was so provocative, attested so easy a virtue, that Mr Hutton took fright. He was on the brink once more – on the brink. He must draw back, oh! quickly, quickly, before it was too late. The girl continued to look up at him.

'*Ha chiamato?*' she asked at last.

Stupidity or reason? Oh, there was no choice now. It was imbecility every time.

'*Scendo*,' he called back to her. Twelve steps led from the garden to the terrace. Mr Hutton counted them. Down, down, down, down. . . . He saw a vision of himself descending from one circle of the inferno to the next – from a darkness full of wind and hail to an abyss of sinking mud.

5

For a good many days the Hutton case had a place on the front page of every newspaper. There had been no more popular murder trial since George Smith had temporarily eclipsed the European War by drowning in a warm bath his seventh bride. The public imagination was stirred by this tale of a murder brought to light months after the date of the crime. Here, it was felt, was one of those incidents in human life, so notable because they are so rare, which do definitely justify the ways of God to man. A wicked man had been moved by an illicit passion to kill his wife. For months he had lived in sin and fancied security – only to be dashed at last more horribly into the pit he had prepared for himself. Murder will out, and here was a case of it. The readers of the newspapers were in a position to follow every movement of the hand of God. There had been vague, but persistent, rumours in the neighbourhood; the police had taken action at last. Then came the exhumation order, the post-mortem examination, the inquest, the evidence of the experts, the verdict of the coroner's jury, the trial, the condemnation. For once Providence had done its duty, obviously, grossly, didactically, as in a melodrama. The newspapers were right in making of the case the staple intellectual food of a whole season.

Mr Hutton's first emotion when he was summoned from Italy to give evidence at the inquest was one of indignation. It was a monstrous, a scandalous thing that the police should take such idle, malicious gossip seriously. When the inquest was over he would bring an action for malicious prosecution against the Chief Constable; he would sue the Spence woman for slander.

The inquest was opened; the astonishing evidence unrolled itself. The experts had examined the body, and had found traces of arsenic; they were of opinion that the late Mrs Hutton had died of arsenic poisoning.

Arsenic poisoning. . . . Emily had died of arsenic poisoning? After that, Mr Hutton learned with surprise that there was enough arsenicated insecticide in his greenhouse to poison an army.

It was now, quite suddenly, that he saw it: there was a case against him. Fascinated, he watched it growing, growing, like some monstrous tropical plant. It was enveloping him, surrounding him; he was lost in a tangled forest.

When was the poison administered? The experts agreed that it must have been swallowed eight or nine hours before death. About lunch-time? Yes, about lunch-time. Clara, the parlour-maid, was called. Mrs Hutton, she remembered, had asked her to go and fetch her medicine. Mr Hutton had volunteered to go instead; he had gone alone. Miss Spence – ah, the memory of the storm, the white aimed face! the horror of it all! – Miss Spence confirmed Clara's statement, and added that Mr Hutton had come back with the medicine already poured out in a wine-glass, not in the bottle.

Mr Hutton's indignation evaporated. He was dismayed,

frightened. It was all too fantastic to be taken seriously, and yet this nightmare was a fact – it was actually happening.

M'Nab had seen them kissing, often. He had taken them for a drive on the day of Mrs Hutton's death. He could see them reflected in the wind-screen, sometimes out of the tail of his eye.

The inquest was adjourned. That evening Doris went to bed with a headache. When he went to her room after dinner, Mr Hutton found her crying.

'What's the matter?' He sat down on the edge of her bed and began to stroke her hair. For a long time she did not answer, and he went on stroking her hair mechanically, almost unconsciously; sometimes, even, he bent down and kissed her bare shoulder. He had his own affairs, however, to think about. What had happened? How was it that the stupid gossip had actually come true? Emily had died of arsenic poisoning. It was absurd, impossible. The order of things had been broken, and he was at the mercy of an irresponsibility. What had happened, what was going to happen? He was interrupted in the midst of his thoughts.

'It's my fault – it's my fault!' Doris suddenly sobbed out. 'I shouldn't have loved you; I oughtn't to have let you love me. Why was I ever born?'

Mr Hutton didn't say anything, but looked down in silence at the abject figure of misery lying on the bed.

'If they do anything to you I shall kill myself.'

She sat up, held him for a moment at arm's length, and looked at him with a kind of violence, as though she were never to see him again.

'I love you, I love you, I love you.' She drew him, inert and passive, towards her, clasped him, pressed herself against him. 'I didn't know you loved me as much as that, Teddy Bear. But why did you do it – why did you do it?'

Mr Hutton undid her clasping arms and got up. His face became very red. 'You seem to take it for granted that I murdered my wife,' he said. 'It's really too grotesque. What do you all take me for? A cinema hero?' He had begun to lose his temper. All the exasperation, all the fear and bewilderment of the day, was transformed into a violent anger against her. 'It's all such damned stupidity. Haven't you any conception of a civilized man's mentality? Do I look the sort of man who'd go about slaughtering people! I suppose you imagined I was so insanely in love with you that I could commit any folly. When will you women understand that one isn't insanely in love? All one asks for is a quiet life, which you won't allow one to have. I don't know what the devil ever induced me to marry you. It was all a damned stupid, practical joke. And now you go about saying I'm a murderer. I won't stand it.'

Mr Hutton stamped towards the door. He had said horrible things, he knew – odious things that he ought speedily to unsay. But he wouldn't. He closed the door behind him.

'Teddy Bear!' He turned the handle; the latch clicked into place. 'Teddy Bear!' The voice that came to him through the closed door was agonized. Should he go back? He ought to go back. He touched the handle, then withdrew his fingers and quickly walked away. When he was half-way down the stairs he halted. She might try to do something silly – throw herself out of the window or God knows what! He listened attentively; there was no sound. But he pictured her very clearly, tiptoeing across the room, lifting the sash as high as it would go, leaning out into the cold night air. It was raining a little. Under the window lay the paved terrace. How far below? Twenty-five or thirty feet? Once, when he was walking along Piccadilly, a dog had jumped out of a third-storey window of the Ritz. He had seen it fall; he had heard it strike the pavement. Should he go back? He was damned if he would; he hated her.

He sat for a long time in the library. What had happened? What was happening? He turned the question over and over in his mind and could find no answer. Suppose the nightmare dreamed itself out to its horrible conclusion. Death was waiting for him. His eyes filled with tears; he wanted so passionately to live, 'Just to be alive.' Poor Emily had wished it too, he remembered: 'Just to be alive.' There were still so many places in this astonishing world unvisited, so many queer delightful people still unknown, so many lovely women never so much as seen. The huge white oxen would still be dragging their wains along the Tuscan roads, the cypresses would still go up, straight as pillars, to the blue heaven; but he would not be there to see them. And the sweet southern wines – Tear of Christ and Blood of Judas – others would drink them, not he. Others would walk down the obscure and narrow lanes between the bookshelves in the London Library, sniffing the dusty perfume of good literature, peering at strange titles, discovering unknown names, exploring the fringes of vast domains of knowledge. He would be lying in a hole in the ground. And why, why? Confusedly he felt that some extraordinary kind of justice was being done. In the past he had been wanton and imbecile and irresponsible. Now Fate was playing as wantonly, as irresponsibly, with him. It was tit for tat, and God existed after all.

He felt that he would like to pray. Forty years ago he used to kneel by his bed every evening. The nightly formula of his childhood came to him almost unsought from some long unopened chamber of the memory. 'God bless Father and Mother, Tom and Cissie and the Baby, Mademoiselle and Nurse, and everyone that I love, and make me a good boy. Amen.' They were all dead now – all except Cissie.

His mind seemed to soften and dissolve; a great calm descended upon his spirit. He went upstairs to ask Doris's forgiveness. He found her lying on the couch at the foot of the bed. On the floor beside her stood a blue bottle of liniment, marked 'Not to be taken'; she seemed to have drunk about half of it.

'You didn't love me,' was all she said when she opened her eyes to find him bending over her.

Dr Libbard arrived in time to prevent any very serious consequences. 'You mustn't do this again,' he said while Mr Hutton was out of the room.

'What's to prevent me?' she asked defiantly.

Dr Libbard looked at her with his large, sad eyes. 'There's nothing to prevent you,' he said. 'Only yourself and your baby. Isn't it rather bad luck on your baby, not allowing it to come into the world because you want to go out of it?'

Doris was silent for a time. 'All right,' she whispered. 'I won't.'

Mr Hutton sat by her bedside for the rest of the night. He felt himself now to be indeed a murderer. For a time he persuaded himself that he loved this pitiable child. Dozing in his chair, he woke up, stiff and cold, to find himself drained dry, as it were, of every emotion. He had become nothing but a tired and suffering carcass. At six o'clock he undressed and went to bed for a couple of hours' sleep. In the course of the same afternoon the coroner's jury brought in a verdict of 'Wilful Murder', and Mr Hutton was committed for trial.

6

Miss Spence was not at all well. She had found her public appearances in the witness-box very trying, and when it was all over she had something that was very nearly a breakdown. She slept badly, and suffered from nervous indigestion. Dr Libbard used to call every other day. She talked to him a great deal – mostly about the Hutton case. . . . Her moral indignation was always on the boil? Wasn't it appalling to think that one had had a murderer in one's house? Wasn't it extraordinary that one could have been for so long mistaken about the man's character? (But she had had an inkling from the first.) And then the girl he had gone off with – so low class, so little better than a prostitute. The news that the second Mrs Hutton was expecting a baby – the posthumous child of a condemned and executed criminal – revolted her; the thing was shocking – an obscenity. Dr Libbard answered her gently and vaguely, and prescribed bromide.

One morning he interrupted her in the midst of her customary tirade. 'By the way,' he said in his soft, melancholy voice, 'I suppose it was really you who poisoned Mrs Hutton.'

Miss Spence stared at him for two or three seconds with enormous eyes, and then quietly said 'Yes'. After that she started to cry.

'In the coffee, I suppose.'

She seemed to nod assent. Dr Libbard took out his fountain-pen, and in his neat, meticulous calligraphy wrote out a prescription for a sleeping-draught.

V. S. Pritchett

THE FLY IN THE OINTMENT

IT was the dead hour of a November afternoon. Under the ceiling of level mud-coloured cloud, the latest office buildings of the city stood out alarmingly like new tombstones, among the mass of older buildings. And along the streets the few cars and the few people appeared and disappeared slowly as if they were not following the roadway or the pavement but some inner, personal route. Along the road to the main station, at intervals of two hundred yards or so, unemployed men and one or two beggars were dribbling slowly past the desert of public buildings to the next patch of shop fronts.

Presently a taxi stopped outside one of the underground stations and a man of thirty-five paid his fare and made off down one of the small streets.

Better not arrive in a taxi, he was thinking. The old man will wonder where I got the money.

He was going to see his father. It was his father's last day at his factory, the last day of thirty years' work and life among these streets, building a business out of nothing, and then, after a few years of prosperity, letting it go to pieces in a chafer of rumour, idleness, quarrels, accusations and, at last, bankruptcy.

Suddenly all the money quarrels of the family, which nagged in the young man's mind, had been dissolved. His dread of being involved in them vanished. He was overcome by the sadness of his father's situation. Thirty years of your life come to an end. I must see him. I must help him. All the same, knowing his father, he had paid off the taxi and walked the last quarter of a mile.

It was a shock to see the name of the firm, newly painted too, on the sign outside the factory and on the brass of the office entrance, newly polished. He pressed the bell at the office window inside and it was a long time before he heard footsteps cross the empty room and saw a shadow cloud the frosted glass of the window.

'It's Harold, Father,' the young man said. The door was opened.

'Hullo, old chap. This is very nice of you, Harold,' said the old man shyly, stepping back from the door to let his son in, and lowering his pleased, blue eyes for a second's modesty.

'Naturally I had to come,' said the son, shyly also. And then the father, filled out with assurance again and taking his son's arm, walked him across the floor of the empty work-room.

'Hardly recognize it, do you? When were you here last?' said the father.

This had been the machine-room, before the machines had gone. Through another door was what had been the showroom, where the son remembered seeing his father, then a dark-haired man, talking in a voice he had never heard before, a quick, bland voice, to his customers. Now there were only dust-lines left by the shelves on the white brick walls, and the marks of the showroom cupboards on the floor. The place looked large and light. There was no throb of machines, no hum of voices, no sound at all, now, but the echo of their steps on the empty floors. Already, though only a month bankrupt, the firm was becoming a ghost.

The two men walked towards the glass door of the office. They were both short. The father was well-dressed in an excellent navy-blue suit. He was a vigorous, broad man with a pleased impish smile. The sunburn shone through the clipped white hair of his head and he had the simple, trim, open-air look of a snow-man. The son beside him was round-shouldered and shabby, a keen but anxious fellow in need of a hair-cut and going bald.

'Come in, Professor,' said the father. This was an old family joke. He despised his son, who was, in fact, not a professor but a poorly paid lecturer at a provincial university.

'Come in,' said the father, repeating himself, not with the impatience he used to have, but with the habit of age. 'Come inside, into my office. If you can call it an office now,' he apologized. 'This used to be my room, do you remember, it used to be my office. Take a chair. We've still got a chair. The desk's gone, yes, that's gone, it was sold, fetched a good price – what was I saying?' he turned a bewildered look to his son. 'The chair. I was saying they have to leave you a table and a chair. I was just going to have a cup of tea, old boy, but – pardon me,' he apologized again, 'I've only one cup. Things have been sold for the liquidators and they've cleaned out nearly everything. I found this cup and teapot upstairs in the foreman's room. Of course, he's gone, all the hands have gone, and when I looked around just now to lock up before taking the keys to the agent when I hand over today, I saw this cup. Well, there it is. I've made it. Have a cup?'

'No, thanks,' said the son, listening patiently to his father. 'I have had my tea.'

'You've had your tea? Go on. Why not have another?'

'No, really, thanks,' said the son. 'You drink it.'

'Well,' said the father, pouring out the tea and lifting the cup to his soft rosy face and blinking his eyes as he drank, 'I feel badly about this. This is terrible. I feel really awful drinking this tea and you standing there watching me, but you say you've had yours – well, how are things with you? How are you? And how is Alice? Is she better? And the children? You know I've been thinking about you – you look worried. Haven't lost sixpence and found a shilling have you, because I wouldn't mind doing that?'

'I'm all right,' the son said, smiling to hide his irritation. 'I'm not worried about anything. I'm just worried about you. This' – he nodded with embarrassment to the dismantled show-room, the office from which even the calendars and wastepaper-basket had gone – 'this' – what was the most tactful and sympathetic word to use? – 'this is bad luck,' he said.

'Bad luck?' said the old man sternly.

'I mean,' stammered his son, 'I heard about the creditors' meeting. I knew it was your last day – I thought I'd come along, I . . . to see how you were.'

'Very sweet of you, old boy,' said the old man with zest. 'Very sweet. We've cleared everything up. They got most of the machines out today. I'm just locking up and handing over. Locking up is quite a business. There are so many keys. It's tiring, really. How many keys do you think there are to a place like this? You wouldn't believe it, if I told you.'

'It must have been worrying,' the son said.

'Worrying? You keep on using that word. I'm not worrying. Things are fine,' said the old man, smiling aggressively. 'I feel they're fine. I *know* they're fine.'

'Well, you always were an optimist,' smiled his son.

'Listen to me a moment. I want you to get this idea,' said his father, his warm voice going dead and rancorous and his nostrils fidgeting. His eyes went hard, too. A different man was speaking, and even a different face; the son noticed for the first time that like all big-faced men his father had two faces. There was the outer face like a soft warm and careless daub of innocent sealing-wax and inside it, as if thumbed there by a seal, was a much smaller one, babyish, shrewd, scared and hard. Now this little inner face had gone greenish and pale and dozens of little veins were broken on the nose and cheeks. The small, drained, purplish lips of this little face were speaking. The son leaned back instinctively to get just another inch away from this little face.

'Listen to this,' the father said and leaned forward on the table as his son leaned back, holding his right fist up as if he had a hammer in his hand and was auctioning his life. 'I am sixty-five. I don't know how long I shall live, but let me make this clear: if I were not an optimist I wouldn't be here. I wouldn't stay another minute.' He paused, fixing his son's half-averted eyes to let the full meaning of his words bite home. 'I've worked hard,' the father went on. 'For thirty years I built up this business from nothing. You wouldn't know it, you were a child, but many's the time coming down from the North I've slept in this office to be on the job early the next morning.' He looked decided and experienced like a man of forty, but now he softened to sixty again. The ring in the hard voice began to soften into a faint whine and his thick nose sniffed. 'I don't say I've always done right,' he said. 'You can't live your life from A to Z like that. And now I haven't a penny in the world. Not a cent. It's not easy at my time of life to begin again. What do you think I've got to live for? There's nothing holding me back. My boy, if I wasn't an optimist I'd go right out. I'd finish it.' Suddenly the father smiled and the little face was drowned in a warm flood of triumphant smiles from the bigger face. He rested his hands on his waistcoat and that seemed to be smiling too, his easy coat smiling, his legs smiling and even winks of light on the shining shoes. Then he frowned.

'Your hair's going thin,' he said. 'You oughtn't to be losing your hair at your age. I don't want you to think I'm criticizing you, you're old enough to live your own life, but your hair you know – you ought to do something about it. If you used oil every day and rubbed it in with both hands, the thumbs and forefingers is what you want to use, it would be better. I'm often thinking about you and I don't want you to think I'm lecturing you, because I'm not, so don't get the idea this is a lecture, but I was thinking, what you want, what we all want, I say this for myself as well as you, what we all want is ideas – big ideas. We go worrying along but you just want bigger and better ideas. You ought to think big. Take your case. You're a lecturer. I wouldn't be satisfied with lecturing to a small batch of people in a university town. I'd lecture the world. You know, you're always doing yourself injustice. We all do. Think big.'

'Well,' said his son, still smiling, but sharply. He was very angry. 'One's enough in the family. You've thought big till you bust.'

He didn't mean to say this, because he hadn't really the courage, but his pride was touched.

'I mean,' said the son, hurriedly covering it up in a panic, 'I'm not like you ... I ... '

'What did you say?' said the old man. 'Don't say that.' It was the smaller of the two faces speaking in a panic. 'Don't say that. Don't use that expression. That's not a right idea. Don't you get a wrong idea about me. We paid sixpence in the pound,' said the old man proudly.

The son began again, but his father stopped him.

'Do you know,' said the bigger of his two faces, getting bigger as it spoke, 'some of the oldest houses in the city are in Queer Street, some of the biggest firms in the country? I came up this morning with Mr Higgins, you remember Higgins? They're in liquidation. They are. Oh yes. And Moore, he's lost everything. He's got his chauffeur, but it's his wife's money. Did you see Beltman in the trade papers? Quarter of a million deficit. And how long are Prestons going to last?'

The big face smiled and overflowed on the smaller one. The whole train, the old man said, was practically packed with bankrupts every morning. Thousands had gone. Thousands? Tens of thousands. Some of the biggest men in the City were broke.

A small man himself, he was proud to be bankrupt with the big ones; it made him feel rich.

'You've got to realize, old boy,' he said gravely, 'the world's changing. You've got to move with the times.'

The son was silent. The November sun put a few strains of light through the frosted window and the shadow of its bars and panes was weakly placed on the wall behind his father's head. Some of the light caught the tanned scalp that showed between the white hair. So short the hair was that the father's ears protruded and, framed against that reflection of the window bars, the father suddenly took (to his son's fancy) the likeness of a convict in his cell and the son, startled, found himself asking: Were they telling the truth when they said the old man was a crook and that his balance sheets were cooked? What about that man they had to shut up at the meeting, the little man from Birmingham, in a mackintosh . . . ?

'There's a fly in this room,' said the old man suddenly, looking up in the air and getting to his feet. 'I'm sorry to interrupt what you were saying, but I can hear a fly. I must get it out.'

'A fly?' said his son, listening.

'Yes, can't you hear it? It's peculiar how you can hear everything now the machines have stopped. It took me quite a time to get used to the silence. Can you see it, old chap? I can't stand flies, you never know where they've been. Excuse me one moment.'

The old man pulled a duster out of a drawer.

'Forgive this interruption. I can't sit in a room with a fly in it,' he said apologetically. They both stood up and listened. Certainly in the office was the small dying fizz of a fly, deceived beyond its strength by the autumn sun.

'Open the door, will you, old boy,' said the old man with embarrassment. 'I hate them.'

The son opened the door and the fly flew into the light. The old man struck at it but it sailed away higher.

'There it is,' he said, getting up on the chair. He struck again and the son struck too as the fly came down. The old man got on top of his table. An expression of disgust and fear was curled on his smaller face; and an expression of apology and weakness.

'Excuse me,' he said again, looking up at the ceiling.

'If we leave the door open or open the window it will go,' said the son.

'It may seem a fad to you,' said the old man shyly. 'I don't like flies. Ah, here it comes.'

They missed it. They stood helplessly gaping up at the ceiling where the fly was buzzing in small circles round the cord of the electric light.

'I don't like them,' the old man said.

The table creaked under his weight. The fly went on to the ceiling and stayed there. Unavailingly the old man snapped the duster at it.

'Be careful,' said the son. 'Don't lose your balance.'

The old man looked down. Suddenly he looked tired and old, his body began to sag and a look of weakness came on to his face.

'Give me a hand, old boy,' the old man said in a shaky voice. He put a heavy hand on his son's shoulder and the son felt the great helpless weight of his father's body.

'Lean on me.'

Very heavily and slowly the old man got cautiously down from the table to the chair. 'Just a moment, old boy,' said the old man. Then, after getting his breath, he got down from the chair to the floor.

'You all right?' his son asked.

'Yes, yes,' said the old man out of breath. 'It was only that fly. Do you know, you're actually more bald at the back than I thought. There's a patch there as big as my hand. I saw it just then. It gave me quite a shock. You really must do something about it. How are your teeth? Do you have any trouble with your teeth? That may have something to do with it. Hasn't Alice told you how bald you are?'

'You've been doing too much. You're worried,' said the son, soft with repentance and sympathy. 'Sit down. You've had a bad time.'

'No, nothing,' said the old man shyly, breathing rather hard. 'A bit. Everyone's been very nice. They came in and shook hands. The staff came in. They all came in just to shake hands. They said, "We wish you good luck."'

The old man turned his head away. He actually wiped a tear from his eye. A glow of sympathy transported the younger man. He felt as though a sun had risen.

'You know –' the father said uneasily, flitting a glance at the fly on the ceiling as if he wanted the fly as well as his son to listen to what he was going to say – 'you know,' he said, 'the world's all wrong. I've made my mistakes. I was thinking about it before you came. You know where I went wrong? You know where I made my mistake?'

The son's heart started to a panic of embarrassment. For heaven's sake, he wanted to shout, don't! Don't stir up the whole business. Don't humiliate yourself before me. Don't start telling the truth. Don't oblige me to say we know all about it, that we have known for years the mess you've been in, that we've seen through the plausible stories you've spread, that we've known the people you've swindled.

'Money's been my trouble,' said the old man. 'I thought I needed money. That's one thing it's taught me. I've done with money. Absolutely done and finished with it. I never want to see another penny as long as I live. I don't want to see or hear of it. If you came in now and offered me a thousand pounds I should laugh at you. We deceive ourselves. We don't want the stuff. All I want now is just to go to a nice little cottage by the sea,' the old man said. 'I feel I need air, sun, life.'

The son was appalled.

'You want money even for that,' the son said irritably. 'You want quite a lot of money to do that.'

'Don't say I want money,' the old man said vehemently. 'Don't say it. When I walk out of this place tonight I'm going to walk into freedom. I am not going to think of money. You never know where it will come from. You may see something. You may meet a man. You never know. Did the children of Israel worry about money? No, they just went out and collected the manna. That's what I want to do.'

The son was about to speak. The father stopped him.

'Money,' the father said, 'isn't necessary at all.'

Now, like the harvest moon in full glow, the father's face shone up at his son.

'What I came round about was this,' said the son awkwardly and dryly. 'I'm not rich. None of us is. In fact, with things as they are we're all pretty shaky and we can't do anything. I wish I could, but I can't. But' – after the assured beginning he began to stammer and to crinkle his eyes timidly – 'but the idea of your being – you know, well short of some immediate necessity, I mean – well, if it is ever a question of – well, to be frank, *cash*, I'd raise it somehow.'

He coloured. He hated to admit his own poverty, he hated to offer charity to his father. He hated to sit there knowing the things he knew about him. He was ashamed to think how he, how they all dreaded having the gregarious, optimistic, extravagant, uncontrollable, disingenuous old man on their hands. The son hated to feel he was being in some peculiar way which he could not understand, mean, cowardly and dishonest.

The father's sailing eyes came down and looked at his son's nervous, frowning face and slowly the dreaming look went from the father's face. Slowly the harvest moon came down from its rosy voyage. The little face suddenly became dominant within the outer folds of skin like a fox looking out of a hole of clay. He leaned forward brusquely on the table and somehow a silver-topped pencil was in his hand preparing to note something briskly on a writing-pad.

'Raise it?' said the old man sharply. 'Why didn't you tell me before you could raise money? How can you raise it? Where? By when?'

Evelyn Waugh

MR LOVEDAY'S LITTLE OUTING

I

'You will not find your father greatly changed,' remarked Lady Moping, as the car turned into the gates of the County Asylum.

'Will he be wearing a uniform?' asked Angela.

'No, dear, of course not. He is receiving the very best attention.'

It was Angela's first visit and it was being made at her own suggestion.

Ten years had passed since the showery day in late summer when Lord Moping had been taken away; a day of confused but bitter memories for her; the day of Lady Moping's annual garden party, always bitter, confused that day by the caprice of the weather which, remaining clear and brilliant with promise until the arrival of the first guests, had suddenly blackened into a squall. There had been a scuttle for cover; the marquee had capsized; a frantic carrying of cushions and chairs; a table-cloth lofted to the boughs of the monkey-puzzler, fluttering in the rain; a bright period and the cautious emergence of guests on to the soggy lawns; another squall; another twenty minutes of sunshine. It had been an abominable afternoon, culminating at about six o'clock in her father's attempted suicide.

Lord Moping habitually threatened suicide on the occasion of the garden party; that year he had been found black in the face, hanging by his braces in the orangery; some neighbours, who were sheltering there from the rain, set him on his feet again, and before dinner a van had called for him. Since then Lady Moping had paid seasonal calls at the asylum and returned in time for tea, rather reticent of her experience.

Many of her neighbours were inclined to be critical of Lord Moping's accommodation. He was not, of course, an ordinary inmate. He lived in a separate wing of the asylum, specially devoted to the segregation of wealthier lunatics. These were given every consideration which their foibles permitted. They might choose their own clothes (many indulged in the liveliest fancies), smoke the most expensive brands of cigars and, on the anniversaries of their certification, entertain any other inmates for whom they had an attachment to private dinner parties.

The fact remained, however, that it was far from being the most expensive kind of institution; the uncompromising address, 'COUNTY HOME FOR MENTAL DEFECTIVES', stamped across the notepaper, worked on the uniforms of their attendants, painted, even, upon a prominent hoarding at the main entrance, suggested the lowest associations. From time to time, with less or more tact, her friends attempted to bring to Lady Moping's notice particulars of sea-side nursing homes, of 'qualified practitioners with large private grounds suitable for the charge of nervous or difficult cases', but she accepted them lightly; when her son came of age he might make any changes that he thought fit; meanwhile she felt no inclination to relax her economical régime; her husband had betrayed her basely on the one day in the year when she looked for loyal support, and was far better off than he deserved.

A few lonely figures in great-coats were shuffling and loping about the park.

'Those are the lower-class lunatics,' observed Lady Moping. 'There is a very nice little flower garden for people like your father. I sent them some cuttings last year.'

They drove past the blank, yellow brick façade to the doctor's private entrance and were received by him in the 'visitors room', set aside for interviews of this kind. The window was protected on the inside by bars and wire netting; there was no fireplace; when Angela nervously attempted to move her chair further from the radiator, she found that it was screwed to the floor.

'Lord Moping is quite ready to see you,' said the doctor.

'How is he?'

'Oh, very well, very well indeed, I'm glad to say. He had rather a nasty cold some time ago, but apart from that his condition is excellent. He spends a lot of his time in writing.'

They heard a shuffling, skipping sound approaching along the flagged passage. Outside the door a high peevish voice, which Angela recognized as her father's, said: 'I haven't the time, I tell you. Let them come back later.'

A gentler tone, with a slight rural burr, replied, 'Now come along. It is a purely formal audience. You need stay no longer than you like.'

Then the door was pushed open (it had no lock or fastening) and Lord Moping came into the room. He was attended by an elderly little man with full white hair and an expression of great kindness.

'That is Mr Loveday who acts as Lord Moping's attendant.'

'Secretary,' said Lord Moping. He moved with a jogging gait and shook hands with his wife.

'This is Angela. You remember Angela, don't you?'

'No, I can't say that I do. What does she want?'

'We just came to see you.'

'Well, you have come at an exceedingly inconvenient time. I am very busy. Have you typed out that letter to the Pope yet, Loveday?'

'No, my lord. If you remember, you asked me to look up the figures about the Newfoundland fisheries first?'

'So I did. Well, it is fortunate, as I think the whole letter will have to be redrafted. A great deal of new information has come to light since luncheon. A great deal. . . . You see, my dear, I am fully occupied.' He turned his restless, quizzical eyes upon Angela. 'I suppose you have come about the Danube. Well, you must come again later. Tell them it will be all right, quite all right, but I have not had time to give my full attention to it. Tell them that.'

'Very well, Papa.'

'Anyway,' said Lord Moping rather petulantly, 'it is a matter of secondary importance. There is the Elbe and the Amazon and the Tigris to be dealt with first, eh, Loveday? . . . *Danube* indeed. Nasty little river. I'd only call it a stream myself. Well, can't stop, nice of you to come. I would do more for you if I could, but you see how I'm fixed. Write to me about it. That's it. *Put it in black and white.*'

And with that he left the room.

'You see,' said the doctor, 'he is in excellent condition. He is putting on weight, eating and sleeping excellently. In fact, the whole tone of his system is above reproach.'

The door opened again and Loveday returned.

'Forgive my coming back, sir, but I was afraid that the young lady might be upset at his lordship's not knowing her. You mustn't mind him, miss. Next time he'll be very pleased to see you. It's only today he's put out on account of being behind-hand with his work. You see, sir, all this week I've been helping in the library and I haven't been able to get all his lordship's reports typed out. And he's got muddled with his card index. That's all it is. He doesn't mean any harm.'

'What a nice man,' said Angela, when Loveday had gone back to his charge.

'Yes. I don't know what we should do without old Loveday. Everybody loves him, staff and patients alike.'

'I remember him well. It's a great comfort to know that you are able to get such good warders,' said Lady Moping; 'people who don't know, say such foolish things about asylums.'

'Oh, but Loveday isn't a warder,' said the doctor.

'You don't mean he's cuckoo, too?' said Angela.

The doctor corrected her.

'He is an *inmate*. It is rather an interesting case. He has been here for thirty-five years.'

'But I've never seen anyone saner,' said Angela.

'He certainly has that air,' said the doctor, 'and in the last twenty years we have treated him as such. He is the life and soul of the place. Of course he is not one of the private patients, but we allow him to mix freely with them. He plays billiards excellently, does conjuring tricks at the concert, mends their gramophones, valets them, helps them in their crossword puzzles and various – er – hobbies. We allow them to give him small tips for services rendered, and he must by now have amassed quite a little fortune. He has a way with even the most troublesome of them. An invaluable man about the place.'

'Yes, but why is he here?'

'Well, it is rather sad. When he was a very young man he killed somebody – a young woman quite unknown to him, whom he knocked off her bicycle and then throttled. He gave himself up immediately afterwards and has been here ever since.'

'But surely he is perfectly safe now. Why is he not let out?'

'Well, I suppose if it was to anyone's interest, he would be. He has no relatives except a step-sister who lives in Plymouth. She used to visit him at one time, but she hasn't been for years now. He's perfectly happy here and I can assure you *we* aren't going to take the first steps in turning him out. He's far too useful to us.'

'But it doesn't seem fair,' said Angela.

'Look at your father,' said the doctor. 'He'd be quite lost without Loveday to act as his secretary.'

'It doesn't seem fair.'

2

Angela left the asylum, oppressed by a sense of injustice. Her mother was unsympathetic.

'Think of being locked up in a looney bin all one's life.'

'He attempted to hang himself in the orangery,' replied Lady Moping, *'in front of the Chester-Martins.'*

'I don't mean Papa. I mean Mr Loveday.'

'I don't think I know him.'

'Yes, the looney they have put to look after Papa.'

'Your father's secretary. A very decent sort of man, I thought, and eminently suited to his work.'

Angela left the question for the time, but returned to it again at luncheon on the following day.

'Mums, what does one have to do to get people out of the bin?'

'The bin? Good gracious, child, I hope that you do not anticipate your father's return *here*.'

'No, no. Mr Loveday.'

'Angela, you seem to me to be totally bemused. I see it was a mistake to take you with me on our little visit yesterday.'

After luncheon Angela disappeared to the library and was soon immersed in the lunacy laws as represented in the encyclopedia.

She did not re-open the subject with her mother, but a fortnight later, when there was a question of taking some pheasants over to her father for his eleventh Certification Party she showed an unusual willingness to run over with them. Her mother was occupied with other interests and noticed nothing suspicious.

Angela drove her small car to the asylum, and after delivering the game, asked for Mr Loveday. He was busy at the time making a crown for one of his companions who expected hourly to be anointed Emperor of Brazil, but he left his work and enjoyed several minutes' conversation with her. They spoke about her father's health and spirits. After a time Angela remarked, 'Don't you ever want to get away?'

Mr Loveday looked at her with his gentle, blue-grey eyes. 'I've got very well used to the life, miss. I'm fond of the poor people here, and I think that several of them are quite fond of me. At least, I think they would miss me if I were to go.'

'But don't you ever think of being free again?'

'Oh yes, miss, I think of it – almost all the time I think of it.'

'What would you do if you got out? There must be *some-thing* you would sooner do than stay here.'

The old man fidgeted uneasily. 'Well, miss, it sounds un-grateful, but I can't deny I should welcome a little outing, once, before I get too old to enjoy it. I expect we all have our secret ambitions, and there *is* one thing I often wish I could do. You mustn't ask me what. . . . It wouldn't take long. But I do feel that if I had done it, just for a day, an afternoon even, then I would die quiet. I could settle down again easier, and devote myself to the poor crazed people here with a better heart. Yes, I do feel that.'

There were tears in Angela's eyes that afternoon as she drove away. 'He *shall* have his little outing, bless him,' she said.

3

From that day onwards for many weeks Angela had a new purpose in life. She moved about the ordinary routine of her home with an abstracted air and an unfamiliar, reserved courtesy which greatly disconcerted Lady Moping.

'I believe the child's in love. I only pray that it isn't that un-couth Egbertson boy.'

She read a great deal in the library, she cross-examined any guests who had pretensions to legal or medical knowledge, she showed extreme goodwill to old Sir Roderick Lane-Foscote, their Member. The names 'alienist', 'barrister' or 'government official' now had for her the glamour that formerly surrounded film actors and professional wrestlers. She was a woman with a cause, and before the end of the hunting season she had triumphed. Mr Loveday achieved his liberty.

The doctor at the asylum showed reluctance but no real opposition. Sir Roderick wrote to the Home Office. The necessary papers were signed, and at last the day came when Mr Loveday took leave of the home where he had spent such long and useful years.

His departure was marked by some ceremony. Angela and Sir Roderick Lane-Foscote sat with the doctors on the stage of the gymnasium. Below them were assembled everyone in the institution who was thought to be stable enough to endure the excitement.

Lord Moping, with a few suitable expressions of regret, presented Mr Loveday on behalf of the wealthier lunatics with a gold cigarette case; those who supposed themselves to be emperors showered him with decorations and titles of honour. The warders gave him a silver watch and many of the non-paying inmates were in tears on the day of the presentation.

The doctor made the main speech of the afternoon. 'Remember,' he remarked, 'that you leave behind you nothing but our warmest good wishes. You are bound to us by ties that none will forget. Time will only deepen our sense of debt to you. If at any time in the future you should grow tired of your life in the world, there will always be a welcome for you here. Your post will be open.'

A dozen or so variously afflicted lunatics hopped and skipped after him down the drive until the iron gates opened and Mr Loveday stepped into his freedom. His small trunk had already gone to the station; he elected to walk. He had been reticent about his plans, but he was well provided with money, and the general impression was that he would go to London and enjoy himself a little before visiting his step-sister in Plymouth.

It was to the surprise of all that he returned within two hours of his liberation. He was smiling whimsically, a gentle, self-regarding smile of reminiscence.

'I have come back,' he informed the doctor. 'I think that now I shall be here for good.'

'But, Loveday, what a short holiday. I'm afraid that you have hardly enjoyed yourself at all.'

'Oh yes, sir, thank you, sir, I've enjoyed myself *very much*. I'd been promising myself one little treat, all these years. It was short, sir, but *most* enjoyable. Now I shall be able to settle down again to my work here without any regrets.'

Half a mile up the road from the asylum gates, they later discovered an abandoned bicycle. It was a lady's machine of some antiquity. Quite near it in the ditch lay the strangled body of a young woman, who, riding home to her tea, had chanced to overtake Mr Loveday, as he strode along, musing on his opportunities.

Graham Greene

ACROSS THE BRIDGE

'They say he's worth a million,' Lucia said. He sat there in the little hot damp Mexican square, a dog at his feet, with an air of immense and forlorn patience. The dog attracted your attention at once; for it was very nearly an English setter, only something had gone wrong with the tail and the feathering. Palms wilted over his head, it was all shade and stuffiness round the bandstand, radios talked loudly in Spanish from the little wooden sheds where they changed your pesos into dollars at a loss. I could tell he didn't understand a word from the way he read his newspaper – as I did myself picking out the words which were like English ones. 'He's been here a month,' Lucia said. 'They turned him out of Guatemala and Honduras.'

You couldn't keep any secrets for five hours in this border town. Lucia had only been twenty-four hours in the place, but she knew all about Mr Joseph Calloway. The only reason I didn't know about him (and I'd been in the place two weeks) was because I couldn't talk the language any more than Mr Calloway could. There wasn't another soul in the place who didn't know the story – the whole story of the Halling Investment Trust and the proceedings for extradition. Any man doing dusty business in any of the wooden booths in the town is better fitted by long observation to tell Mr Calloway's tale than I am, except that I was in – literally – at the finish. They all watched the drama proceed with immense interest, sympathy and respect. For, after all, he had a million.

Every once in a while through the long steamy day, a boy came and cleaned Mr Calloway's shoes: he hadn't the right words to resist them – they pretended not to know his English. He must have had his shoes cleaned the day Lucia and I watched him at least half a dozen times. At midday he took a stroll across the square to the Antonio Bar and had a bottle of beer, the setter sticking to heel as if they were out for a country walk in England (he had, you may remember, one of the biggest estates in Norfolk). After his bottle of beer, he would walk down between the money changers' huts to the Rio Grande and look across the bridge into the United States: people came and went constantly in cars. Then back to the square till lunch-time. He was staying in the best hotel, but you don't get good hotels in this border town: nobody stays in them more than a night. The good hotels were on the other side of the bridge: you could see their electric signs twenty storeys high from the little square at night, like lighthouses marking the United States.

You may ask what I'd been doing in so drab a spot for a fortnight. There was no interest in the place for anyone; it was just damp and dust and poverty, a kind of shabby replica of the town across the river: both had squares in the same spots; both had the same number of cinemas. One was cleaner than the other, that was all, and more expensive, much more expensive. I'd stayed across there a couple of nights waiting for a man a tourist bureau said was driving down from Detroit to Yucatán and would sell a place in his car for some fantastically small figure – twenty dollars, I think it was. I don't know if he existed or was invented by the optimistic half-caste in the agency; anyway, he never turned up and so I waited, not much caring, on the cheap side of the river. It didn't much matter; I was living. One day I meant to give up the man from Detroit and go home or go south, but it was easier not to decide any-thing in a hurry. Lucia was just waiting for a car going the other way, but she didn't have to wait so long. We waited together and watched Mr Calloway waiting – for God knows what.

I don't know how to treat this story – it was a tragedy for Mr Calloway, it was poetic retribution, I suppose, in the eyes of the shareholders he'd ruined with his bogus transactions, and to Lucia and me, at this stage, it was pure comedy – except when he kicked the dog. I'm not a sentimentalist about dogs, I prefer people to be cruel to animals rather than to human beings, but I couldn't help being revolted at the way he'd kick that animal – with a hint of cold-blooded venom, not in anger but as if he were getting even for some trick it had played him a long while ago. That generally happened when he returned from the bridge: it was the only sign of anything resembling emotion he showed. Otherwise he looked a small, set, gentle creature with silver hair and a silver moustache, and gold-rimmed glasses, and one gold tooth like a flaw in character.

Lucia hadn't been accurate when she said he'd been turned out of Guatemala and Honduras; he'd left voluntarily when the extradition proceedings seemed likely to go through and moved north. Mexico is still not a very centralized state, and it is possible to get round governors as you can't get round cabinet ministers or judges. And so he waited there on the border for the next move. That earlier part of the story is, I suppose, dramatic, but I didn't watch it and I can't invent what I haven't seen – the long waiting in ante-rooms, the bribes taken and refused, the growing fear of arrest, and then the flight – in gold-rimmed glasses – covering his tracks as well as he could, but this wasn't finance and he was an amateur at escape. And so he'd washed up here, under my eyes and Lucia's eyes, sitting all day under the bandstand, nothing to read but a Mexican paper, nothing to do but look across the river at the United States, quite unaware, I suppose, that everyone knew everything about him, once a day kicking his dog. Perhaps in its semi-setter way it reminded him too much of the Norfolk estate – though that, too, I suppose, was the reason he kept it.

And the next act again was pure comedy. I hesitate to think what this man worth a million was costing his country as they edged him out from this land and that. Perhaps somebody was getting tired of the business, and careless; anyway, they sent across two detectives, with an old photograph. He'd grown his silvery moustache since that had been taken, and he'd aged a lot, and they couldn't catch sight of him. They hadn't been across the bridge two hours when everybody knew that there

were two foreign detectives in town looking for Mr Calloway—
everybody knew, that is to say, except Mr Calloway, who
couldn't talk Spanish. There were plenty of people who could
have told him in English, but they didn't. It wasn't cruelty, it
was a sort of awe and respect: like a bull, he was on show, sitting
mournfully in the plaza with his dog, a magnificent spectacle
for which we all had ring-side seats.

I ran into one of the policemen in the Bar Antonio. He was
disgusted; he had had some idea that when he crossed the
bridge life was going to be different, so much more colour and
sun, and – I suspect – love, and all he found were wide mud
streets where the nocturnal rain lay in pools, and mangy dogs,
smells and cockroaches in his bedroom, and the nearest to
love, the open door of the Academia Comercial, where pretty
mestizo girls sat all the morning learning to typewrite. Tip-
tap-tip-tap-tip – perhaps they had a dream, too – jobs on the
other side of the bridge, where life was going to be so much
more luxurious, refined and amusing.

We got into conversation; he seemed surprised that I knew
who they both were and what they wanted. He said, 'We've
got information this man Calloway's in town.'

'He's knocking around somewhere,' I said.

'Could you point him out?'

'Oh, I don't know him by sight,' I said.

He drank his beer and thought a while. 'I'll go out and sit in
the plaza. He's sure to pass sometime.'

I finished my beer and went quickly off and found Lucia.
I said, 'Hurry, we're going to see an arrest.' We didn't care a
thing about Mr Calloway, he was just an elderly man who
kicked his dog and swindled the poor, and who deserved anything he got. So we made for the plaza; we knew Calloway
would be there, but it had never occurred to either of us that
the detectives wouldn't recognize him. There was quite a
surge of people round the place; all the fruit-sellers and boot-
blacks in town seemed to have arrived together; we had to
force our way through, and there in the little green stuffy
centre of the place, sitting on adjoining seats, were the two
plain-clothes men and Mr Calloway. I've never known the

place so silent; everybody was on tiptoe, and the plain-clothes men were staring at the crowd looking for Mr Calloway, and Mr Calloway sat on his usual seat staring out over the money-changing booths at the United States.

'It can't go on. It just can't,' Lucia said. But it did. It got more fantastic still. Somebody ought to write a play about it. We sat as close as we dared. We were afraid all the time we were going to laugh. The semi-setter scratched for fleas and Mr Calloway watched the U.S.A. The two detectives watched the crowd, and the crowd watched the show with solemn satisfaction. Then one of the detectives got up and went over to Mr Calloway. That's the end, I thought. But it wasn't, it was the beginning. For some reason they had eliminated him from their list of suspects. I shall never know why. The man said:

'You speak English?'

'I *am* English,' Mr Calloway said.

Even that didn't tear it, and the strangest thing of all was the way Mr Calloway came alive. I don't think anybody had spoken to him like that for weeks. The Mexicans were too respectful – he was a man with a million – and it had never occurred to Lucia and me to treat him casually like a human being; even in our eyes he had been magnified by the colossal theft and the world-wide pursuit.

He said, 'This is rather a dreadful place, don't you think?"

'It is,' the policeman said.

'I can't think what brings anybody across the bridge.'

'Duty,' the policeman said gloomily. 'I suppose you are passing through.'

'Yes,' Mr Calloway said.

'I'd have expected over here there'd have been – you know what I mean – life. You read things about Mexico.'

'Oh, life,' Mr Calloway said. He spoke firmly and precisely, as if to a committee of shareholders. 'That begins on the other side.'

'You don't appreciate your own country until you leave it.'

'That's very true,' Mr Calloway said. 'Very true.'

At first it was difficult not to laugh, and then after a while there didn't seem to be much to laugh at; an old man imagining all the fine things going on beyond the international bridge. I think he thought of the town opposite as a combination of London and Norfolk – theatres and cocktail bars, a little shooting and a walk round the field at evening with the dog – that miserable imitation of a setter – poking the ditches. He'd never been across, he couldn't know that it was just the same thing over again – even the same layout; only the streets were paved and the hotels had ten more storeys, and life was more expensive, and everything was a little bit cleaner. There wasn't anything Mr Calloway would have called living – no galleries, no book-shops, just *Film Fun* and the local paper, and *Click* and *Focus* and the tabloids.

'Well,' said Mr Calloway, 'I think I'll take a stroll before lunch. You need an appetite to swallow the food here. I generally go down and look at the bridge about now. Care to come, too?'

The detective shook his head. 'No,' he said, 'I'm on duty. I'm looking for a fellow.' And that, of course, gave *him* away. As far as Mr Calloway could understand, there was only one 'fellow' in the world anyone was looking for – his brain had eliminated friends who were seeking their friends, husbands who might be waiting for their wives, all objectives of any search but just the one. The power of elimination was what had made him a financier – he could forget the people behind the shares.

That was the last we saw of him for a while. We didn't see him going into the Botica Paris to get his aspirin, or walking back from the bridge with his dog. He simply disappeared, and when he disappeared, people began to talk, and the detectives heard the talk. They looked silly enough, and they got busy after the very man they'd been sitting next to in the garden. Then they, too, disappeared. They, as well as Mr Calloway, had gone to the state capital to see the Governor and the Chief of Police, and it must have been an amusing sight there, too, as they bumped into Mr Calloway and sat with him in the waiting-rooms. I suspect Mr Calloway was generally shown in first, for everyone knew he was worth a million. Only in Europe is it possible for a man to be a criminal as well as a rich man.

Anyway, after about a week the whole pack of them returned by the same train. Mr Calloway travelled Pullman, and the two policemen travelled in the day coach. It was evident that they hadn't got their extradition order.

Lucia had left by that time. The car came and went across the bridge. I stood in Mexico and watched her get out at the United States Customs. She wasn't anything in particular, but she looked beautiful at a distance as she gave me a wave out of the United States and got back into the car. And I suddenly felt sympathy for Mr Calloway, as if there were something over there which you couldn't find here, and turning round I saw him back on his old beat, with the dog at his heels.

I said 'Good afternoon', as if it had been all along our habit to greet each other. He looked tired and ill and dusty, and I felt sorry for him – to think of the kind of victory he'd been winning, with so much expenditure of cash and care – the prize this dirty and dreary town, the booths of the money-changers, the awful little beauty parlours with their wicker chairs and sofas looking like the reception rooms of brothels, that hot and stuffy garden by the bandstand.

He replied gloomily 'Good morning', and the dog started to sniff at some ordure and he turned and kicked it with fury, with depression, with despair.

And at that moment a taxi with the two policemen in it passed us on its way to the bridge. They must have seen that kick; perhaps they were cleverer than I had given them credit for, perhaps they were just sentimental about animals, and thought they'd do a good deed, and the rest happened by accident. But the fact remains – those two pillars of the law set about the stealing of Mr Calloway's dog.

He watched them go by. Then he said, 'Why don't you go across?'

'It's cheaper here,' I said.

'I mean just for an evening. Have a meal at that place we can see at night in the sky. Go to the theatre.'

'There isn't a chance.'

He said angrily, sucking his gold tooth, 'Well, anyway, get away from here.' He stared down the hill and up the other side. He couldn't see that that street climbing up from the bridge contained only the same money-changers' booths as this one.

I said, 'Why don't *you* go?'

He said evasively, 'Oh – business.'

I said, 'It's only a question of money. You don't *have* to pass by the bridge.'

He said with faint interest, 'I don't talk Spanish.'

'There isn't a soul here,' I said, 'who doesn't talk English.'

He looked at me with surprise. 'Is that so?' he said. 'Is that so?'

It's as I have said; he'd never tried to talk to anyone, and they respected him too much to talk to him – he was worth a million. I don't know whether I'm glad or sorry that I told him that. If I hadn't, he might be there now, sitting by the bandstand having his shoes cleaned – alive and suffering.

Three days later his dog disappeared. I found him looking for it, calling it softly and shamefacedly between the palms of the garden. He looked embarrassed. He said in a low angry voice, 'I *hate* that dog. The beastly mongrel', and called 'Rover, Rover' in a voice which didn't carry five yards. He said, 'I bred setters once. I'd have shot a dog like that.' It reminded him, I *was* right, of Norfolk, and he lived in the memory, and he hated it for its imperfection. He was a man without a family and without friends, and his only enemy was that dog. You couldn't call the law an enemy; you have to be intimate with an enemy.

Late that afternoon someone told him they'd seen the dog walking across the bridge. It wasn't true, of course, but we didn't know that then – they'd paid a Mexican five pesos to smuggle it across. So all that afternoon and the next Mr Calloway sat in the garden having his shoes cleaned over and over again, and thinking how a dog could just walk across like that, and a human being, an immortal soul, was bound here in the awful routine of the little walk and the unspeakable meals and the aspirin at the *botica*. That dog was seeing things he couldn't see – that hateful dog. It made him mad – I think literally mad. You must remember the man had been going on for months. He had a million and he was living on two pounds a week, with nothing to spend his money on. He sat there and brooded on the hideous injustice of it. I think he'd have crossed over one day in any case, but the dog was the last straw.

Next day when he wasn't to be seen, I guessed he'd gone across and I went too. The American town is as small as the Mexican. I knew I couldn't miss him if he was there, and I was still curious. A little sorry for him, but not much.

I caught sight of him first in the only drug-store, having a Coca-cola, and then once outside a cinema looking at the posters; he had dressed with extreme neatness, as if for a party, but there was no party. On my third time round, I came on the detectives – they were having Coca-colas in the drug-store, and they must have missed Mr Calloway by inches. I went in and sat down at the bar.

'Hello,' I said, 'you still about.' I suddenly felt anxious for Mr Calloway, I didn't want them to meet.

One of them said, 'Where's Calloway?'

'Oh,' I said, 'he's hanging on.'

'But not his dog,' he said, and laughed. The other looked a little shocked, he didn't like anyone to *talk* cynically about a dog. Then they got up – they had a car outside.

'Have another?' I said.

'No thanks. We've got to keep moving.'

The men bent close and confided to me, 'Calloway's on this side.'

'No!' I said.

'And his dog.'

'He's looking for it,' the other said.

'I'm damned if he is,' I said, and again one of them looked a little shocked, as if I'd insulted the dog.

310

I don't think Mr Calloway was looking for his dog, but his dog certainly found him. There was a sudden hilarious yapping from the car and out plunged the semi-setter and gambolled furiously down the street. One of the detectives – the sentimental one – was into the car before we got to the door and was off after the dog. Near the bottom of the long road to the bridge was Mr Calloway – I do believe he'd come down to look at the Mexican side when he found there was nothing but the drug-store and the cinemas and the paper-shops on the American. He saw the dog coming and yelled at it to go home – 'home, home, home', as if they were in Norfolk – it took no notice at all, pelting towards him. Then he saw the police car coming, and ran. After that, everything happened too quickly, but I think the order of events was this – the dog started across the road right in front of the car, and Mr Calloway yelled, at the dog or the car, I don't know which. Anyway, the detective swerved – he said later, weakly, at the inquiry, that he couldn't run over a dog, and down went Mr Calloway, in a mess of broken glass and gold rims and silver hair, and blood. The dog was on to him before any of us could reach him, licking and whimpering and licking. I saw Mr Calloway put up his hand, and down it went across the dog's neck and the whimper rose to a stupid bark of triumph, but Mr Calloway was dead – shock and a weak heart.

'Poor old geezer,' the detective said, 'I bet he really loved that dog', and it's true that the attitude in which he lay looked more like a caress than a blow. I thought it was meant to be a blow, but the detective may have been right. It all seemed to me a little too touching to be true as the old crook lay there with his arm over the dog's neck, dead with his million between the money-changers' huts, but it's as well to be humble in the face of human nature. He had come across the river for something, and it may, after all, have been the dog he was looking for. It sat there, baying its stupid and mongrel triumph across his body, like a piece of sentimental statuary: the nearest he could get to the fields, the ditches, the horizon of his home. It was comic and it was pitiable, but it wasn't less comic because the man was dead. Death doesn't change comedy to tragedy, and if that last gesture was one of affection, I suppose it was only one more indication of a human being's capacity for self-deception, our baseless optimism that is so much more appalling than our despair.

Angus Wilson

RASPBERRY JAM

'How are your funny friends at Potter's Farm, Johnnie?' asked his aunt from London.

'Very well, thank you, Aunt Eva' said the little boy in the window in a high prim voice. He had been drawing faces on his bare knee and now put down the indelible pencil. The moment that he had been dreading all day had arrived. Now they would probe and probe with their silly questions and the whole story of that dreadful tea party with his old friends would come tumbling out. There would be scenes and abuse and the old ladies would be made to suffer further. This he could not bear, for although he never wanted to see them again and had come, in brooding over the afternoon's events, almost to hate them, to bring them further misery, to be the means of their disgrace would be worse than any of the horrible things that had already happened. Apart from his fear of what might follow he did not intend to pursue the conversation himself, for he disliked his aunt's bright patronizing tone. He knew that she felt ill at ease with children and would soon lapse into that embarrassing 'leg pulling' manner which some grown ups used. For himself, he did not mind this but if she made silly jokes about the old ladies at Potter's Farm he would get angry and then Mummy would say all that about his having to learn to take a joke and about his being highly strung and where could he have got it from, not from her.

But he need not have feared. For though the grown ups continued to speak of the old ladies as 'Johnnie's friends', the topic soon became a general one. Many of the things the others said made the little boy bite his lip, but he was able to go on drawing on his knee with the feigned abstraction of a child among adults.

'My dear,' said Johnnie's mother to her sister, 'you really

must meet them. They're the *most* wonderful pair of freaks. They live in a great barn of a farmhouse. The inside's like a museum, full of old junk mixed up with some really lovely things all mouldering to pieces. The family's been there for hundreds of years and they're madly proud of it. They won't let anyone do a single thing for them, although they're both well over sixty, and of course the result is that the place is in the most *frightful* mess. It's really rather ghastly and one oughtn't to laugh, but if you could *see* them, my dear. The elder one, Marian, wears a long tweed skirt almost to the ankles, she had a terrible hunting accident or something, and a school blazer. The younger one's said to have been a beauty, but she's really rather sinister now, inches thick in enamel and rouge and dressed in all colours of the rainbow, with dyed red hair which is constantly falling down. Of course, Johnnie's made tremendous friends with them and I must say they've been immensely kind to him, but what Harry will say when he comes back from Germany, I can't think. As it *is*, he's always complaining that the child is too much with women and has no friends of his own age.'

'I don't honestly think you need worry about that, Grace' said her brother Jim, assuming the attitude of the sole male in the company, for of the masculinity of old Mr Codrington their guest he instinctively made little. 'Harry ought to be very pleased with the way old Miss Marian's encouraged Johnnie's cricket and riding; it's pretty uphill work, too. Johnnie's not exactly a Don Bradman or a Gordon Richards, are you, old man? I like the old girl, personally. She's got a bee in her bonnet about the Bolsheviks, but she's stood up to those damned council people about the drainage like a good 'un; she does no end for the village people as well and says very little about it.'

'I don't like the sound of "doing good to the village" very much' said Eva 'it usually means patronage and disappointed old maids meddling in other people's affairs. It's only in villages like this that people can go on serving out sermons with gifts of soup.'

'Curiously enough, Eva old dear,' Jim said, for he believed

in being rude to his progressive sister, 'in this particular case you happen to be wrong. Miss Swindale is extremely broad-minded. You remember, Grace,' he said, addressing his other sister 'what she said about giving money to old Cooper, when the rector protested it would only go on drink – "You have a perfect right to consign us all to hell, rector, but you must allow us the choice of how we get there." Serve him damn well right for interfering too.'

'Well, Jim darling' said Grace 'I must say she could hardly have the nerve to object to drink – the poor old thing has the most dreadful bouts herself. Sometimes when I can't get gin from the grocer's it makes me absolutely livid to think of all that secret drinking and they say it only makes her more and more gloomy. All the same I suppose *I* should drink if I had a sister like Dolly. It must be horrifying when one's family-proud like she is to have such a skeleton in the cupboard. I'm sure there's going to be the most awful trouble in the village about Dolly before she's finished. You've heard the squalid story about young Tony Calkett, haven't you? My dear, he went round there to fix the lights and apparently Dolly invited him up to her bedroom to have a cherry brandy of all things and made the *most* unfortunate proposals. Of course I know she's been very lonely and it's all a ghastly tragedy really, but Mrs Calkett's a terrible silly little woman and a very jealous mother and she won't see it that way at all. The awful thing is that both the Miss Swindales give me the creeps rather. I have a dreadful feeling when I'm with them that I don't know who's the keeper and who's the lunatic. In fact, Eva my dear, they're both really rather horrors and I suppose I ought never to let Johnnie go near them.'

'I think you have no cause for alarm, Mrs Allingham' put in old Mr Codrington in a purring voice. He had been waiting for some time to take the floor, and now that he had got it he did not intend to relinquish it. Had it not been for the small range of village society he would not have been a visitor at Mrs Allingham's, for, as he frequently remarked, if there was one thing he deplored more than her vulgarity it was her loquacity. 'No one delights in scandal more than I do, but it is always a little distorted, a trifle *exagéré*, indeed where would be its charm, if it were not so! No doubt Miss Marian has her solaces, but she remains a noble-hearted woman. No doubt Miss Dolly is often a trifly naughty' he dwelt on this word caressingly 'but she really only uses the privilege of one, who has been that rare thing, a beautiful woman. As for Tony Calkett it is really time that that young man ceased to be so unnecessarily virginal. If my calculations are correct, and I have every reason to think they are, he must be twenty-two, an age at which modesty should have been put behind one long since. No, dear Mrs Allingham, you should rejoice that Johnnie has been given the friendship of two women who can still, in this vulgar age, be honoured with a name that, for all that it has been cheapened and degraded, one is still proud to bestow – the name of a lady.' Mr Codrington threw his head back and stared round the room as though defying anyone to deny him his own right to this name. 'Miss Marian will encourage him in the manlier virtues, Miss Dolly in the arts. Her own water colours, though perhaps lacking in strength, are not to be despised. She has a fine sense of colour, though I could wish that she was a little less bold with it in her costume. Nevertheless with that red-gold hair there is something splendid about her appearance, something especially wistful to an old man like myself. Those peacock blue linen gowns take me back through Conder's fans and Whistler's rooms to Rossetti's Mona Vanna. Unfortunately as she gets older the linen is not overclean. We are given a Mona Vanna with the collected dust of age, but surely,' he added with a little cackle 'it is dirt that lends patina to a picture. It is interesting that you should say you are uncertain which of the two sisters is a trifle peculiar, because, in point of fact, both have been away, as they used to phrase it in the servants' hall of my youth. Strange,' he mused, 'that one's knowledge of the servants' hall should always belong to the period of one's infancy, be, as it were, eternally outmoded. I have no conception of how they may speak of an asylum in the servants' hall of today. No doubt Johnnie could tell us. But, of course, I forget that social progress has removed the servants' hall from the ken of all but the most privileged children. I wonder now whether that is a loss or a blessing in disguise.'

'A blessing without any doubt at all' said Aunt Eva, irrepressible in the cause of Advance. 'Think of all the appalling inhibitions we acquired from servants' chatter. I had an old nurse who was always talking about ghosts and dead bodies and curses on the family in a way that must have set up terrible phobias in me. I still have those ugly, morbid nightmares about spiders' she said, turning to Grace.

'I refuse' said Mr Codrington in a voice of great contempt, for he was greatly displeased at the interruption, 'to believe that any dream of yours could be ugly; morbid, perhaps, but with a sense of drama and artistry that would befit the dreamer. I confess that if I have inhibitions, and I trust I have many, I cling to them. I should not wish to give way unreservedly to what is so unattractively called the libido, it suggests a state of affairs in which beach pyjamas are worn and jitterbugging is compulsory. No, let us retain the fantasies, the imaginative games of childhood, even at the expense of a little fear, for they are the true magnificence of the springtime of life.'

'Darling Mr Codrington' cried Grace 'I do pray and hope you're right. It's exactly what I keep on telling myself about Johnnie, but I really don't know. Johnnie, darling, run upstairs and fetch Mummy's bag.' But his mother need not have been so solicitous about Johnnie's overhearing what she had to say, for the child had already left the room. 'There you are, Eva,' she said 'he's the strangest child. He slips away without so much as a word. I must say he's very good at amusing himself, but I very much wonder if all the funny games he plays aren't very bad for him. He's certainly been very peculiar lately, strange silences and sudden tears, and, my dear, the awful nightmares he has! About a fortnight ago, after he'd been at tea with the Miss Swindales, I don't know whether it was something he'd eaten there, but he made the most awful sobbing noise in the night. Sometimes I think it's just temper, like Harry. The other day at tea I only offered him some jam, my best home-made raspberry too, and he just screamed at me.'

'You should take him to a child psychologist' said her sister.

'Well, darling, I expect you're right. It's so difficult to know whether they're frauds, everyone recommends somebody different. I'm sure Harry would disapprove too, and then think of the expense. . . . You know how desperately poor we are, although I think I manage as well as anyone could' . . . At this point Mr Codrington took a deep breath and sat back, for on the merits of her household management Grace Allingham was at her most boring and could by no possible stratagem be restrained.

Upstairs, in the room which had been known as the nursery until his eleventh birthday, but was now called his bedroom, Johnnie was playing with his farm animals. The ritual involved in the game was very complicated and had a long history. It was on his ninth birthday that he had been given the farm set by his father. 'Something a bit less babyish that those woolly animals of yours' he had said, and Johnnie had accepted them, since they made in fact no difference whatever to the games he played; games at which could Major Allingham have guessed he would have been distinctly puzzled. The little ducks, pigs, and cows of lead no more remained themselves in Johnnie's games than had the pink woollen sheep and green cloth horses of his early childhood. Johnnie's world was a strange compound of the adult world in which he had always lived and a book world composed from Grimm, the Arabian Nights, Alice's adventures, natural history books, and more recently the novels of Dickens and Jane Austen. His imagination was taken by anything odd – strange faces, strange names, strange animals, strange voices and catchphrases – all these appeared in his games. The black pig and the white duck were keeping a hotel; the black pig was called that funny name of Granny's friend – Mrs Gudgeon-Rogers. She was always holding her skirt tight round the knees and warming her bottom over the fire – like Mrs Coates, and whenever anyone in the hotel asked for anything she would reply 'Darling, I can't stop now. I've simply got to fly', like Aunt Sophie, and then she would fly out of the window. The duck was an Echidna, or Spiny Anteater who wore a picture hat and a fish train like in the picture of

Aunt Eleanor; she used to weep a lot, because, like Granny, when she described her games of bridge, she was 'vulnerable' and she would yawn at the hotel guests and say 'Lord I am tired' like Lydia Bennet. The two collie dogs had 'been asked to leave', like in the story of Mummy's friend Gertie who 'got tight' at the Hunt Ball, they were going to be divorced and were consequently wearing 'co-respondent shoes'. The lady collie who was called Minnie Mongelheim kept on saying 'That chap's got a proud stomach. Let him eat chaff' like Mr F's Aunt in Little Dorrit. The sheep, who always played the part of a bore, kept on and on talking like Daddy about 'leg cuts and fine shots to cover'; sometimes when the rest of the animal guests got too bored the sheep would change into Grandfather Graham and tell a funny story about a Scotsman so that they were bored in a different way. Finally the cat who was a grand vizier and worked by magic would say 'All the ways round here belong to me' like the Red Queen and he would have all the guests torn in pieces and flayed alive until Johnnie felt so sorry for them that the game could come to an end. Mummy was already saying that he was getting too old for the farm animals: one always seemed to be getting too old for something. In fact the animals were no longer necessary to Johnnie's games, for most of the time now he liked to read and when he wanted to play games he could do so in his head without the aid of any toys, but he hated the idea of throwing things away because they were no longer needed. Mummy and Daddy were always throwing things away and never thinking of their feelings. When he had been much younger Mummy had given him an old petticoat to put in the dustbin, but Johnnie had taken it to his room and hugged it and cried over it, because it was no longer wanted. Daddy had been very upset. Daddy was always being upset at what Johnnie did. Only the last time that he was home there had been an awful row, because Johnnie had tried to make up like old Mrs Langdon and could not wash the blue paint off his eyes. Daddy had beaten him and looked very hurt all day and said to Mummy that he'd 'rather see him dead than grow up a cissie'. No it was better not to do imitations oneself, but to leave it to the animals.

This afternoon, however, Johnnie was not attending seriously to his game, he was sitting and thinking of what the grown ups had been saying and of how he would never see his friends, the old ladies, again, and of how he never, never wanted to. This irrevocable separation lay like a black cloud over his mind, a constant darkness which was lit up momentarily by forks of hysterical horror, as he remembered the nature of their last meeting.

The loss of his friendship was a very serious one to the little boy. It had met so completely the needs and loneliness which are always great in a child isolated from other children and surrounded by unimaginative adults. In a totally unself-conscious way, half crazy as they were and half crazy even though the child sensed them to be, the Misses Swindale possessed just those qualities of which Johnnie felt most in need. To begin with they were odd and fantastic and highly coloured, and more important still they believed that such peculiarities were nothing to be ashamed of, indeed were often a matter for pride. 'How delightfully odd', Miss Dolly would say in her drawling voice, when Johnnie told her how the duck-billed platypus had chosen spangled tights when Queen Alexandra had ordered her to be shot from a cannon at Brighton Pavilion. 'What a delightfully extravagant creature that duck-billed platypus is, *caro* Gabriele', for Miss Dolly had brought back a touch of Italian here and there from her years in Florence, whilst in Johnnie she fancied a likeness to the angel Gabriel. In describing her own dresses, too, which she would do for hours on end, extravagance was her chief commendation, 'as for that gold and silver brocade ball dress' she would say and her voice would sink to an awed whisper 'it was richly fantastic.' To Miss Marian, with her more brusque, masculine nature, Johnnie's imaginative powers were a matter of far greater wonder than to her sister and she treated them with even greater respect. In her bluff, simple way like some old-fashioned religious army officer or overgrown but solemn schoolboy, she too admired the eccentric and unusual. 'What a lark!' she would say, when Johnnie told her how the Crown Prince had slipped in some polar bears dressed in pink ballet skirts to sing 'Ta Ra Ra boomdeay' in the middle of a boring school concert which his royal duties had forced him to attend. 'What a nice chap he must be to know.' In talking of her late father, the general, whose memory she worshipped and of whom she had a never ending flow of anecdotes, she would give an instance of his warm-hearted but distinctly eccentric behaviour and say in her gruff voice 'Wasn't it rum? That's the bit I like best.' But in neither of the sisters was there the least trace of that self-conscious whimsicality which Johnnie had met and hated in so many grown ups. They were the first people he had met who liked what he liked and as he liked it.

Their love of lost causes and their defence of the broken, the worn out, and the forgotten met a deep demand in his nature, which had grown almost sickly sentimental in the dead practical world of his home. He loved the disorder of the old eighteenth-century farm house, the collection of miscellaneous objects of all kinds that littered the rooms, and thoroughly sympathized with the sisters' magpie propensity to collect dress ends, feathers, string, old whistles, and broken cups. He grew excited with them in their fights to prevent drunken old men being taken to workhouses and cancerous old women to hospitals, though he sensed something crazy in their constant fear of intruders, Bolsheviks, and prying doctors. He would often try to change the conversation when Miss Marian became excited about spies in the village, or told him of how torches had been flashing all night in the garden and of how the vicar was slandering her father's memory in a whispering campaign. He felt deeply embarrassed when Miss Dolly insisted on looking into all the cupboards and behind the curtains to see, as she said 'if there were any eyes or ears where they were not wanted. For, *caro* Gabriele, those who hate beauty are many and strong, those who love it are few.'

It was, above all, their kindness and their deep affection which held the love-starved child. His friendship with Miss Dolly had been almost instantaneous. She soon entered into his fantasies with complete intimacy, and he was spellbound by her stories of the gaiety and beauty of Mediterranean life. They would play dressing up games together and enacted all his favourite historical scenes. She helped him with his French too, and taught him Italian words with lovely sounds; she praised his painting and helped him to make costume designs for some of his 'characters'. With Miss Marian, at first, there had been much greater difficulty. She was an intensely shy woman and took refuge behind a rather forbidding bluntness of manner. Her old-fashioned military airs and general 'manly' tone, copied from her father, with which she approached small boys, reminded Johnnie too closely of his own father. 'Head up, me lad' she would say 'shoulders straight.' Once he had come very near to hating her, when after an exhibition of his absentmindedness she had said 'Take care, Johnnie head in the air. You'll be lost in the clouds, me lad, if you're not careful.' But the moment after she had won his heart for ever, when with a little chuckle she continued 'Jolly good thing if you are, you'll learn things up there that we shall never know.' On her side, as soon as she saw that she had won his affection, she lost her shyness and proceeded impulsively to load him with kindness. She loved to cook his favourite dishes for him and give him his favourite fruit from their kitchen garden. Her admiration for his precocity and imagination was open-eyed and childlike. Finally they had found a common love of Dickens and Jane Austen, which she had read with her father, and now they would sit for hours talking over the characters in their favourite books.

Johnnie's affection for them was intensely protective, and increased daily as he heard and saw the contempt and dislike with which they were regarded by many persons in the village. The knowledge that 'they had been away' was nothing new to him when Mr Codrington had revealed it that afternoon. Once Miss Dolly had told him how a foolish doctor had advised her to go into a home 'for you know, *caro*, ever since I returned to these grey skies my health has not been very good. People here think me strange, I cannot attune myself to the cold northern soul. But it was useless to keep me there, I need beauty and warmth of colour, and there it was so drab. The people, too, were unhappy crazy creatures and I missed my music so dreadfully.' Miss Marian had spoken more violently of it on one of her 'funny' days, when from the depredations caused by the village boys to the orchard she had passed on to the strange man she had found spying in her father's library and the need for a high wall round the house to prevent people peering through the telescopes from Mr Hatton's house opposite. 'They're frightened of us, though, Johnnie,' she had said. 'I'm too honest for them and Dolly's too clever. They're always trying to separate us. Once they took me away against my will. They couldn't keep me, I wrote to all sorts of big pots, friends of Father's, you know, and they had to release me.' Johnnie realized, too, that when his mother had said that she never knew which was the keeper, she had spoken more truly than she understood. Each sister was constantly alarmed for the other and anxious to hide the other's defects from an un-understanding world. Once when Miss Dolly had been telling him a long story about a young waiter who had slipped a note into her hand the last time she had been in London, Miss Marian called Johnnie into the kitchen to look at some pies she had made. Later she had told him not to listen if Dolly said 'soppy things' because being so beautiful she did not realize that she was no longer young. Another day when Miss Marian had brought in the silver framed photo of her father in full dress uniform and had asked Johnnie to swear an oath to clear the general's memory in the village, Miss Dolly had begun to play a mazurka on the piano. Later, she too, had warned Johnnie not to take too much notice when her sister got excited. 'She lives a little too much in the past, Gabriele. She suffered very much when our father died. Poor Marian, it is a pity perhaps that she is so good, she has had too little of the pleasures of life. But we must love her very much, *caro*, very much.'

Johnnie had sworn to himself to stand by them and to fight the wicked people who said they were old and useless and in the way. But now, since that dreadful tea-party, he could not fight for them any longer, for he knew why they had been shut up and felt that it was justified. In a sense, too, he understood that it was to protect others that they had to be restrained, for the most awful memory of all that terrifying afternoon was the thought that he had shared with pleasure for a moment in their wicked game.

It was certainly most unfortunate that Johnnie should have been invited to tea on that Thursday, for the Misses Swindale had been drinking heavily on and off for the preceding week, and were by that time in a state of mental and nervous excitement that rendered them far from normal. A number of events had combined to produce the greatest sense of isolation in these old women whose sanity in any event hung by a precarious thread. Miss Marian had been involved in an unpleasant scene with the vicar over the new hall for the Young People's Club. She was, as usual, providing the cash for the building and felt extremely happy and excited at being consulted about the decorations. Though she did not care for the vicar, she set out to see him, determined that she would accommodate herself to changing times. In any case, since she was the benefactress, it was, she felt, particularly necessary that she should take a back seat, to have imposed her wishes in any way would have been most ill-bred. It was an unhappy chance that caused the vicar to harp upon the need for new fabrics for the chairs and even to digress upon the ugliness of the old upholstery, for these chairs had come from the late General Swindale's library. Miss Marian was immediately reminded of her belief that the vicar was attempting secretly to blacken her father's memory, nor was the impression corrected when he tactlessly suggested that the question of her father's taste was unimportant and irrelevant. She was more deeply wounded still to find in the next few days that the village shared the vicar's view that she was attempting to dictate to the boys' club by means of her money. 'After all,' as Mrs Grove at the Post Office said, 'it's not only the large sums that count, Miss Swindale, it's all the boys' sixpences that they've saved up.' 'You've too much of your father's ways in you, that's the trouble, Miss Swindale,' said Mr Norton, who was famous for his bluntness 'and they won't do nowadays.'

She had returned from this unfortunate morning's shopping to find Mrs Calkett on the doorstep. Now the visit of Mrs Calkett was not altogether unexpected, for Miss Marian had guessed from chance remarks of her sister's that something 'unfortunate' had happened with young Tony. When, however, the sharp-faced unpleasant little woman began to complain about Miss Dolly with innuendos and veiledly coarse suggestions, Miss Marian could stand it no longer and drove her away harshly. 'How dare you speak about my sister in that disgusting way, you evil-minded little woman,' she said. 'You'd better be careful or you'll find yourself charged with libel.' When the scene was over, she felt very tired. It was dreadful of course that anyone so mean and cheap should speak thus of anyone so fine and beautiful as Dolly, but it was also dreadful that Dolly should have made such a scene possible.

Things were not improved, therefore, when Dolly returned from Brighton at once elevated by a new conquest and depressed by its subsequent results. It seemed that the new conductor on the Southdown 'that charming dark Italian-looking boy I was telling you about, my dear' had returned her a most intimate smile and pressed her hand when giving her change. Her own smiles must have been embarrassingly intimate, for a woman in the next seat had remarked loudly to her friend, 'These painted old things. Really, I wonder the men don't smack their faces.' 'I couldn't help smiling,' remarked Miss Dolly, 'she was so evidently *jalouse*, my dear. I'm glad to say the conductor did not hear, for no doubt he would have felt it necessary to come to my defence, he was so completely *épris*.' But, for once, Miss Marian was too vexed to play ball, she turned on her sister and roundly condemned her conduct, ending up by accusing her of bringing misery to them both and shame to their father's memory. Poor Miss Dolly just stared in bewilderment, her baby blue eyes round with fright, tears washing the mascara from her eyelashes in black streams down the wrinkled vermilion of her cheeks. Finally she ran crying up to her room.

That night both the sisters began to drink heavily. Miss Dolly lay like some monstrous broken doll, her red hair streaming over her shoulders, her corsets unloosed and her fat body poking out of an old pink velvet ball dress – pink with red hair was always so audacious – through the most un-expected places in bulges of thick blue-white flesh. She sipped at glass after glass of gin, sometimes staring into the distance with bewilderment that she should find herself in such a con-dition, sometimes leering pruriently at some pictures of Johnny Weismuller in swimsuits that she had cut out of *Film Weekly*. At last she began to weep to think that she had sunk to this. Miss Marian sat at her desk and drank more deliberately from a cut glass decanter of brandy. She read solemnly through her father's letters, their old-fashioned, earnest Victorian sentiments swimming ever more wildly before her eyes. But, at last, she, too, began to weep as she thought of how his memory would be quite gone when she passed away, and of how she had broken the promise that she had made to him on his deathbed to stick to her sister through thick and thin.

So they continued for two or three days with wild spasms of drinking and horrible, sober periods of remorse. They cooked themselves odd scraps in the kitchen, littering the house with unwashed dishes and cups, but never speaking, always avoiding each other. They didn't change their clothes or wash, and indeed made little alteration in their appearance. Miss Dolly put fresh rouge on her cheeks periodically and some pink roses in her hair which hung there wilting; she was twice sick over the pink velvet dress. Miss Marian put on an old scarlet hunting waistcoat of her father's, partly out of maudlin sentiment and partly because she was cold. Once she fell on the stairs and cut her forehead against the banisters; the red and white handkerchief which she tied round her head gave her the appearance of a tipsy pirate. On the fourth day, the sisters were reconciled and sat in Miss Dolly's room. That night they slept, lying heavily against each other on Miss Dolly's bed, open-mouthed and snoring, Miss Marian's deep guttural rattle contrasting with Miss Dolly's high-pitched whistle. They awoke on Thursday morning, much sobered, to the realization that Johnnie was coming to tea that after-noon.

It was characteristic that neither spoke a word of the late debauch. Together they went out into the hot July sunshine to gather raspberries for Johnnie's tea. But the nets in the kitchen garden had been disarranged and the birds had got the fruit. The awful malignity of this chance event took some time to pierce through the fuddled brains of the two ladies, as they stood there grotesque and obscene in their staring pink and clashing red, with their heavy pouchy faces and blood-shot eyes showing up in the hard, clear light of the sun. But when the realization did get home it seemed to come as a confirmation of all the beliefs of persecution which had been growing throughout the drunken orgy. There is little doubt that they were both a good deal mad when they returned to the house.

Johnnie arrived punctually at four o'clock, for he was a small boy of exceptional politeness. Miss Marian opened the door to him, and he was surprised at her appearance in her red bandana and her scarlet waistcoat, and especially by her voice which, though friendly and gruff as usual, sounded thick and flat. Miss Dolly, too, looked more than usually odd with one eye closed in a kind of perpetual wink, and with her pink dress falling off her shoulders. She kept on laughing in a silly, high giggle. The shock of discovering that the raspberries were gone had driven them back to the bottle and they were both fairly drunk. They pressed upon the little boy, who was thirsty after his walk, two small glasses in succession, one of brandy, the other of gin, though in their sober mood the ladies would have died rather than have seen their little friend take strong liquor. The drink soon combined with the heat of the day and the smell of vomit that hung around the room to make Johnnie feel most strange. The walls of the room seemed to be closing in and the floor to be moving up and down like sea waves. The ladies' faces came up at him sud-denly and then receded, now Miss Dolly's with great blobs of blue and scarlet and her eyes winking and leering, now Miss Marian's a huge white mass with her moustache grown large and black. He was only conscious by fits and starts of what they were doing or saying. Sometimes he would hear Miss Marian speaking in a flat, slow monotone. She seemed to be reading out her father's letters, snatches of which came to him clearly and then faded away. 'There is so much to be done in our short sojourn on this earth, so much that may be done for good, so much for evil. Let us earnestly endeavour to keep the good steadfastly before us,' then suddenly 'Major Campbell has told me of his decision to leave the regiment. I pray God hourly that he may have acted in full consideration of the Higher Will to which . . . ', and once grotesquely, 'Your Aunt Maud was here yesterday, she is a maddening woman and I consider it a just judgement upon the Liberal party that she should espouse its cause.' None of these phrases meant anything to the little boy, but he was dimly conscious that Miss Marian was growing excited, for he heard her say 'That was our father. As Shakespeare says, "He was a man take him all in all" Johnnie. We loved him, but there were those who sought to destroy him, for he was too big for them. But their day is nearly ended. Always remember that, Johnny.' It was difficult to hear all that the elder sister said, for Miss Dolly kept on drawling and giggling in his ear about a black charmeuse evening gown she had worn, and a young donkeyboy she had danced with in the fiesta at Asti. '*E come era bello, caro Gabriele, come era bello*. And afterwards . . . but I must spare the ears of one so young the details of the *arte dell' amore*' she added with a giggle and then with drunken dignity 'it would not be immodest I think to mention that his skin was like velvet. Only a few lire, too, just imagine.' All this, too, was largely meaningless to the boy, though he remembered it in later years.

For a while he must have slept, since he remembered that later he could see and hear more clearly though his head ached terribly. Miss Dolly was seated at the piano playing a little jig and bobbing up and down like a mountainous pink blancmange, whilst Miss Marian more than ever like a pirate was dancing some sort of a hornpipe. Suddenly Miss Dolly stopped playing. 'Shall we show him the prisoner?' she said solemnly. 'Head up, shoulders straight,' said Miss Marian in a parody of her old manner, 'you're going to be very honoured, me lad. Promise you'll never betray that honour. You shall see one of the enemy punished. Our father gave us close instructions "Do good to all" he said "but if you catch one of the enemy, remember you are a soldier's daughters." We shall obey that command.' Meanwhile Miss Dolly had returned from the kitchen, carrying a little bird which was pecking and clawing at the net in which it had been caught and shrilling incessantly – it was a little bullfinch. 'You're a very beautiful little bird,' Miss Dolly whispered, 'with lovely soft pink feathers and pretty grey wings. But you're a very naughty little bird too, *tanto cattivo*. You came and took the fruit from us which we'd kept for our darling Gabriele.' She began feverishly to pull the rose breast feathers from the bird, which piped more loudly and squirmed. Soon little trickles of red blood ran down among the feathers. 'Scarlet and pink a very daring combination,' Miss Dolly cried. Johnnie watched from his chair, his heart beating fast. Suddenly Miss Marian stepped forward and holding the bird's head she thrust a pin into its eyes. 'We don't like spies around here looking at what we are doing,' she said in her flat, gruff voice. 'When we find them we teach them a lesson so that they don't spy on us again.' Then she took out a little pocket knife and cut into the bird's breast; its wings were beating more feebly now and its claws only moved spasmodically, whilst its chirping was very faint. Little yellow and white strings of entrails began to peep out from where she had cut. 'Oh!' cried Miss Dolly, 'I like the lovely colours, I don't like these worms.' But Johnnie could bear it no longer, white and shaking he jumped from his chair and seizing the bird he threw it on the floor and then he stamped on it violently until it was nothing but a sodden crimson mass. 'Oh, Gabriele, what have you done? You've spoilt all the soft, pretty colours. Why it's nothing now, it just looks like a lump of raspberry jam. Why have you done it, Gabriele?' cried Miss Dolly. But little Johnnie gave no answer, he had run from the room.

FOR THE BEST IN PAPERBACKS, LOOK FOR THE

In every corner of the world, on every subject under the sun, Penguin represents quality and variety – the very best in publishing today.

For complete information about books available from Penguin – including Pelicans, Puffins, Peregrines and Penguin Classics – and how to order them, write to us at the appropriate address below. Please note that for copyright reasons the selection of books varies from country to country.

THE PENGUIN BOOK OF AMERICAN
SHORT STORIES
Edited by James Cochrane

This collection offers twenty-one short stories from the
literature of America, a nation which has always been
particularly at home with this form, and which has
produced many of its masters. Some of the stories included
– those by Poe, James and Hemingway for example – are
already widely known. Some of the others will be less
familiar to the English reader. The collection as a whole
should serve as an introduction to the rich diversity of
pleasures that the American short story at its best can offer.

THE NEW PENGUIN BOOK OF
SCOTTISH SHORT STORIES
Edited by Ian Murray

This new Penguin collection contains stories laced with
humour or Calvinist guilt, dealing in folklore or the dis-
appearing rural traditions and linked – like those of James
Hogg, John Buchan and Muriel Spark – by a thread of the
supernatural. It also includes an early nineteenth-century plea
for women's liberation by John Galt, a tale from Samoa by
Robert Louis Stevenson, stories of life in Edinburgh and
Glasgow, 'A Wee Nip' by Edward Gaitens and an Orkney
classic by Eric Linklater, as well as contributions from Naomi
Mitchison, George Mackay Brown, Ian Crichton Smith and
more of Scotland's finest living writers.

HOW TO BECOME RIDICULOUSLY
WELL-READ IN ONE EVENING
Compiled and Edited by E. O. Parrott

This superbly efficient book allows one to savour the wealth of great literature without the time-consuming tedium of having to read it. It contains some 150 succinct and entertaining encapsulations of the best-known books in the English language including a few foreign works familiar to us in translation. Through them you will rapidly acquire nearly all that is worth knowing about the books.

MORE TALES OF THE
UNEXPECTED
Roald Dahl

Roald Dahl can stand you on your head, twist you in knots, tie up your hands and leave you gasping for more. In this, his latest, selection of short stories the surprises are as wicked and witty as ever. Taken from *Someone Like You*, *Kiss Kiss* and *The Wonderful World of Henry Sugar*, PLUS FOUR BRAND NEW STORIES, they lure you into a world as full of unease, coincidence and black humour as you could wish.

MRS REINHARDT AND
OTHER STORIES
Edna O'Brien

'The stories are . . . varied in setting, in style and in execution . . . they retain the odd, stubborn energy, the baffled resilience that triumphs over humiliation of spirit and circumstance . . . the sensuous perception which brings such pleasure to her readers' – Frank Tuohy in *The Times Literary Supplement*

NO COUNTRY FOR YOUNG MEN
Julia O'Faolain

The author unleashes a brilliant and devastating story of human and political relations in contemporary Ireland. Past and present: memory, madness and buried trauma shift in a disturbing kaleidoscope as four generations of the O'Malleys and Clancys attempt to come to terms with the after-affects of the Irish Civil War – the 'troubles' of the 1920s.

'A marvellous novel' – John Braine

No Country for Young Men was nominated for the Booker Prize.

MIDSUMMER NIGHT MADNESS
Sean O'Faolain

'One salutes, in these stories, an immense creative humour, as broad in speech as Joyce's gloom' – Graham Greene

Alight with a young man's idealism in *Midsummer Night Madness*, stories about the Troubles, or turning his ripening genius to the Irish character and Catholicism in *A Purse of Coppers* and *Theresa* – Sean O'Faolain's prose is by turns lyrical, exuberant, austere, and his stories the cream of Irish writing this century.

HEARTS OF GOLD
Clive Sinclair

Winner of the Somerset Maugham Award 1981

'Extremely sexy, wry, likeable, tortured, these stories crackle with talent' – Jacky Gillott in *The Times*

'If you can imagine a Borgesian Joseph Heller, or a Nabokovian Isaac Bashevis Singer, you have something of his tone . . . a striking collection' – Malcolm Bradbury in *The Times Literary Supplement*

Penguin Omnibus Editions

THE PENGUIN COMPLETE NOVELS OF JANE AUSTEN

With their supremely spirited and attractive heroines, Jane Austen's novels portray the minutiae of life in country houses, and society in Bath and Georgian London. Perhaps because – in very different ways – they are classic stories of love and marriage with happy endings, the novels in this collection represent for us, as no others, everything that is comic, delightful and wise in English fiction.

THE PENGUIN COMPLETE SHORT STORIES OF FRANZ KAFKA

From 'Metamorphosis' to 'In the Penal Colony', Kafka's stories create a paradoxical world where individuals faced with the absurdity of existence continue to search for the truth.

'The author who comes nearest to bearing the same kind of relationship to our age as Dante, Shakespeare and Goethe bore to theirs ... Kafka is important to us because his predicament is the predicament of modern man' – W. H. Auden

THE PENGUIN COMPLETE LONGER NON-FICTION OF GEORGE ORWELL

All the force of George Orwell's vision, compassion and candour went into the making of these three books. In *Down and Out in Paris and London* he brings the poor of two capitals to life with eerie intensity; in *The Road to Wigan Pier* he exposes, in a series of painfully vivid descriptions, a cruel system; and in *Homage to Catalonia* he memorably describes the bright hopes and cynical betrayals of the Spanish Civil War.